MATTHEW'S STORY

**Center Point
Large Print**

OTHER BOOKS IN THE JESUS CHRONICLES

John's Story: The Last Eyewitness
Mark's Story: The Gospel According to Peter
Luke's Story: By Faith Alone

**This Large Print Book carries the
Seal of Approval of N.A.V.H.**

THE JESUS CHRONICLES

Book Four

MATTHEW'S STORY

FROM SINNER TO SAINT

TIM LAHAYE

and

JERRY B. JENKINS

CENTER POINT PUBLISHING
THORNDIKE, MAINE

This Center Point Large Print edition is published in the year 2010 by arrangement with G. P. Putnam's Sons, a member of Penguin Group (USA) Inc.

This is a work of fiction based on characters and events depicted in the Bible. Scripture is from the New King James Version®. Copyright © 1982 by Thomas Nelson, Inc. All rights reserved. Used by permission.

The text of this Large Print edition is unabridged. In other aspects, this book may vary from the original edition. Printed in the United States of America on permanent paper. Set in 16-point Times New Roman type.

ISBN: 978-1-60285-739-1

Library of Congress Cataloging-in-Publication Data

LaHaye, Tim F.
  Matthew's story / Tim LaHaye and Jerry B. Jenkins. -- Center Point large print ed.
    p. cm. -- (The Jesus chronicles ; bk. 4)
  ISBN 978-1-60285-739-1 (lib. bdg. : alk. paper)
  1. Matthew, the Apostle, Saint--Fiction.
    2. Bible. N.T.--History of Biblical events--Fiction. 3. Large type books.
  I. Jenkins, Jerry B. II. Title.
  PS3562.A315M38 2010b
  813'.54--dc22
2009052565

To
MISSIONARIES,
*who let their lights so shine
before men and women
that they see their good works
and glorify their Father in heaven*

There my burdened soul
found liberty
at Calvary.

PART ONE

LEVI'S RESOLVE

Thus says the LORD:

"A voice was heard in Ramah,
Lamentation *and* bitter weeping,
Rachel weeping for her children,
Refusing to be comforted for her children,
Because they *are* no more."

—JEREMIAH 31:15

The Palace of Herod the Great, Jerusalem
The king toddled like a baby in the wee hours of the morning, gingerly favoring hips and knees worn from more than seven decades of use. Shuffling across vast marble floors, he drew his robe tight around his neck and settled heavily on the portico steps.

Herod's chief aide maintained an appropriate distance.

"Ariel, come," the king said, sighing. "Sit with me."

Ariel hastened to the stairs, bowed, and sat two steps below the king.

"You can tell I am vexed," Herod said. "Can you not?"

"Of course, Majesty. Allow me to send for some wine perhaps. Ale? Water?"

With a dismissive wave, Herod shook his head and looked away, gazing out over his expansive gardens, lit by the dancing flames of torches. "The stargazers," he muttered. "What did you make of them?"

Ariel shrugged. "I made of them what you made of them, Sire."

"And you know my assessment?"

"Of course. For all their finery and diplomacy and scholarship, they made a grave error. Asking the King of the Jews for news of the birth of the King of the Jews—verily!"

Herod stood and tottered down the steps, and Ariel immediately began to rise. "Stay put," the king said. "I am going nowhere." He placed a hand against a column and stared at the floor. "The Roman Senate themselves made me King of Judea! My subjects can call me half a Jew all they want—don't look at me as if you are unaware. You are surprised that I know?"

"Somewhat."

"You should know better by now. I know all. Has it been too long since Marc Antony and Octavian themselves walked me from the meeting in Rome and allowed me to sacrifice to their gods?"

Ariel nodded. "I daresay many have no knowledge of it, except what they've heard from their elders. You were a young man."

"Thirty. But it's history, man! To be taught from birth! When Octavian defeated Antony and became Augustus, I confessed that I had been loyal to his foe. I hid nothing! I pledged myself to him thenceforth, and he himself told me Judea was too small for a man like me."

"And everyone knows he added territories to your kingdom, Highness."

"Then how is it that the so-called wise men did not seem to know?"

"They showed you great deference, sir."

Herod sat again. "You said yourself, they asked me—*me!*—about the newborn King of the Jews!"

"And may I say, Highness, your response was priceless."

"It was, wasn't it?"

"Persuading them to bring you news of him so you yourself could worship him!"

Herod had to laugh, though he convulsed into a spasm of coughs. "Could they have been blinded by the splendor of my kingdom and thus unaware of my determination?"

"That is all I can surmise. Though your passion is not secret . . ."

Herod held up a hand. "Please, don't speak of it. My brother-in-law, three of my sons, my mother-in-law . . ."

"Their demises at your hand merely confirm your resolve to preserve your power, Sire."

"Could these men not know that I spared not even my own beloved?"

"They must, sir."

"I miss her."

"After all this time? You've had nine others."

Herod nodded miserably. "It is not guilt, Ariel. Just melancholy. I love her still."

"But you could countenance no threat to your throne."

Herod sat in silence, staring into the heavens. "And I am not about to start now."

"Are you not tired, Majesty?"

"Of course. But how can I sleep? You know this child is the prophesied Messiah."

"So the scribes say."

Herod shifted his eyes to the arched ceiling. "The priests confirm it! The child the seers seek is to be the Christ."

Ariel leaned back and stretched. "Born in Bethlehem."

"So the prophets write," Herod whispered.

"And when the men from the East bring you news of him?"

"I will invite him here, of course!"

Ariel laughed. "And worship him . . ."

"No doubt! I'll worship him with a sword."

Ariel eventually persuaded the elderly king to fill his belly with wine. "It always makes you drowsy."

Herod slept fitfully nonetheless, and after a morning bath in one of his magnificent pools, he summoned his aide again. "What news of the magi?"

"None, Sire."

"Bethlehem is but a village. Surely they are conspicuous."

"I'll send scouts."

"I want those foreigners here with news—if not with the infant himself—by nightfall. They have had more than enough time to find him and report back to me."

ONE

Bet Guvrin, 20 miles southwest of Bethlehem

Levi loved being the older brother, but at nearly eight years old, he was not allowed to carry little Chavivi, who had just learned to walk. The toddler provided no end of delight to Levi, who followed him about, calling his name, and trying everything he could to amuse the boy. To hear a giggle or to see a flash of those few tiny teeth was all Levi was after. How he wished he could hold the baby the way his parents did.

"You are lithe and lanky," his mother said. "And you will one day be tall and strong. But Chavivi is fragile, understand?"

Levi nodded, but that didn't keep him from pleading his case to his father when he returned from his day's work at the tannery just beyond the village market. Levi sat on his father's lap smelling the pungent leather on the man and tracing his orange tinted hands with his own fingers.

"But I'm strong, Father, and I won't drop him."

"You know the rules," Alphaeus said. "When your mother and I are present, you may hold the lad."

"Even now?"

"Of course. Bring him to me."

Levi ran off to get his brother, his father calling after him, "Remember, don't try to lift him until you get him in here!"

Chavivi sat on the ground near where his mother was checking the risen barley dough, preparing to bake it. "Come!" Levi called out, and the little one leapt to his feet with a smile and scampered away. "No! We're not playing chase! Come see Father!"

But the boy was headed for the goat pen, where he held his nose and looked back at Levi. The older son overtook him and grabbed his hand, making him laugh. He pulled Chavivi to the side of the house, where his father was washing up.

"Cha-cha!" Alphaeus roared, quickly drying his hands and squatting, opening his arms. Chavivi ran to him and jumped, and his father swung him in the air. "Now let Levi hold you."

Levi reached for the boy, but his father made him sit on the ground first. Yet when he was settled, Chavivi wriggled to stay with his father, laughing when he plopped him into Levi's lap. Soon he seemed to have had enough of that and ran off again to find his mother.

"Keep him from the fire," Alphaeus said, as Levi rose to follow. He would never allow his little brother to be hurt, though once he had neglected him for only a few seconds and was startled by his cries. The boy had tripped over donkey dung and landed atop the pile. Levi's mother made him wash Chavivi, then she checked the baby over carefully, sniffing his whole body before dressing him afresh.

Now as the family lit the candelabrum and sat for dinner, Levi asked if they were still planning on a trip to Jerusalem the next day. Once each month his father picked up raw hides at a trading center near the Holy City. Twice a year he took the family along.

Alphaeus nodded. "Tomorrow is Wednesday, when the Damascus traders arrive with their goods. Mary, rumor has it they will have silk from the east."

Levi's mother smiled. "You know as well as I that I can only look. We can't afford such . . ."

"I know," Alphaeus said. "But you can dream. And perhaps they'll have trinkets for Chavivi again."

She smiled. "Trinkets I can afford." She turned to the child and broke off a small piece of bread, tucking it into his mouth. "You want a toy, little one? Do you?"

Chavivi's eyes widened and he smiled, the bread slipping from his mouth. Mary pressed it back in and drew her finger across his cheek, causing the baby to grin again, the bread to reappear, and the family to laugh. Levi couldn't wait until the next morning. On their last trip, Chavivi slept on the long wagon ride into Jerusalem, but that had been half a year ago. He would be more alert now, and it would be fun to see his face when he saw the bustle of the city and especially the pageantry at the temple.

. . .

LEVI HAD LEARNED to read at a young age, and at five years old began the daily reading of the Torah, looking forward to the day he could join his older friends at the synagogue school to study the Oral Law, commentaries from sages on biblical passages. His parents sat with him, huddled over a lamp, helping him sound out all the words and then explaining them to him. It was as if he could feel himself becoming smarter every day.

He knew friends who dreaded the daily readings and did not look forward to turning ten and starting to really study at the synagogue. But that was not true with Levi. He took pride in his name and his future, especially in his parents' expectations for him. Often they had talked about how he would not have to break his back farming or tanning or shaping pottery. He would be a priest, called out, separated for the service of the Lord God Almighty. "You will never have riches," his mother would say, "but you will be richly blessed in the service of the one true God."

Levi dreamed of someday taking his place in the Levite choir that sang at the daily sacrificial service at the holy temple in Jerusalem. On the few occasions when his parents had taken him there, he was fascinated by the signal for the choir to begin—the dropping of the rake used to clean the altar. Lyres, harps, cymbals, and trumpets accompanied the dozen or so singers, who had a different song for each day. Levi's father explained that each song represented one day of the creation week.

The last time Levi had heard the choir had been on a Friday, when they commemorated the crowning completion of creation by singing a psalm:

The LORD reigns, He is clothed with majesty;
the LORD is clothed,
He has girded Himself with strength.
Surely the world is established, so that it
*   cannot be moved.*
Your throne is established from of old;
You are from everlasting.
The floods have lifted up, O LORD,
the floods have lifted up their voice;
the floods lift up their waves.
The LORD on high is mightier
than the noise of many waters,
than the mighty waves of the sea.
Your testimonies are very sure;
holiness adorns Your house,
O LORD, forever.

Levi had asked his father if the Lord was clothed with majesty the same as King Herod was, not realizing until he saw his father's face cloud over that he had apparently made a grave mistake.

"You are young, son, and so can be forgiven for

mentioning the name of our evil king in the same breath with that of our great Lord and the God of our fathers Abraham, Isaac, and Jacob."

"I'm sorry, Father."

"The song refers not to God's clothes but to His majesty. Today, the sixth day, was the day man was created, and of all God's handiworks, only man is able to recognize God's true greatness and become His subject."

Levi felt bad because he had clearly displeased his father, though his question had been innocent. He had hoped to suggest that the family complete that visit to Jerusalem with a walk past Herod's palace inside the city's southern walls, but in light of his father's reprimand, that was clearly out of the question, but still, although his parents despised the king, it had not stopped them from gazing at the palace before.

Tomorrow's visit would be better. He would know not to compare Herod with God. Plus Levi had never been to the holy temple on a Wednesday. "What will the choir sing tomorrow, Father?"

Alphaeus glanced at his wife, his brow furrowed. "Hmm. The fourth day is Psalm Ninety-four, Mary, is it not?"

Levi's mother nodded. "Son," she said, "keep Chavivi occupied while I tidy up, then I want to hear your prayer, as you will not be doing your reading in the morning."

Levi was amused by the baby. Chavivi always grew sleepy after eating, especially in the evening. Now he sat on the floor, staring. His eyelids drooped, leading to long, slow blinks. He nodded like a man who had imbibed too much wine and Levi laughed, rousing the boy, but he started to nod off again a few seconds later.

"He's falling asleep, Mother!"

"Prepare his mat and put him down then, but be careful."

Sometimes the baby fought being put to bed, but not tonight. He appeared to be trying to stay awake, staring wide-eyed at Levi and then at his mother as she bustled about. Finally he turned and shut his eyes. Levi draped a small blanket over him.

"Sing him your prayer, Levi," his mother said.

"Yes," his father said. "And do it perfectly, every word. I have two prutahs here that will afford you a dessert of pears and honey from the vendors tomorrow."

"Oh, Alphaeus," his mother said. "He should do it for its own sake."

"I will!" Levi said. "But I will enjoy the treat too."

He cleared his throat and chanted softly, " 'Hear, O Israel: The Lord our God, the Lord is one! You shall love the Lord your God with all your heart, with all your soul, and with all your strength. And it shall be that if you earnestly obey My commandments which I command you today, to love the Lord your God and serve Him with all your heart and with all your soul, then I will give you the rain for your land in its season, the early rain and the latter rain, that you may gather in your grain, your new wine, and your oil. And I will send grass in your fields for your livestock, that you may eat and be filled.

" 'Take heed to yourselves, lest your heart be deceived, and you turn aside and serve other gods and worship them, lest the Lord's anger be aroused against you, and He shut up the heavens so that there be no rain, and the land yield no produce, and you perish quickly from the good land which the Lord is giving you.

" 'Therefore you shall lay up these words of Mine in your heart and in your soul, and bind them as a sign on your hand, and they shall be as frontlets between your eyes. You shall teach them to your children, speaking of them when you sit in your house, when you walk by the way, when you lie down, and when you rise up. And you shall write them on the doorposts of your house and on your gates, that your days and the days of your children may be multiplied in the land of which the Lord swore to your fathers to give them, like the days of the heavens above the earth.' "

"Excellent!" his father announced, proffering the coins.

Levi helped him pull the table to the wall and

move the chairs. He then laid out his parents' and his own mats, not far from the baby's. With the setting of the sun the air grew cold, and his father brought fresh charcoal for the brazier. That was Levi's favorite way to sleep—a cool night with the air stealing in around the shutters on one side, the fire warming him on the other.

TWO

Herod's Palace
As darkness settled over Jerusalem, the king paced.

"No word from the scouts, Ariel?"

Herod's aide shook his head. "I expect them momentarily. They were to report at nightfall."

"Well, night has fallen, hasn't it? Send for Caiaphas and have him bring the scroll of the prophets."

"The entire . . ."

"You know what portion I wish to hear! Now, with dispatch!"

Ariel assigned a courier to fetch the chief priest. "Highness, he'll be none too pleased to have to return so soon."

"Let him say that to my face," Herod hissed. "I will deal with him as I plan to with these magi." He cursed. "How hard can it be to find these men in Bethlehem?"

"I cannot imagine."

"If these scouts have been slothful, I'll . . ."

"You may rest assured, Your Majesty, that they are among your finest armed guards."

"If they are not here in due time, they will be among my late armed guards."

Caiaphas arrived quiet and clearly in a bad mood, a cylinder tucked under his arm. The willowy cleric followed Ariel and the king to an inner room and opened the scroll on a limestone table. Without hesitating he pointed to the passage in question and intoned: " 'But you, Bethlehem, in the land of Judah, are not the least among the rulers of Judah; for out of you shall come a Ruler Who will shepherd My people Israel.' "

"I know what you're thinking, Rabbi. You're thinking I should have been able to memorize that, or at the very least not forget it."

Caiaphas shrugged and rolled the scroll. "Will there be anything else?"

"Yes, you can interpret it for me! And no sighing!"

The chief priest shook his head. "I am at your service, sir, but this passage strikes me as quite literal."

"So these wise men have come to see the Messiah?"

"Clearly they believe they have."

"What are you saying?"

"Nothing here indicates timing. The men spoke of following a star in the East. Studying the heavens is their pursuit, not mine, but have you seen any such star?"

Herod shook his head. "So, they're wrong? Dreaming? Think they've seen something?"

"I cannot say. They could be right. I pray they are right. We have prayed for our Messiah for centuries."

Herod hesitated and glanced at Ariel. "Well, of course you have. We all have. How old would this child be?"

"Based on what they said, somewhere between six months and a year old."

"But you're saying this may not be the time?"

"I don't know. I suppose if they find a child and bring him to you, we'll know."

"I will summon you immediately, Rabbi."

Caiaphas raised a brow. "Just here to serve, Excellency."

When he was gone, Herod limped out to the front portico and into the street, where he could look to the west and see where the scouts would come through the Citadel Gate near David's Tower.

"Sire," Ariel said, quickly overtaking him, "I'd really rather you not expose yourself to the elements—or to your detractors."

Herod whirled to face him. "My detractors? They would be wise to not expose themselves to me!"

"Please, sir! Step back inside. I will inform you when the scouts return."

"If they are not back within minutes, send out a garrison of soldiers to find them!"

"Your Highness, the Romans will want nothing to do with this."

"I don't care what they want! I pay for those soldiers!"

"Here they come, sir."

"I will assign centurions to arrest the scouts and then to—"

"Sir, the riders approach."

The scouts' horses skittered to a stop before the king. "What news?" he said. "I demand to know where—"

"No sign of them, my king," the leader said.

"How is that possible?" Herod fumed. "What took so long?"

"We knew this was important, sir. We searched every home in the village."

"And what did the citizens say? Had the magi been there?"

"Some thought they had seen foreigners, but there is no sign of them now."

"Did you say why you were looking for them?"

"Yes, we said you wanted to worship the infant king. The citizenry were unaware of such a child, but intrigued."

"Excellent. And children?"

"Sire?"

"Babies between six months and a year! How many did you see?"

"We did not realize we were to look for children, Your Highness," he said, looking to the others. "But we saw several that age, certainly."

"How many?"

"More than a dozen, perhaps. But we would not have seen them all."

"Get yourselves something to eat," Herod said, "but stay at hand. I may have another task for you tonight. And you will need to be fully armed."

"As you wish."

Herod grabbed Ariel's sleeve and dragged him back into the palace. "If it were entirely up to me I would send Roman soldiers to execute every child in Bethlehem and its surrounding districts."

"You'll risk your relationship with Rome if you do that without authorization."

"*They* named me King of the Jews!"

"But the execution of children, Sire . . ."

"I have executed members of my own family, Ariel! I should ignore a usurper to my throne?"

"Of course not. But you don't need the complication of using Roman soldiers for such an odious task, especially without approval."

"Then I'll use my own men! Those scouts owe me. How many more do we need?"

"What is your aim, sir?"

"Need you ask? I am decreeing the deaths of every child in the Bethlehem district under the age of two!"

"And how do you propose to effect this decree?"

25

"By the sword this very night."

"You will need at least two teams of a half dozen men each."

"Two? Why?"

"As soon as this purge begins, word will spread fast. Parents with infants will flee."

"Good thinking! Two teams it is. See to it immediately."

"Let me be certain I understand, Your Highness."

"I cannot be clearer, Ariel! They go house to house, executing every child under two. I have never countenanced any threat to my throne. I am not about to start now."

Bet Guvrin

Levi was startled awake, but not by any noise he was aware of. Suddenly he found himself sitting up straight, alarmed that his mother was standing by the window, the shutter open a few inches. She was wrapped in a blanket.

Levi's father stood and tiptoed to her. "What is it, Mary?"

"I heard something," she whispered. "Levi, go back to sleep."

Levi lay back down, but of course he would not sleep until his parents returned to their mats.

"Your imagination?" his father said.

She shook her head. "Perhaps an animal, but it sounded like a scream."

"A jackal or a hyena," he suggested. "Come back to bed. There are but a few hours before dawn."

Levi's mother was quietly pressing the shutter closed when a scream pierced the night, and it was no animal. Levi bolted straight up again, and his mother whimpered, "Alphaeus! Someone's in trouble."

"It sounds far away," he said, just as the scream turned to shrieks and then wailing.

"Someone has died," she whispered.

"You don't know that."

"I know."

Now men's voices, shouting, horses' hooves. The clamor became so great that Mary reached for Chavivi, still sound asleep. Levi leapt to his feet, surprised his parents didn't send him back to bed. He peeked around his father as Alphaeus opened the shutter. Torchlights lit the horizon in the distance, and from the noise it was clear that people were racing through the village.

"Who *is* that?" Levi's father muttered, peering out. "He's riding a donkey!"

"Hide your children!" the man cried. "Hide your children! Herod's men are slaughtering them!"

"Alphaeus!"

"To the roof! Now! Go!"

His mother rushed outside to the stairs.

"I'll stay with you, Father!"

"No, Levi! Go with your mother now!"

But as he stepped outside, six horsemen thundered up and one bounded directly from his steed to the middle of the stone staircase, blocking his mother's path. "No!" she screamed.

"How old are your children?" the leader demanded.

Levi's father emerged from the tiny house shouting, "There are no children here!" But he fell silent as he took in the scene. The man on the stairs was wrestling with Mary over Chavivi.

"No! Alphaeus!"

Levi froze as his father flew up the steps and knocked the armed man to the ground. Immediately the others slid from their mounts, pulling swords and knives. As Alphaeus dropped onto the man, he was pulled off by two others, one of whom wrapped an arm around his neck with a dagger at his throat.

Levi's mother rushed toward the roof, and as two gave chase, Levi grabbed the second from behind, only to be shaken off and thrown back down the steps. They quickly overtook his mother on the roof and one rushed back down, the now squalling baby in his arms. The other stood on the roof with a knife to Mary's throat.

Still she fought and thrashed. "If you mean to harm my baby, kill me too!"

"What is happening?" Levi shouted, as the man took the baby around the side of the house. Chavivi suddenly stopped crying. The other men released his parents as the now limp and bloody baby was brought back and handed to Alphaeus.

The horsemen remounted and galloped off as Levi dropped to his knees, breathless and silent. His father, howling like a wild animal, staggered back and fell to his seat, cradling the baby. Mary crept down the steps, trembling, eyes afire, jaw set. As she joined her husband, they both enveloped the tiny body, rocking, weeping.

Levi had never heard such a haunting tone from his mother, repeating, "My baby, my life, why, why, why?"

"Did they kill him?" Levi said, finally able to breathe.

"Alphaeus, tend to Levi," she managed, struggling to her feet and taking the lifeless child inside.

"Father, what?"

Alphaeus gathered the boy to himself. "I don't know," he said, rigid with rage. "But someone will pay."

Levi heard his mother crying and pulled away to head inside, but his father held him back.

A neighbor approached, a farmer. "Not Chavivi, Alphaeus. Please no."

Levi's father nodded. "I don't understand."

"All the children under two," the man said. "Herod is making sure he eliminates the Christ child, the Messiah."

"But why Cha-cha?"

"The king does not know whom to target. Three others have already been lost in our village. Many more in Bethlehem. I'm so sorry, Alphaeus."

Levi's father could only nod, pulling Levi close and leading him into the house. His mother had laid the baby on the table and set lamps around his body. When she noticed Levi she quickly covered Chavivi with a clean blanket. The blood-sopped one lay in a corner.

She was ashen and looked smaller than Levi had ever thought of her. "Alphaeus," she said softly, "they ran him through the heart."

"Herod's men," Alphaeus said, but she shushed him. "The king—"

"I don't care," she said. "I don't want to know. There is no why. I wish they had killed me."

"Don't say that, Mother!"

"Oh, Levi! I'm so sorry for you!"

She turned and embraced him, and Levi had never felt so helpless.

She held him tight as she began to wail, her forlorn sobs carrying in the night and joining with others in the distance. Levi sensed his father was fighting sobs as well, but the man soon surrendered to his own emotions. His bitter cries scared Levi as much as Herod's soldiers had, and all he could do was join his parents in loudly mourning his baby brother.

After nearly an hour, Levi said, "I want to see Chavivi."

"Not yet," his mother managed. "Let me prepare him. Alphaeus, bring water."

Alphaeus wiped his face and reached for Levi and walked hand in hand with him to where they stored urns full from the village well. After he had delivered a large urn to Mary, he sat on the floor in a corner where he held Levi in his arms. Levi sat watching his mother, horrified, as she seemed in a trance. She closed the baby's eyes and gently kissed all over his face. It was more than Levi could bear. He buried his face in his father's chest and sobbed.

After what seemed a very long time, during which his mother washed the body, wrung out the cloths, and washed him again and again, she spoke in a voice so soft he barely heard her. "Levi?"

He sat up. "Yes?"

"Would you like to help?"

He stood quickly. "What can I do?"

"From the chest, bring me nard and myrrh."

Glad for something to do, Levi quickly returned with the vials. His mother took them without a word and began anointing the body. Levi turned with a start when his father said, "I want to kill someone. I want to kill Herod."

"Alphaeus, please. The boy."

"*I* want to kill him too," Levi blurted.

Mary turned and faced her husband, and Levi thought she would fall. Alphaeus rose and hurried to her. "We must somehow get through this," she whispered, but she collapsed into moans so mournful that Levi had to sit on the floor and bury his head in his hands, covering his ears.

For the next few hours before sunup, his mother alternated between weeping in her husband's arms and making her way between the chest and the table, where she bound the baby's hands and feet in linen strips, gently placed a clean cloth over his face, and finally wrapped his body.

Levi could barely stand to look at the small white bundle on the table, so sickened had he been by what he had seen and how horrible he felt for his baby brother.

The family sat weeping until the sun began to peek through the shutters. "We must bury him before noon," Levi's mother said.

Alphaeus nodded. "We will not be alone. I shudder to think how many others there will be."

"And then you must get started toward Jerusalem."

"Oh, Mary, I wouldn't even consider it."

"No, you must, Alphaeus! We can't afford for you to forfeit the payment."

"I'll find someone else to go for me. Someone surely will have pity on us."

THREE

The horror made sleep impossible for Levi, not that he was even aware of fatigue. Fear, confusion, and a terrible rage roiled within him. It broke his heart to see his mother kneeling before the tiny wrapped bundle on the table, her shoulders heaving.

Levi's father whispered, "Son, we will take Chavivi to the roof where our neighbors and relatives will come to pay their respects. I want you to stay close by your mother's side, as I have important duties I must attend to."

"Doesn't the Torah say you are to do no work for the first thirty days of mourning?"

"I am allowed to do what is necessary. People must be informed and invited. And I must hire flautists and mourners and arrange for someone else to make the trek to Jerusalem today."

By dawn, Levi's parents had changed into mourning garments. His father neither washed nor shaved and wore old, dirty, tattered clothes Levi had seen him in only when he last patched the roof. He also wore a loincloth of camel's hair Levi recognized from his readings as a sign of sorrow.

Levi's mother had changed into a long dress made of sackcloth. Levi had never seen her so pale and shaky, even when she had been ill. Her eyes looked empty, as if she herself were dead, but he also noticed that they darted at any sound.

Part of Levi wanted to leave the room, to not have to look at Chavivi lying there. He wished he could go to the stable and just curl into a ball. He would pray this had been a bad dream, and when he awakened, his little brother would be teasing him to play, flashing that pretend look of fright when Levi would chase him.

His father was speaking quietly to his mother, and when the sun was fully up, he helped her stand.

"Please, I don't want the baby left alone even for an instant," she said.

"I understand. I will carry him, and Levi will help you up the stairs."

"I am too unsteady, and he is too small."

"Then I will take the baby up and Levi will wait with him while I return for you. Can you do that, Levi?"

He nodded, though it was the last thing in the world he wanted to do.

It appeared to the boy that his father was trying to be strong. He gently lifted the body and slowly made his way out to the steps, nodding that Levi should follow. His mother guided him out and waited at the bottom.

When his father reached the roof, he asked Levi to slide a wooden bench over, where he would lay the baby. But when it was in place it seemed his father was reluctant to release the body. He stood there, lips quivering and pressed tight, eyes filling. Finally his breath rushed from his nose and he cradled Chavivi close to his chest and began weeping again.

Levi wanted to comfort his father, but what could he say? He reached to touch his father's arm, and the man sat heavily on the bench, head bowed over the infant, rocking and sobbing. Levi wanted to suggest that his father fetch his mother, but when he opened his mouth, everything that had assaulted his every sense had conspired to strike him dumb.

Suddenly his mother appeared, accompanied by the local rabbi. Levi's father immediately stood and gently laid the baby on the bench, then wiped his tears.

"Rabbi," he said, "thank you for coming."

"Of course, of course." He stood among the family before the slain child, hands clasped before him, bowing from the waist and praying softly.

"Thank you," Mary whispered.

"I know it does not assuage your grief to know you are not alone. Three other families in this very village have suffered."

"Who?" she said.

The rabbi named them, and Mary clutched her sackcloth to her neck, trembling afresh. "That's not the worst of it," he added. "Nearly two dozen more in Bethlehem and its environs."

Levi's mother looked as if she might collapse,

and both the rabbi and her husband reached for her. Soon the rabbi began discussing details of the day, telling Levi's parents that everyone would have to exhibit patience and understanding. The visits to the homes of the grieving would take longer than normal, due to the number. Some of the parents may not be able to pay their respects to the others.

"I will visit them all," Mary said.

"Are you sure?" Alphaeus said. "They would understand if you did not."

"I will go if someone will stay with Chavivi."

"Of course."

"And the procession to the graves," the rabbi said, "will be corporate. The mothers will lead the way, carrying their own if they are able, and we will have a brief ceremony at each tomb."

Levi's family's tomb was rough-hewn out of a cliff some one hundred or so cubits from the stable. Most other families had made similar arrangements.

"I will be back in due time," the rabbi said.

"I'll go with you," Alphaeus said, glancing at Levi with a look that told him to take care of his mother. Levi nodded, still entirely unable to speak.

The rabbi cupped Levi's face in his hands and gave him a look of pity so painful that the boy could hardly stand it. He had so many questions, so many charges, such unsatisfied anger and vengeance that he felt he could split in two. And yet he could not even talk.

Levi found a chair for his mother, and when she opened her arms to him he sat in her lap. She wrapped one arm around him and held him close, as if desperate to not let him go. She laid her free hand on the baby's little belly and stared at the white bundle.

About an hour later, people began arriving, making their way up the steps and hesitantly approaching. All cooed sympathy and whispered their horrified regrets. Mary merely nodded to each, saying nothing, and Levi could only imitate her.

Presently Levi's father returned with one flautist and one mourner. They immediately began wailing and playing, and he explained that while he had hoped for two of each, "There simply weren't enough to go around. And, Mary, no one is available to go to Jerusalem in my place today."

"Then you must go. I will be all right."

"I couldn't."

"Alphaeus, everyone will understand. You have no choice. The wagon and the steeds are rented—"

"He will refund—"

"But the Damascus traders will not. Your business will surely be ruined."

Levi thought his father wanted to argue, but he fell silent. It must be true. To miss a scheduled shipment for any reason was a breach that could not be fixed. Levi had been along before when his father dealt with the traders. Everything seemed to favor them. It was, his father always said, a seller's market. If he did not purchase the agreed-upon stock of raw goods, his business would fail. As it was, the tannery provided only enough income to keep the family alive.

"I will speak to the rabbi about it," Alphaeus said at last, his shoulders drooping.

He asked Levi to accompany his mother to the homes of the other grieving families, and the boy wondered how she could endure it. To think that the king of all the land, the King of the Jews, had done this to his own people was more than Levi could take in. Was the man at war with his own kingdom? It made no sense.

By the middle of the morning, just less than eight hours after the killings, the entire village gathered for the procession to the tombs. Levi had never seen anything so ghastly. Four mothers staggered along the paths, each with a lifeless child in her arms, leading husbands and other children, relatives, friends, and dozens of neighbors. A flautist and a mourner had been assigned each family, and they accompanied the somber parade, the flutes emitting a mournful dirge as the mourners added high-pitched wails that echoed off the hills and turned the heads of curious sheep and goats.

The entire gathering stopped at each tomb as the fathers laid their babies inside and the mothers surrounded the bodies with piles of aromatic herbs and spice. Village men helped the fathers wall the graves shut while the rest of the family arranged a neat pile of stones of remembrance.

The rabbi spoke briefly at each site and prayed, "May the prayers and the entreaties of all the people of Israel be received before their Father who is in heaven."

It had been agreed that under the circumstances the traditional funeral meal, the bread and wine of mourning, would be held at the synagogue rather than at the individual houses. Levi was struck that not one citizen of the village seemed unaffected by the massacre. Even his friends, who normally romped and played after Shabbat services, now sat motionless and appeared stunned. None seemed to know what to say to him and so said nothing, for which he was grateful.

When the family made its way home, Levi trudged along barely listening to his parents. The rabbi had determined that Alphaeus was free to go to Jerusalem, and his mother wanted him to take Levi along. Alphaeus insisted that Levi should stay at home with his mother.

"He needs to be with you," she said urgently. "And I need to be alone."

"Are you sure you will be all right?"

"Alphaeus, I will never be all right again. But

do not condescend to me. I expect even more visitors, those who were not able to get here in time."

"I should be here for that," he said.

"We have already decided that you are going. And now I'm saying I want you to take the boy."

Levi's father looked away and shook his head, as if frustrated but knowing that he should not force his will on her, especially now. "I have actually had in mind that I might exact some revenge at the palace," he said.

"Don't speak like that," she said. "This is hard enough. That is not our way."

"Is that why you want me to take Levi? So I will not act on my impulses?"

"I can only pray so."

Knowing he had no say in the matter, still Levi was torn. He wanted to be near his mother, to comfort her and to have her comfort him. But he also wanted to be as far from the scene of the murder as he could. On the other hand, that meant visiting the very city where the evil king lived. Levi no longer had any interest in seeing the grand palace. He once had been enamored of its splendor and had not fully understood why his parents so loathed the king. They didn't seem the jealous type, so although his father groused that the king lived high and mighty on the purses of his subjects, he thought it went deeper than simply the money.

But Levi would never look at the palace the same again. From then on it would represent only evil and bloodshed.

BY THE MIDDLE of the afternoon the horse-drawn wagon his father had hired for the day rumbled to the outskirts of Jerusalem and connected with the Damascus traders who had set up their wares in a huge clearing. Levi had always been fascinated by the foreigners and their camels and caravans and hard-selling ways.

He had finally found his voice but was grateful his father seemed in no more mood to talk than he did. Occasionally he noticed the man weeping as he drove. Levi couldn't imagine having any more tears to shed, yet he felt as if he were crying on the inside.

"Stay right here," his father said, climbing down to find his contact. Slaves mingled nearby, waiting to be assigned to load various wagons. Levi was stunned to see his father speak briefly with the trader and then simply pay him, pointing out the wagon where the hides were to be loaded. The last two times Levi had accompanied his father he had enjoyed the bantering and negotiating. Both times voices were raised, arms waved about, and his father had pretended to give up in disgust and return to the wagon without buying. Then the trader would run up and make one last concession that finally sealed the deal—then trudge away muttering that he had made no money.

Now it was obvious that his father was in no mood to quibble, and the worldly trader—who had always seemed so cold to Levi—actually put his hand on his father's shoulder and seemed to speak softly. There was no mistaking Alphaeus's mourning garb, and surely the traders had heard all that had taken place.

The slaves loaded the wagon high with hides, and Levi's father carefully watched, being sure he got the number and quality he had paid for.

The trader approached. "And your wife?"

"She is deeply wounded, of course."

"Of course." The man turned to a group of slaves and clicked his fingers. One approached and the man whispered in his ear. The slave returned presently with a bolt of linen. "Please," the man said to Levi's father. "A gift for her."

"You are too kind."

The trader turned to Levi with a sad smile. "And for you, little one? A trinket perhaps?"

Levi had in his pocket the prutahs with which he had planned to buy something for Chavivi. He held them out to the man.

"No, no. A gift and my sympathies." And he dug from his sack a small carved camel.

"Thank the man, Levi."

Then both Alphaeus and the trader had to pay the tax collector. That Levi had never understood.

Everyone despised the collector, and he seemed to do nothing for the privilege of exacting a tax on both buyer and seller. His father had to pay a tax on everything he bought, on the horses that pulled the wagon, and on each axle. But when the man tried to charge a tax on the bolt of linen, Alphaeus said, "It was a gift."

"A gift from a trader? That's a laugh."

"It's true, sir, please, and I have no more money."

"Then that is between you and the trader. Someone has to pay the tax on the linen."

The trader rushed over and told Alphaeus to pull out. He screamed at the tax collector gesturing and pointing. "I will pay the tax, but you, sir, are scum!"

As his father carefully maneuvered the wagon around to head back home, Levi saw the high temple towers in the distance. "I wonder what the Levite choir sang today."

"I told you yesterday," Alphaeus said. "On the fourth day it's Psalm Ninety-four."

"Can we go hear them?"

"And leave your mother alone another minute longer?"

"Of course not, Father. I'm sorry, you're right."

"They would have already sung today anyway."

"All right."

"You have memorized that psalm already, have you not?"

"Probably."

"Probably? Either you have or you haven't, Levi."

"I should have. How does it begin?"

" 'O Lord God, to whom vengeance belongs—O God, to whom vengeance belongs, shine forth!' "

"I think I know some of it. 'Rise up, O Judge of the earth; render punishment to the proud. Lord, how long will the wicked, how long will the wicked triumph? They utter speech, and speak insolent things; all the workers of iniquity boast in themselves. They break in pieces Your people, O Lord, and afflict Your heritage. They slay the widow and the stranger, and murder the fatherless. Yet they say, "The Lord does not see, nor does the God of Jacob understand." ' "

"I think that's all I know."

"That will be a good one for you when you begin reading again."

Levi nodded. But something troubled him from deep within. For the first time in his life he wasn't sure himself whether the Lord really saw or understood. How could He allow such evil to befall Levi's family? Did He not care that Herod had broken his family into pieces?

FOUR

By the time Levi and his father had traveled all the way back to their own village and had unloaded the hides at the tannery, it was well after dark. Alphaeus's fellow craftsmen and one of his apprentices assured him that they would carry his workload the best they could for the next thirty days while he mourned and cared for his wife.

The lack of sleep caught up with Levi on the short walk home. With all the emotions raging inside, he was aware of an exhaustion that went far past any fatigue he could ever remember. He dreaded returning to the little home and the patch of dirt that had been his and Chavivi's world. Would anything there ever interest him again?

He missed his mother and was eager to see her, but what could he say or do? He fingered the carved camel in his pocket and decided he would show it to her and tell her the surprising story of the kind trader. She had seen these men in action over the years. She would be as astounded as he had been to see another side to the man.

When they arrived home, it was clear that someone had helped Levi's mother light the large, high torches that illuminated the stable. There stood two horses, three donkeys, even two camels Levi didn't recognize. Inside the house were relatives, some he remembered, some he had never met, and some distant friends who had not been able to reach the village before the burials and the mourning bread meal.

His mother buried herself in Alphaeus's embrace, and Levi sensed she was eager for the family to be alone again. The mourners kept rising and bowing to the family until everyone had done this seven times. The professional mourner and flautist were back, wailing and playing, and Levi knew the memory of this dreadfulness would haunt him the rest of his life.

The friends and relatives were kind enough, but their concerned and sorrowful looks helped nothing. His baby brother had been massacred almost before his eyes, and there was simply nothing anyone could say or do to change that.

His mother seemed to be striving to be hospitable while sleepwalking through this unspeakable tragedy. Levi got the impression that if she allowed herself, she would scream and wail like the professional mourner. Only she would mean it.

Would he ever see her smile again? Would he himself ever find anything amusing or even pleasing? He could not imagine it.

When everyone finally took their leave, Levi and his parents just sat as if unable to move. His mother spoke in a flat, quiet tone, as if any effort was more than she could manage. "I would like you to sleep with us tonight, Levi."

"Do I have to?"

"Levi!" his father scolded. "Of course you will do whatever your mother suggests."

"Yes, I'm sorry."

"I just want you close," she said softly.

"All right, Mother."

"Have you eaten, Mary?" Levi's father said. She shook her head. "I couldn't."

"You should."

"I'm not hungry."

"I'm not either, but I know I must. For the sake of all of us. Is there any bread left?"

She nodded. "Levi, did you eat your treat?"

"No, I wasn't hungry either. But I am now."

His father fetched the round loaf and broke off large chunks for each of them. Alphaeus seemed to slump wearily as he ate.

"Are we not to wash before eating?" Levi said.

His father held up a hand and finished swallowing. "Not while we are in mourning."

"I will be in mourning forever," Levi said.

"It feels that way to me right now too," his father said. "Mary, please try to eat."

She held her piece in one hand and shook her head. "Perhaps later."

"You need strength, dear."

"I need Chavivi ben Alphaeus," she said. "You must pray God will be my comfort, because I am at the end of myself." And suddenly Levi was no longer hungry either.

"I will, Mary, but you must force yourself to eat

47

just a couple of bites. You too, Levi. Now, please."

The boy forced himself, but even though his mother had once told him that hunger was the best seasoning—and he had to be hungry whether he felt so or not—never had bread tasted so flat.

"Mary," his father said softly but directly, "take a little bread, and then I will stop pestering you. You know it's because I care."

"I care about nothing but my—"

"I know, beloved. I know."

Levi was relieved to see her eat a bit, though it seemed so painful to her that he could barely watch. Finally, when it was clear no one wanted any more, his father covered the rest of the bread and set it aside.

"Lord," he said, "thank You for this, our daily bread. Please provide us with what we need. Thank You for our precious baby and welcome him to Your bosom. Help us. Help us."

THAT NIGHT Levi slept between his parents as he had been asked. He would not have slept well anyway with so much on his mind, but he was aware how tightly his mother pulled him to her at times. And when he did finally drowse, he was awakened several times when she moaned to his father that she kept imagining the screaming that had awakened her the night before.

Alphaeus shushed her and caressed her, but at about the same hour of the night she had risen at the noise, she suddenly stood and moved to the window, again wrapped in a blanket, opening the shutter.

"Mary, please," Alphaeus whispered. "There's nothing there."

When she did not move he finally joined her, wrapping an arm around her shoulders, which made her weep again. He closed the shutter and led her back to the mat, where she lay whimpering until dawn.

Levi could not have known what to expect during the mourning period, as it was, of course, all new to him. He did not know whether he was expected to cry the whole time or—as the adults were directed by the Torah—not even respond to a greeting in the street.

It was strange to have his father there all day every day, but Levi was certainly glad he was. He alone would not have been able to comfort his mother, past hugging her and sitting with her and letting her talk about Chavivi. At times she seemed not herself, almost as if she weren't there. She stared at nothing, not even out the window, and Levi was sure she was seeing the baby in her mind, remembering everything about him.

That was all Levi could think of, and it made him so sad he didn't know what to do with himself. Sometimes he would sit near the stable for hours, playing with his new toy. Sometimes he caught himself wanting to show Chavivi something or tell him something, only to be stabbed afresh by the reality that the boy was gone forever.

After a few days of the whole family going through the routine of each day with barely a word, fetching water from the well, his mother baking bread, and sitting around doing hardly much of anything, Levi's father suggested that the boy might want to get back to his daily reading of the Torah.

That caused a strange reaction in Levi's mind. He knew he couldn't, but he wanted to tell his father no. He wanted to say that there was nothing he would less rather do. It held no appeal to him, and it was more than simply because he was mourning his little brother.

Levi was angry. In fact, anger was not a strong enough word for what he felt. He was furious. Everything he had read about God in the past had made him see the Lord as a Person, a Supreme Being who knew him and loved him and cared about him and wanted to talk to him.

Before, when he or anyone in the family prayed, Levi had the feeling they were not just going through some ritual but were actually talking to God. God had never spoken to him, except through His word, but that had always been enough. Levi didn't understand all of it—in fact he understood precious little of it. But he had gotten the point. Now he didn't know if he believed or accepted any of it.

Levi tried a stalling tactic and told his father that he would be happy to begin reading the Torah again, except that he did not want to be responsible for his parents' having to work during the mourning period.

"I can consult the rabbi if you wish," his father said. "But I believe I know what he would say—that this falls into the same category of my making the buying trip to Jerusalem. And I also believe he would find it a worthy diversion from my grief. Anyway, you don't require much work on our parts. We just listen. Now, read."

"What shall I read?"

"Where did you leave off?"

"The Torah, I believe. But I would like to read a psalm, if you don't mind."

"I think anything would be fine," his father said, handing him the scroll.

Levi searched until he found the psalm the Levite choir would have sung on the Wednesday they were in Jerusalem. Something about the vengeance of God seemed just right today, and he wanted to read more of it.

"Listen, Father," he said. "Let me read the psalm for the fourth day of creation, and maybe you can explain it to me. 'Understand, you senseless among the people; and you fools, when will you be wise? He who planted the ear, shall He not hear? He who formed the eye, shall He not see? He who instructs the nations, shall He not correct, He who teaches man knowledge? The Lord knows the thoughts of man, that they are futile. Blessed is the man whom You instruct, O Lord, and teach out of Your law, that You may give him rest from the days of adversity, until the pit is dug for the wicked. For the Lord will not cast off His people, nor will He forsake His inheritance. But judgment will return to righteousness, and all the upright in heart will follow it. Who will rise up for me against the evildoers? Who will stand up for me against the workers of iniquity? Unless the Lord had been my help, my soul would soon have settled in silence. If I say, "My foot slips," Your mercy, O Lord, will hold me up. In the multitude of my anxieties within me, Your comforts delight my soul. Shall the throne of iniquity, which devises evil by law, have fellowship with You? They gather together against the life of the righteous, and condemn innocent blood. But the Lord has been my defense, and my God the rock of my refuge. He has brought on them their own iniquity, And shall cut them off in their own wickedness; the Lord our God shall cut them off.' "

Levi looked up at his father, noticing that his mother had come in and sat to listen too. "The Lord will give us rest from adversity? You told me what adversity is, and we're in it, aren't we?"

His mother nodded. "We are."

"Is the mourning period our rest, since we're not

supposed to work? Because that is not enough for me."

"What do you mean by that?" his father said.

"I want rest," Levi said. "I do not feel rest from my adversity."

"Neither do I," his mother said.

Levi warmed to it now. "Didn't Herod condemn innocent blood? Will God really bring down on him his own iniquity and cut him off? And what does it mean to be cut off?"

"That's what I want to know," Levi's mother said. "Because I am going to hold God to that promise."

"Be careful how you speak, Mary," Alphaeus said. "Who are we to hold God to anything?"

"Who am I? Who am *I?* I am one whose child was murdered before my eyes! If vengeance is the Lord's, I want Him to exact it. And if I am impudent for requiring something of Him, could He punish me more?"

Levi was alarmed at his mother's tone, and yet something deep within told him she was saying things he wanted to say. There were some deep, heavy promises in this psalm. Were they real? Could they be taken literally? Was the psalmist not promising that God would avenge the evil-doers?

Levi wanted that, expected that. And while he may not have been saying so aloud, as his mother was, he also demanded it.

FIVE

Levi was not blind to something strange and terrible going on inside him. Though young, he understood that he was being raised by devout Jews who lived their entire lives in the service of God. Everything they did and said was intended to glorify God. They considered all of life sacred, even their work, their bread, their clothes.

He somehow knew his mother would return to her passion and devotion to God. Somehow she would begin trusting Him again. Though she seemed to look older to Levi every day, she slowly, slowly, became more active. She spent less time sitting and staring and more time busying herself with chores.

Levi hesitated to bring up Chavivi, because he did not want to upset his mother. But when the baby had been on his mind for hours, he just had to remind someone of a cherished memory, some antic, or some look. When he dared mention Chavivi's name to his mother, he was surprised that her eyes brightened and she gave him her full attention. It was as if she *wanted* to be reminded of the baby, and while Levi wouldn't call her look an actual smile—the pain was apparently too sharp and fresh for that—she sometimes looked closer to her old self than she had since that ghastly night.

Eventually Levi's father went back to work, and that seemed the best thing for him as well. While he wasn't there to look after Mary during the day, he came home more talkative, more eager to see both his wife and his son. Gradually life began to return to normal, and yet Levi realized it would never really be the same.

Even when the family went about their routines, the thought of Chavivi was never far from his mind, and he knew it was the same for his parents. He could see it in their eyes, particularly his mother's. She had, he feared, been wounded forever.

When he was fully back into his daily rhythms after several weeks, a dark secret planted itself deep within his soul, and every day it seemed to grow. He could not tell his parents, not yet. He didn't know what to think about it himself.

The problem was that the more he read and studied and learned, the more he realized that he lacked the love of and devotion to God required of a future priest. Even as a youngster he had once enjoyed a passion, an enthusiasm for God and for the Word of God. Now, the deeper he got into the Scripture, the more it repulsed him. Oh, he had long known that the Lord was not just a God of love and mercy but also of justice and sometimes vengeance. Even if Levi could not blame on God the unspeakable crime against his family, could not the righteous Creator of the universe have protected them from it? Why did the most precious, most innocent among them have to die?

The Scripture said it was not right to question God, and Levi knew that if he dared speak his mind about not only his questions, but also his very hatred of God, he would terribly vex his parents. They certainly didn't need that. Not now.

HIS MOTHER, after many months, began to pray again. It sounded so strange to hear her talk to God, to thank Him for His daily provisions. Occasionally she would thank Him for the blessing of having been able to enjoy the beautiful Chavivi, even if for so short a time. But she never—at least in her vocal prayers—asked to know why He had allowed the baby to be taken.

Levi didn't know—nor did he dare ask—whether that was because his mother had somehow come to accept it. He could not imagine.

Levi's strange new thinking affected even his sleep. It wasn't that he dreaded his daily morning readings—he didn't. It's just that he looked at them in a whole new light. He was no longer reading for the edifying of his soul, as the rabbi put it. Nor was he reading solely for his education—though he sensed that was a great benefit too.

No, now he was reading furiously with a definite, specific purpose, one that would horrify the rabbi and his parents and anyone who knew him.

He was studying and learning all he could about God and the Word of God, and he was even looking forward to learning other languages—but all for a reason he dared not speak aloud: Levi had become an enemy of God.

It wasn't that he was losing his faith or belief. No, he still believed in God, that there was a God, that He was an all-powerful Being. He had no doubt about God's existence. The truth that appalled even Levi himself was that he despised God so much. The seed of bitterness that had taken root in his soul the night Chavivi was murdered had permeated his whole being.

DAY AFTER DAY for the next several years, Levi worked at hiding his terrible secret. He learned to smile again, as did his mother—though he always detected a deep sadness in her eyes. He was diligent in his reading, and when it came time for him to attend daily lessons at the synagogue, he quickly became recognized as the brightest in his class of twenty-five students. He became as proficient in Hebrew and Greek as in Aramaic, and it was not uncommon for the rabbi to tell his parents how pleased he was with Levi's scholarship and leadership.

"He is an example to the other lads," the rabbi would say, beaming.

During Levi's tenth year, his parents sat him down one evening and said they had wonderful news. "The Lord has blessed us," Alphaeus said, "and your mother is again with child."

It was plain that they expected him to be as overjoyed as they, but he could not force a smile, and he knew it was obvious. "Levi, dear," his mother said, "no new brother or sister will ever replace Chavivi. To welcome a new sibling will not diminish our love for your brother, nor do we expect it to diminish yours."

Levi just nodded. He knew he should be excited about the arrival of a new baby, but his mother had been exactly right. The very idea that anything or anyone could make up for the loss of the precious Chavivi was absurd.

As the weeks and months passed and his mother's abdomen grew, Levi was reminded of when she had carried his little brother. While he still tried to remain neutral about the whole idea, his parents' enthusiasm began to affect him. But their continual praise to God for this new life was lost on him. How could God allow them to be nearly destroyed because of a horrible, violent act and then expect them to feel blessed by a new child a few years later?

IN THE MIDDLE of a particularly cold early spring night, Levi's mother awoke with a moan and urged Alphaeus to fetch the midwife. He told Levi to dress quickly, and they rushed out into the darkness. Levi was dropped off at the home of friends, and Alphaeus went on to find the midwife.

In the morning, just before Levi was to walk to the synagogue, the midwife stopped by on her way home and told him to go and see his new baby brother. Levi knew better than to expect the newborn baby to look like Chavivi, but he was struck by how tiny and loud and red the infant was. He frankly wasn't sure what to make of this new member of the family. But the baby certainly seemed to make his mother happy, and Levi understood that she would be very busy with him for a long time. That had to be good.

But eight days later when the local *mohel* circumcised the baby and Alphaeus announced that his name would be James, Levi was stunned. What was it about that name that gave him pause? He couldn't put his finger on it immediately, but he had already had so much language training for a young age that he knew he had run across it before.

The next day he asked the rabbi if the name James had a special meaning.

"It does, my son," the rabbi said. "Like Jacob, it means *supplanter* or *replacement*."

Levi fumed all day and ran all the way home when classes were over. "I know why Father named the baby James," he told his mother. "I know what it means."

"We just liked the sound of it," she said.

"Verily? Mother, I have never known you to lie to me before."

"Levi! How impudent to accuse me of such a thing! Now, apologize!"

"I won't! You know as well as I do what James means. I may never even call the baby that! He will never replace Chavivi!"

"I'm going to have to tell your father what you've said and how you spoke to me."

"I'll tell him myself. He named this baby. Is he going to tell me he didn't know what the name meant either?"

THAT EVENING, after a similar encounter with his father, Levi was asked to join Alphaeus for a stroll after dinner.

"I am very disappointed in you, son."

"I am disappointed in you too."

"And perhaps we were wrong to name your brother James after assuring you that he was not here to replace Chavivi. And he is not. We will love him and cherish him and care for him in a whole new way, for he is a whole new person."

"Then why name him James?"

His father sighed. "That is our right and responsibility, and I have chosen what I have chosen. You may choose to not accept it, but it shall not change. As you grow to become a man, you may not agree with everything we say or do or decide, but you will talk to us with respect, and you will obey. And whatever you do, do not take out your frustration or anger on your brother. He is innocent in all of this. He did not come to us from God in order to take Chavivi's place. We must accept him for who he is. I believe he will bring his own joy into our home."

Angry as Levi was, he knew his father was right, at least about the innocence of James. He would try to be a good brother, and he couldn't imagine calling the baby anything but his given name. But he was not going to be happy about it.

The root of bitterness toward God continued to grow in him, and he realized he was excelling at his studies for a reason that would alarm and deeply distress his parents and the rabbi if they knew of it. When he grew up, he wanted nothing to do with the God of the Torah. His goal was to make a success of himself, to gain wealth, to become independent of the Lord and everyone else.

SIX

Word spread fast and wide when King Herod the Great died a horrible death, his body putrefied and worm-infested. While the succession to the throne of his sons brought no encouragement to the citizenry, Levi for one exulted in the man's horrific demise. If he had only lingered longer in pain, depression, and paranoia, Levi might have found more satisfaction in his suffering. Maybe God had exacted His vengeance after all.

But that did not remedy Levi and his family's loss. The joy had wholly been ripped from Levi's life, and it was obvious to everyone. His parents seemed to study him with concern on their faces. And he had to be badgered to spend time with baby James the way he had with Chavivi. He found the child precocious and even cute at times, but as Levi grew older, his mind and his interests were elsewhere. Though he vowed he would never marry or have a family—his way of getting back at God for allowing such deep sorrow to his own parents—he began to notice the girls who hung around the synagogue at the end of the school day. Though they were not allowed in the classes, they were often nearby. They had been a nuisance to the boys when they were younger, but now as the boys neared their thirteenth birthdays and their *bar mitzvahs*, more and more were taking an interest in talking and playing with the girls.

But while Levi enjoyed looking at them and sometimes talking with one or two, he also viewed them with suspicion. If one seemed to like him, he tended to ignore her. Though the attention was flattering, a relationship with one would lead to marriage and a family—and that he could not countenance.

Levi could be kind enough to his little brother,

and it often fell to him to keep track of the child. But their relationship was not at all what his and Chavivi's had been. That baby had brought Levi no end of delight and humor. Cute as James could be, Levi saw him as a responsibility.

Simply, Levi had gone from being a happy, smiling child engaged with life and learning, to a quiet, sullen young man near his coming of age. He was anything but lazy and did all his chores. But he could be insolent, short-tempered, and sarcastic. More than once his father had to punish him, and while Levi took it, never did he apologize.

His deportment and attitude became a deep concern for both the rabbi and the *hazzan*—the schoolmaster. It was not uncommon for one or the other to visit Levi's home or invite Alphaeus to the synagogue for a discussion about the lad.

Just before Levi's *bar mitzvah*, both parents and child were asked to come to the temple for such a meeting. A synagogue aide entertained three-year-old James outside.

"We have a very interesting situation here," the rabbi began. "Levi is our brightest, most accomplished student by far. That is a most valuable trait in a future priest, because, as you know, if you have knowledge, you have everything. If you do not possess knowledge, you possess nothing."

Levi's mother spoke quietly. "He certainly seems to possess knowledge."

"Oh, without question," the rabbi said. "The problem I see here is that Levi has no passion for what he is pursuing. Rare is the day when the schoolmaster or I see a smile on his face, and when we do, it is usually at the expense of one of his classmates. His tongue is sharp, his attitude haughty. He is aware of his place above the others in his mastery of the languages and the Torah. When the *hazzan* calls upon him to recite, Levi does it perfectly but without enthusiasm."

"Is he respectful of the *hazzan*, whom we know is to be treated as the messenger of the Almighty?"

The rabbi seemed to hesitate. "I have no reports of outright insolence, but as I say, we're looking for enthusiasm—which we do not see. I have no doubt that he will fulfill all the requirements of his *bar mitzvah*, but I have to wonder if he really has interest in continuing on his educational path toward becoming a priest."

"Of course he does," Alphaeus said. "Don't you, Levi?"

So there it was. It was one thing to harbor his secret resentment of God and his resolve to run as far from his parents' religion as he could when the time was right. It was quite another to admit it aloud, knowing the turmoil it would cause.

"Father, it is said that a child ought to be fattened with the Torah as an ox is fattened in the stall. Well, I feel fat as an ox."

This elicited smiles all around, but Levi's father continued to press. "That doesn't answer the question, son. Our hope and prayer—which we assumed was yours as well—was that you would go beyond your *bar mitzvah* and begin the perfecting of your knowledge. To become a priest you must go to Jerusalem and join one of the *beth ha-midrash* and be taught by the elite doctors of the Law."

In truth, Levi had wanted to wait a couple of years to reveal to his parents his own plans. His plan was to continue his studies, yes in Jerusalem, but certainly not with the aim his parents assumed. He wanted all the education and training the religious studies offered, but not to make him a religious man—it was for his own gain. He would not change his mind about that, but the longer he protected his mother and father from what they would see as an awful truth, the more he would honor them—wouldn't he?

He respected them, even admired them. He loved them. He even loved his little brother, although he could never replace Chavivi. His plans had nothing to do with dishonoring them or hurting them or getting back at them for anything. The devastation of their family was in no way their fault—though Levi would have loved to see his father follow through on his early threats against Herod. Even more fulfilling than hearing of the king's final days would have been the knowledge that one of the parents of the innocents had had the honor of beheading him.

But that was not his father's way. Alphaeus left such things to God.

And now the man had put to Levi the question he had hoped not to have to answer for several more years. Even now he could not bring himself to tell the whole truth, because he did not wish to inflict that much pain on his parents. It would be bad enough for them to learn that he had decided on a future that in no way included or even resembled the priesthood.

"We need to know, son," his mother said, as he sat there wondering how to phrase his answer. "We gave you to God, dedicated you and your future to Him, and we believe He would have you become a priest. Everything about your life and training has prepared you for this. Is the rabbi right? Is the *hazzan* right? Do you need to recapture your passion and enthusiasm for it?"

Levi sighed and looked at the floor. They really wanted to know, did they? "They are right," he said at last. "I am not interested in the priesthood."

"Levi!" his mother blurted, her hand to her throat. "What are you saying?"

"I cannot be more clear, Mother. If I have learned anything from all this training, it is to be direct. A priest must love the Lord with all his heart and soul and mind and treat his neighbor as himself. He must love God's Word and God's ways."

"Yes!" his mother said. "And that describes you perfectly, does it not?"

"It does not."

"Levi!" she said again, but Alphaeus laid a hand on hers.

"Son," he said, "you will be *bar mitzvahed*, no?"

"I will. I recognize that I must fulfill certain requirements so that I can go on and finish my education."

His mother said, "But you said—"

"I said I do not want to study for the priesthood."

"You will serve God another way?"

Why would she not let up? He knew she didn't want to hear this devastating news. "Mother, I do not plan to serve God."

This elicited a gasp even from the rabbi. "Tread carefully, young man. You are sitting in the very house of God."

"It isn't that I don't respect you, Rabbi, or my parents. They know I do. But if you must know, I do not love God. I do not love His Word or His ways. I go with my father twice a year to trade in the markets, and we visit the temple in Jerusalem for the feasts and holy days. They have been diligent in teaching me everything I must know. They have not, however, succeeded in explaining why God allowed what happened to our family."

The rabbi began to speak, but Alphaeus interrupted. "I do not believe that is something we are to know in this life."

"I agree. I will never understand it. But I do not accept it. It would be easier, believe me, if I simply stopped believing in God. I could have decided that an all-powerful God would not have allowed such crimes, and thus He doesn't exist. Somehow I have not been able to accomplish this in my mind. I do believe in Him. I just don't agree with Him, don't like Him, and will not serve Him."

With that the rabbi stood and began bowing and praying, beseeching the Lord's forgiveness for allowing such blasphemy in His temple.

Levi's mother, her eyes filling, stared at her son, appearing eager to speak but plainly waiting for the prayer to end. As soon as the rabbi finished, she said, "My son, I have failed you. I did not know you still harbored bitterness over our loss. I shared your anger and grief at first, you know I did. But the Lord became my portion, my comfort. Forgive me for not realizing that you had not come to the same place of acceptance. Had I only known, I would have—"

"You would have what? Somehow persuaded me that this was part of some plan? Mother, I *saw* you get over this."

"I did not get over it, Levi! How could I?"

"How could you indeed? Somehow you were able to set it aside, live with it, get on with your life. Maybe I should be proud of you for that. I don't resent you for it. Maybe I wish I could have come to the same place. But I couldn't, and I don't want to."

"I don't understand! Why have you been so diligent in your studies? What do you want for yourself?"

"Do you really want to know? Do you really want me to say, when the news of my rejecting the priesthood is already so hard for you to take?"

"Yes! I want to know."

"But," the rabbi said, "I need to know whether you plan to blaspheme the name of the Lord again. If you do, I must ask that we continue this discussion outside."

Levi ran his hands through his hair. "I believe I can express myself without defiling the temple, Rabbi. Forgive me."

"Carry on."

Levi wasn't sure he wanted to carry on. In fact, he was pretty sure he didn't want to. But he owed his parents this much, didn't he? After having opened this door, he could not retreat now. They deserved to hear it all.

Levi's father said, "We are heartbroken, son. But your mother is right. We want to know. I want to know. What will become of you if you turn your back on your God?"

"On *your* God, you mean."

"He is your God too, Levi, whether you acknowledge Him or not."

"Are you implying He will make me pay for this decision?"

"We pray not," his mother said. "We will pray that He will draw you back to Himself. We would dread your becoming an object of God's wrath."

"Chavivi was an object of someone's wrath, and what did he ever do to deserve that?"

Now Levi realized he had gone too far. He had heaped pain upon pain, and although he was too far into this to back out now, he wished he could touch his mother, apologize to her, put her mind at ease. He knew she had not really ever gotten over her loss, nor would she. And he had to admire that she somehow remained devoted to God.

But that wasn't for him. "I'd rather not say more just now," he said, haltingly.

"You must!" his mother said. "The only thing that would make this worse is for you to force us to learn more—the worst of it—over time."

"Yes," Alphaeus said. "You've begun this, now finish it. What do you want to do with your life, if not serve the Lord?"

Levi knew there was no way out of it, but still he stalled. He gazed at the ceiling, then the floor, then out the window. He looked at the rabbi, who looked as if his own son had told him similar news. Levi rubbed his eyes, then scratched his chest.

"Father, do you want to know what impressed me most on all those trips to buy raw goods?"

"The traders? You envy their wealth? You know that they are pagans who—"

"It was not the traders, Father. Who really profits from all the trade?"

Levi let the question hang in the air until he saw the looks of recognition on every face.

"Oh, Levi!" his father moaned. "The publicans? Tax gatherers? They are lower than pagans! They are despised by all but their own, and with good reason! They lie, they cheat, they steal! Not only do they not serve the one true God, they serve Rome! Surely, you're not saying—"

"Then why do you pay them, Father? You pay for the horses, the wagon, the axles, the road, the goods."

"I have no choice! Distasteful as it is, it is part of our life. It is a cost of doing business, a business that puts bread on our table, bread in your mouth."

"So this evil, as you call it, is accepted. It's simply the way things are."

"Sadly, yes."

"Then it will make me a wealthy man."

Levi's mother stood. "My son," she said flatly. "Not a priest. Not even a man of God. No longer a Jew. You would be a servant of Rome, a cheat, a user of your own people?"

"Worse," Alphaeus said, tugging at her sleeve until she sat again. "He would use the very educa-

71

tion our faith allowed to give him the skills for this odious work."

"You wanted the truth," Levi said, but later he wept bitterly recalling the pain on their faces caused by his words.

SEVEN

By the time of Levi's *bar mitzvah*, the word had blazed through Bet Guvrin of his abandonment of the faith. He was banned from the temple and not allowed to study at the religious institutions in Jerusalem. Witnessing the shame his parents bore—very nearly as devastating to them as the grief over the slaughter of their baby five years before—turned Levi's heart cold as stone. Seeing people treat them that way, when his actions were entirely his own, made Levi all the more determined to leave as soon as he was of age.

He knew he had caused this, destroyed his family's reputation, even damaged his father's business. And though he wasn't there to witness it, his friends told him his parents were all but shunned at the synagogue. It fell to them to raise a son in the nurture and admonition of the Lord. And Alphaeus and Mary had failed.

To their credit, they did not lay at Levi's feet the sharp decline in his father's business. But Levi soon wearied of the tears, the lectures, the prayers, the pleading that he return to the Lord. All he wanted was to get out on his own, to study the languages more, to learn the trade of the publican, including *tachygraphy,* the special sort of abbreviated writing that would allow him to quickly record all transactions—even conversations.

In an attempt to escape the disgrace, the family migrated to Cana, north of Jerusalem and just west of the Sea of Galilee. There were plenty of tanners already plying their trade, so Alphaeus tried his hand at pottery, only to realize he had no aptitude for it. With no other choice, he returned to tanning, apprenticing under a man much younger than himself. Though he would eventually become known as a master craftsman in the new town, he never again saw the success he enjoyed in Bet Guvrin.

While the humiliation from their hometown did not follow them to Cana—at least with such intensity—Levi was aware that it quickly became known in the area that they were the family with the wayward son. He had asked around, asked a thousand questions, and as soon as he turned fifteen, he would be off to Jerusalem to study for his eventual profession. Levi would study and live at a school designed to train tax collectors. It was housed not far from Herod's palace—now occupied by his son, Herod Antipas. Jews in the area avoided the building the way they would a house of ill repute or a palace that bore statuary lauding Greek or Roman gods.

Levi knew that people assumed he wanted to become a publican just to get rich. That was all right. Riches would serve him just fine. He could trust money, and if there was one thing he was sure of, it was that he could trust no man. Besides, serving as a publican was as far from serving God as he could imagine.

Informing his parents of his plan had not been easy. The day he packed to leave, his mother bore that pale, faraway look he remembered so intensely from the days after the slaughter of his little brother. She did not cry in front of him, but it was obvious she had been weeping in private.

The arguing and the pleading were past now. Levi's father merely reminded him that they would be praying for him, particularly that God would somehow bring him back to Himself without having to punish Levi too severely.

Knowing his parents were devout and true was the only thing that gave Levi pause. Though he had turned against God, he could find no fault in them. He would miss James, of course, but he had hardened himself against drawing too close to the lad. James was a good enough child and could be most engaging, but Levi would not allow himself to be so wounded again. If something were to happen to another member of his family . . . well, he didn't know what he would do. But he could certainly force himself not to become so enamored of a baby brother again.

"You know," Alphaeus told his son as he helped gather his things for the journey, "while our people are repelled by the school itself, they save their most vehement wrath for the students. You will be most reviled."

"I know, Father, and as I have told you, that is something I simply don't care about."

Levi knew himself well enough to know that few people anywhere could like him. He didn't want to be liked. He wanted to exact revenge against a king long dead, and short of that, revenge against the evil Roman government who sanctioned such a ruler. He understood deep inside that there was no vengeance possible against the God of his forefathers, who had allowed the tragedy. Perhaps turning his back on his faith and religion and family was all he could do. It would have to be enough.

"You have no need to be liked by anyone?" his father pressed. "The Romans will use you gladly, but they will neither like you nor will they trust you."

"That will be mutual."

"Then what is this all about, Levi? Will you merely live off the Jews and the Romans for your own gain for the rest of your days? That will be your life?"

"What if it is?"

"That is no life worth living."

"You should know."

Alphaeus sighed but did not speak, causing Levi to regret his words, at least for a moment. There was no sense in further hurting his father. In fact, once he made a name for himself in his chosen profession, Levi would help out his parents. He would see how dead set against riches they would be then.

He could not despise or revile them. But neither could he respect their devotion to a God so capricious and spiteful that He would allow what He had allowed to happen to Chavivi. In some small way, Levi wished he shared even a bit of his parents' obvious despair over his leaving. In truth he was eager to just get out and get going. He was anxious about the future, how he would fare, who he would meet, whether he would succeed. He did not doubt his intellect or his abilities. He fully expected to dominate his class. And his goal was nothing short of becoming the wealthiest, most famous, and most hated tax collector in the land. It might take years, but this would allow him to decide his own fate, control his own future. He could think of nothing better.

Levi was already fluent in Hebrew, Greek, and Aramaic, so while he would be forced to study all those again to prove himself, they would take little work. He was also proficient in calculation, a talent indispensable to the trade. What he needed to learn were all the ins and outs of the job: how to determine a tax, how to collect it, how to exact the highest amount possible.

Levi suspected that he would learn as much away from the school as in it, as he would be paying for his education by apprenticing under a veteran tax collector. He could hardly wait to discover who that would be and where.

As he made the long journey south to Jerusalem, both the love and admonition of his parents rang in his ears with every step or borrowed wagon ride. His father had continued to remind him that he didn't have to do this, that he could change his mind, stay home, come back to the Lord, petition to be welcomed back into the temple, even still become a priest.

Levi's mother, however, had gone about the farewell with her jaw set and eyes fixed. She had embraced him hard and long before he set out, but it was clear she had resigned herself to this. He wished she didn't wear her dishonor as personal failure. This was on Levi, on himself alone. It was his decision.

Also fixed in his mind was the sweet expression on young James. Plainly the boy did not understand all of what was going on, but he was timid and shy and quiet, saying nothing but good-bye. What would become of him? Spared a horrid tragedy, he would likely study the holy books and become the priest his parents so wanted to come from the family.

The farther Levi traveled from Cana, the more nervousness grew in his gut. But he was not scared. He was excited. A whole world awaited him. On the one hand he was eager to prove himself and impress his peers and his superiors. On the other, he cared about none of them—whoever they might prove to be. They were not people to be admired or trusted. They were people from whom he would glean everything he could, trying not to alienate them until he was independent enough not to care what they thought.

But what would his quarters look like, his classroom? What would his duties and studies entail? More important, how long would it take him to earn the tax collector's stick that was used to rummage through goods and even to hold a man back who wanted to pass without paying an appropriate—or inappropriate—toll? And how long before he wore the telltale brass breastplate that identified him? Someday he simply wanted to be known for the profession he had chosen. And he would be known as the most feared.

Something about that very idea excited Levi. If it were in his power, he would skip all the instruction and training and get on with his career. Nothing else loomed on the horizon for him, so he just wanted to get on with it.

If Levi were to be despised and rejected and looked down upon, the sooner the better. He would proudly stick out his chest until the breast-plate glinted in the sun.

If anyone had an opinion, something they wanted to say to the publican, the tax collector, the traitor, the cheat, the scoundrel, the sinner, let them say it to his face or keep their mouth shut.

EIGHT

The head of the publican training facility proved to be an enormous fat man named Chaklai who grunted as he rose to welcome Levi into his modest office. He seemed to move with great difficulty, and sweat poured from him. His head and face were a mass of tangled black-and-white curls, the beard and mustache hiding his lips.

He shook Levi's hand with his own thick, greasy fingers, forcing a quickly fading smile that revealed brown teeth. Over the man's shoulder Levi noticed a plate that appeared to contain the remnants of lamb and beef—rich man's fare—and a chunk of bread. Levi wiped his hand on his tunic as Chaklai pointed to a chair, and they both sat.

"Tall and fair and young," the fat man said. "I like that. And from the tribe of Levi?"

"My parents could only wish."

"They are not favorable toward this?"

"Hardly."

Chaklai cleared his throat loudly, mouth open,

and Levi smelled his breath. "Families are never lukewarm about us, son. They either disown us or fully embrace the idea for themselves and their progeny. For instance, I am merely one in a long line of publicans."

"And I am likely the first and last in my family."

Chaklai pressed his lips together and seemed to study the young man. He shook his head. "Not if you prove worthy of the calling. Then everyone in your family will envy you and begin inquiring discreetly how they too can succeed like you."

Levi held his tongue. He knew his family better than this crude man did.

Chaklai drummed his fingers on the wood table. "So you will work for your education . . ."

"Whatever is necessary. Cleaning, errands . . ."

"We have slaves for that. Your work will involve learning the business. You are fluent in Aramaic, and I know you were raised speaking Hebrew. Now you know you must also learn the language of Rome."

"It happens that I am fluent in that too," Levi said in Greek, causing the man to raise a brow.

"Indeed?"

"Sir, I want to know how this works. I know I will study, learn tachygraphy, become even more proficient at calculations, be taught all the taxes and so on, but I need to know how one acquires his own tax area."

"Oh, you do, do you?" Chaklai bellowed,

leaning back and laughing. "You're already a man now, prepared to supervise your own tax office?"

"Well, no, certainly not. But that is my aim."

"And only the aim of everyone else here! All in due time, son. Believe me, if you prove yourself, your horizon is limitless. But it takes a certain, special kind of a man to do well at this work. We will have to see if you have what it takes."

"Believe me, I do."

"Is that so? You know, I'm sure, how we are viewed by our countrymen."

"Of course."

"Can you bear up under that? We tend to keep to ourselves, as no one else will have us."

"That suits me."

"Indeed? Our own people are angry enough that they are not masters of their own fate but are counted like cattle and taxed for everything imaginable. It galls them to no end that we, their brothers, work for the foreigners who subject them. It also makes us their vilest enemies."

Levi knew what the man wanted to hear. "The Jews are also excused from military service, so they pay nothing to Rome in the way of their own blood."

"So let them be taxed!" Chaklai roared. "Am I right? Tell me if I am not right!"

"Let them be taxed and let me collect it," Levi said, enjoying entertaining the man so.

"We are going to get along well," Chaklai said

with a grin. "As for how you do that and how you go about procuring your own area, that is what we teach here. You will study under Divri, a most eloquent teacher. Anything you need to know, he will instruct you. If you do not master it, that will be to your charge and certainly not to his. But first I would like to show you to your chambers, which you will share with Efah, one of our brighter students."

"One of but not *the* brightest?" Levi said.

Chaklai narrowed his eyes. "That is your aim too? To be the best student?"

"Nothing less."

"Follow me."

Levi had to keep himself in check not to overcome and step on the heels of the big man's sandals as Chaklai trudged ponderously to the dormitory. The man left in his wake a stench that made Levi hold his breath.

He was stunned to find the minuscule rooms in which two mats were separated by a tiny table and one chair. There was little room to move and mere pegs protruded from the walls on either side, apparently for hanging garments.

"You and Efah will trade off studying here or in our library. He is on assignment in Bethany today and will be back in time for the evening meal."

"Where will I be assigned?"

"That will be up to Divri, but you have much to learn first, young man."

• • •

THE TEACHER PROVED Chaklai's opposite, at least in appearance. Tall and lithe, he appeared to have bathed recently. He was clean-shaven with short, wavy hair and sat placidly with his hands folded before him on a desk. He spoke precisely and softly and smiled a lot, but still Levi got the impression the man was looking down his nose at him. His aim was to not allow that for long.

"I generally advise younger pupils to remain silent at first. Do a lot of observing and listening. If you have aptitude, your time will come. And your practical training will quickly prove to us whether you are meant for this work."

"Believe me, I'm meant for it," Levi said.

"We will be the judge of that. And like I said, silence is more prudent than boastfulness."

Perfect, Levi thought. *I hate him already.*

"I won't need to boast any longer once I prove myself to you, will I, sir?"

Maddeningly, Divri acted as if he had not even heard the question. He sat perfectly still, as if at peace with the world. Levi had to wonder how the man felt about himself and his profession. He was the teacher, the instructor, the guide who made this most hated caste of people proficient at their odious tasks. And yet here he sat, smug and self-assured. Levi was convinced he could do Divri's job better than the man himself could, given time to learn what he needed to know.

One thing Levi did not lack was confidence—in his intellect, his memory, and his ability to master whatever he set his mind to. These people could look down on him, doubt him, laugh at him, he didn't care. Once he proved himself they would have to accept, even if begrudgingly, that he was worth the trouble, because for every shekel he brought in, they would get a piece. He was determined to be worth a fortune to them. They didn't have to respect or like him; they would have to put up with him because he would shine.

"This will prove your last day of respite, young man," Divri said. "We rise early and study long and hard, and your assignment will begin immediately."

"Where will that be?"

"What, you're worried I was going to forget to tell you? Perhaps I would require you to just guess?"

Levi knew he was expected to apologize for pestering, but no. Never. There would be no apologizing to this preening fool.

"I am wondering when we're finally going to get to the business at hand."

"Oh, you are? We will cover the pertinent aspects of our work in the order I deem appropriate. Understood?"

Levi shot him a look.

"Well, do you understand or not?"

Levi sighed. "You would do well to spare me the

parental tone. As I told Chaklai, I am fluent in three languages and have already mastered calculation. In my opinion, all I really need to learn now is the tachygraphy."

"That's all, is it? You have no idea how difficult it is, and you may think you have mastered calculation, but let me assure you, there is a vast difference between figuring out simple problems and adding and subtracting and multiplying in your head while the citizenry is alternately trying to cheat you and wishing you dead. You think you're prepared for that?"

"Try me."

Finally Levi had elicited some animation from Divri. The man put his hands in his lap and leaned forward, fully engaged. "All right. A man has brought to the market four wagons, sixty head of cattle, two dozen sheep, two slaves to sell, and forty bushels of wheat." Divri then rattled off the amount of the tax on everything, including the axles of the wagons. "Even before he sells anything, what does he owe?"

Levi announced the total immediately. While he knew Divri would never show he was impressed, Levi was pleased to see that this had given him pause. The man then recited the sale price of everything the merchant sold and the standard percentage he would owe the tax collector for each.

Levi quickly calculated the total.

"Incorrect!" Divri said, chortling. "And you think you are—"

"Why? You think it's twenty percent too high?"

The man's smile disappeared. "Exactly."

"You didn't think I would exact my own profit from the transaction?"

"Well, I—uh, yes that would be correct. All right, and if the trader balks . . ."

"I tell him that the extra is to keep me from reporting to Rome that he was also smuggling illegal goods."

"And if he denies this?"

"I will tell him where to report for a hearing so he may take it up with Rome. He will pay."

Divri squinted. "Tell me. Just how is it you are so conversant in this?"

"I am not stupid," Levi said. "I listen. This happened so many times to my own father that I . . ."

"And he came to accept it as a cost of doing business."

"Naturally."

"What happens when, every so many years, the citizens become fed up and threaten to revolt?"

"That's up to Herod. He has given reprieves and refunds, just like his evil father did."

"You were no fan of Herod the Great?"

Levi would not get into this. "The king, whoever he is at the time of a tax revolt, must do what he has to do to preserve his kingdom. But until he decrees otherwise, I will push for every mite owed."

"And a few more for your own pocket."

"As much as the market will bear."

"You seem to have the personality for it. A tax collector must be persistent and persuasive."

"*Feared* is the word you're looking for."

"You don't seem so fearsome."

"Give me a stick and a breastplate and then tell me what you think."

EFAH PROVED A gloomy sort about ten years Levi's senior. Levi thought the man looked Greek, trim and athletic with short black hair and beard. Efah let his bag slip from his shoulder and stashed it in the corner, hanging his cloak on a peg. "So you're the new man."

Levi hated someone stating the obvious. "When's the evening meal?"

Efah eyed him. "Nice to meet you too."

"I'm hungry, that's all. That all right with you?"

"I was told only yesterday I would have a chamber mate," Efah said. "I'm no more happy about this arrangement than you are."

"How many get their own quarters?"

"I was the last. But I earned it. I have seniority."

"How long have you been here?"

"Just over two years."

"I don't plan to be here that long."

Efah smirked and motioned for Levi to follow, leading him down labyrinthine staircases to a long narrow room crowded with tables. Levi smelled fish and bread. "I expected better fare," he said.

"Not used to poor man's food? An aristocrat, are you?"

"Hardly, but publicans—"

"Are rich men, no? You expect to eat like the fat man immediately? Have you not been told that you must pull your weight from the beginning? I'm surprised they're not charging you until you begin to pay your own way."

"We have an understanding," Levi said, immediately regretting that he felt the slightest obligation to explain himself to a fellow student. "Trust me, I'll begin paying my way soon enough, and I won't be here any two years, let alone more."

"We'll see."

Levi and Efah fell into a mostly silent truce that found them largely grunting acknowledgment of each other's presence each day. Levi was assigned an internship in Lod, about twice as far west of Jerusalem as Bethany was east. There he reported to a middle-aged publican who ran a small tax office that levied charges on goods coming into the village from the port at Jaffa and from Jerusalem, and of course on goods that went to those cities as well.

Levi was expected to watch and listen. He was struck by how normal and even friendly the tax collectors were with one another, but how their ruthless nastiness was manifest against the citizens. There seemed no attempt to work with anyone in a businesslike manner. Publicans were stationed at every major thoroughfare, identified by their breastplates and rapacious in their manner.

They stepped directly in front of carts and wagons, fully expecting them to stop immediately without a word or a signal—which they did. Every word to the public bore a tone of condescension and suspicion. It was as if each question carried an accusation of dishonesty. Commerce—the lifeblood of the village—was suspected and treated like a nuisance. Levi learned that regardless what the tax man said to the traders, it sounded like some variation of, "What do you mean trying to ply your illegal business in my town? What are you smuggling? Who are you trying to defraud?"

The tax men wielded their sticks with alacrity, using them to push beasts and slaves aside, to lift tarpaulins off loads, to pop lids off barrels and bins and baskets, to dig through grain as if expecting to find contraband. As they dug and commented and made lists, the assistant or an intern like Levi was expected to record everything they said.

Levi had taken to tachygraphy as if born to it, quickly outdistancing his classmates in recording every word Divri said during instruction. Some suspected him of having learned it before, and even Efah said he had an inhuman knack for it, almost as if he bore an evil spirit. Levi only wished that were so. Perhaps his hatred of God was evidence that he did.

The day he was privileged to take notes for the Lod chief tax man himself, Levi found himself scolded in the man's office at the end of the day.

"I had heard of your talents," he said. "And I was not disappointed. You do, however, need to learn the art and not just the craft."

"The art?"

"When I begin listing the items and the tax and the percentages, what is your charge, your task, your responsibility?"

"To record it as quickly and accurately as possible."

"No!"

"No?"

"Do you not see that we are all in this together? Do you not want your education paid for and to add a little to your pouch as well?"

"Well, yes, sure."

"Do you not understand that these men know exactly how much they are bringing to market?"

"I assume they know."

"Then when I say they are to pay a tax on four head of oxen and two wagons and eight wheels and four axles, they would have cause to charge us if we listed that incorrectly, wouldn't they?"

Levi nodded.

"But what are they to say if I announce eight

bushels of wheat, sixteen gallons of oil, and so forth, and when your list is tallied, it shows more than that?"

"I don't suppose they could argue."

"You don't suppose. Of course they can argue! But will they? Do they want to call me—or you—a liar? How might their transactions go the next time they come through here? I am old and an expert. I read off the amounts, you record them, and they pay what we say. Understand?"

"I do."

"Prove it tomorrow."

LEVI HAD PROVEN it not only the next day, but the next and the next and the next, soon becoming the most outstanding student the publican training facility had ever seen. He became, he knew, an object of jealous and angry ridicule on the part of his fellow students, but nothing stopped him.

Levi was out of the school and quickly pressed into work before he was even seventeen years old, just as he had boasted. Soon after he was awarded the breastplate and stick, he became known as one of the fiercest and most feared tax collectors in Judea. Levi was assigned to apprentice under an aging publican in Capernaum on the northern shore of the Sea of Galilee, and there he began to make his fortune.

It was then that he finally found the time to venture back to Cana to visit his family for the first time. He had sent word that he was prospering and had heard back that they were all fine. But Levi also expected a scolding for not having maintained more frequent contact.

While first his mother and then his father heartily embraced him and the young James shyly shook his hand, it became quickly clear that his mother bore an offense. She neither smiled nor maintained eye contact with him, and Levi's father seemed to chatter to cover the tension. Levi found himself watching James at play, but his brother appeared to have little curiosity about Levi or any interest in interacting with him.

"I've missed you, Mother," Levi said.

"I doubt that," she said.

"How can you say that? Every man misses his mother when he moves away."

"Is that so? How would I have known? Had it not been for the occasional report from someone who happened to visit Capernaum, I would barely have known you were still alive. And I don't suppose you have returned to the temple."

Levi glanced at his father, who quickly left the room and busied himself with James. "I have not, nor do I plan to. I know this pains you, so why do you raise the subject?"

"A mother can hope and pray."

"And a man can make his own decisions."

"A man. To me you seem barely of age."

Levi pulled a pouch from his sack and plopped

it on the table, the mass of coins rattling. "Is this the gift from a child?"

"Gift?"

"It's yours. I have not forgotten or abandoned you or Father. With this he could take a year off from his work or at least reduce his load and take things easier for a while."

Levi's father reentered. "What are you talking about? I do not work merely for money, and I am not at all looking to quit or take things easier."

Levi opened the pouch and upended it, quickly corralling rolling coins. "You will notice," he said, "that while much of this is Roman currency bearing the Caesar's own image, I had some denarii changed into *zuzim*."

This brought both his parents closer to the table, where they bent to peer at the silver coins struck by the Phoenician bankers at Tyre. "Now *that* was thoughtful," his father said softly. "The temple leaders prefer the offering come in these kinds of coins, but we rarely see them."

"This is not our money," Levi's mother said. "I will not make an offering of profits swindled from our own countrymen, no matter what form of coin it is in."

"Not so fast," her husband said. "Neither will I accept such a gift from a tax collector—"

"Can I not, just for today, be only your son?"

"Our son?" Levi's mother said. "Coming to us with such a gift? No."

"—but I would gladly present the *zuzim* at temple, Mary," Alphaeus said.

"Even this?" she said.

"Even this. But, Levi, change out the rest as well, or keep it."

"So you can give it all to the temple?" he said, gathering the coins and returning them to his pouch. "Forget I made the gesture."

"Gladly," his mother said.

When Levi bade his farewell, he bore the ominous feeling that he might never see his parents—or his little brother—again.

NINE

Despite all the claims and promises of Chaklai and Divri, it was not until Levi found himself in Capernaum that he really learned how one went about securing one's own territory.

Once he had endeared himself to Ziya, the chief tax collector, it became clear that Levi had shot past his new colleagues as the favorite to succeed his superior when he finally retired. Suddenly the normal camaraderie among the publicans—which always included sarcasm and ribald teasing anyway—turned openly hostile. Levi was at first shunned, then loudly ridiculed by anyone within earshot.

It was one thing to be hated by the citizenry. That was to be expected and was considered evidence of efficiency. The most despised tax collectors were generally the toughest and most profitable. But the collectors counted on their colleagues as the only ones who understood them. While they suspected one another and were jealous of anyone who made more money, they often socialized and traded what they considered the privilege of hosting feasts for all.

But now Levi, besides being the youngest tax collector in Capernaum, had found favor in the boss's eyes and was vigorously ostracized by the others.

Late one evening, the wizened chief collector asked to see him after dark. They strolled deserted streets in the coolness near the shores of the Sea of Galilee.

"You must decide," the old man said, his left hand bearing a constant tremor, "whether you care more about the esteem of your co-workers or your personal fortune. You realize that if you succeed me, you may hire whom you want and fire whom you want."

"I can?"

"Of course!" Ziya said. "If I tell Rome that you should be the first considered to buy this territory, all you will need is enough capital to pay. Leave the collection of the direct taxes—on property and holdings and such—to agents of the royal treasury. The money, the margin, is in the indirect taxes we concern ourselves with."

Levi was well aware what was meant by indirect taxes. He had collected them at bridges, cross-roads, town borders, and markets. What he wanted was to be the farmer-general, the one who reported to the Roman knight who served as financial procurator. To do that, according to Ziya—his own farmer-general—he would have to sign a five-year contract with Rome and agree to pay a fixed amount for the right to collect all the indirect taxes.

"I'm not sure I have enough yet," Levi told his boss.

"Find it. It will be worth it to you. Then you can fire your enemies and surround yourself with friends. Maybe a few of them can be your partners, but the sooner you buy out their interests, the better it will go for you."

Levi stopped and warmed his hands over a public grill. "The problem, sir, is that I have no friends. And I don't want any of my current colleagues as partners."

"I don't blame you. Tell me, which student did you most dislike at training?"

"I don't even have to think about that," Levi said. "It was my own roommate, Efah."

"I've heard of him. What was your problem with him?"

"His attitude. Sarcastic. Condescending."

"People here say the same about you."

Levi chuckled. "And they are right."

"Did he perform better than you?"

"Sometimes. Not often. But he was among the best, that is certain."

"Might he have enough resources to become your partner someday?"

"If it were only a matter of money, probably yes."

"Such profit all coming from Bethany?" Ziya said. "That is saying something, my friend."

Levi followed as the man began strolling again. "I'm not sure I could trust him, sir."

"That's wise," the old man said. "You know no one trusts a tax collector."

They both laughed.

"But yet you are recommending offering a partnership to such a man . . ."

"Only if you can afford to be the majority holder. Before long you buy him out, and if he has been profitable to you, you decide whether to keep him on."

ON HIS NEXT OFF DAY, Levi made the trek to Bethany to seek out Efah. From the moment Efah saw him, he was clearly wary.

"Why me?" he said after hearing the proposal.

"First, I need you and your share. But also, competing against each other made us both better. Anyway, you need to get out of this hamlet and come to where the great trade routes intersect. We collect taxes from every direction, including the sea."

"Do you think I want to report to someone so much younger than I?"

"I think you want to work in a fertile field. I'll tell you what: You may bring with you the number of publicans that matches the percentage of your investment. You supervise them directly and take the larger share of the commission."

Levi knew when he saw a flash in Efah's eyes that the man would go for the deal. Levi was not altogether at peace about it, but he almost immediately began dreaming about being the youngest farmer-general in the history of Judea. With his and Efah's own people in place, it would be only a matter of time before he became a very wealthy man. Let Efah profit for a while. It would be only temporary. Levi would have the majority of the staff and would get a portion of everyone's take. Soon he would be the sole owner of the territory.

Riches were only part of the appeal for Levi, of course. He would use every trick and tool of the trade to not only maximize his profits but also exploit Rome as much as he took advantage of the citizens. He was no friend of Rome. He wondered only how much he could take from the pockets of the sponsors of Herod the Great to make up for the loss he had suffered at the evil king's hand.

Twenty-three years later
Now in his forties, Levi was one of the wealthiest men in all of Judea. Of all the men Efah had brought to his tax office from Bethany, only a few remained, the others having moved on to other areas. Efah and Levi had become friends of sorts, conspiring to benefit each other by getting along, even long after Levi had bought out Efah's share of the partnership.

Efah became, in essence, Levi's right-hand man, supervising the rest of the staff while Levi—the owner—enjoyed most of the spoils. Levi owned a palatial estate, to which he added bordering plots of land as they became available and on which he built more and more barns and banquet halls, along with guest residences he decorated elaborately but rarely used.

He had never married, which became another issue between him and Efah. The older man had married and enjoyed a houseful of children now coming of age. This had seemed to take the edge off Efah's temper and attitude, though he was still a ruthless and thus effective publican. He and Levi often entertained the rest of the staff, spreading lavish feasts of meat and bread and wine, some of which lasted for days—to the merriment of the employees.

Levi's relationship with his younger brother James was an awkward affair punctuated by mostly bad or mixed news. The last two times Levi had seen James had been at the funerals of first their aged father Alphaeus and then, three years later, their mother Mary.

Levi had sat at these somber affairs fully aware of the spiteful looks and the cold shoulders of his parents' friends. He had dreaded the events and wondered whether some modicum of regret or remorse would invade his spirit. He found himself melancholy and full of memories, but he did not come to regret his painful decision to part ways with them to the point where he rejected their faith and religion.

Levi did find himself reminiscing for days after each memorial. But the seed of bitterness that had taken root in his soul the night his baby brother was murdered had become a carefully tilled thicket over the years.

Ironically, but as expected, James had become a priest and even, for many years, sang in the Levite choir at the temple in Jerusalem. Following their mother's burial, James had prevailed upon Levi to promise to visit sometime and hear him sing and witness him perform his duties. Against his better judgment and wondering what had come over him, Levi had agreed. He had business in Jerusalem a few months later and so fulfilled his promise.

The ceremonies brought back poignant memories, and while he was cordial and even congratulatory to his brother, still he would not allow any regrets or second thoughts to penetrate his conscience. Once, when a council meeting of priests was held in the synagogue at Capernaum, James timidly sent word asking if he might be privileged to visit his older brother.

Levi let the request sit for several days before finally replying that he not only welcomed James to his home, but also invited him to stay for the length of his meetings. His brother gratefully accepted, and when the time came, the reunion began pleasantly, if awkwardly. Levi instructed his household staff to withhold nothing from James, lavishing on him a beautiful guest's robe, and serving him bountiful quantities of the types of foods he would not likely usually enjoy. Levi also invited his entire staff to a two-day feast in his brother's honor, but being that he was a man of God, the usual bawdy entertainment and excess wine were replaced with self-conscious soberness and decorum.

James expressed deep appreciation for every consideration, but Levi was much relieved when his brother was gone. He later heard that James was called before the Sanhedrin and counseled to be careful about associating with tax collectors and sinners and escaped censure only because Levi was his brother.

LEVI'S CHIEF ROLE became to work with Efah at teaching the rest of his staff how to exact the absolute most out of every transaction. A couple of times a week he ventured out from his tax office to watch his charges do their work. Nothing pleased him more than stepping in with his own stick and taking over, showing the younger men—or even the older Efah—how it should be done.

He had become a lonely, bitter man, and his simmering fury was unleashed on his fellow Jews—not to mention his staff—when transactions stalled. His goal in life remained to get the best of everyone, chiefly Rome. As long as they received the basic taxes, they looked the other way when it became obvious that he was squeezing the citizens for every possible shekel.

The day came, however, when Levi was brought up short by a family dressed in mourning clothes. He was watching Efah and another collector dig through their wagon and was about to step in and make things worse for the couple when the husband began desperately pleading with Efah.

"Have mercy, sir! We are not trying to avoid any tax, but we have just buried our daughter and wish to simply pay and then be on our way."

"That is none of my concern," Efah railed. "Now unload your entire wagon so I can see what you have hidden—"

"Let me take this," Levi said.

"I've got it, chief," Efah said, peeling back the tarpaulin with his stick.

"I said I will take it!" Levi said, making Efah's face redden as he backed away.

Levi counted the bushels and barrels and whispered to the man, "All seems in order. How old was your daughter?"

"Three years, sir, and as you can imagine, we are most devastated."

"Of course. And how did she die?"

"An accident in our fields. Trampled by oxen."

"How awful. I am sorry."

"Wealthy farmers," Efah spat. "They should not be trading during their mourning period anyway!"

Levi remembered his father having to make the buying trip to Jerusalem the day Chavivi was buried.

"Keep out of this, Efah."

He turned back to the man and announced the tax, which was exactly what Rome required and not a farthing more.

"Don't forget our margin!" Efah called out, and Levi leveled a look at him that finally shut him up.

"Thank you, sir!" the farmer whispered, then spoke earnestly to his wife, who looked up at Levi with such a look of gratitude that he had to look away.

As Levi and Efah made their way back to the tax office, Efah held his silence for a long time. But finally he shook his head and said, "You're losing your edge. What got into you?"

"Speak no more of it," Levi said.

"But I have seen you—"

"Not another word, Efah."

TEN

Levi found himself somber and lonely at sundown one Friday, and naturally most of Capernaum was silent as the Jewish population observed Shabbat. He was finishing his ciphering by lamplight as Efah and some of his staff stopped in at the tax office on their way home from their various stations throughout the region.

As the others left, Levi's subordinate leaned against the door frame and watched as he recorded the last bits of income from the day—asking Efah to rehearse how the transactions had gone. As Efah spoke and Levi quickly wrote, his longtime associate shook his head.

"You have never lost that gift," Efah said. "You were always the best, and I daresay you're as fast and accurate now as you have ever been."

Levi shrugged. "I take pride in not having to go back and rewrite any of it."

"That is the wonder of it. To be so proficient and legible besides. I don't know how you do it."

"I try not to think about it," Levi said. "I don't want to study it for fear I might lose it."

"After all this time? Not likely."

"I like to think I can record an entire conversation and not miss a syllable."

"Remarkable."

Levi stored his records and doused the lamp. "I have a freshly butchered lamb at home," he said. "Enjoy it with me and we'll take some of my best wine as well, just the two of us."

Efah hesitated. "Normally I would embrace that opportunity; you know I would. But my wife has a meal waiting for me. And I must be back here tomorrow evening."

"On a Saturday? Why?"

"Two of the fishing families have asked for a meeting."

"Who?"

"The sons of Zebedee. John and—I forget the other's name . . ."

"James, my brother's namesake. And?"

"Simon and Andrew."

"Boat owners all. What do they want?"

"Need you ask?"

Levi snorted. "I suppose not. Are they representing the others again?"

"Of course. They always claim to speak for the lot of them. I could recite their arguments before they begin."

"Perhaps you should. Take some of the wind from their sails."

As the men stepped out into the chilly evening

air, Efah said, "That's a good idea. I'll ask if they have anything new since last time or are they going to begin their litany of why all the fishermen of the Sea of Galilee should be given special consideration. 'The less we pay in taxes, the more we can put into our equipment, then our businesses will be more profitable, and in the long run Rome will make even more money from us.'"

Levi chuckled. "You know that makes some sense."

"Sure it does. But they should make such concessions from their own margins. Why should we lend them money by easing their taxes?"

"We shouldn't," Levi said. "Unless they are ready to make us partners. The question is whether they really speak for the lot of the fishermen. If the whole of the industry is threatening to revolt, I must inform the financial procurator. I want no surprises."

Efah shrugged. "If history serves, what's the worst they can do? Stop paying, stop fishing, and get the rest of the populace up in arms over the dwindling supply."

"Talk sense to them, Efah. It could take them years to make up for lost profits if they tried a scheme like that."

Efah nodded. "I've found I can reason with Andrew. Simon not so much. He can be forceful."

"And the sons of Zebedee?"

"They amuse me."

"How so?"

"They grow angry and incoherent as soon as they recognize that I will not budge."

"When are they coming?"

"After three stars appear in the sky tomorrow evening."

"I have no plans," Levi said. "How about I come and record the meeting for you, implying that I am doing this for the sake of Rome? That should alarm them."

THE LONGTIME ASSOCIATES agreed on the plan, and Levi found himself eagerly anticipating it, if for no other reason than that he was alone and bored. His staff prepared the fresh lamb and he ate by himself. Normally fresh lamb pleased him, but with no one to enjoy it with him, the pleasure was gone; he ate too much and was then uncomfortable. When he found sleep elusive, he wandered his vast estate.

Something was nagging at him, something he had not concerned himself with for years. The fact was that he had succeeded at everything he had set his hand to since the moment he decided to turn his back on his parents and their God. Short of finding some pleasure in but missing the satisfaction of having been in any way responsible for Herod's horrible end, Levi had made of himself exactly what he wished. He was the best at what he did, and he had succeeded in plying his trade, seeking vengeance for the loss of his brother by misusing the so-called children of God and by also exploiting the Romans who employed him.

It had all worked perfectly. The rub was that it had fallen so short of accomplishing what he hoped it would that he barely remembered what that was anymore. Levi had wished, he supposed, that perfecting his craft and building his own wealth off the income of others would somehow bring about a feeling of contentment. He had assuaged any guilt over his actions by reminding himself daily that he deserved every coin he could exact from his victims. Yet any feeling of vindication, vengeance, or justice eluded him.

For months he had been sleeping less, thinking more, growing more restless. What had he made of his life? What had he really accomplished? Certainly he was the envy of every other publican in Israel. They were jealous of his role as chief publican on the Via Maris, the main trade route between Damascus and Egypt. But what had that brought him? He had been estranged from his now late parents, from his brother James, and naturally from God.

Whatever he had achieved—and he couldn't imagine what more he could have done—it was not enough. All the diligence, all the study, all the work, the perfecting of his skills—it all led to emptiness. And he was convinced it was way too late to change his ways now.

The night sky was clear and star-filled, so Levi rested on a small outcropping of rock, allowing his feet to dangle as he took in the expanse of the heavens. How much easier this all would have been, had he been able to push from his mind and heart the very existence of God. It wasn't as if he hadn't tried. Deep within he knew it would have been easier to accept the capricious nature of the awful end of his precious baby brother if he could simply decide there was no God, no Supreme Being who cared.

Unable to shake free from that last vestige of his childhood—the infuriating deep-seated belief that there was one true God—Levi had mired himself into an ugly opposition to the creator, the God of Abraham, Isaac, and Jacob. As he tried to take in the breadth of the heavens, he was only reminded of what a lonely, bitter battle this was.

Levi suddenly stood and drew his cloak more tightly around him. He was shaken by a sudden inclination to pray, to talk to his chief enemy, to tell Him what he really thought. But what would be the profit in that? God would not answer him, nor was He required to. Levi cast his eyes down and hurried back to his home and to his bed, determined to evade the urge by no longer gazing at the stars.

THE FOLLOWING DAY, Levi was still out of sorts. He had barely slept, and though his staff prepared his favorite breakfast, nothing appealed and he left his plate largely untouched. He spent much of the rest of the day wandering his gardens, watching his staff, and dozing in the sun.

But the naps could not make up for the solid hours of sleep he required, and he was left feeling logy and frustrated. Was this to be his life then? A vague empty feeling that he had wasted his best years doing what he had set out to do, only to find that in the end it added up to nothing?

Levi looked forward to the evening meeting with Efah and the fishermen, if for no other reason than it would give him something else to think about. Self-loathing was hardly profitable. He had to set his mind on other things—like recording the meeting so thoroughly that the fishermen would fear the report getting back to Rome.

LEVI WAS NOT used to being defensive. Normally it was he who intimidated the other party—unless it happened to be Roman dignitaries or specifically Leontius, the Roman knight to whom he reported. But as soon as he arrived at the tax office and was confronted by the four fishermen, his plan to unnerve them was quickly foiled.

"My name is Simon, Levi, and I'm glad you're here."

"I know who you are, sir, and I need to tell you that my role this evening will be to—"

"Your job is to record this meeting, Levi," the

110

plain-speaking man announced. "You are known as a man who writes quickly and accurately, and we need to know that our ideas will be heard and passed on to Rome."

"Sit, gentlemen, sit," Efah said. "There is no need to involve Rome. That's why we are here. We will hear your concerns and—"

"We have been told that before," James said, joining his brother John and Simon's brother Andrew on a long wooden bench. "Now we really must insist that you make note of—"

"I will record the meeting," Levi said, spreading out his papyrus and writing implements. "But I will decide what is communicated to Rome, not you. Is that understood?"

The fishermen glanced at one another, glowering, and James began to speak again before Simon cut him off. "Friend, we agreed I would do the talking. Now, let me. And I should say, Levi and Efah, when I talk, I am speaking for—"

"All the fishermen," Efah said. "We know."

"They're waiting for a good word from us," Simon said. "And you know as well as we do how many there are and how much of the local trade depends on us."

"Because poor people eat fish," Levi said, beginning to write.

"Is there something wrong with being poor?" Simon said.

"Come, come," Levi said. "You are business

111

owners. Surely you do not number yourselves among your customers."

"Of course we do!" John said indignantly before Simon shushed him.

"Yes, we do," Simon said. "Unlike you, we don't brag about our profits. We worked for years to build our businesses and own our boats. And now, because of all that Rome and you and the temple demand of us—"

Levi looked up sharply. "Don't lay on us any burden the Pharisees place on you. That is between you and them. If you want to revolt against taxes, revolt against those."

Simon lowered his voice. "The Pharisees think less of you than you do of them."

Efah laughed aloud. "No doubt, though that would take some doing! Now, Simon, let me ask that you direct your comments to me and allow the chief publican to concentrate on his work. Tell me what it is that brings you to our office tonight, and please spare me the usual list of grievances and unacceptable suggestions for solutions."

"But that's the problem, sir," Simon said. "We are humble, hardworking men. We do not work to line our own pockets. We try to serve our fellow citizens and provide for our families. It's good for Capernaum if we succeed."

"It benefits Capernaum if you pay your taxes."

"At cost to our businesses? How does that help anyone but you?"

"You would be advised to not make this personal," Efah said.

"It's personal to us!" James thundered.

"John," Simon said, "take your brother for a walk, would you?"

"I don't need to be treated like a child!" James said.

"Apparently you do. Now go."

As John tugged his raging brother toward the door, James hissed over his shoulder, "You had better succeed, Simon. Don't let them put you off again. Don't believe their empty promises."

"I'm sorry, Efah," Simon said. "Both sons of Zebedee have short tempers. But I must also say that they are right. This *is* personal. We and our fellow fishermen are the lifeblood of this region. We feed the masses. We know what we're doing and we keep trying to get better at it, but our sails are old and worn and our nets are mostly in shreds. By the time we pay taxes on our property—"

"An obligation that is none of our business," Efah said. "That is a direct tax paid to the royal treas—"

"It all goes to Rome!" Simon said. "But, all right, forget the direct taxes, though they can sometimes account for twenty-five percent of our assets. Paying you for every catch, every trip to the market, and even for the use of the sea leaves us with barely enough to feed and clothe our families and provide them shelter. All we are asking for is a short break. We promise to use every bit of it to fix our equipment and make us more productive. That will mean more business for us and more taxes for you!"

"For Rome, you mean."

"Oh, I'm sorry. I did not realize you were on fixed salaries regardless of the amount of taxes you collect."

Even the otherwise silent Andrew laughed at that.

"You know full well we take no salary," Efah said. "So what you are asking is for us to lend you money, to take it from our own pockets to your benefit."

"To *your* benefit in the long run," Simon said.

"Perhaps we are not interested in the long run," Efah said. "Perhaps we are interested in the here and now."

"A true pagan," Simon muttered.

"What did you say?" Levi said.

"Nothing."

"I heard that."

"Gentlemen," Simon said. "We don't want to have to stop fishing. Surely you don't want Rome hearing that the fishermen of Galilee have shut down their businesses. The people will go hungry, and it won't be long before they rise up. What will you do, feed them meat from your rich tables?"

"Do *not* threaten us," Efah said. "Now, as we are

on record and as the chief publican has said that he will decide what is communicated to Rome, let me speak my piece. Your request is denied, your threat is acknowledged, and my suggestion to Rome will be that they send their best and most industrious fishermen to replace you and fish these waters. Your buyers will have grown hungry enough to not care who puts the food on their tables."

Levi was impressed. Efah had come up with a capital plan, and it was clear from the shock on Simon and Andrew's faces that he had got their attention. Rome would leap at such a prospect. Future-thinking young businessmen would invest in such a scheme and Romans would strike out for the Sea of Galilee to make their fortunes. The problem was, despite the brilliance of the plan, it was just wrong. Such enterprising men would not pay taxes to Levi but directly to Rome, so besides putting the fishermen out of business, the plan would cost him money. It would destroy families who had been fishermen for centuries. Their income would dry up, their families would go hungry. It was almost as despicable as sending armed horsemen out in the middle of the night to slaughter innocent children.

"Excuse me, Efah," Levi said, fully aware that he was about to embarrass, perhaps even humiliate, his subordinate. "Allow me to reason with Simon here, as he speaks for the fishing trade. If your taxes were to be suspended for two months, would that provide enough income to mend your nets and repair your boats?"

"It would, sir."

Levi held up a hand. "And would you then be willing to pay back the temporary savings by having your taxes increased by twenty-five percent for each of the following four months?"

"Levi!" Efah cried. "Surely, you're not—"

"Well, I—"

"You said yourself that the improvement to your equipment would increase your business to higher levels than ever."

"Yes, we would be willing to take that risk."

"And if we agree to such an arrangement, may I inform Rome so they will not feel compelled to take action due to a temporary drop in tax revenue?"

"Certainly," Simon said with a wary tone, as if he knew he shouldn't believe this.

Efah stood. "Levi, surely you're not actually going to—"

"As always," Levi said, "I am going to do what I decide to do in the best interests of this region and Rome. And what I have decided is that this makes sense. Simon, we have you and your compatriots within sight every day. We will know at once if you seem to be taking advantage of my good graces and fail to uphold your end of the bargain."

Simon nodded, still plainly wary. "Can I tell the others?"

"With one caveat. The public at large must know nothing of it."

"That will not be easy. The men will want to tell their wives and close friends."

"They must not. If word gets back to this office that others want a similar consideration, the arrangement is rescinded."

Efah sat and then stood quickly again when Levi rose and thrust out a hand to Simon. "You're actually going to do this," Efah said.

Again Levi silenced him with a gesture and a look. Simon shook both their hands vigorously and said, "You won't be sorry! Thank you, gentlemen! You'll see that this is good for all." Andrew merely nodded as they left, and Levi heard excited talking among the two sets of brothers as they headed away.

Efah sat heavily on the bench and crossed his legs and arms. "Well?" he said.

"Well what?"

"I'm waiting for an explanation, Levi."

"And where did you get the notion that I am required to explain myself to you? I have to answer to Rome for this decision, so—"

"You certainly do! And if you do not report it accurately, I will."

"I need not remind you, Efah, that you do not report to Rome. You answer to me. *I* answer to Rome."

117

"They are not unaware of my role here, chief."

"That's because I inform them."

"That's not the only reason."

"Oh, you inform them too? Well, fine. You should know by now that they listen to the jangling of coins, not the breast-beating of proud birds."

"I remain stunned by what you have done."

"Spend the rest of the evening with me, and we will talk it through."

Efah ran his hands through his hair. "I told my wife not to expect me home before the midnight watch. But I confess I am not happy with you just now."

"That's plain. I did not invite you to be charming company but rather so that we can dine and talk."

Efah rose and strode past Levi into the night, and as Levi bent to douse the lamps, he realized that he had not noticed before that his old classmate's hair was already turning gray. It wouldn't be long before his own did the same. And again he was stabbed with the knowledge that his life was passing with little to show for it beyond what he had tried to accrue for himself. There had been no satisfaction, no relief, nothing gained by shaking his fist in the face of God.

TWO OF LEVI'S SERVANTS were idly chatting when he and Efah approached. One ran to him and asked what he would like. Levi ordered quantities of roast lamb, fresh bread, and his finest wine.

Half an hour later the feast seemed wasted on Efah, who spent more time talking than eating, which did nothing for Levi's appetite. Finally Levi shoved his plate aside and dismissed the servants.

"You made me look the fool," Efah said.

"That was not my intent."

"The decision was mine to make, Levi."

"Unless the chief publican disagreed with it, and I did. My friend, this seems obvious. We may not have liked what the fishermen said or the way they said it, but they were right, and in the end we will profit more."

"And if we don't?"

"Then you will have been right, I will have been humiliated in the eyes of Rome, and all those men will lose their livelihoods."

"That is my prophecy."

"Indeed? And you don't see that if you are right, you will suffer financially?"

"Oh, no, sir. *You* might. But I won't. I will succeed you."

ELEVEN

Ten days into the new arrangement with the local fishermen, Levi made his way to the northern shore of the Sea of Galilee to see if he might be able to determine whether they were wisely using their tax breaks. Around midday his patience was rewarded when Simon and Andrew's crew came ashore and began processing their catch.

"We're already doing better!" Simon called out with a wave.

Levi pressed a finger to his lips to remind the man to not speak publicly about their deal. Simon drew closer and spoke in low tones. "See the repaired nets and a few new ones? And see that resealing of the hull? All impossible without your favor. We appreciate it very much."

"Let us not appear too friendly," Levi said. "I have a reputation to maintain."

"Understood. Scold me, yell at me if you must."

"That will not be necessary. I'll be on my way now. I was only checking on your progress. You need to vindicate me in the eyes of Rome."

"We're doing all we can, sir."

LEVI ARRIVED BACK at the tax office to find a sealed message from Rome, informing him that Knight Leontius would be arriving in two days. "I am in receipt of your report concerning the arrangement with the fishermen and wish to discuss it in person. There shall be twelve in our party and, as usual, we will plan to lodge and dine with you."

Levi sat back and sighed, aware Efah was watching him. The seal had not been broken, but it would not have surprised Levi if the man knew what the message said. He was certain something was afoot, though it was also possible that the financial procurator would have sought such a meeting based on Levi's input alone.

But what more could he have told his superior? What else was there to say? He had recorded virtually every word of the meeting with the two sets of brothers and even noted Efah's opposition to his decision. But he had also written out all the calculations, showing that the temporary shortfall would result in much heavier profits for all in just a few months.

All he needed was the pomp and ceremony of a visit from Leontius. The man enjoyed being transported about Judea in a four-posted sedan carried by two teams of four servants each, both led and trailed by a Roman soldier in a chariot. Those ten, along with his top aide and the knight himself, would make up the twelve. Why he needed to be transported like a Caesar was beyond Levi, but he was used to the ritual.

There had never been even the hint of a threat on the man's life. Indeed, the citizenry barely knew who he was or what he did. But with all the pageantry and colors flying, onlookers stopped and gaped as the caravan slowly made its way from the port to Jerusalem and then up to Capernaum. That his scheduled arrival was so soon meant that the knight had already arrived in Israel.

Levi sent a runner to his estate to inform his staff so they would have time to stock up on the finest meat and cheese and wine and bread, plus foodstuffs for the horses. The lodging had to be just so as well, as Leontius preferred a window on one side of his room that greeted the rising sun and one on the other side that allowed him to also watch the sunset.

Levi couldn't imagine why that was so important, because to his knowledge, based on several previous visits over the past two decades, the man had never seen a sunset. By the time the sun disappeared, Leontius was full-bellied, still drinking, and demanding entertainment. By the time his aide hauled him off to bed, it was well past the midnight watch.

"I'm off to supervise the closing of the markets," Efah said, throwing his cloak over his shoulders. "Will you want me in attendance when you entertain Rome?"

"I'll let you know," Levi said slowly.

"I did not read your message, if that's what you're wondering. I just noticed the seal and drew a conclusion. I shall await word of any need for me."

"Naturally. Tell me, Efah, have you been promised anything yet? Should I begin packing?"

"What? No! Why would you say such a thing? You have just renewed your contract. You would have to be in egregious breach of it to necessitate any such drastic change here."

"You yourself prophesied you would replace me."

"Oh, that! You know it was said in anger, in haste. I should like to think I would be your choice to replace you someday, when you have had enough of this."

Levi waved Efah in and asked him to sit.

"I really must be going."

"Just a moment," Levi said.

Efah sat.

"Do you think I'm going to retire like my predecessor? I mean, I just might, but do not forget that you are nearly ten years my senior. You are more likely to quit before I do."

"Let us be frank," Efah said. "Neither of us is ready for pasture, and the benefits are too lucrative."

Levi nodded sadly. He could not argue.

"And yet, you seem to have lost the passion, Levi. Are you growing soft? Do you wish to see the end of this?"

"Are you that eager to take my place? And do you have the resources?"

"Not yet. But perhaps by the end of your current agreement."

Efah leaned as if awaiting permission to stand and leave, and Levi nodded. As the man towered over him, Levi said, "Perhaps that would not be an unwise goal."

"I should plan for that, then? It is a good thing to know and prepare for."

"With this stipulation," Levi said, as Efah hesitated at the door. "I do not want you working behind my back, plotting with Leontius. I have options other than you as my successor, you know. And if you weary me with too much opposition to my decisions, I reserve the right to change my mind."

THERE HAD BEEN A TIME when Levi actually looked forward to hosting his superior. Leontius always insisted that he enjoyed crowds, and so Levi was instructed to invite his entire staff and their spouses for at least one evening at the estate. This filled his house and grounds for a lavish feast. He had long wondered why his people so seemed to enjoy these bacchanals, only to finally be told that the wives especially liked the novelty of trying to impress royalty—or at least a secondary dignitary.

Levi knew that was his own motivation as well. He had always worked to fulfill Leontius's every desire and to show well at being a good host. He spared no expense and basked in his superior's praise. Never before, however, had the knight specifically mentioned a matter of concern he wished to discuss, and so perhaps this visit would be different.

Still Levi assembled his staff and told them of the planned visit, inviting them to a banquet on the second night of Leontius's stay. No surprise, they seemed excited to get home and tell their wives.

LEVI KNEW to have his entire tax office staff working every thoroughfare the afternoon the knight was expected, with runners and couriers at the ready to get word to him of the progress of the trip. Leontius enjoyed being appropriately welcomed at the tax office on his way to Levi's estate, where he expected to be received by the host himself, to have his feet washed, and to be given a cool cup of water. As Leontius's feet never touched solid ground from the time he disembarked from the ship until he was helped from the covered sedan, first at the tax office and finally at Levi's, why he needed them washed was beyond his host. But Levi would do his duty.

He gathered citizens outside the tax office to celebrate the knight's arrival, then rushed ahead to his own home to be there in time for that reception. Every time before, Levi had done this with a certain amount of excitement. He'd had a reason, an aim. He would subject himself to this pompous man as a means to an end. And that end was his own elevation in the eyes of Rome—not because he cared what they thought of him, but so he would be in a better position to take advantage of them.

But by now, in the twilight of his career, Levi had accomplished that and more. He realized that Rome expected publicans, particularly chief publicans, to take as much as they could get away with. As long as the government got enough, that was all they cared about. Besides the fact that all he had garnered for himself had not come even close to avenging his loss, Rome's effectual complicity in his own scheme tempered any satisfaction he might have gotten from it.

Now the pomposity Leontius embodied so repelled Levi that it was all he could do to fake the least passion for his subservient act. The centurions would bark orders at him and his servants, and he and they would rush about, bowing, scraping, washing, pouring, opening doors, pulling out chairs, laughing at lame jokes, nodding as if interested in every boring story.

The knight always seemed to feel obligated to rehearse his entire trip, from the trek to the ship to every turn of the weather or bout with seasickness and from the port all the way to Capernaum. It rarely changed, nor did anything interesting really happen, but still Levi felt compelled to maintain eye contact and feign wholehearted interest.

This trip proved true to form, and by the time Levi himself had finished drying the man's feet and sat sipping cold water with him, it was all he could do to keep from falling asleep due to sheer boredom. Finally, to Levi's great relief, Leontius himself suggested they complete their business before the evening meal.

They moved from Levi's welcoming parlor to a tile-roofed portico that overlooked his vineyards. Out of the presence of his lackeys, some of Leontius's haughtiness abated. He lifted his toga and sat, stretching as if the long journey had been tedious, though of course he had not lifted a finger, let alone a foot.

"The Pharisees," he said at last. "How are they treating you?"

"The usual," Levi said. "They hate us as they always have. Constantly at the edges of the crowd, yipping at us, berating us. We'd feel neglected if they quit."

Leontius laughed. "And Efah? Is he still working out for you?"

"Let's not pretend we're both unaware of his relationship with me, and with you."

"With me?" the knight said. "He has no contract with us."

"But he wants one badly enough to be able to taste it."

"That shouldn't threaten you, Levi. You have long been the prime example of a chief publican, leading the way in profits, known throughout Judea—and Rome, naturally—as the toughest negotiator, the fastest recorder, and the best calculator."

"Did I say Efah's ambition threatened me?"

"You seemed sensitive about his approach to us."

"Should I not? That is insubordination, a dismissal-level offense."

"He worries about you, that's all. And why shouldn't he? He tells me you let a farm couple off with the minimum tax. That's not like you. How do you expect to make a profit and pay your people?"

"What does Rome care about that as long as it gets its share?"

"We got the entirety of that payment, Levi. You must admit it was out of character."

Levi sighed. "Must we be inhumane, sir? Did Efah also tell you the couple was in mourning?"

"He did. That never got in your way before."

"Perhaps it should have."

"So you're saying you plan to make a habit of this?"

"Of what? Lightening the burden, forgoing my margin for any couple that has recently buried a child? Maybe I will. Rest assured, I will however squeeze from them every shekel you require."

Leontius slowly turned and looked into Levi's eyes. "You are bordering on sarcasm and insolence, my friend."

"I apologize. But let me worry about my own

profits. I'm not asking Rome to partner with me in allowing any credit."

"Not even to the fishermen?"

"Only temporarily, as you know."

"I do not understand it."

"Of course you do, sir. You know enough about business to comprehend that a wise investment now can soon pay deep dividends. That is all I am allowing—these men to have some relief from their tax burden in order to improve their business long-term. Surely you see the wisdom in it."

"You ascribe to yourself wisdom now?"

"Frankly, I always have. I do not apologize for thoroughly giving myself to my craft, and while this latest stratagem may seem unique, it fits my pattern of slowly, carefully, creatively building my business by allowing some of my best accounts to build theirs."

Leontius sat in silence for a few minutes, and Levi did not feel obligated to say more. Finally the knight shifted his weight and spoke softly. "I need not remind you that you are fresh into your current contract. Like you, I have a superior, and may I say that he is not as reasonable as I. He will not long countenance a drop in income. All that to say, we will be watching. If you are right and in the long run we come out ahead, that will accrue only to the enhancing of your already fine reputation. Short of that, despite your stellar record, I can make no promises."

"I understand."

"Now, on to more pleasant topics. When do your guests arrive and what shall I look forward to this evening?"

"Oh, sir, just a sumptuous meal with your staff and me tonight. The celebratory feast in your honor is set for the morrow."

"Oh! That will not do! Is it too late to get word to your people—and to whoever you have arranged for our entertainment—to favor us this very evening?"

"My apologies, sir. I am afraid it *is* too late. I had no inkling that you were not able to stay over as you usually do."

"Admittedly it *was* a late change of plans. I am to investigate a rabble-rouser, some sort of troublemaker in the Judean wilderness ranting about Herod Antipas and what he calls his seduction of Herodias, the wife of one of his half brothers."

Levi smiled. "It's true, isn't it?"

"Well, everyone knows that," Leontius said, "but sane people don't rush about criticizing the king."

"This madman is not the first and will not be the last. Is anyone taking him seriously?"

"Oh, he has quite a following, despite that he dresses like a wild animal and claims he is preparing the way of the Messiah."

"The Messiah again."

"Say, you were the son of a priest, were you not?"

"I was the son of a tanner."

"But your name . . ."

"Yes, they wanted me to become a priest. I preferred, shall we say, a more comfortable living."

"Well this man, who goes by John, is the son of a priest. Can you imagine the family's shame?"

"Oh, believe me, Leontius, they are likely quite proud of him. The religious leaders are as upset with the king and his wife as any of the populace are."

Leontius stood. "I am growing hungry."

"We'll eat within the hour, sir."

"Good. It will be an early evening for me tonight, as I leave at first light tomorrow to see if I can join the throngs who clamor to hear this insurrectionist."

"Will he not temper his opinions if he sees a Roman dignitary in the crowd?"

They began walking back inside. "Quite the contrary, I understand. I am told I should expect to be called down, challenged to speak for Rome in denouncing the king and his immorality. Imagine."

TWELVE

Levi was not surprised to learn, just a few days after Leontius's departure, that the madman John had been arrested and thrown into prison. What did he expect? The son of a priest, indeed, prophesying about the coming Messiah. Didn't he realize that the king's own father, Herod the Great, had likely taken the life of the Christ shortly after he was born some thirty years before?

Stories began circulating of the man in prison and what he had been preaching, but Levi gave the matter little more thought until he received word from his brother James that he wished to come and visit him again soon.

"I wish to speak with you about the condemned man," his brother wrote. "I'm sure you've heard of him."

It was unusual that James would visit again so soon, but what might he possibly have to say about this John? Had he seen the man, heard him, met him? From what little he knew of his own brother, James was a steady, most levelheaded scholar. Surely he wasn't becoming a rumor-monger, especially not about a mischief maker.

During the days he waited for James to arrive, Levi found himself listening to more and more of the talk about what might become of the man who had been preaching and baptizing hundreds in the Jordan. Something about him had proved appealing to the masses. Could there be any shred of credibility to this baptizer?

James's arrival—he was carrying his simple sack over his shoulder and walking a donkey—was in such contrast to Leontius's grand entrance that Levi had to smile at the memory of it. How nice to have a normal person visit, a man just as happy with a piece of grilled fish, a crust of bread, and a cup of wine, one on whom all the flurry of meats and entertainment would be lost. Levi found himself warmer and more forthcoming with his brother than he had ever been. He was genuinely curious about the man and his life, an entirely new interest on his part.

But after having his feet washed and being refreshed with water, James was eager to get to the matter at hand. And he was clearly exercised. "Tell me anything you may know of John the baptizer," James said.

"Just what's going around, brother. Most see him as a lunatic but admire his boldness in openly challenging the king. I don't know what people think about his claims to be preparing the way for the long-awaited Messiah."

"Well, that's why I'm here."

"So your message said."

From his bag James produced scrolls. "You brought Scriptures?" Levi said. "This is not like you."

"I know, but I do not want to rely only on my memory."

"Which is as good as mine was, if our father and mother could be believed."

"It is a strength of mine, Levi. But here, allow me to show you this."

Levi led him to a table where he could unroll the

documents, and he quickly found his place. He rested his finger on it, then looked at his brother. "I was assigned to go hear the man and report back to the elders."

"Did you meet him?"

James shook his head. "But at one point I was close enough that I could have touched him."

"Really? He mingled with the crowds while his life was in such danger?"

"Levi, he was fearless! And I know what he says sounds extreme, but never have I met a man with such passion. I came away knowing, *knowing,* that if nothing else, he thoroughly believed everything he was saying."

"And what was he saying, besides calling the Pharisees vipers and the king immoral?"

Levi had never seen James so excited. He was by nature calm and thoughtful, befitting his station. But now he looked at his older brother with fire in his eyes. "What the baptizer said was that people should repent, for the kingdom of heaven is at hand."

Levi nearly laughed but caught himself. "Sit, brother. Tell me what you think the man meant by that."

"I will sit, but first let me show you this." He pointed to the ancient passage. "Is it possible that this John is the one referred to by the prophet Isaiah?"

Levi looked over James's shoulder and read, *"The*

voice of one crying in the wilderness: 'Prepare the way of the Lord; Make His paths straight.'

"Oh, I don't know, James. You know I haven't studied this for more than two decades. You think this man is the fulfillment of some prophecy? You haven't said that about any of the other magicians or sorcerers who make claims of divinity."

They sat, James seemingly unable to relax. "But he makes no such claims! He spoke of one who is to come after him who he said was 'mightier than I, whose sandals I am not worthy to carry.' He said this Man will baptize with the Holy Spirit and fire."

"What does that mean?"

"I don't know. But here was this impassioned man, dressed in camel hair and wearing a leather belt, baptizing people from all over the region who came to him confessing their sins."

"He holds some sway over them," Levi said. "Where were all these people coming from?"

"Jerusalem, all Judea, and all the region around the Jordan. And when he noticed Pharisees and Sadducees in the crowd, he asked them, 'Who warned you to flee from the wrath to come?'"

"Again, James, what was he saying and who was he talking about?"

"That's the reason I'm here, Levi."

"I know! You wouldn't come all this way to tease me with riddles, would you? Surely this is leading somewhere."

"John said he baptized with water unto repentance, but that the One who is to come after him 'will thoroughly clean out His threshing floor, and gather His wheat into the barn; but He will burn up the chaff with unquenchable fire.' "

Levi did not want to offend his brother, but he could not hide his amusement. "Well, I guess we'll just have to see who comes after John and whether he can keep from the baptizer's own fate."

"He has already come, Levi, and he may be the Messiah."

Levi was stunned to silence. Finally he managed, "You're serious?"

"Witnesses say that not long before John was arrested and imprisoned, a Man of about thirty came from Galilee to the Jordan to be baptized by him. They say John at first tried to prevent Him, saying, 'I need to be baptized by You, and are You coming to me?'

"This Man answered that John should permit it because it was fitting for them to fulfill all righteousness. People say that when John baptized this Man, He came up immediately from the water and the heavens were opened and a dove alighted upon Him. And suddenly a voice came from the clouds, saying, 'This is My beloved Son, in whom I am well pleased.' "

"And you believe this?"

"I am fascinated by it."

"Who wouldn't be? Where is this Messiah now?"

"No one has seen Him for more than a month. But, Levi, listen. You always told me how and why our brother was killed. If the Messiah *was* born around that time, could this Man be Him?"

"Anything is possible. But why has He disappeared? If He is who you think He could be, does He not have a lot to accomplish?"

James stood and paced. "Should I be offended at your tone? I can tell you are merely humoring me."

"I mean you no offense, brother. But you come to me with this wild tale about the kingdom of God being at hand and perhaps the Messiah arriving. What am I supposed to think?"

"That it could be true."

"As I say, anything is possible, but it could also not be true."

"Let me show you one more passage." James moved to the scroll, and Levi sighed as he rose to follow. "Look here."

He found a text that read: "The land of Zebulun and the land of Naphtali, by the way of the sea, beyond the Jordan, Galilee of the Gentiles . . ."

James kept his finger there and looked up at Levi. "Would you not agree that describes Capernaum?"

"Yes, but—"

"Listen. 'The people who sat in darkness have

seen a great light, And upon those who sat in the region and shadow of death Light has dawned.'"

Levi cupped his brother's face in his hands. "So when this mystery Man reappears, you think he's coming here."

"I do."

"I will let you know."

"That is all I ask."

"No, it isn't. You require more of me. You ask that I remain open to His actually being the Messiah."

"What I'm asking, Levi, is that you allow in your mind the possibility that there may be some validity to this, especially if this Man *does* come to the 'land of Zebulun and the land of Naphtali, by the way of the sea, beyond the Jordan, Galilee of the Gentiles.'"

Levi smiled and clapped his brother on the back, surprised to feel that he was leaner, bonier than he recalled.

"Are you losing weight?"

"Brother, I am asking you a serious question! If this Man appears near here, you will know of it. Will you send word immediately?"

"How will I know of it? What does He look like? Who am I looking for?"

"If He is the Messiah, He will preach, He will draw more people to Himself than this John has."

"And won't He overthrow the government? I remember that much from my childhood studies."

"I know you are taking this lightly, Levi. I am not. If Messiah should come in our lifetimes, imagine it! I would not want to miss any of it."

"You know as well as I that I am in no position to be welcoming the Messiah."

"Your decision is final, then? You turned your back on our God once and forever?"

Levi felt as if he had been struck speechless. Not long ago he would have answered with venom, insisting that this was exactly the case. God had failed him, disappointed him, proved Himself weak or incompetent or capricious at best. But his recent battles with sleeplessness and restlessness and disappointment in his own life had given him pause. His problem, he now knew, was that despite his deep feelings of anger and resentment and even abandonment, he missed God.

He finally found his voice and whispered, "I suppose if God chose this time to send Messiah, He might rekindle my attention."

Levi was embarrassed by his own admission and realized that he had tempered his own self-assured image in the eyes of his younger brother. "Come," he said more brightly. "Let's walk my vineyard. And you need to tell me why you are growing thinner."

James rerolled the scrolls, then followed Levi out. "It is nothing," he said. "I confess both my appetite and my sleep have been affected by my recent assignment. It falls to me to investigate this

Man for the Sanhedrin and to watch for any evidence proving He could not be the Messiah."

Levi stopped and pressed a grape between his thumb and forefinger, then plucked it and popped it into his mouth. "I should think they would want evidence that He *is* Messiah."

"Oh, I think they would like nothing more. But rumor has it that the man baptized by John in the Jordan is a carpenter from Nazareth."

Levi threw back his head and laughed. "Nazareth! Well, that simply wouldn't do, would it?"

"That's not the worst of it. Some have said he may be related to John and that this whole thing may simply be something they have devised as a scheme."

"To what end?"

James shook his head. "I cannot make sense of it. I don't see how they profit from this, unless they begin raising money for some cause. The people were enamored of John. What might they think of this other Man?"

"And how do those who suspect a plot explain the voice from heaven?"

"I don't know," James muttered. "Maybe they are in on it."

"Let me ask you this," Levi said. "What about your new task costs you sleep and your appetite?"

James sighed. "I suppose because I so badly want it to be true. I have looked forward to the coming of Messiah since I was old enough to understand the prophecies. To think that He may come in my lifetime . . ."

"Come, brother. You realize how unlikely this all is."

"Yes. Sadly, I do."

"If I were you, I would eat more and try to get some sleep."

As they walked back toward the house, James said, "You know, Levi, one of the reasons this is so important to me is the impact it would have on you."

"On me?"

"Tell me you wouldn't have to reconsider your entire attitude toward God if He sent Messiah to Galilee."

Levi laughed again. "You have always been such a dreamer."

"How would you know?"

PART TWO

LEVI'S CALL

THIRTEEN

When James departed Capernaum for Jerusalem, Levi realized for the first time how abjectly empty he felt. He was overwhelmed with a desolation that seemed to eat at him, and he missed his brother immediately, for more reasons than his own loneliness. This visit had brought memories of his parents flooding back. Though James was not a man who worked with his hands, and he did not have that big, broad frame of their father, still he bore a distinct resemblance to the man, especially in his jaw and chin.

And in James's manner and tone, his loving spirit, Levi recognized his mother.

Whatever his problems with God were, had he had to be so cruel to Alphaeus and Mary? His intent was to make plain his bitterness and to flee from the plans they had for him. And while he had never been overtly hostile, his mere absence and silence—he knew—spoke loudly. As he walked to the office the morning following his brother's visit he realized that he loved James and was still stung by his brother's retort, asking how he could have known whether the man was a dreamer.

The implication, of course, was that he had hardly known James as a lad. And it was true. Levi had protected his heart from another tragic disappointment and by the time James was old enough to truly engage as a brother, Levi had left home. Over the years, while they had cordially visited occasionally, they were more acquaintances—not even friends—than brothers.

LEVI HAD WALKED PAST the local synagogue hundreds, yea thousands, of times on his way to work over the years. Never before had it given him pause. He had never so much as hesitated in its shadow, let alone been tempted to enter for any other reason than business—and his business there was infrequent. The leaders cared even less for him than he did for them.

Yet this morning, not two weeks since his brother had visited, Levi's gait seemed to slow involuntarily. Was it time to slip inside and acknowledge God? He had not prayed since leaving home. And if he prayed, what would he say? Could he say he was sorry, that he had been mistaken? He still didn't feel that. Yes, the ancient manuscripts made clear that no man should question the mind of God. No one who had not hung the stars or created the earth should dare question the great God and Father of the faith.

So, what was the point? Would there be any value in just standing in the house of God as a form of communicating that perhaps—just perhaps—Levi was open to being persuaded that God had some purpose behind what He had allowed some thirty years before?

Levi stopped, but he could not force himself to take a step toward the entrance. What would people think? What would they say? He had never cared before, but a reputation, especially in his profession, was precious. Why did that still matter? Was he not coming to the conclusion that for all he had accomplished and achieved, his life was empty and meaningless?

A heartbeat from creeping into the synagogue, Levi froze at the sound of voices from within. And then the young students came running. Some skidded to a stop before him and one shouted, "Publican! Sinner! Traitor!"

This was nothing he hadn't heard countless times before—usually from adults—but always in the past he had grinned or smirked or scowled or snarled. Let them think and say what they wanted was his attitude, as long as they knew who he was and that he would not allow them to pay a shekel less than what he decreed.

But now he was unable to make a face, let alone form any response. *Yes,* he thought. *You have described me most accurately if not well.*

The *hazzan* quickly followed the boys out, scolding them and telling them to mind their own business. But even he shot Levi a glance, glaring and furrowing his brow as if he had found donkey dung in the middle of the road.

It was less than a quarter of a mile from the synagogue to the tax office, but Levi found it surprisingly long and slow. Whatever had been working on his mind the last few months, it had succeeded in taking all his motivation from living. What was his purpose? What was the point? He had become what everyone accused him of: a heartless, mean-spirited man.

He arrived at his office surprised to see Efah waiting for him. "I thought you were supervising at the harbor. Do we not expect cargo ships this morning?"

"It is all in hand," Efah said. "Let me worry about my staff, if you would."

"Don't forget that your staff is only my staff that I have assigned to you."

"Then allow me to do my job."

"That's my question, Efah. How can you do your job here when there is cargo to tax at the harbor?"

"My people will handle it, and if we are short, you may take it up with me. I am wondering where we stand with the fishermen at this point."

"That's why you stand idle here? To question me, the owner, your boss?"

"You are evading the question, Levi. It has now been two months since we gave them the break."

"So now you wish for me to go and demand payment?"

"When was the last time you checked on them?"

"I told you about that. I saw the new and mended nets, the repaired boats. And Simon him-self reported bigger catches already."

"He reported. Did you do any counting?"

"Efah, really! Do you really intend to insult me? I hold your fate in my hands."

"You have less sway over my fate than you may think. I am asking only the questions Rome will ask. If I am to inherit this territory, I want it in the healthiest state possible."

"That is four years from now! Are you not getting ahead of yourself?"

Efah shook his head. "You answer questions with questions! Do you need me to accompany you to the shore?"

"I had not forgotten, if that is your concern. Would you feel better about being at the harbor if you were aware that I was at the fishermen's shore?"

"I would."

"Then set your mind at ease, please, Efah, by all means. For I am on my way."

Maddeningly, Efah continued to wait as if making sure Levi actually headed out to the seashore, making Levi delay and find things to do. It made him feel childish, and when Efah finally asked, "Are you going?" Levi had had enough.

"Honestly, Efah! I am not your employee! You are mine! Now, get yourself to your appointed station or I shall replace you."

Efah reddened and began slamming things around, yanking on his cloak and muttering. Finally he said, "It is not I whose hold on this region is tenuous. You are the one who ought to be worried about his future."

"That may be, but for now, you remain subordinate to me."

"We'll see for how long."

"Yes, we will. Perhaps not beyond today if you cannot find it within yourself to do as you are instructed."

Levi allowed Efah a half mile or so head start so he would not have to deal with him along the way. When finally he reached the fishing boats and began watching for the brothers, Levi quickly became aware of the stares and glares that always greeted the tax collector. He was puzzled at this today, however, because it had seemed the fishermen had been easier on him since he had offered the temporary tax break. Had something changed, or with the end of the reprieve was everything back to normal?

He approached a boat where three men sat mending nets. They glanced at him and looked away. "I am looking for your spokesman," Levi said.

"Of course you are," one muttered.

"He is not on the water today, sir."

"You're sure?"

"I'm sure."

"Where is he? Do you know?"

The man shrugged. "Perhaps listening to the prophet on the eastern shore."

"The prophet?"

"Some of the early morning men returned with stories of a man over there carrying on about the kingdom of God."

Levi felt a chill. "Anyone going that way yet today?"

"We are if we can get this work done."

"Might I catch a ride with you? Surely it would be faster than walking."

"What, is a tax due for preaching?"

The men laughed, and to stay in their good graces and gain passage, Levi chuckled along. "I am just curious. And perhaps I will meet with Simon."

"We'll be another hour."

"Would it be more prudent for me to walk?"

"You'd be ahead if you could find a cart ride right now. Otherwise, we'll take you."

Levi busied himself while waiting by observing other boats coming and going, offloading fish, and making small repairs. Presently he came upon the elderly Zebedee, whose wispy white hair sprouted from a leathery brown head. The old man was slowly folding a net, appearing to conserve his waning strength. They greeted each other and Levi asked after James and John.

Zebedee looked surprised, as if he found it difficult to believe the chief publican cared about his sons. "Well, they are all right," he said, a slight smile revealing toothless gums. "They, and all of us, have very much appreciated your consideration these last two months."

In truth, Levi was not in the habit of congenial conversation. "Well, you should appreciate it. And the benefits to the business had better show, and soon."

Zebedee's smile faded and he nodded, turning back to his work.

THREE HOURS LATER Levi disembarked on the eastern shore with a less than effusive thank-you to his hosts. Hundreds of people were milling about, talking excitedly. He overheard a woman say, "I have never heard anything like it!"

"Pardon me, madam," Levi said, "what did I miss?"

"You didn't hear the Preacher?"

"I only just arrived."

"He spoke as One with authority."

"What did He say?"

"He said what the baptizer had been saying, to repent, for the kingdom of God is at hand."

"What did He mean?"

"I don't know, but I will hear Him again."

Levi searched in vain for Simon or Andrew and eventually resorted to getting a slow ride all the way around to the northern end of sea on an oxcart. All the way back he planned what he would write to his brother. No, he had not seen the Man in question, but yes, it had to be the one James was assigned to follow.

And yet, too, the more Levi thought about the fact that Simon and perhaps his brother had been distracted from their work and business so soon after benefiting from his largesse, the angrier he became. He was grateful to find the brothers securing their boat when finally he arrived back.

"What do you mean by taking the day off when you are behind in your taxes?"

Simon normally retorted angrily when Levi challenged him, especially publicly. But now his eyes seemed to dance. "We didn't take the entire day off, friend. In fact, we just finished processing a decent catch just before you arrived. I was on the eastern shore where—"

"So I heard. Listening to a Preacher?"

"More of a prophet. He was most impressive. He—"

"I know, I know. Don't make a habit of this while trying to make up for the tax break."

"You should hear Him, sir."

"Perhaps I will! But you have responsibilities. After your work is finished tomorrow, I want you to come by the tax office."

"Must I?"

"You must! Rome will have no more patience with you than I do."

IT WAS DARK by the time Levi reached the tax office, where he planned to simply be certain all was in order before penning his missive to his brother and heading home. Though it was dusk, he was surprised to see more people than usual milling about in the streets. They were speaking excitedly, as those on the other side of the Galilee had been, and Levi realized that for the second time in one day, he had just missed the Prophet, or Teacher, or Preacher, or impostor—whichever it was he might be.

Naturally Levi suspected the last, but he couldn't deny the stir caused by the Man. A passerby said, "He taught in the synagogue, preaching the gospel of the kingdom! And rumor has it He then went out and healed all kinds of sickness and all kinds of disease among the people!"

Levi had seen fake healers before. They paid people to feign maladies, which they then miraculously cured. Their fame was brief, as they were soon found out. He hurried to the synagogue, where the rabbi was surrounded by citizens, all clamoring for answers.

"I do not know what to make of Him any more than you do," he was saying.

"Yes, but you allowed Him inside to read the Scriptures and teach! Is He a rabbi?"

"He certainly spoke like one," the rabbi said. "Didn't He?"

"But if you don't know Him, how could you allow—"

"He asked my permission. He introduced himself as Jesus bar Joseph of Nazareth, and—"

"Is He a rabbi there?"

The rabbi threw up his hands. "Not to my knowledge. He said His trade was carpentry."

"Carpentry! Are you not to guard the gate of the temple the way a shepherd protects the flock? What possessed you to allow Him that place of honor when He has no training?"

The rabbi hesitated. "I don't know. All I can say is that His tone, His very visage, gave me confidence that He was sincere and had a word for us. Plus crowds followed Him here, so I knew they were already persuaded that He was worth hearing. And did you not hear Him? Could you argue with a single point He made?"

"I did not understand Him," a woman called out.

"Neither did I!" a man said. "He spoke mysteries."

"Yet He made sense," the rabbi said. "And I would welcome Him again."

"And I would hear Him again!"

"Me too!"

"Did you hear about the healings?"

The rabbi nodded. "I heard, but I did not witness anything of the sort, so I will withhold judgment and comment on that."

Levi stepped forward. "What if He turns out to be a sorcerer, a charlatan?"

155

"Then we will have all been played for fools," the rabbi said. "And I the chief among you."

"Don't include me," Levi said. "I am not convinced."

"You heard Him and were not impressed?" a young man said.

And Levi was caught. All he had heard was what others had said, but admitting that would render his opinion moot. He swore. "I heard all I needed to hear. I am not swept along by every wind that passes through Capernaum."

"Watch your language!" the rabbi said.

"And go back to your overflowing purse!" a woman said. "We stopped caring what you thought years ago."

Levi waved them off as he skulked back to his office. He scratched neatly on a piece of papyrus, "James, the object of your investigation is here. Jesus bar Joseph of Nazareth. The populace is in an uproar. I cannot imagine he is who you hope him to be, but you might want to come in haste."

FOURTEEN

The night proved long and particularly lonely for Levi, especially since he knew that his message to his brother would not even begin its way to Jerusalem until the next morning. Perhaps James would have already heard the clamor that had to be spreading throughout the land.

If this Jesus was from Nazareth, even if He was the right age to be the Messiah, the Christ who had supposedly been born thirty years before, how had He escaped Herod's sword? Levi soon recognized the illogic of his own question. Surely God would find a way to protect the Messiah.

Levi ate listlessly and found himself barking at the servants over minor matters. He nearly apologized, alarming himself by some new sensitivity that had seemed to come over him. He talked himself out of it, though he knew the problem was his, not theirs. Nothing and no one could please him this night.

Sleep eluded him and he walked the grounds, the gardens, the vineyard. Levi found himself wishing, hoping, everything but praying that this Nazarene would still be in Capernaum the next day. He would see Him, hear Him, perhaps even question Him, whatever it took. And he would look forward to his brother's arrival, which would likely be only days away. James would be versed in all the evidences necessary to identify whether this Man fit the prophetic description of Messiah.

Levi finally drifted into a fitful sleep a few hours after midnight and found himself waking every hour or so before dawn. He ate a light breakfast and was at the tax office to address the staff before they headed out to their various posts. Efah seemed offended that Levi would address them all, when in recent years Levi had left direct supervision of them to him.

"I have an appointment here at the end of the day with the spokesmen for the fishermen," Levi announced. "But I want you all to be on the lookout for this Preacher, Jesus of Nazareth, and send word to me immediately if He appears near your area."

UNFORTUNATELY, the word Levi was looking for did not come until the end of the day, and it came from the shores. Jesus had been spotted interacting with the fishermen themselves. Levi was tempted to rush there, but he feared he would be too late and would then miss his appointment with Simon. Simon was expected soon, so perhaps he would be able to tell Levi something more about the Man and what he was up to.

But Simon never showed up. More than an hour after Simon was supposed to be there, Levi was pacing and trying to decide whether to make his way to the shore when one of his young tax collectors hurried in. "You were at the shore today, no?" Levi said.

"Yes!" the man said, out of breath. "And I spotted your Man, the one you were looking for!"

"Is he still there?"

"No, he was not there long."

"And what of Simon? Is he on his way here?"

"No, sir! Let me tell you what happened. This

Man was walking by the sea and stopped when He saw Simon and his brother casting a net. He called out to them, 'Follow Me, and I will make you fishers of men.' "

"Fishers of men? What did he mean?"

"I don't know, master, but Simon and Andrew immediately dropped their nets and left with Him."

Levi could not make sense of this. "They left their new nets?"

The young man nodded. "Others of their crew immediately took over their work, but the brothers are gone, following this Man."

"Following Him where?"

"They headed north. And when they came to the sons of Zebedee, in the boat with their father mending their nets, this Man called out to them too, and immediately they left the boat and their father and followed Him."

Levi realized he was trembling and interlocked his fingers to hide it. "Do you value your job, young man?"

"Of course I do, sir."

"Did you collect taxes from these men before they left? They owe for each boat, each net, each crew member, and every fish they caught."

"I know, but you seemed so urgent this morning about hearing word of the Preacher that I came immediately to tell what I had seen."

"Get back there and collect those taxes! These

men had better not have left their businesses for good. Who will make up for the break they were given to improve their income?"

"It may be too late for today, master, but I will do my best."

"Do that, and if no one remains there to pay, find them tomorrow. And if you hear anything about where they went with this stranger, bring me word of that too. I will be at home."

THAT NIGHT LEVI was listlessly dining alone when he heard activity at the front gate. He wiped his mouth and waited until a servant told him an employee wished to see him.

"Send him in."

The young man entered and apologized for interrupting his meal.

"Not at all. What news?"

"Today's taxes were paid in full by all the fishermen, and I have been assured they will be paid daily from here on out, even by the crews who have lost their owners."

"Lost? So Simon and Andrew and Zebedee's sons are gone?"

"They are, sir. Gone to be disciples of the Preacher."

"That makes no sense."

"It puzzled me too. But they tell me that the crowds hearing Him speak and watching Him heal people have grown to many hundreds."

"I am curious about this Man and should hear him. Where would I do that?"

"He is dwelling in Capernaum now."

"You don't say." Levi smiled. "He will become a taxpayer. I have official reasons to meet Him now."

"I believe he is staying at Simon's house, sir."

"Hmm. So just a visitor. Where might I hear Him speak and watch Him perform his so-called miracles?"

"No one knows. But when crowds begin to gather, as they seem to whenever He appears, follow the crowd."

"I do not want to miss this."

"I understand, sir. I will keep an eye out for Him and tell the others to do the same."

THE MAN CREATING the stir was living in Capernaum. James would make a huge assumption from that. All it told Levi was that he would do what his young employee suggested. He would pack a satchel with papyrus, ink, and quills, and he would be at the ready when crowds began to form around this Man. Levi would use one of his greatest talents—his proficiency at tachygraphy—to record every word Jesus said. Then he would have time to pore over it with his brother and decide whether there was anything legitimate about Him.

HIS MERE EXCITEMENT over the possibility would have kept Levi awake yet another night had it not been for his fatigue. He had walked more the last few days than in weeks before that, and his concern over both the man of mystery and the tax obligations of the fishermen weighed on him. Levi was sleeping soundly at dawn when he was awakened by his main servant.

"A thousand apologies, master, but a runner has arrived, sent by one of your employees."

"What's the trouble?"

"The message is that crowds are gathering in anticipation of the Galilean, and your man was certain you would want to be made aware."

"Yes! Thank you! Prepare a horse and cart and driver."

Levi hurriedly bathed and dressed, and another servant drove him into his office in minutes. People were streaming alongside the road, hurrying into the city. And when Levi arrived at the tax office, it was plain the multitudes were now heading north and west.

"He's up there!" someone shouted, and many ran ahead.

Levi had never seen so much excitement. He filled his shoulder bag with papyrus and writing supplies, planning to join the throng. He still had not caught sight of the Man.

On his way out he was brought up short by Efah. "How many of us may take the day off for the spectacle?"

"None!"

"You are our leader, and you find diversion while we work?"

"Precisely. I cannot imagine it will take long."

"How will you discipline someone who follows your example?"

Levi stopped. "I will sever my relationship with *you* if you cause me any further delay! And anyone who misses his daily quota will not have to be told the consequences."

Levi hurried out into the street and fell in with the crowd, now moving swiftly. He quickly became aware of his age, as he was soon panting, his knees and ankles aching. He needed to find a place to be able to sit with his bag in his lap to serve as a foundation for his papyrus. It would not do for him to be in the middle of a jostling crowd.

Levi increased his pace to where he was trotting, passing men and women and families, including many carrying sick and crippled friends and relatives. They would know soon enough if the Preacher/Healer was genuine.

As he finally neared the front of the pack, now trudging up into the foothills, Levi caught sight of Jesus. He strode along at a steady pace, surrounded by perhaps twenty men, including the four fishermen Levi recognized even from behind. He was of a mind to demand of them how they could leave their businesses at such a crucial time, but for now he would see how their pledges to his employee worked out. They had said they would pay, even though their boats and nets were under new management. Well, someone would pay, that was certain.

As Jesus climbed the hill in the distance, He turned, and for the first time, Levi got a good look at Him. He was rather plain-looking, of medium height and build, and He clearly followed the Jewish custom of not cutting His hair or beard. Levi was not close enough to see His eyes, but from a distance He did not appear to be striking or handsome.

The Man appeared surprised at the size of the crowd and briefly spoke to a few of the men near Him. They pointed farther up to a mountain, and suddenly they all turned and began the climb in earnest. Levi was already exhausted, but he had figured out where the men were headed, and he was determined to beat everyone else there so he could situate himself to hear clearly and be able to write. If he was correct, the Man would speak at one particular spot near the top, which benefited from the shade of a small grove of olive trees. Levi could sit with his back against a large rock on the left.

By the time he had hurried past the others and even Jesus and His friends, Levi was sweating and gasping. He situated himself where he guessed he would have the best view and be able to hear clearly. But just as he set the papyrus in his lap and pulled out his first quill, Jesus Himself and a few of the men approached him.

"Would you mind if I sat right there to address the crowd?" Jesus said. "You need move just a few feet."

"Certainly, sir," Levi said, gathering his things and quickly scooting to about four feet below the Man. *Kind* was the word that came to mind when he saw Jesus' eyes and heard His voice for the first time. He didn't know what he had expected, but this simply seemed like a pleasant person. What was it about Him that drew so many people? Perhaps His healing tricks? No, it had to be more than that, because so many talked about what He had to say and how it was unique.

Jesus stood just beyond the shade in bright morning sunlight that made Him easy to see for the more than a thousand people who began gathering and sitting on the long incline below Him. He folded His hands in front of Him, bowed his head, and closed his eyes. After a few moments, he opened His eyes and raised His head, seeming to simply watch as the people slowly settled.

When Jesus had stood there nearly twenty minutes in silence, Levi finally forced himself to stand and look to see what He was waiting for. He was astounded to see that people were still coming, more and more of them, doubling the original crowd and seeming to fill the mountainside. How would this soft-spoken Man be able to be heard by all?

The crowd was active and noisy, and only when

it appeared that all who wished to be there had gathered, Jesus held up one hand. An eerie silence descended on the place. Jesus lowered His hand, continued to gaze at his audience, and sat atop the rock. His disciples came to Him and gathered around Him, and finally He opened his mouth to speak.

Levi was stunned when from this normal-sized man came a voice that rang clear and loud without being offensive. Surely everyone was able to hear every word. And from the first, Levi understood what had caused all the excitement.

"Blessed are the poor in spirit, for theirs is the kingdom of heaven."

Jesus paused, as if to let this make its impression on His listeners. Levi didn't know what the others were thinking, but as he quickly jotted it, he ran it through his mind, pondering it and turning it over. The poor in spirit own the kingdom of heaven? Jesus said it as if He knew it as well as He knew His own name. But who was He, this Nazarene carpenter, to know such a thing?

"Blessed are those who mourn, for they shall be comforted."

Suddenly Levi stopped questioning the Man's authority. He could not evade the words. He himself was one who mourned and had been mourning for three decades. That he could be comforted had never entered his mind. *I shall?* he wondered. *I shall be comforted? When? How? By whom?*

"Blessed are the meek, for they shall inherit the earth."

Astounding!

"Blessed are those who hunger and thirst for righteousness, for they shall be filled."

Filled with righteousness? Levi wondered if he had ever hungered or thirsted for anything but vengeance.

"Blessed are the merciful, for they shall obtain mercy."

Levi wrote as quickly as he could, but he was shaken. When had he ever been merciful? When he took pity on the mourning couple? And when he had given the fishermen the break? Did that result in his obtaining mercy? Perhaps that's what this privilege of hearing the Master was! Mercy.

"Blessed are the pure in heart, for they shall see God."

And for the first time since the night his brother was murdered, Levi's eyes filled. He quickly wiped the tears so they would not fall onto the ink and spoil the page. Pure in heart! He was *not* that! Never! Not even close to that. And yet the pure in heart shall see God? He wanted to see God!

"Blessed are the peacemakers, for they shall be called sons of God."

O God, O God, forgive me! I have never been a peacemaker. I can never be called a son of God!

Jesus continued this beautiful, powerful, poetic litany, and Levi kept writing, turning his head now to let the tears roll off his cheeks to the ground, not wanting to miss a word. It was too much, too rich, too deep. He would have to record it all and ponder it later.

"Let your light so shine before men, that they may see your good works and glorify your Father in heaven."

I have no light! I perform no good works that would make people glorify God!

No one stirred as Jesus continued, speaking of the commandments and how people have misunderstood them. And He added, "Unless your righteousness exceeds the righteousness of the scribes and Pharisees, you will by no means enter the kingdom of heaven."

Levi knew well enough what Jesus meant by that. No one could live up to the rules and regulations of the pious religious leaders—not even they themselves.

As Jesus continued, Levi wrote as fast as he could, unable to keep up in his mind. He turned to be sure no one who recognized him could see him weeping, thoroughly confused himself at what had come over him.

"Give to him who asks you, and from him who wants to borrow from you do not turn away. You have heard that it was said, 'You shall love your neighbor and hate your enemy.' But I say to you, love your enemies, bless those who curse you, do good to those who hate you, and pray for those who spitefully use you and persecute you . . ."

This was profound and paradoxical! Who else had ever thought, let alone expressed, such a revolutionary idea? Could Levi do this? He could not imagine.

"For if you love those who love you, what reward have you? Do not even the tax collectors do the same?"

Levi looked up quickly, only to find the preacher gazing directly at him. Did this Man know who he was, or was this just coincidence?

"And if you greet your brethren only, what do you do more than others? Do not even the tax collectors do so?"

Someone had to have told him! Regardless, Levi could not be angry. He had been given too much to think about, all of it a mystery.

The teacher had much to say about generosity and humility and prayer. He warned against praying in public to impress people. "In this manner, therefore, pray:

Our Father in heaven, hallowed be Your name.
Your kingdom come. Your will be done on earth as it is in heaven.
Give us this day our daily bread.
And forgive us our debts, as we forgive our debtors.

And do not lead us into temptation, but deliver us from the evil one.

For Yours is the kingdom and the power and the glory forever. Amen.

"For if you forgive men their trespasses, your heavenly Father will also forgive you. But if you do not forgive men their trespasses, neither will your Father forgive your trespasses."

Jesus seemed to be talking directly to Levi again when he said, "Do not lay up for yourselves treasures on earth, where moth and rust destroy and where thieves break in and steal; but lay up for yourselves treasures in heaven, where neither moth nor rust destroys and where thieves do not break in and steal. For where your treasure is, there your heart will be also."

My heart has always been in my riches! My entire life has been about storing up treasures on earth for me.

"No one can serve two masters; for either he will hate the one and love the other, or else he will be loyal to the one and despise the other. You cannot serve God and mammon. Therefore I say to you, do not worry about your life, what you will eat or what you will drink; nor about your body, what you will put on. Is not life more than food and the body more than clothing?"

Yes, but my life has been the only thing I have ever worried about.

"Look at the birds of the air, for they neither sow nor reap nor gather into barns; yet your heavenly Father feeds them. Are you not of more value than they? Which of you by worrying can add one cubit to his stature? So why do you worry about clothing? Consider the lilies of the field, how they grow: they neither toil nor spin; and yet I say to you that even Solomon in all his glory was not arrayed like one of these.

"Now if God so clothes the grass of the field, which today is, and tomorrow is thrown into the oven, will He not much more clothe you, O you of little faith?

"Therefore do not worry, saying, 'What shall we eat?' or 'What shall we drink?' or 'What shall we wear?' . . . For your heavenly Father knows that you need all these things.

"But seek first the kingdom of God and His righteousness, and all these things shall be added to you."

It's too late! Too late! How can I seek the kingdom of God and His righteousness now?

"Ask, and it will be given to you; seek, and you will find; knock, and it will be opened to you. For everyone who asks receives, and he who seeks finds, and to him who knocks it will be opened. . . . Whatever you want men to do to you, do also to them, for this is the Law and the Prophets."

Who is this Man?

"Not everyone who says to Me, 'Lord, Lord,'

shall enter the kingdom of heaven, but he who does the will of My Father in heaven."

He refers to himself as Lord?

"Therefore whoever hears these sayings of Mine, and does them, I will liken him to a wise man who built his house on the rock: and the rain descended, the floods came, and the winds blew and beat on that house; and it did not fall, for it was founded on the rock.

"But everyone who hears these sayings of Mine, and does not do them, will be like a foolish man who built his house on the sand: and the rain descended, the floods came, and the winds blew and beat on that house; and it fell. And great was its fall."

And suddenly the teaching was finished. With the warning ringing in his ears that if he had heard these sayings and did not do them, he was a foolish man, Levi wiped his tears and packed away his writing tools. It was obvious from the looks on their faces and their hushed tone that everyone else was as astonished as Levi was. He heard a woman say, "He teaches as One having authority, and not as the scribes."

FIFTEEN

When Jesus came down from the mountain, great multitudes followed Him. Levi wished he could speak personally with Jesus, but he was certain everyone else had the same idea. Anyway, he had to get back to his office.

But as he moved along with the crowd, not far from Jesus, a local leper came and bowed down before Him, saying, "Lord, if You are willing, You can make me clean."

So this was the true test. If Jesus was able to heal this man, what would that say to the rest of the sick and afflicted who had come to hear Him? Without hesitation, Jesus touched him, saying, "I am willing; be cleansed." And immediately the man was healed.

Levi was astounded beyond words. Any vestige of skepticism melted away, and he only wished his brother had been there. Surely he was in the presence of the divine. His life up to this moment seemed so pedestrian, so mundane, it repelled him to think of the waste he had made of it. Though he knew he must get back to the tax office, he didn't feel like a tax collector anymore. He was moved to do right by everyone, to apologize to anyone he had ever wronged or even slighted or insulted. Where he had overcharged taxes—and he would not be able to dredge up the memory of all of those times—he wished he could make restitution several-fold.

His very gait was different; he carried his head higher. Levi noticed things that had not made an impression on him in years—the beauty of the creation, the feel of a cool breeze in his face, even the sounds of birds. He had many questions for Jesus if he ever got the opportunity to talk with Him privately, but he had no doubt who the Man was.

As they re-entered Capernaum, a centurion came to Jesus, saying, "Lord, my servant is lying at home paralyzed, dreadfully tormented."

Jesus said, "I will come and heal him."

But the centurion said, "Lord, I am not worthy that You should come under my roof. But only speak a word, and my servant will be healed. For I also am a man under authority, having soldiers under me. And I say to this one, 'Go,' and he goes; and to another, 'Come,' and he comes; and to my servant, 'Do this,' and he does it."

Jesus turned to those who followed and said, "Assuredly, I say to you, I have not found such great faith, not even in Israel!" He turned back to the man and said, "Go your way; and as you have believed, so let it be done for you."

Levi vowed to somehow follow up on that, to find that man and see what he learned when he got home.

Meanwhile it was clear that Jesus and His disciples were heading to Simon's home, where the former fisherman lived with his family, including his mother-in-law. How Levi wished he would be invited in, but people outside his own circle of publicans were not in the habit of including him.

Levi made his way back to the tax office, which was largely abandoned this time of day. Only two staff members monitored commercial traffic there as the rest manned their stations throughout the territory. Even this place looked different to Levi. It looked foreign, as if it were not the place he had conducted business for his entire adult life. It was as if he no longer belonged. Finishing out the more than four more years under his contract with Rome seemed like a prison sentence to him now.

Late in the afternoon, as his assistants began to appear from their various stations, Efah showed up in a slightly different mood than he had exhibited that morning.

"Well, I hope you got your fill of the Preacher today, chief!" he said. "You'll be happy to know that I too saw Him."

"You did? You were there?"

"No, I only saw Him coming from Simon's house with his gaggle of worshipers. So, tell me, did He live up to His reputation?"

"Actually, He did, Efah, and I would urge you to witness it for yourself. The next time He is speaking anywhere, or healing the sick, I want you to be sure to be there."

"And neglect my work?"

"You will find it profitable."

"Indeed? You too have been swept along by the crowd?"

"Oh, no, Efah. It was as if I were the only one there."

Efah fell silent and seemed to study him. "Well, I have more news. I made sure to remind Simon that he had missed his meeting with you and that if he knew what was good for him, he would get himself in here. You know, he seemed genuinely sorry. He had entirely forgotten about it. He asked me to beg your forgiveness and promised to come by here at his first opportunity."

"Oh, I appreciate that, Efah, but it won't be necessary. I have been assured that those who were left with his business will follow through on our new agreement."

"And you believe that."

"Why shouldn't I?"

"Oh, I don't know. Perhaps because you have no history with them. They have no experience running a business. And everyone we know tries to get out of every obligation they have."

"I choose to believe them until they prove otherwise."

Efah squinted at Levi. "Is this a new man I see before me?"

"Perhaps it is."

THAT NIGHT AT HOME, Levi sat until past midnight reading over and over the entire record of what he had written that day. And to his great astonishment, the tears poured afresh. "God," he prayed silently, "have You blessed me by letting me meet Messiah? I believe You have! Can You forgive me of my sins?"

In the morning he once again rode to the office in a horse-drawn cart, hoping to follow Jesus wherever He went to teach or heal. But Jesus was nowhere to be seen, and rumors abounded. Levi asked in the square what anyone had heard, and a man told him that Jesus had healed Simon's mother-in-law of a fever by just touching her hand, and she immediately arose and served Him and His disciples.

A woman said, "Last evening many brought to Him those who were demon-possessed. And He cast out the spirits with a word, and healed all who were sick."

Levi was immediately reminded of an ancient passage from Isaiah about which he would have to ask James. Isaiah had prophesied that Messiah "took our infirmities and bore our sicknesses."

"Might I still find Him at Simon's house?"

"Oh, no, sir. He and His disciples left by boat late last night when the crowds grew too great at the house."

"To what destination?"

"I don't believe anyone knows."

Levi returned to the tax office, again imploring his employees to send word if they saw Jesus anywhere in the area that day. It was the middle of the afternoon before an assistant entered and said, "Master, Simon is here to see you."

"Simon!" Levi cried, rising and embracing the man. "Come, walk with me and let's talk! Where is your Master?"

Simon appeared amused and in good spirits. "He is back at my house, resting. We had quite a night, and may I say, quite a morning."

"Tell me all about it!"

"I will, I will," Simon said, "but slow down, sir. Are we hurrying somewhere?"

"Not unless I am welcome at your house. I must meet this man!"

"Oh, in due time, Levi, perhaps I can arrange it. But not now. The crowds have been pressing, and we must let Him rest."

"Very well."

"I saw you yesterday, you know. On the mount."

"Did you? I was most impressed."

"I could tell. You know, a publican shedding tears in public just won't do!"

Levi looked up to see Simon grinning broadly, and they laughed. "Have you ever heard anyone so profound?"

"Of course not."

"You see why I would give up anything and everything and follow Him anywhere?"

"I do. Tell me, Simon, the centurion who approached him—"

"—sent word that he got home to learn his servant was healed the very hour Jesus told him it would be so!"

"Amazing."

"That's the least of it. My mother-in-law was sick with—"

"A fever, yes, I heard about this."

"It's true. He healed her immediately. And when people learned of it, they brought many, many more to be healed."

"And the crowds grew so great you had to leave?"

"He told us He wanted to go to the other side of the sea. He immediately fell asleep, but on our short voyage suddenly a great tempest arose, so that the boat was covered with the waves. Levi, most of us have been fishermen all our lives, and we thought we were going to perish! We woke Him and said, 'Lord, save us!' Do you know what He replied?"

"Tell me!"

"He asked why we were fearful. Why? Because we know that sea and what it can do to a small vessel when the winds and the waves conspire. He called us 'you of little faith,' then He arose and rebuked the winds and the sea, and there was a great calm."

"No!"

"Yes! We marveled and asked ourselves, 'Who can this be, that even the winds and the sea obey

Him?' This morning, when we came to the country of the Gergesenes, two demon-possessed men came out of the tombs, exceedingly fierce, and cried out, 'What have we to do with You, Jesus, You Son of God? Have You come here to torment us before the time?' "

"They called Him that? Son of God? They knew?"

Simon nodded. "Jesus cast the demons out of the men, and they entered a herd of swine that stampeded over a cliff and drowned in the sea. The swineherds fled into the city and must have told all they had seen, because it seemed the whole city came out to meet Jesus. They begged Him to depart from their region."

"Where did you all go from there?"

"We returned to the boat and came back here. And almost immediately, someone brought to Him a paralyzed man lying on a bed. Jesus said that their faith was obvious, so He said to paralytic, 'Son, be of good cheer; your sins are forgiven you.'

"Well, Levi, you know that anywhere the public gathers, the scribes and Pharisees cannot be far. Some of the scribes were scowling at Him, and He read their thoughts. He said, 'Why do you think evil in your hearts?' and told me later that they had been thinking He was a blasphemer. He said to them, 'Which is easier, to say, "Your sins are forgiven you," or to say, "Arise and walk"? But that you may know that the Son of Man has power on earth to forgive sins'—then He said to the paralytic, 'Arise, take up your bed, and go to your house.' And he did. The multitudes marveled and glorified God."

"As do I."

"Levi, I must get back. I want to be there and available when He awakes, in case He needs me. I do not know where He will go next, but I want to be there."

"Certainly. Thank you, Simon."

LATE THAT AFTERNOON, as Levi sat in the tax office eagerly writing as much as he could remember of Simon's report, he began daydreaming of when his brother would arrive and the pleasure he would have in listening to Jesus with James. From outside he heard a clamor and realized that a great crowd was passing. That could mean only one thing. Jesus was passing by.

Levi pulled back a drape, hoping to catch a glimpse of the Man, and there stood Jesus before the open window. His gaze seemed to bore into Levi's soul. Levi wanted to smile but could not move. He wanted to greet Jesus, but he could not speak. The man whose name was on everyone's lips seemed focused on Levi alone.

Jesus whispered, "Follow me," and Levi immediately arose with only his papyrus and sack of supplies and hurried outside. Jesus embraced him and said, "From henceforth I shall call you Matthew, which means gift from God."

Gift from God? How could anyone, let alone this miracle worker, see Levi as a gift? He was not worthy of the name and couldn't imagine he ever would be. But one thing was certain. Levi immediately realized that his days as a tax collector were over. He instantly became a disciple of Jesus, and he had an idea. "Lord, will you and your friends dine at my home tonight?"

"Certainly, thank you."

Levi, already seeing himself as Matthew, pressed a coin into the palm of a young lad and quickly whispered in his ear to run to his estate and tell the servants how many to expect for dinner.

And as they continued along the way, greater and greater crowds packed the road, then sat to listen as Jesus spoke, and watched as He healed all the sick and lame that were brought to Him.

Matthew could not wait for James to come.

SIXTEEN

Matthew invited his entire staff and tax collectors from surrounding areas to a great feast at his home that evening in honor of his new Master. The house was full and noisy, and it was all he could do to not fawn and bow at Jesus' feet. He washed His feet and gave Him water, but Jesus seemed so humble and loving that He set Matthew at ease, thanking him and looking at him as if He truly saw His host as a gift from God. Matthew still found that impossible to comprehend.

Just before they gathered around the great banquet tables, Efah pulled Matthew aside. "Levi," he said, "I need to know—"

"Call me Matthew, please."

"Matthew?"

"That is what the Master calls me, so I am Levi no longer."

"Anyone else can call you whatever they want," Efah said, "but to me you will always be Levi. I need to know your intentions. Are you, like the fishermen, leaving your business?"

"Not only my business, but also my name and my entire life. I have sent for my personal belongings and my writing supplies."

"You will not be back at the tax office?"

"I will not."

"Does Rome know?"

"I assume you will tell them."

"You are leaving the business to me, then?"

"That will be between you and Rome."

"Thank you, Levi!"

"Please, Efah. We have never been close, but can you not afford me this one courtesy?"

"All right, Matthew."

"But don't thank me. In fact I should probably apologize. While the business is strong, owning it will cost you, and as I say, Rome may have other ideas for who should succeed me."

"They will have to beat my bid."

"True enough. I wish you the best with it. I also urge you to listen to Jesus, should He choose to speak tonight."

"I have no interest, and frankly, had I known His presence would attract the Pharisees, I would not have come."

Matthew looked past Efah. "Pharisees? Where? I invited no Pharisees and doubt they would have accepted if I had."

"Outside your gate. A gaggle of them."

"Please stay and enjoy the meal, Efah. And do listen."

Matthew hurried out the front, his stomach turning as he saw the holy men clustered just outside the entrance. Surprisingly, however, he did not feel his usual hatred for this enemy. He felt overcome with pity for them, but he was also concerned about the offense to his guests.

"What is your business?" he said as politely as he was able. The day before he would have gestured and cursed and ordered them off his land.

"We have questions for the sorcerer!" one called out.

"Gentlemen, He is no sorcerer, and if you had listened and observed, you would know that."

"We would speak with Him!"

"Not this evening, please! You know He speaks and teaches openly nearly every day."

"He defiles the temple!"

"Then wait for Him there. I am certain He would be glad to answer—"

"If you will not send Him out, we will wait!"

"Must I spirit Him away? What if I invite Him to spend the night?"

"And all his disciples?"

"What is that to you? I consider myself one."

This was met with hilarity. "You? He has chosen wisely!"

"Gentlemen, please. Let the Man rest and enjoy His meal. He will be available tomorrow."

"We will wait all night if we must."

"Suit yourselves."

But as Matthew returned inside, he heard the men murmuring and wondered what they were up to. The servants waited with heaping trays of meat and fish and bread and wine. "As soon as I usher Jesus to the place of honor, I will signal you to fill the tables."

Matthew found Jesus and beckoned Him to follow. As he pointed out His place, Jesus whispered, "Thank you. I would like to bless the food, and while I am praying, I would like for you to invite them in."

Matthew flinched. "Them?"

"Those who await Me at your gate."

"But they are Phar—"

"Will you do that, Matthew?"

"I will do anything you ask, Master. But—"

"Thank you. Now go."

As Matthew hurried out he heard Jesus thanking him for his hospitality and praying over the food. When he emerged from the front of the house, the Pharisees suddenly quieted and glared at him.

"Would you care to join us?" he said. "We have plenty."

"What! You know better than that! We would not lower ourselves to recline at table with your kind!"

"But you are welcome," Matthew said. "And our supplies are great."

"No! Just send the blasphemer out here!"

Matthew sat next to Jesus and told him, "They would not come."

"Of course. But they cannot say they were not invited."

"You will want to avoid the front gate on the way out. Or, even better, You and Your disciples are welcome to spend the night."

"I will not avoid them. They are of no danger to Me until My time has come."

"I don't understand."

"You will. All in good time."

Jesus did not choose to speak formally that evening, but rather He engaged Matthew and his friends in casual conversation. At one point Jesus drew Matthew close and whispered, "You know that the Son of Man has nowhere to lay His head. Following Me means that you won't either."

There was something about the way Jesus spoke, with such earnest, quiet directness, that caused Matthew to understand fully His entire meaning. Jesus told Matthew where to meet Him and the other disciples the next day, and Matthew knew he would never again return to his beautiful estate. That evening, he would inform his house staff and urge them to find new masters.

When the festivities were over and people began leaving, Efah thanked Matthew and said, "He seemed pleasant enough."

"You should come and hear Him teach."

"I would, but you see I have just been given much more responsibility in my job . . ."

Matthew smiled. "Make the time, friend."

Finally Matthew walked out with Jesus and the other disciples. No surprise, the Pharisees remained outside the gate. "Say, fisherman!" one called out to Simon. "Why does your Teacher eat with sinners?"

But before he could answer, Jesus said, "Those who are well have no need of a physician, but those who are sick. If you want something to think about, go and learn what this means: '*I desire mercy and not sacrifice.*' For I did not come to call the righteous, but sinners, to repentance."

When Jesus followed His disciples out the gate and past the Pharisees, Matthew was abashed to see that He had left them speechless. Matthew did not know what Jesus had meant either, but he certainly knew how important sacrifices were to the Pharisees. To imply that they should show mercy rather than judging everyone was to deeply insult them.

That night after speaking with his servants and setting out his coat and cloak and sandals for the next day, Matthew realized that he would be leaving everything else behind. In the bag he would sling over his shoulder, he would pack his papyrus, quills, and ink. All the rest of his earthly belongings, including all his clothes, would remain. A bright moon streamed through the window as Matthew lay on his back on his mat, feeling a strange refreshed exhaustion and knowing he would sleep deeply and soundly, despite one question still naggling at his mind. Matthew felt an excitement and an anticipation, not to mention a deep commitment to both learn from and selflessly serve his Master. How much more fulfilling this would be than spending his entire life trying to accumulate wealth that never satisfied! Already he was grateful to have learned that he could talk to Jesus like an old friend—no, better than that. This was a Teacher, a Rabbi, a Man sent from God, and Matthew believed Him to be the long-sought and prophesied Messiah.

That meant He could answer the deepest question of Matthew's heart. Chavivi.

• • •

THE NEXT MORNING Matthew met Jesus and the other disciples—who numbered more than two dozen at that point—and the Master sat in their midst and told them what was to happen that day. He would once again teach in an open area and heal all the injured, diseased, and afflicted.

"Then we will enjoy a dinner of roasted fish and bread at the shore and talk over the events of the day around a fire."

Nothing could have sounded better to Matthew. He would look for an opportunity to speak to Jesus privately, and he would also keep watch for his brother, who should be on his way from Jerusalem by now.

Just before they started out, a man in a ruler's purple robes rushed to Jesus and fell at His feet. "My daughter has just died," he said, weeping, "but come and lay Your hand on her and she will live."

Jesus merely nodded and stood, following the man with all His disciples behind Him. As they hurried along, great crowds appeared and began to grow, clamoring to get close to Jesus. Suddenly a woman pushed past Matthew. When she got near Jesus she fell to her hands and knees and crawled close enough to touch the hem of His garment.

Jesus turned and lifted her by the hand. "Be of good cheer, daughter," He said. "Your faith has made you well."

As Jesus moved on, the woman turned her face to the sun and raised her hands. Matthew said, "Are you well?"

"I am!" she said. "I had an issue of blood for twelve years, but I knew if I could just touch the hem of His garment . . ."

When Jesus and His party finally reached the ruler's house, the flute players and noisy mourners were already playing and wailing. Matthew was chilled, remembering the single player and mourner who had accompanied his pitiful family for Chavivi's burial.

Jesus quieted them, saying, "Make room, for the girl is not dead, but sleeping."

The flute player laughed and the others jeered. "Who says? We have seen her, and she is dead! What do you know?"

"Clear everyone out of the house," Jesus said, and when it was empty, He entered. Just as Matthew crossed the threshold, He saw Jesus take the dead girl by the hand, and she immediately arose.

The flautist and the mourners screamed and ran, shouting about ghosts and spirits, as did many onlookers. But Matthew also knew the report of what Jesus had done was quickly spreading throughout the land.

When Jesus departed from there, the crowds were even larger and infused by pockets of men in pharisaical garb. They were also followed by two blind men who cried out, "Son of David, have mercy on us!"

Jesus said to them, "Do you believe that I am able to do this?"

They said, "Yes, Lord."

He touched their eyes. "According to your faith let it be to you." Immediately it was obvious both could see. And Jesus sternly warned them, "Say nothing to anyone. See that no one knows it."

It was all Matthew could do to keep from laughing. The entire crowd knew! And as the men ran off, they shouted, "Jesus healed us! We were blind and now we see!"

Matthew would have to ask Jesus about that around the fire that evening.

Soon the crowd brought to Him a man who could not speak and was demon-possessed. Jesus commanded the demon to come out of him, and when the man arose, he could speak. It was obvious to Matthew that the multitudes were astonished, and he heard several say, "I've never seen anything like this!"

But the Pharisees at the edge of the crowd said, "He casts out demons under the authority of the ruler of the demons." Matthew wondered if they did not recognize the lunacy of that statement and he added one more item to his mental list of things to ask the Master that evening.

SEVENTEEN

Matthew sat on the shore of the Sea of Galilee with the other disciples—more than two dozen. He was sore from his hair to his toes after walking and sometimes running to keep up with Jesus all day.

Jesus had urged the men to bathe in the sea while a few roasted dinner. Matthew kept an eye on his satchel, then had to laugh. If he could not trust these men, whom could he trust? He simply wanted to eat quickly, then write as much as he could remember of the events of the day before taking notes on whatever Jesus had to say.

Matthew had barely realized how hungry he was until the simple meal of fish and bread proved as delicious to him as the feast he had thrown for Jesus at his own home the night before. He felt self-conscious pulling out his writing materials in front of so many strangers. The fishermen were familiar to him, of course, and he had done business with a few of the others. But most of the rest of the men were entirely new to him.

Matthew wondered if all had left their homes and families and work, and he was curious about where they would sleep. Did they have as many questions as he did? For himself, giving little or no thought to the future was novel. He had been a man of planning and structure. He had had an idea what every day would bring and what he wanted to accomplish. Now he had simply abandoned all, virtually without thinking, to follow Jesus. He would do anything the Master asked, and he would listen, learn, watch, and write. He would give no thought to what he would eat or where he would sleep or what tomorrow would bring.

To Matthew's delight, after Jesus discussed the events of the day, He asked if anyone had any questions. It was clear from the cacophony of voices that Matthew would not likely have to say a word. The first question would have been his too.

"Why did You tell the blind men not to tell anyone You had healed them? Can you imagine anyone in all of the land of Israel who is unaware of it?"

The men chuckled and Jesus smiled. "Let me ask you this," he said. "Do you recall what those men called me?"

"Yes! They called you Son of David."

"And did you also notice that I did not respond at first?"

"Not for a long time actually. Why?"

"Their persistence proved their faith. But that they called me Son of David showed that they know who I am."

Matthew realized immediately that Jesus was acknowledging that his brother James was right. Son of David was a common Jewish title for the long-promised Deliverer. He was Messiah, who would rule over the coming kingdom of God.

"The time for Me to be revealed has not come. As you know, I already have many enemies. They must not have cause to hinder Me until the due time."

"But you have been performing miracles in plain sight for days!"

Jesus nodded. "I am here to do the will of My Father. These men sought me humbly, pleading for mercy. If you have studied the ancient texts, you know that 'the Lord is gracious and merciful, slow to anger and great in loving-kindness,' and that He 'is good to all, and His mercies are over all His works.'"

"I am curious," Andrew, Simon's brother, said. "Why did You ask them if they believed You were able to heal them? Was that not quite obvious?"

"Yes, I knew their trust was genuine. They had followed for a great distance, and they knew who I was. I wanted everyone to hear them express their faith."

The men talked until well into the night. Then Jesus announced that He and Simon (whom He began calling Peter), Andrew, and a few of the others were returning to Simon's home to sleep. "The rest of you make camp here, and we will meet you in the morning."

MATTHEW WROTE UNTIL the embers began fading, then slept the sleep of the dead. He was awakened just before dawn by whistling. As soon as he recognized the tune as something his mother had hummed to him as a child, he bolted upright and looked around. His brother James waved shyly from several feet away, and Matthew ran to him.

"I was told I would find you here," James said.

"By whom?"

"Efah at the tax office."

"He's there already?"

"And busy. He told me everything! Is it true?"

"James, you must follow us today! By the noontime you will know this Man is Messiah."

For the next hour Matthew regaled James with every detail he could remember, frequently referring to his notes. As soon as Jesus and the others arrived, Matthew pulled James over to meet Him.

James gushed, "I confess I am here at the behest of the Sanhedrin in Jerusalem. They have asked me to determine—"

"I know why you are here, My friend. You are welcome to accompany us today and to observe."

"Thank you, sir. If I can merely confirm for myself even a little of all that I have already been told, I will able to report—"

"That you do not return will be your report."

"Oh, but, Rabbi, I am expected—"

"That you do not return will be your report. Will you join us for breakfast?"

James appeared speechless and looked to Matthew, puzzled. "Levi, I—"

"James, you have been invited to dine with the Master and us. Say something."

"Yes! Thank you."

That day Jesus visited several cities and villages, teaching in their synagogues, preaching the gospel of the kingdom, and healing every sickness and every disease among the people.

Matthew noticed that James wept when first he saw Jesus begin healing. "I had no idea," he said.

"I tried to tell you."

"I know, but this is something you have to see for yourself. Maybe you wrote this, but I was unaware that He heals everyone, not just some. Truly this is the Messiah."

As the multitudes grew ever larger, it appeared to Matthew that Jesus was moved with compassion for them. When tears trickled down Jesus' face, Matthew drew near and asked if He was all right.

"They are weary and scattered," he said, "like sheep having no shepherd. Gather the others, Matthew, please."

With merely a gesture, Matthew beckoned the rest to surround the Master.

"Listen to me," He said, sitting. "The harvest truly is plentiful, but the laborers are few. Therefore pray the Lord of the harvest to send out laborers into His harvest."

"We don't know what you mean, Lord," Simon Peter said.

"My work has only just begun," He said. "Soon I will select from among you a small group who will be asked to suffer with Me all the way to the end."

"Suffer with you?" Peter said.

"Much will be required of you. I will become known throughout all of Syria, and the people will bring to Me many afflicted with various diseases and torments, and those who are demon-possessed, epileptics, and paralytics. I will heal them and I will also preach to and teach the multitudes. The need is great. But beware, for the opposition will be greater."

"Who could be more powerful than You?" Peter said.

"Only those who are allowed, for My Father's purposes. All will be made clear to you, but not today."

When Jesus rose and the group began on its way again, Matthew approached Him quietly. "I do not know if I am to be one of the select, but—"

"You are."

"You may not want to decide that until—"

"I have decided."

"I am honored by Your confidence, Lord, but I am deeply troubled in my own mind."

"Your sins have been forgiven you."

"I know, but—"

"Your whole life is not counted against you any longer."

"I am grateful, Master. But my soul is vexed still at—"

"I know, Matthew. Your loss."

"Yes. I don't understand. I never have."

"I know. Listen carefully to Me, Matthew. Your ways are not God's ways. He has plans you know not of. Life is full of deep mysteries that may come with great sorrow. I understand your anger and I empathize with your pain. I know that is difficult to comprehend now, but there will come a day when you will learn that what I tell you is the truth, and in that day you will know the depth of My love for you. Trust Me, and I will show you the goodness of your Heavenly Father even in the midst of grief. I am not promising that you will endure no more pain or sorrow, but I am promising that if you trust Me, you will experience the glory of the goodness of the Father in ways now unimaginable.

"Can you do that? Will you?"

Matthew did not know what to say, but he felt embraced in Jesus' love, and so he said, "I will."

OVER THE NEXT FEW DAYS greater crowds than ever followed Jesus—from Galilee, Decapolis, Jerusalem, Judea, and beyond the Jordan—everywhere He went. They awaited Him at dawn when He set out from Peter's house and stayed with Him to sunset when His many disciples finally spirited Him away to where they could gather with Him around a fire and discuss all that had happened. To His friends He explained Himself and His actions more fully, and while Matthew admitted to his brother that he often understood little more than any of the others, he grew to cherish these times with Jesus apart from the multitudes.

Finally, late one evening as the fire was dying, Jesus said, "The time has come for Me to thank all of you for standing with Me and send most of you on your way. From henceforth, I wish to be accompanied by only the following: Peter and Andrew his brother; James and John, the sons of Zebedee; Matthew and James, the sons of Alphaeus; Philip, Bartholomew, Thomas, Lebbaeus Thaddaeus, Simon the Cananite, and Judas Iscariot."

Jesus spent much of the next hour bidding farewell individually to the many others who had served Him for many days. He spoke quietly to each, prayed with some, and embraced them all. When the last was gone, He called the twelve back around the fire, and several, led by Simon of Cana, also known as Simon the Zealot, added more kindling to make it roar.

"Tonight," Jesus said, "I am going to impart to you power over unclean spirits."

"Power as you have," Bartholomew said, "to cast them out?"

"Yes, and to heal all kinds of sickness and all

kinds of disease. We have much to do and many places to go. In this way, I multiply Myself through you. Tomorrow I will send you out in pairs, but not to the Gentiles for now, and do not enter a city of the Samaritans. That will come later. Go rather to the lost sheep of the house of Israel. And as you go, preach, saying, 'The kingdom of heaven is at hand.' Heal the sick, cleanse the lepers, raise the dead, cast out demons. Freely you have received, freely give. Take neither gold nor silver nor copper in your money belts, nor bag for your journey, nor two tunics, nor sandals, nor staffs. As you work, your Father will provide for you.

"Now whatever city or town you enter, lodge with a household that proves friendly to you and seeks after God. Stay there until you leave for your next destination. If the household is worthy, bless it with your peace. But if it does not receive you, do not bless it. Whoever will not receive you nor hear your words, when you depart from that house or city, shake off the dust from your feet.

"Assuredly, I say to you, it will be more tolerable for the land of Sodom and Gomorrah in the day of judgment than for that city! I send you out as sheep in the midst of wolves. Therefore be wise as serpents and harmless as doves. Beware of men who would deliver you up to councils and scourge you in their synagogues as one day they will do to Me. You will be brought before governors and kings for

My sake, as a testimony to them and to the Gentiles."

"Lord," Peter said, "we are willing. But what shall we do when that happens?"

"When they deliver you up, do not worry about how or what you should speak. For the Father will give to you in that hour what you should speak; for it will not be you who speaks, but the Spirit of your Father who speaks in you. You will be hated for My name's sake. But he who endures to the end will be saved. When they persecute you in one city, flee to another. Assuredly, you will not have reached all the cities of Israel before the Son of Man is revealed.

"What I have taught you in the dark, speak in the light; and what you have heard Me say, preach on the housetops. Do not fear those who can kill the body, because they cannot kill your soul. Rather fear Him who is able to destroy both soul and body in hell."

"What if we *are* fearful, Master?" Philip said. "For I confess I am."

"Fear not, My friends. Are not two sparrows sold for a copper coin? Not one of them falls to the ground apart from your Father's will. The very hairs of your head are all numbered. How can you be afraid when you are of more value than many sparrows? Whoever confesses Me before men, him I will also confess before My Father who is in heaven. But whoever denies Me before men, him I will also deny before My Father who is in heaven."

EIGHTEEN

In the morning, Jesus paired up the disciples, teaming James with Peter's brother Andrew, and Matthew with Thomas, whom he had not known before. Before they could get acquainted, Jesus continued to admonish them all.

"Do not think that I came to bring peace on earth. I did not come to bring peace but a sword. For I have come to *'set a man against his father, a daughter against her mother, and a daughter-in-law against her mother-in-law'*; and *'a man's enemies will be those of his own household.'*"

Matthew was thoroughly confused, and though he was writing every word he heard, he made a note to ask Jesus about this by the fire that night. The evening ritual of bathing in the sea and taking turns roasting fish and baking bread became such a welcome event that Matthew found himself looking forward to it all day. When the sun baked him and his feet and ankles were sore from so much walking, and when sweat mixed with the dust and he wondered whether he could ever be clean again, he daydreamed of the refreshing dip into the water. Stretching out on the sand in a clean, dry garment, relaxing, enjoying olives and grapes with the main staples . . . all this pointed to the long discussions with Jesus as the moon traversed the sky.

It had also become understood that Matthew got to sit closest to the fire so he could write by its light. Somehow Peter and John seemed to have assumed the favored spots on either side of Jesus—Peter because he was a forceful personality and simply elbowed his way into position; John because Jesus often beckoned him to His side. John was the youngest and smallest, and though he had a temper like his brother James, it was apparent that Jesus had taken him under His wing.

Matthew wondered what Peter and John thought of this current discourse. What was Jesus saying? No doubt even they would have questions when the twelve reconvened at the prearranged spot that night.

Jesus continued, "He who loves father or mother more than Me is not worthy of Me. And he who loves son or daughter more than Me is not worthy of Me. And he who does not take his cross and follow after Me is not worthy of Me."

Matthew knew Jesus was aiming at some truth about priorities—that a man's relationship with God and with Messiah had to take precedence over all other attachments—but "take his cross"? Matthew had too many times witnessed the spectacle of a condemned man carrying his cross to the site of his own execution. The final act in itself was ghastly enough, but making a person trudge along with his own crossbeam, scraping the flesh from his shoulders, causing him to stagger and stumble, all the while being harassed and humiliated by people who found some enjoyment in watching such things . . . it was horrible by any standard. The populace had long ridiculed Matthew, when he was Levi, for being scum, a sinner, a tax collector. Perhaps they assumed he was one who might enjoy seeing some criminal suffer his just rewards. But Matthew, even at his worst, ofttimes had to look away when even the basest of offenders bowed low beneath his last burden, trudging to a place alongside the road where he would hang in public for as long as it took for him to die.

And now Jesus wanted His disciples, His friends, to take up their crosses and follow Him? Surely this was figurative, symbolic. While Jesus warned daily that He had enemies—and the snarling, sniping Pharisees seemed ever-present— was it really to end in mortal danger to the Master? For all their criticism and charges that He was a blasphemer, could they not see what His miraculous powers had brought to the lives of so many? What had they ever done to improve life in Israel?

In just a matter of several days, Matthew found his love and admiration for Jesus growing so deeply within that he found himself agreeing even with the boisterous Peter when he vowed to never let any harm come to Him. Matthew had never worked with his hands, had not developed the fisherman's physique, and yet he felt he would throw himself into any fracas that threatened his Lord.

Sometimes, when Jesus talked more quickly than Matthew could write, Matthew would just gesture to Him to pause for a moment so he could catch up. He had to do that now as Jesus began a litany so profound that the twelve not only remained silent but seemed not to breathe, let alone move.

"He who finds his life will lose it, and he who loses his life for My sake will find it. He who receives you receives Me, and he who receives Me receives Him who sent Me. He who receives a prophet in the name of a prophet shall receive a prophet's reward. And he who receives a righteous man in the name of a righteous man shall receive a righteous man's reward."

Thomas, who had already been designated Matthew's partner for the next several days of ministry, apparently did not want to wait until the end of the day for clarification. "Forgive me, Lord, but what exactly are you saying here?"

Jesus paused and looked around as the usual crowds began to gather. It was apparent He didn't want them to hear what He was saying to only His friends, and so he drew the twelve closer and spoke softly. "He who has ears, let him hear."

All this sounded so earnest and sincere, besides

being profound, but Matthew was lost. They all had ears, yet he doubted any of them understood this any better than the others. He knew Jesus was saying that if one had understanding one could grasp it, and it was frustrating to realize he didn't have that kind of ears.

Families drew close, and Jesus' eyes always lit up when he was in the presence of children, to whom He often spoke directly. He gestured toward them and whispered, "And whoever gives one of these little ones only a cup of cold water in the name of a disciple, assuredly, I say to you, he shall by no means lose his reward."

Matthew would be glad to be as compassionate as Jesus in serving people, especially children—to whom he himself had always been drawn (even when he was a despised tax collector). But what was this reward he would preserve? He wanted nothing more than to be Jesus' friend.

JESUS REMINDED THEM where they were to reconvene at dusk that evening and assigned each pair to a different town or city. "Tell them I am coming," He said, "and I will get to each place in due time. Tell them the kingdom of God is at hand and that I have a message for them. Do not hesitate to tell them what that message will be—that they should repent of their sins and be prepared for God to dwell with them. If they will not hear you, perhaps they will hear Me."

"They will when they see You perform miracles!" Peter said.

"But you have been imbued with the same power, so they will see that you have authority. Now go, and prepare the way for Me."

Matthew and Thomas were assigned to Tiberias, where Jesus was to come second, around the noon hour. They arrived there in the middle of the morning, having discussed all along the way their strategy of gaining attention and drawing a crowd. They also became acquainted with each other, talking of their pasts, but mostly Matthew tried to steer the conversation to where Thomas would agree to be the primary speaker, at least at first.

"I'd be delighted," Thomas said. "But you must be the first to minister to the afflicted. Do you have faith, Matthew, that you can do this?"

"I shouldn't," Matthew said. "I have never so much as touched a stranger, let alone even considered the idea of healing someone. But had I not seen it with my own eyes, I would not have believed Jesus could heal the sick or lame either. He tells me I have been given this power, His power, to heal, and so I will attempt it with confidence. It certainly will not be in my own power that I do this."

It was a particularly hot day, so when Matthew and Thomas arrived in Tiberius they went straightaway to the communal well, where both townspeople and travelers took turns drawing water and refreshing their animals and themselves and filling pots and pitchers to take with them.

Matthew was impressed that Thomas kept his nerve and called out, "Men and women of Tiberius and travelers, I come to you today with news of the coming kingdom of God!"

Matthew saw smiles and heard snickering, and some shouted, "What news? Is He here?"

"As a matter of fact, the Christ is coming."

"So the prophecies have said for centuries! But this shall not happen in our lifetimes!"

"He will be here at midday!"

"And how will we know Him?"

"He will preach repentance and the coming kingdom, as we do! And He will heal the sick and the lame, also as we will do!"

More laughter and jeering, and the crowd that had begun to gather now began to disperse. But a woman stepped forward, holding the hand of a young girl who limped. Many in the crowd seemed to know them. "Heal her!"

"Yes! Show us something!"

Thomas looked to Matthew, who suddenly felt emboldened. "This is not a trick, nor is it for your amusement. Bring the girl to me, and as is your faith, may it be done to you."

Matthew looked carefully at the countenance of the mother to see whether she was skeptical, challenging, or hopeful. The fact was, she appeared desperate. And when he saw the little girl's foot,

Matthew nearly lost his faith and resolve. Her ankle looked as if bones were missing. Her foot flopped and there seemed no muscle, bone, or tendon in it.

The girl looked shy and fearful. Matthew reached for her and said, "Come to me."

The crowd quieted and pressed close as the girl minced toward Matthew. He put an arm gently around her shoulders and found her trembling.

"Would you be healed?" he said.

She nodded, looking at her mother.

"God loves you, and your faith will make you whole. Do you believe?"

"I believe," she said quietly.

Matthew knelt before her and cupped her destroyed ankle in his hands. He looked to the heavens. "In the name of Jesus the Christ and our Father in heaven, be healed."

Matthew felt a surge of warmth through his body, from the top of his head through his chest and arms. The girl threw her head back and shuddered, and as Matthew loosened his grip, he felt the joint being restored and the foot turning to the front. As he pulled his hands away, the foot looked strong and new.

The mother fell to her knees and the girl gingerly tried her new limb. Within seconds she began leaping and twirling and dancing, and many in the crowd fell on their faces, weeping.

"Healed!" the girl squealed. "Healed! I'm healed!"

"Praise God!" her mother said.

"Wait here!" a man shouted. "I must bring my wife! She has been sick many years!"

"Yes! Wait! My son is deaf and mute!"

For more than an hour, Thomas preached repentance and the coming kingdom and Matthew healed all who were brought to him. Soon, of course, the local temple clergy arrived and watched from a distance, scowling. When Thomas reminded the people that Jesus the Christ would be there around midday, some ran off and returned with more scribes and Pharisees. The crowd swelled as more and more travelers paused in their journey to watch and wait for Jesus.

Thomas was preaching in the heat of a cloudless sky when Matthew saw Jesus on the road. He slipped away, but when he reached the Master, two other men had just gotten to Him.

"We are disciples of John the Baptist," one said. "Our master in prison has heard about your works and wants us to ask of you, 'Are You the Coming One, or do we look for another?' "

Matthew was puzzled by this, as he knew that John was the one who had baptized Jesus and had himself proclaimed Him the One. Perhaps his imprisonment had given him second thoughts.

Jesus said, "I want you to go and tell John the things which you hear and see: The blind see and the lame walk; lepers are cleansed and the deaf

210

hear; the dead are raised up and the poor have the gospel preached to them."

As they departed, Jesus began to say to the multitudes, "Among those born of women there has not risen one greater than John the Baptist. He who has ears to hear, let him hear! The Son of Man came eating and drinking, and they say, 'Look, a glutton and a winebibber, a friend of tax collectors and sinners!' But woe to you who see My mighty works but do not repent! For if the mighty works which were done in you had been done in the abominable cities of Tyre and Sidon, even they would have repented long ago in sackcloth and ashes. But I say to you, it will be more tolerable for Tyre and Sidon in the day of judgment than for you."

As the scribes and Pharisees drew close, their countenances clouded with what appeared to Matthew to be contempt, Jesus said, "I thank You, Father, Lord of heaven and earth, that You have hidden these things from the wise and prudent and have revealed them to babes. No one knows the Son except the Father. Nor does anyone know the Father except the Son, and the one to whom the Son wills to reveal Him.

"Come to Me, all you who labor and are heavy laden, and I will give you rest. Take My yoke upon you and learn from Me, for I am gentle and lowly in heart, and you will find rest for your souls. For My yoke is easy and My burden is light."

NINETEEN

That night as Matthew sat by the crackling fire, he recalled the events of the morning. He had been used by God to perform miracles—an experience so foreign to his life up to that point that he knew he would never be the same.

All the disciples seemed energized by what they had experienced that day, and it was all they could do to wait their turn to tell their stories. But Simon the Cananite was most exercised. "We should all be zealots," he said. "No king but Messiah. No tax but the temple's. And no friend but the zealot."

The others smiled and shook their heads, bemused. Thomas was the one who asked the question foremost on Matthew's mind. "Tell us more, Master," he said, "about the willingness to forsake all for Your sake. That *is* what you were saying, isn't it, about pitting us against our families?"

James weighed in. "Yes, Lord, tell about Your bringing a sword rather than peace. Because, as you know, we expect Messiah to bring deliverance for Israel and to bring an eternal kingdom of righteousness and peace. The ancient texts called You the Prince of Peace and speak of Your reign."

Jesus nodded. "But I must prepare you for My rejection and suffering, and also yours. Mine is a gospel of peace, but because of sin, men and women will reject it. Some of your enemies will be the people closest to you."

"Why did You say we had to take up our crosses to follow You?" Matthew said. "We all have seen the thousands crucified along the road after the rebellion. Are we to die for You in this horrible way?"

"I pray you will not," Jesus said. "Yet everything may be required of all of us. But as I said, if you lose your life for My sake, you will find it."

Several began to speak and question, but Jesus silenced them with a hand. "He who has ears, let him hear."

ON THE NEXT Sabbath the disciples were with Jesus as He wandered through a grain field, followed by the seemingly ever-present Pharisees. Matthew knew the others had to be as hungry as he. They began to pluck heads of grain and to eat.

Suddenly the Pharisees shouted, "Look! Your disciples are doing what is not lawful to do on the Sabbath!"

Jesus stopped and turned and let the holy men catch up to Him. "Have you not read what David did when he was hungry, he and those who were with him: how he entered the house of God and ate the showbread which was not lawful for him to eat, nor for those who were with him, but only for the priests? Or have you not read in the law that on the Sabbath the priests in the temple profane the Sabbath, and yet are blameless?

"Yet I say to you that in this place there is One greater than the temple. But if you had known what this means, *'I desire mercy and not sacrifice,'* you would not have condemned the guiltless. For the Son of Man is Lord even of the Sabbath."

Matthew caught James's eye and could see in his visage the same wonder he felt at merely hearing this Man talk. He did not deserve to have the privilege to get a glimpse of the Messiah, the Son of God, let alone to be called His friend and His disciple. He had lived his whole life at war with God, yet now He felt forgiven and cleansed. Even better, his days were filled with the presence of a Man so wise, so profound, that it was all he could do to remember everything in order to be able to record it.

FROM THERE, Jesus went into town and entered the synagogue. A man with a withered hand approached him, but the Pharisees immediately said, "Is it lawful to heal on the Sabbath?" It was obvious they were looking for something they could use to accuse Him.

Jesus said, "Is there a man among you who has one sheep, and if it falls into a pit on the Sabbath, will not lay hold of it and lift it out? Of how much more value then is a man than a sheep? Therefore it is lawful to do good on the Sabbath."

He turned to the afflicted man. "Stretch out your hand." And when he did, it was restored as whole as the other.

The Pharisees immediately rushed out, and Jesus said to His disciples, "Let's withdraw. They are plotting how they might destroy Me."

But as they left, great multitudes followed, and He healed them all. Again Jesus warned them not to make Him known. James hurried to Matthew's side and said, "Do you recall that which was written by Isaiah the prophet?"

Matthew shook his head. "Remind me."

"He wrote, *'Behold! My Servant whom I have chosen, My Beloved in whom My soul is well pleased! I will put My Spirit upon Him, and He will declare justice to the Gentiles. He will not quarrel nor cry out, nor will anyone hear His voice in the streets. A bruised reed He will not break, and smoking flax He will not quench, till He sends forth justice to victory; and in His name Gentiles will trust.'*"

When Jesus and the disciples were back at Peter's house in Capernaum, one was brought to Him who was demon-possessed, blind, and mute. And Jesus healed him. The crowds murmured excitedly and someone said, "Could this be the Son of David?"

Jesus had his eye on the Pharisees at the edge of the crowd and whispered to Matthew, "They are saying again that I cast out demons by Beelzebub, the ruler of the demons."

He turned to them. "I know your thoughts," He said. "But every kingdom divided against itself is brought to desolation, and every city or house divided against itself will not stand. If Satan casts out Satan, he is divided against himself. How then will his kingdom stand? But if I cast out demons by the Spirit of God, surely the kingdom of God has come upon you.

"He who is not with Me is against Me. Every sin and blasphemy will be forgiven men, but the blasphemy against the Spirit will not be forgiven men. Anyone who speaks a word against the Son of Man, it will be forgiven him; but whoever speaks against the Holy Spirit, it will not be forgiven him, either in this age or in the age to come.

"Brood of vipers! How can you, being evil, speak good things? For out of the abundance of the heart the mouth speaks. A good man out of the good treasure of his heart brings forth good things, and an evil man out of the evil treasure brings forth evil things. But I say to you that for every idle word men may speak, they will give account of it in the day of judgment. For by your words you will be justified, and by your words you will be condemned."

Some of the scribes and Pharisees answered, "Teacher, we want to see a sign from You."

Jesus shook His head. "An evil and adulterous generation seeks after a sign, and no sign will be given to it except the sign of the prophet Jonah. For as Jonah was three days and three nights in the belly of the great fish, so will the Son of Man be three days and three nights in the heart of the earth. The men of Nineveh will rise up in the judgment with this generation and condemn it, because they repented at the preaching of Jonah; and indeed a greater Man than Jonah is here. Indeed a greater Man than Solomon is here."

Matthew was stunned that Jesus would be so bold as to draw attention to Himself as the One who was greater than Jonah and even Solomon, if His intention was to stay out of the way of the scheming Pharisees. But who was he to counsel the Master?

While Jesus was still talking to the multitudes, Philip said, "Master, Your mother and Your brothers are outside, seeking to speak with You."

"Philip," Jesus said, "who is My mother and who are My brothers?"

He gestured toward His disciples and said, "Here are My mother and My brothers! For whoever does the will of My Father in heaven is My brother and sister and mother."

LATER THAT SAME DAY, Jesus left the house and sat by the sea where great crowds gathered. There were so many that to be heard He got into a boat and sat, and the whole multitude stood on the shore.

When He began to speak, Matthew immediately began writing.

"Behold, a sower went out to sow. And as he sowed, some seed fell by the wayside; and the birds came and devoured them. Some fell on stony places, where they did not have much earth; and they immediately sprang up because they had no depth of earth. But when the sun was up they were scorched, and because they had no root they withered away. And some fell among thorns, and the thorns sprang up and choked them. But others fell on good ground and yielded a crop: some a hundredfold, some sixty, some thirty. He who has ears to hear, let him hear!"

When the disciples got time with Jesus alone later, Matthew said, "Why do You speak to them in parables?"

"Because it has been given to you to know the mysteries of the kingdom of heaven, but to them it has not been given. For whoever has, to him more will be given, and he will have abundance; but whoever does not have, even what he has will be taken away from him. Therefore I speak to them in parables, because seeing they do not see, and hearing they do not hear, nor do they understand. And in them the prophecy of Isaiah is fulfilled, which says: *'Hearing you will hear and shall not understand, and seeing you will see and not perceive; for the hearts of this people have grown dull. Their ears are hard of hearing, and their eyes they have closed, lest they should see with their eyes and hear with their ears, lest they should understand with their hearts and turn, that I should heal them.'*

"But blessed are your eyes for they see, and your ears for they hear; for assuredly, I say to you that many prophets and righteous men desired to see what you see, and did not see it, and to hear what you hear, and did not hear it.

"Therefore hear the parable of the sower: When anyone hears the word of the kingdom, and does not understand it, then the wicked one comes and snatches away what was sown in his heart. This is he who received seed by the wayside. But he who received the seed on stony places, this is he who hears the word and immediately receives it with joy; yet he has no root in himself, but endures only for a while. For when tribulation or persecution arises because of the word, immediately he stumbles.

"Now he who received seed among the thorns is he who hears the word, and the cares of this world and the deceitfulness of riches choke the word, and he becomes unfruitful. But he who received seed on the good ground is he who hears the word and understands it, who indeed bears fruit and produces: some a hundredfold, some sixty, some thirty."

Another parable Jesus told the multitudes compared the kingdom of heaven to a man who sowed good seed in his field, but while he slept his enemy sowed tares among the wheat and went his way.

"When the grain had sprouted and produced a crop, then the tares also appeared. So the servants of the owner came and said to him, 'Sir, did you not sow good seed in your field? How then does it have tares?'

"He said, 'An enemy has done this.'

"The servants said, 'Do you want us then to go and gather them up?'

"But he said, 'No, lest while you gather up the tares you also uproot the wheat with them. Let both grow together until the harvest, and at the time of harvest I will say to the reapers, "First gather together the tares and bind them in bundles to burn them, but gather the wheat into my barn."'"

Later, back in Peter's home, James said, "Matthew, He spoke to them that way that it might be fulfilled which was spoken by the prophet, saying: *I will open My mouth in parables; I will utter things kept secret from the foundation of the world.*'"

Matthew was familiar with the prophecy, yet he still had trouble understanding all that Jesus taught. The others also seemed confounded. Peter said, "Master, explain to us the parable of the tares of the field."

Jesus said, "He who sows the good seed is the

Son of Man. The field is the world, the good seeds are the sons of the kingdom, but the tares are the sons of the wicked one. The enemy who sowed them is the devil, the harvest is the end of the age, and the reapers are the angels.

"Therefore as the tares are gathered and burned in the fire, so it will be at the end of this age. The Son of Man will send out His angels, and they will gather out of His kingdom all things that offend, and those who practice lawlessness, and will cast them into the furnace of fire. There will be wailing and gnashing of teeth. Then the righteous will shine forth as the sun in the kingdom of their Father. He who has ears to hear, let him hear!

"Again, the kingdom of heaven is like treasure hidden in a field, which a man found and hid; and for joy over it he goes and sells all that he has and buys that field.

"Again, the kingdom of heaven is like a merchant seeking beautiful pearls, who, when he had found one pearl of great price, went and sold all that he had and bought it.

"Again, the kingdom of heaven is like a dragnet that was cast into the sea and gathered some of every kind, which, when it was full, they drew to shore; and they sat down and gathered the good into vessels, but threw the bad away. So it will be at the end of the age. The angels will come forth, separate the wicked from among the just, and cast them into the furnace of fire. There will be wailing and gnashing of teeth."

Matthew looked at the other disciples. How precious the kingdom seemed in the words of Jesus.

The Master said, "My friends, have you understood all these things?"

They said, "Yes, Lord."

PART THREE

LEVI'S ACCOUNT

TWENTY

Over the better part of the next year, Matthew and James enjoyed getting to know each other as they never had as children and young men. They were quite busy every day and spent hours each evening around the fire with Jesus, learning of the kingdom and having Him explain more fully to the twelve all the lessons He had been trying to teach the multitudes.

But before they retired each night—sometimes at Peter's home, sometimes out in the open air, sometimes at the home of some hospitable godly family—the brothers found time to get together. They were paired off with other disciples for their occasional daily sojourns for ministry—Matthew usually with Thomas and James with Andrew—yet Matthew always looked forward to the time with James and never ceased to be amazed at the traits of his parents he recognized in his brother.

James was quiet and studious like his mother, wise and prudent like his father. And he had the gift of memorization that Matthew had enjoyed as a child, but which he feared he had lost in the ensuing years when he quit reading the Scriptures daily. How he wished he still possessed it so he could listen to Jesus and write later, rather than having to write while listening.

The brothers talked much about Jesus' parables

and discussed why it seemed He had so plainly emphasized to the disciples the story of the wheat and the tares, above all the rest. "We are to get that settled in our minds, apparently," James said. "It must be that many who hear His word, and even some who act upon it, will fall away. It is for us to be wise and discerning."

The Master had mentioned numerous times over the last several days His plans to return to His own city of Nazareth to teach in the synagogue. "I am most excited about that trip," Matthew said, "but have you noticed that the Lord does not seem so?"

James nodded. "I have. And I agree with you; it seems He would look forward to returning to His home and His friends and loved ones. How thrilled they must be that someone from their town has become so widely known and beloved, famous for His teaching and His working of wonders."

"It is almost as if He dreads it, James. He has always been wary of the scribes and Pharisees, but surely no one in Nazareth would allow them to harm Him. I should think this would be a respite from the constant pressure from the religious leaders."

The evening before they were to journey to Nazareth, other disciples asked Jesus about His seeming reticence over the visit.

"Hear Me," He said sadly, His voice just above

a whisper. "I long ago told you of when, after My baptism by John, I fasted in the wilderness for forty days and forty nights, tempted by the devil. I returned from there to Nazareth and attempted to teach in the synagogue. Not only was I not received or accepted, but I was also reviled. A mob led Me to the top of a cliff and would have pushed Me to My death, had My Father not allowed Me to disappear from their midst."

"Then why return?" Peter said. "They do not deserve Your presence among them!"

"It is the will of My Father that I return. And I am here to do His will."

IT SEEMED to Matthew that the trek from Capernaum to Nazareth took longer than usual, but it hardly surprised him that when the multitudes that trailed them—first from Capernaum and then from Tiberias—drifted away, they were met by crowds from Nazareth long before they entered the city. By the time they reached the synagogue the throngs had grown to where the disciples had to protect Jesus and keep even His admirers at bay. Peter, as was his wont, kept urging the Master to find shelter to rest and refresh Himself, but Jesus pressed on.

He straightaway entered the temple, and the rabbi seemed to cheerfully step aside and welcome Him. The people filled the place and spilled outside in droves. The Pharisees pushed through the crowds and forced their way in, exercising their authority to remove the last ones in and make them stand outside.

Jesus opened the Scriptures and immediately began reading and teaching, carefully explaining every passage as One with authority. Matthew, who stood between Thomas and James, vigilantly watching both the crowd and the Pharisees for any sign of danger to the Master, was nearly overcome with the privilege of learning under the Messiah Himself.

When Jesus paused to make a point, someone called out, "Where did this Man get this wisdom, and how is He able to do the mighty works we have heard about?"

"Yes!" cried another. "Is this not the carpenter's son? Is not His mother called Mary? And His brothers James, Joses, Simon, and Judas? And His sisters, do they not all live among us? Where, then, did this Man get all these things?"

Peter stepped forward, ready to shout them down, but Jesus put a hand on his shoulder. "Allow me," He said. "Beloved, a prophet is not without honor except in his own country and in his own house."

"We will hear no more! Show us signs and wonders so that we might believe!"

Jesus made His way out of the temple with a look of such abject sorrow that it nearly brought Matthew to tears. And while He healed a few people, Jesus did not do many miracles there, telling the disciples later that it was due to the people's skepticism and unbelief.

As they sat somberly around the fire that night, Jesus said, "Perhaps you recognize that the Sower's seed has fallen on stony ground here, and that is why I have been rejected."

That evening Jesus assigned Matthew and Thomas to steal into Tiberias to learn what they could of the fate of the imprisoned John, the baptizer. "We will meet you back in Capernaum."

Matthew was honored to have such an assignment, but neither he nor Thomas was ignorant of the danger of their mission. Jesus Himself had never set foot in Tiberias, though He had passed that way many times. This was where Herod the Tetrarch, Herod the Great's son, spent most of his time. And it was where John had been imprisoned for publicly proclaiming that the already married Herod had no right to take as his wife Herodias, who was also already married to Herod's own half-brother Philip.

Matthew and Thomas peeled off from the rest of the group as it made its way back to Capernaum, and the crowds were already beginning to again bear down on Jesus.

As they entered the city, Matthew agreed with his partner to split up and begin carefully asking around, trying not to arouse suspicion. John had become such an enemy of the king that anyone who appeared in league with him would also be in danger.

Matthew was taking refreshment in a wayside inn when he overheard several men talking about what had become of the baptizer. "It's no wonder," one said. "He told the king to his face, 'It is not lawful for you to have her.' "

Matthew joined in as if he knew the story. "I'm surprised he was only imprisoned. The king could have had him put to death."

"And have the multitude on his neck? Most of the people consider John a prophet!"

When he and Thomas met up again later that night, they shared what they had learned. Thomas said, "I was getting nowhere trying to innocently ask around, but word apparently got to some of John's disciples. One came out of hiding and approached me. He asked why I was interested in John. I told him I was a disciple of Jesus and that the Master was asking after him. He promised to send word if anything changed."

SEVERAL DAYS LATER, when the disciples and Jesus were all together again at Peter's house in Capernaum, word came that two of John's disciples were outside, asking to speak with Thomas and Matthew. They rushed out to find the men distraught.

"Your Master will want to know that John is dead," one said.

"No!" Matthew cried. "If Herod meant to kill him, why didn't he do that in the first place?"

"Let me get Jesus," Thomas said, running back into the house.

When Jesus and Thomas joined Matthew and John's disciples outside, they retreated to a grove of trees and sat.

"Bad news, I'm afraid, Master," Matthew said.

Jesus nodded sadly, and one of John's disciples told the story. "At Herod's birthday party, Herodias's daughter danced for him and pleased him. Apparently he promised her anything she wanted, and—prompted by her mother—she asked for John's head on a platter. He was bound to honor his pledge, of course. Several of us went to the prison yesterday and took the body and buried it."

Matthew had not seen Jesus weep before, and it moved him deeply. "I need to be by Myself," He said. "Have Peter and Andrew prepare Me a vessel, and I will go to the other side of the Sea of Galilee."

It seemed a simple request, but Matthew found that the crowds had scouts who seemed to watch everything Jesus and His disciples did. It wasn't long before thousands of people followed Him. As usual, Peter wanted to send them all away, and Matthew couldn't blame him. He too wished the Master could get a little time to Himself.

But when Jesus saw the great multitude, it was

obvious from the look on His face that He was moved with compassion for them. He allowed them to gather, their number extending as far as Matthew could see, and all day He healed their sick.

When the sun began to set, Matthew drew near Jesus and whispered, "Lord, this is a deserted place, and the hour is already late. Send the multitudes away, that they may go into the villages and buy themselves food."

But Jesus said, "They do not need to go away. You give them something to eat."

"But, Master, there are thousands of them, and we have here only five loaves and two fish."

"Bring them to Me."

Matthew brought them, wondering what the Lord had in mind. Then Jesus commanded the multitudes to sit down on the grass. He took the five loaves and the two fish, and looking up to heaven, He blessed and broke the loaves and the fish and gave them to the disciples; and the disciples passed them out to the multitudes.

The supply never ran out. Matthew trembled as he watched the people eat, every one, and they were all filled. He and the others then gathered up twelve baskets full of the fragments that remained.

"I counted the men alone!" Peter exulted. "And there were about five thousand. Imagine the total, including women and children!"

Jesus drew Matthew and Peter near and said, "You and the others take the boat to the other side. I will send the people away and go up on the mountain alone to pray."

Peter looked troubled. "You're sure You will be all right?"

Jesus merely nodded, but Matthew threw his head back and laughed. "Peter! He has just fed five thousand men, not to mention their families, with one serving of fish and five loaves of bread! Do you not think He can take care of Himself?"

TWENTY-ONE

For years, Matthew, as Levi the despised tax collector, had seen many Galilean fishermen ply their trade. He had never befriended any of them, but he had on occasion made it his business to notice which ones seemed more proficient than the others.

It was no mystery to him then that Peter had become the spokesman for those in the trade and that his and Andrew's business—along with James and John's—were the most profitable. In the past, Matthew had watched with an eye toward his own profits, for the more successful the business, the more taxes could be charged. But up until now he had not appreciated the seaworthiness of the vessels or the skills of the boatmen for any other reason.

But since joining Jesus and seeing the seafaring duties fall to those four with experience, Matthew had an entirely new appreciation for their abilities. While he had always been slightly put off by Peter's bluster and directness, he couldn't deny that the man knew how to lead others and how to handle a vessel. He and his brother and the brothers Zebedee immediately took charge anytime the Master said where He wanted to sail. They seemed to fly about the boat with ease, securing lines, setting sails, and being sure everything was just so. That freed others to cook meals, help with loading, and minister to Jesus—something Matthew always enjoyed.

This night, when it was just the disciples onboard, with Jesus remaining up in the mountain to pray, the seamen quickly had the craft ready to sail and were soon off. Matthew had grown used to eating on board and had even learned from the fishermen how to avoid seasickness. He sat with his brother and Thomas, eating and talking and watching the sun set.

Soon, however, the waves grew choppy and it seemed to Matthew—despite his inexperience—that the ship was making little progress. Peter and the others maneuvered the sails so they were tacking, trying to make headway by catching the swirling winds. But it was clear that the craft was mostly drifting.

Matthew didn't worry about it until hours later

when the sky was black and the glimpses he caught of the faces of the fishermen showed deep consternation. Peter was high in the rigging while Andrew supervised the others in securing everything that had been brought onboard. "We're expecting a storm, fellows," he said.

"How severe?" Matthew said.

"We're not sure, but we intend to be ready."

When dark clouds blotted out the moon, the sea began to pitch and the boat was soon rolling and rocking on choppy waves. Many of the men went below, but Matthew was intrigued that Andrew watched warily as Peter slowly made his way down. When Peter planted himself at the bow of the bobbing ship as if he intended to stare down the storm, Matthew wished he were brave enough to do the same.

"Coming?" James said as he followed Thomas to the hatch and started down.

"Soon, likely," Matthew said. "But I've never ridden out a tempest before. Let me stay topside as long as I can."

"Just don't be foolish," James said. "I don't want to have to fetch you from the sea."

Matthew laughed and waved him off, having to suddenly grab the side of the ship to keep from falling. Only he and Peter and Andrew remained abovedecks now.

"I judge we're as close to the middle of the sea as we could be!" Peter cried out. "And we may be here for some time! I foresee no break in the weather!"

If Matthew wasn't mistaken, Peter seemed to be enjoying this. He wagered the man had weathered more than a few storms in his day. It wasn't long before Matthew rued his decision to stay topside. Peter and Andrew weren't doing much, for apparently there was little they could do against the wind and waves. The more the boat was tossed, the more Matthew heard shouts from below as the others seemed to be knocking into one another.

"What hour of the night?" Matthew shouted.

"About fourth watch!" Andrew called back.

And just then, the boat rode high on a mountainous wave and slid down, nearly capsizing when the water crashed over it. Matthew held on for all he was worth, and Andrew went sliding up to where Peter held fast. Lightning lit their faces and Matthew was staggered to see that they were as terrified as he.

Now the ship rolled up on its other side and all three men slid about the deck, crashing into the sides and one another, shrieking in fear. The hatch opened and the other nine poured out. "Peter!" someone screamed. "We perish!"

"Hold on!" he called back, but even he had again lost his grip on the side.

Was this how it was to end, then? Would Matthew die merely two years after having been rescued from his miserable life by the Messiah Himself? At least he could be grateful his Lord had stayed behind and would not Himself be robbed of the chance to continue doing the will of His Father.

"Oh, no! No!" Philip hollered, pointing. "Behold, a ghost approaches!"

The others stared with wide eyes and fell over one another trying to again head for the hatch, Matthew among them. But as the figure drew near the boat, He said with a loud voice, "Be of good cheer! It is I! Do not be afraid!"

Peter said, "Lord, if it is You, command me to come to You on the water!"

And Jesus said, "Come."

Peter clambered over the side, and as he reached the water he began to walk on the waves toward Jesus. But as the wind whipped him, he looked fearful and began to sink.

"Lord, save me!"

Jesus reached out and caught him, and said, "O you of little faith, why did you doubt?"

Jesus walked Peter back to the boat and as soon they got in, the wind ceased. Matthew and the others fell to their knees before Jesus and worshiped Him, saying, "Truly You are the Son of God."

WHEN THE BOAT FINALLY reached shore at dawn, the disciples found themselves in the land of

Gennesaret. The people there recognized Jesus and spread the word into the surrounding region. Thousands streamed to Him and brought all who were sick. There were so many that Matthew feared it would take all day for Jesus to minister to them. But they begged Him that they might only touch the hem of His garment, and as many as touched it were made perfectly well.

As usual, Matthew was drawn to the families with small children. As the other disciples worked to keep the crowd from becoming unruly or met with small groups of them to pray while they waited, Matthew sought out those who had little ones in need of healing.

"My son has been mute from birth," a woman told him. "Can the Rabbi heal him?"

Matthew smiled at the boy, who appeared to be fewer than ten years old and was fearful. The lad clung close to his mother.

"I have never seen Him turn away a child," Matthew said. "Indeed He has often asked us to bring the children to Him. Have faith. Notice that He is healing every person who merely touches the hem of His garment."

"I don't know if Timothy will dare do it," she said.

"Jesus will put him at ease."

As Matthew shepherded the family through the line he saw that Jesus was dealing quickly with every afflicted person, as there were so many and the multitude stretched far down the mountain-side. But when the Master noticed the lad, He smiled and stretched out His arms. Timothy looked to his mother, then back at Jesus before shyly approaching.

Jesus gathered the boy into His arms and set Him on His lap.

Timothy's mother said, "He cannot—"

"I know," Jesus said. "But he will speak to Me, and then to you."

The woman immediately fell to her knees.

"Son," Jesus said, "the faith of your mother has made you whole. Tell Me your name."

"Timothy," the boy whispered, and his mother burst into tears.

"And who is this?" Jesus said, pointing to her.

"My mother."

"Why is she weeping?"

"Because she is so happy!"

Timothy's mother embraced Jesus and her son, nearly making the Master topple over. They all laughed and rejoiced, and Jesus said, "Go in peace and praise your Heavenly Father."

LATER THAT DAY James hurried to Matthew's side. "Look! Over there! Those scribes and Pharisees are from Jerusalem—many are my former colleagues."

The religious leaders approached and said, "Why do Your disciples transgress the tradition of the elders? For they do not wash their hands when they eat bread."

Matthew had to smile. It seemed that every day these types of people tried to trick Jesus and catch Him in some detail. But He always proved up to the challenge.

Jesus said, "Why do you also transgress the commandment of God because of your tradition? For God commanded, 'Honor your father and your mother' and, 'He who curses father or mother, let him be put to death.' But you say, 'Whoever says to his father or mother, "Whatever profit you might have received from me is a gift to God"—then he need not honor his father or mother.' Thus you have made the commandment of God of no effect by your tradition.

"Hypocrites! Well did Isaiah prophesy about you, saying:

These people draw near to Me with their mouth, and honor Me with their lips, but their heart is far from Me. And in vain they worship Me, teaching as doctrines the commandments of men."

The scribes and Pharisees scowled and shook their heads as they trudged away. Jesus beckoned the multitude to Himself and said, "Hear and understand: It is not what goes into the mouth that defiles a man, but it is what comes out of his mouth that defiles him."

．　．　．

THAT EVENING as the disciples ate around the fire, Matthew looked up from his writing board and said, "Master, were You aware of how offended the Pharisees were when they heard what You said?"

Jesus nodded. "Hear me. Unless My heavenly Father sows a plant, it will be uprooted. He who has ears, let him hear. Do not worry about the scribes and Pharisees. Let them alone. They are blind leaders of the blind. And if the blind leads the blind, both will fall into a ditch."

Peter said, "But do explain that parable to us about what defiles a man."

Jesus shook his head. "Are you also still without understanding?

"Listen, whatever enters the mouth goes *into* the stomach and is eliminated. But those things which proceed *out* of the mouth come from the heart, and they defile a man. For out of the heart proceed evil thoughts, murders, adulteries, fornications, thefts, false witness, blasphemies. These are the things that defile a man. Eating with unwashed hands does not defile a man."

When they departed from there, Jesus skirted the Sea of Galilee and went up and sat on the mountain there. Again great multitudes came to Him, bringing the lame, blind, mute, maimed, and many others they laid at Jesus' feet. And though Matthew had witnessed this almost daily for more than a year, he remained astonished as his Master healed them all over the next few days.

The multitude marveled when they saw the mute speaking, the maimed made whole, the lame walking, and the blind seeing. They shouted, "Glory to the God of Israel!"

Soon Jesus called His disciples to Himself and said, "I have compassion on the multitude, because they have now continued with Me three days and have nothing to eat. And I do not want to send them away hungry, lest they faint on the way."

James, the brother of John, said, "Where could we get enough bread in the wilderness to fill such a great multitude?"

Matthew wondered if Jesus would miraculously feed the masses again. The Lord said, "How many loaves do you have?"

This time they found seven loaves and a few small fish.

Jesus commanded the multitude to sit on the ground, and He took the loaves and the fish and gave thanks, broke them, and gave them to His disciples. Matthew and the others distributed them to the entire crowd.

Again all ate and were filled, and the disciples collected seven large baskets full of the fragments that were left. Matthew immediately sought out Peter. "How many this time?" he said, smiling.

"Four thousand men, besides women and children."

Jesus sent away the multitude and led the disciples down to the shore and onto the boat. He told Peter to set their course toward Magdala. Then He summoned Matthew to his side.

"Shall I bring my papyrus, Lord?"

"You will not have need of it."

Matthew was aware of the others peering his way as he sat alone with Jesus. Honored as they all were to have a part in ministering to the Lord, it seemed only natural that each coveted a special place with just Him.

"I know your spirit remains troubled, Gift from God."

Jesus seemed to know Matthew better than he knew himself. He thought he had matured in his thinking, but he could not deny that—though he would have had to have been blind to not recognize the Teacher and miracle worker as anyone but Messiah—he still had questions about what God had allowed to happen to his family.

"Yes, Lord. At times I still wonder."

"I want to tell you some of what is to come."

TWENTY-TWO

"I told you when we met that you were a gift to Me from God," Jesus said, as the vessel glided away from the shore.

"Yes, Lord."

"I know you, Matthew."

"I know that You do."

"I know that You see Me doing the will of My Father and performing mighty deeds in His name to glorify Him."

Matthew nodded, wondering what this was all about.

"You understand that these miracles are not to bring attention to Me but rather to show God's power and draw men unto Him."

"I think I understand, Lord, but I am not always sure. Many in the multitudes don't care why You're doing this. All they seem to care about is Your fame or their own benefit. They want signs and wonders in order to believe."

"Blessed is the one who believes without a sign or wonder."

Matthew did not know what to say, and Jesus had fallen silent. Did He expect some response? Jesus gazed at him and he had to look away. Finally Jesus said, "Do you think I have not noticed that you are drawn to the little ones?"

Matthew shrugged. "As you are."

Jesus smiled. "It is true. Theirs is the kingdom of heaven. I so love their pure, simple faith. You know, Matthew, that I understand. You see these miracles and know the power of God and still wonder why He did not prevent what happened to your brother."

"To my brother and my parents, my whole family!"

"To you."

"Yes, Lord, to me! I wasted so many years in pain and bitterness, yet I felt helpless to forgive . . ."

"To forgive God?"

Matthew could not stanch the tears. He nodded miserably. "How does one forgive God?"

"You ask well, Matthew, because My Father is not a mere man who needs the forgiveness of His creation. His ways are not your ways and His purposes are beyond your finding out."

Matthew treasured talking with Jesus, but in spite of himself thought this was not helping. The truth was, Jesus could heal any sickness or affliction. He could disappear from the midst of His enemies. Why could God have not spared Chavivi from the hand of the despised Herod?

Jesus put a hand on Matthew's shoulder, and he had never felt so loved, so cared for. Yet still he remained confused and, he feared, embittered. "As I have asked all those who come to Me for healing, I ask you to have faith, to trust in Me, to believe in Me."

"I do!"

"But I also need you to trust in your Heavenly Father and to know that what men mean for evil, He meant for good."

"The death of an innocent baby? How—"

"It may not be yours to know or understand until you are in paradise with Me. And though as you say you wasted many years in bitterness, this evil wrought against you has also opened your eyes to the tenderness of a mother's love and to the innocence of children. I see it every day in how you interact with them."

Matthew did not want to pretend that whatever softness had been wrought in him was worth the horror of his past, but if he was being asked to merely trust Jesus and his Heavenly Father, he believed he could do that.

After a moment of silence, the only sound the waves lapping against the side of the craft, Matthew said, "You were going to tell me something about what is to come?"

Jesus smiled. "Did you think I had forgotten?"

The absurdity of the notion made Matthew laugh in spite of himself. Jesus was so easy to talk to that Matthew could, for an instant, forget he was in the presence of the Son of God, the Messiah. "Sorry," he said.

Jesus grew serious again. "I have been trying to prepare you and the others for the hour when My enemies will be allowed to have sway over Me."

"May it never be so!"

"This is the will of My Father. I am here to do His will. I tell you this only to remind you that you were never alone in your suffering. Others were plagued with a similar fate."

"I know. Many. Some from my own town."

"And your Heavenly Father."

"I don't understand."

"The day will come when it will be clearer to you. He will suffer a loss as you did. And as you felt abandoned, deserted, forsaken by Him, I will come to experience your pain."

"Master, I know it is not Your intent to more thoroughly confuse me—"

"More I cannot tell you. I want only that you be prepared, have ears to hear and eyes to see. Watch the unfolding of the perfect plan of My Father. And in the meantime, trust Me, trust Him, and use the painful lesson of your childhood to serve Him until then. Do you love Me enough to trust Me and do that?"

"I do, Lord. You know I do."

Jesus stood and drew Matthew close. "Your written record will prove valuable. Many there are who have never heard My voice or seen the wonders God has given Me to perform. Generations yet unborn will know of Me only through what you have written."

As soon as the disciples and Jesus disembarked and the multitudes began to gather, the Pharisees and Sadducees were not far behind. "Rabbi!" they called out from the edge of the crowd, "show us a sign from heaven!"

Jesus gazed at them and said nothing until they pushed their way through to face Him. Then He said, "When it is evening you say, 'It will be fair weather, for the sky is red.' And in the morning you say, 'It will be foul weather today, for the sky is red and threatening.' Hypocrites! You know how to discern the face of the sky, but you cannot discern the signs of the times."

"How dare you? Blasphemer!"

"You come to Me for a sign," Jesus said, "so hear Me. A wicked and adulterous generation seeks after a sign, and no sign shall be given to it except the sign of the prophet Jonah."

"What is that supposed to mean?"

But Jesus left them and departed. When the disciples were alone with Him, He said, "Take heed and beware of the leaven of the Pharisees and the Sadducees."

They had forgotten to bring bread along, so they huddled far from Him and said, "Does He say this because we have brought no bread?"

Matthew should have known Jesus was aware of their thoughts, but he was startled when Jesus said, "O you of little faith, why do you reason among yourselves because you have brought no bread? Do you not yet understand or remember the five loaves of the five thousand and how many baskets you took up? Nor the seven loaves of the four thousand and how many large baskets you took up? How is it you do not understand that I was not speaking to you concerning bread, but was warning you about the leaven of the Pharisees and Sadducees?"

Peter muttered to the others, "The leaven?"

Matthew's brother James said, "He means their doctrine and how it would affect His true teachings of the kingdom."

WHEN THEY CAME into the region of Caesarea Philippi, Jesus appeared weary from all His ministry and travel, not to mention the frustration of having to deal with the scribes and Pharisees and Sadducees. As He settled before His serving of roasted fish and baked bread He sighed and said, "Beloved brothers, who do men say that I, the Son of Man, am?"

"Some say John the Baptist," Matthew said. "Even Herod the Tetrarch was said to have asked if You were he, come back from the grave."

Andrew said, "Others say Elijah, and others Jeremiah or one of the prophets."

Jesus gazed at each of them, as if studying their faces. "But who do you say that I am?"

Peter said, "You are the Christ, the Son of the living God."

Matthew was warmed by Jesus' smile. "Blessed are you, Simon bar Jonah, for flesh and blood has not revealed this to you, but My Father who is in heaven. And I also say to you that you are Peter, and on this rock I will build My church, and the gates of Hades shall not prevail against it." He turned to the others and said, "And I will give you the keys of the kingdom of heaven, and whatever you bind on earth will be bound in heaven, and whatever you loose on earth will be loosed in heaven."

Matthew recognized that they had all experienced a singular moment. No one moved. No one ate, and those who had a bite in their mouth stopped chewing.

"Now hear Me, My friends," Jesus said. "I command you that you should tell no one that I am the Christ. You need to know that I must go to Jerusalem and suffer many things from the elders and chief priests and scribes. In fact, I will be killed and be raised three days later."

Matthew and the others began to protest, but Peter silenced them, rose, and planted himself next to Jesus in the sand. "Far be it from You, Lord! This shall not happen to You!"

Jesus immediately faced Peter and said, "Get behind Me, Satan! You are an offense to Me, for you are not mindful of the things of God, but the things of men."

Peter hung his head and Matthew ached for him. Here he had been lauded for having recognized Jesus as the Christ, and now the Master was so vexed with him that He had called him Satan!

Jesus said softly, "I tell all of you, if anyone desires to come after Me, let him deny himself, and take up his cross, and follow Me. For whoever desires to save his life will lose it, but whoever loses his life for My sake will find it. For what profit is it to a man if he gains the whole world and loses his own soul? Or what will a man give in exchange for his soul? For the Son of Man will come in the glory of His Father with His angels, and then He will reward each according to his works."

Not many days later, as Jesus was traveling throughout the countryside, a young man came to Him and said, "Good Teacher, what good thing shall I do that I may have eternal life?"

Jesus said, "Why do you call Me good? No one is good but One, and that is God. But if you want to enter into life, keep the commandments."

"Which ones?"

Jesus said, " 'You shall not murder,' 'You shall not commit adultery,' 'You shall not steal,' 'You shall not bear false witness,' 'Honor your father and your mother,' and, 'You shall love your neighbor as yourself.' "

The young man smiled. "All these I have kept from my youth. What do I still lack?"

Jesus said, "If you want to be perfect, go, sell what you have and give to the poor, and you will have treasure in heaven; and come, follow Me."

"*All* that I have? I have a lot!"

"Where your treasure is," Jesus said, "there will your heart be also."

The man trudged away, shaking his head.

Jesus said to His disciples, "Assuredly, I say to you that it is hard for a rich man to enter the kingdom of heaven. In fact, it is easier for a camel to go through the eye of a needle than for a rich man to enter the kingdom of God."

Matthew caught his brother's eye and shook his head. James said, "Master, who then can be saved?"

Jesus said, "With men this is impossible, but with God all things are possible."

Peter said, "But, see Lord, we have left all and followed You. Therefore what shall we have?"

"Assuredly," Jesus said, "when the Son of Man sits on the throne of His glory, you who have followed Me will also sit on twelve thrones, judging the twelve tribes of Israel. And everyone who has left houses or brothers or sisters or father or mother or wife or children or lands, for My name's sake, shall receive a hundredfold, and inherit eternal life."

TWENTY-THREE

Several months later . . .

Jesus and the disciples had been slowly traveling throughout the areas south of Capernaum, and Matthew had a sinking feeling that they were making their way toward the Master's destiny. He had been trying to push from his mind Jesus' ominous warnings about His own fate, but he knew better than to even hope that the Son of God Himself might be wrong about the future.

Jesus had been preaching the gospel of the kingdom and healing thousands all along the way, to the growing anger and consternation and even hatred of the scribes and Pharisees. Matthew sensed the religious leaders were up to something and that they would not allow Jesus to continue with what they believed was blasphemy. The closer He and the twelve drew to the city of Jerusalem, the more exercised became the holy men.

Finally one day He drew His disciples away from the multitudes and stopped at the side of the road near Jericho. "Behold," He said wearily, "we are going up to Jerusalem, and the Son of Man will be betrayed to the chief priests and to the scribes; and they will condemn Him to death, and deliver Him to the Gentiles to mock and to scourge and to crucify. And the third day He will rise again."

He had been saying this and similar dire things for weeks, and Matthew had found himself trying to make sense of it. What did He mean about rising again? Surely that was some sort of a parable, a lesson from which they were to glean something. But he was afraid to ask further for fear of being chastised, and for fear of learning something he really did not want to know.

THE NEXT DAY, as Jesus and the twelve walked through Jericho, the party was overtaken by the mother of John and James. She pulled her sons before Jesus and knelt before Him as Matthew and the others looked on.

Jesus greeted her and said, "What do you wish?"

"Grant that these two sons of mine may sit, one on Your right hand and the other on the left, in Your kingdom."

What? Peter immediately stepped forward, as did Matthew and his brother. What an impudent request!

But before anyone else could say anything, Jesus said, "You do not know what you ask. James and John, are you able to drink the cup that I am about to drink, and be baptized with the baptism that I am baptized with?"

They both said, "Yes, Lord, we are able!"

Jesus shook his head, looking sad. "You will indeed drink My cup and be baptized with the baptism that I am baptized with. But to sit on My right hand and on My left is not Mine to give, but it is for those for whom it is prepared by My Father."

Matthew and the others were incensed with the two brothers. But Jesus gathered them around Himself and said, "You know that the rulers of the Gentiles lord it over them, and those who are great exercise authority over them. Yet it shall not be so among you. Whoever desires to become great among you, let him be your servant. And whoever desires to be first among you, let him be your slave—just as the Son of Man did not come to be served, but to serve, and to give His life as a ransom for many."

A ransom for me? Oh, that I could serve others as He has served! Matthew thought to himself.

As they left Jericho, Matthew wondered if the great multitude that followed Jesus would go with Him all the way to Jerusalem. What was to become of Him there? Surely He would not be allowed to preach of the kingdom or heal the sick so close to the temple. Matthew did not want to even entertain the thought of what Jesus had predicted.

When they drew near Jerusalem and came to Bethphage near the Mount of Olives, Jesus sent Matthew and Thomas into the village, telling them they would find a donkey and a colt tied. "Loose them and bring them to Me. And if anyone says anything to you, you shall say, 'The Lord has need of them,' and immediately he will send them."

Matthew felt privileged, but he was puzzled and sought out his brother before he left. "What do you make of it, James?"

"I don't know, but remember what was written by the prophet, 'Tell the daughter of Zion, "Behold, your King is coming to you, lowly, and sitting on a donkey, a colt, the foal of a donkey."'"

Matthew and Thomas hurried off and found the animals. When they returned they draped a cloak over the back of the foal and helped Jesus sit astride it. As soon as the disciples began to lead the donkey toward the city, masses of people from all the surrounding areas pressed in on them, spreading their own cloaks on the road before Him. Others cut branches from the trees and spread them on the road.

Matthew recognized many of the people as those who had heard Jesus preach and teach and had witnessed many of His miracles. It was clear they had no doubt who He was. They crowded all around Him, and the ones in the lead and even those who followed cried out, "Hosanna to the Son of David! *'Blessed is He who comes in the name of the Lord!'* Hosanna in the highest!"

What should have been a joyous parade made Matthew shudder. The people loved Jesus and revered Him, but Matthew felt as if he and his friends were leading Jesus to His doom. When the multitude slowly moved into the great city, it seemed all of Jerusalem was in an uproar with people all about saying, "Who is this?"

The crowds answered, "This is Jesus, the prophet from Nazareth of Galilee!"

When they came to the temple, Jesus appeared troubled and then clearly angry. The merchants who sold doves for the ceremonies and changed money were sitting right in the courtyard of the holy place, doing their business. Jesus leapt from the donkey and drove out all those who bought and sold in the temple, tipping over the tables of the money changers and the seats of those who sold doves.

He shouted, "It is written, *'My house shall be called a house of prayer,'* but you have made it a *'den of thieves'*!"

Suddenly Jesus was surrounded by many who were blind or lame, and He began healing them. Matthew was certain that the indignant merchants would already be plotting revenge and beckoning the authorities, but performing miracles at the temple? The chief priests and scribes arrived in droves as the multitudes were crying out, "Hosanna to the Son of David!"

"Do You hear what they are saying?" the chief priests demanded.

Jesus said, "Yes, I hear them. Have you never read, *'Out of the mouth of babes and nursing infants You have perfected praise'*?"

Matthew was greatly relieved when Jesus straightaway left there and headed to Bethany. He was certain that had Jesus tarried even a few more moments, He would have been seized.

The next morning Jesus set out again for Jerusalem, despite the warnings of His friends. Along the way He said He was hungry and stopped at a fig tree by the road. There was nothing on it but leaves. Jesus said to it, "Let no fruit grow on you ever again." Immediately the tree shriveled.

"How did that happen?" Thomas said, as the

others crowded around, astonished as Matthew was.

Jesus said, "Assuredly, if you have faith and do not doubt, you will not only do what was done to the fig tree, but also if you say to this mountain, 'Be removed and be cast into the sea,' it will be done. And whatever things you ask in prayer, believing, you will receive."

Matthew was fascinated that Jesus did not even seem to hesitate as He reentered Jerusalem and strode straight into the temple. Crowds grew with His every step, and as soon as He was inside and began to teach, the chief priests and elders confronted Him. "By what authority are You doing these things? And who gave You this authority?"

Jesus said, "I also will ask you one thing, and if you tell Me, I will tell you by what authority I do these things: The baptism of John—where was it from? From heaven or from men?"

The holy men moved away from Him to where Matthew could overhear their murmuring. "If we say, 'From heaven,'" one said, "He will say, 'Why, then, did you not believe him?' But if we say, 'From men,' the multitude will turn on us, for they considered John a prophet." They turned back to Jesus and said, "We do not know."

"Then neither will I tell you by what authority I do these things. But what do you think of this? A man had two sons, and he came to the first and said, 'Son, go, work today in my vineyard.'

"The son said, 'I will not,' but afterward he regretted it and went. Then the father went to the second son and said to him likewise. And the son said, 'Yes, sir, I will go,' but he did not go. Which of the two did the will of his father?"

The holy men said, "The first."

Jesus said, "Tax collectors and harlots enter the kingdom of God before you. For John came to you in the way of righteousness, and you did not believe him; but tax collectors and harlots believed him; and when you saw it, you did not afterward relent and believe him.

"Hear another parable: A certain landowner planted a vineyard and set a hedge around it, dug a winepress in it, and built a tower. He leased it to vinedressers and went into a far country. Now when vintage-time drew near, he sent his servants to the vinedressers, that they might receive its fruit.

"But the vinedressers took his servants, beat one, killed one, and stoned another. Again he sent other servants, more than the first, and they did likewise to them. Then last of all he sent his son to them, saying, 'They will respect my son.' But the vinedressers said among themselves, 'This is the heir. Come, let us kill him and seize his inheritance.' So they cast him out of the vineyard and killed him.

"Now, when the owner of the vineyard comes, what will he do to those vinedressers?"

The holy men said, "He will destroy those wicked men miserably and lease his vineyard to other vinedressers who will render to him the fruits in their seasons."

Jesus said, "Have you never read in the Scriptures: *'The stone which the builders rejected has become the chief cornerstone. This was the Lord's doing, And it is marvelous in our eyes'*? Therefore I say to you, the kingdom of God will be taken from you and given to a nation bearing the fruits of it."

The chief priests and Pharisees grumbled among themselves, "He is speaking of us! Seize him!"

"No!" others said. "Not with all these people here. The multitudes take Him for a prophet!"

Matthew heard the Pharisees plotting how they might entangle Jesus as they went out. Not long later they sent others to openly challenge Him.

"Teacher," they said, "we know that You teach the way of God in truth and that You do not care what others think, for You do not regard the person of men. Tell us, therefore, is it lawful to pay taxes to Caesar, or not?"

Jesus smiled and shook His head. "Why do you test Me, you hypocrites? Show Me the tax money." They showed him a denarius coin.

He said, "Whose image and inscription is on this?"

"Caesar's."

"Render therefore to Caesar the things that are

Caesar's, and to God the things that are God's."

Matthew could barely contain his glee as the men marveled and left Him and went their way.

THAT SAME DAY the Sadducees, who Matthew knew believed there would be no resurrection day, came and said, "Teacher, Moses said that if a man dies, having no children, his brother shall marry his wife and raise up offspring for his brother. Now there were with us seven brothers. The first died after he had married, and having no off-spring, left his wife to his brother. Likewise the second also, and the third, even to the seventh. Last of all the woman died also. Therefore, in the resurrection, whose wife of the seven will she be?"

Jesus said, "You are mistaken, not knowing the Scriptures nor the power of God. For in the resurrection they neither marry nor are given in marriage, but are like angels of God in heaven. But concerning the resurrection of the dead, have you not read what was spoken to you by God, saying, *'I am the God of Abraham, the God of Isaac, and the God of Jacob'*? God is not the God of the dead, but of the living."

Soon the Pharisees arrived again and talked among themselves about the fact that Jesus had silenced the Sadducees. One of them, who identi-fied himself as a lawyer, said, "Teacher, which is the great commandment in the law?"

Jesus said, " *'You shall love the Lord your God with all your heart, with all your soul, and with all your mind.'* This is the first and great commandment. And the second is like it: *'You shall love your neighbor as yourself.'* On these two commandments hang all the Law and the Prophets."

Matthew knew the Pharisees could not argue with that, but as they talked among themselves, Jesus said, "Let me ask you, what do you think about the Christ? Whose Son is He?"

They said, "The Son of David."

"Is that right?" He said. "How then does David in the Spirit call Him *'Lord,'* saying: *'The Lord said to my Lord, "Sit at My right hand, till I make Your enemies Your footstool"'*? If David calls Him *'Lord,'* how can He be his Son?"

As Matthew quickly transcribed this conversation, he was immediately struck that those who tested Jesus had no response. And from that day on no one dared question Him anymore.

TWENTY-FOUR

Matthew had been hoping and praying that Jesus would be careful, that He would show the wisdom He had in the past, pushing and challenging the religious leaders but always stopping short of forcing their hand. Matthew knew it would take little more for these men to take action against

Jesus, if for no other reason than to save face. He was making them look bad.

But it soon became clear that Jesus apparently no longer cared about that. He spoke to the multitudes and to His disciples, holding back none of His disdain for the scribes and the Pharisees. At first He sounded conciliatory, but soon His true view of them surfaced.

"Whatever they tell you to observe, that observe and do, but do not do according to their works; for they say, and do not do. They bind heavy burdens on men's shoulders, but they themselves will not move a finger. All their works they do to be seen by men. They make their phylacteries broad and enlarge the borders of their garments. They love the best places at feasts, the best seats in the synagogues, greetings in the marketplaces, and to be called by men, 'Rabbi, Rabbi.' "

Matthew stood hiding his face in his hands, expecting that at any moment Jesus would be taken and tried. It was as if He were begging for it. And He continued:

"But as for you, do not allow yourself to be called 'Rabbi,' for One is your Teacher, the Christ, and you are all brethren. Do not call anyone on earth your father, for One is your Father, He who is in heaven. And do not be called teachers, for One is your Teacher, the Christ.

"He who is greatest among you shall be your servant. Whoever exalts himself will be humbled, and he who humbles himself will be exalted."

Matthew had grown accustomed to such profound teaching that seemed to fly in the face of convention. But just as he was appreciating this wisdom, Jesus again turned against His adversaries.

"Woe to you, scribes and Pharisees, hypocrites! For you shut up the kingdom of heaven against men.

"Woe to you, scribes and Pharisees, hypocrites! For you devour widows' houses, and for a pretense make long prayers. Therefore you will receive greater condemnation.

"Woe to you, scribes and Pharisees, hypocrites! For you travel land and sea to win one proselyte, and when he is won, you make him twice as much a son of hell as yourselves.

"Woe to you, blind guides, who say, 'Whoever swears by the temple, it is nothing; but whoever swears by the gold of the temple, he is obliged to carry out his pledge.' Fools and blind! For which is greater, the gold or the temple that sanctifies the gold? Fools and blind! For which is greater, the gift or the altar that sanctifies the gift?

"Therefore he who swears by the altar swears by it and by all things on it. He who swears by the temple swears by it and by Him who dwells in it. And he who swears by heaven swears by the throne of God and by Him who sits on it.

"Woe to you, scribes and Pharisees, hypocrites!

For you pay tithe of mint and anise and cumin, yet you have neglected the weightier matters of the law: justice and mercy and faith. Blind guides, who strain out a gnat and swallow a camel!

"Woe to you, scribes and Pharisees, hypocrites! For you cleanse the outside of the cup and dish, but inside they are full of extortion and self-indulgence. Blind Pharisee, first cleanse the inside of the cup and dish, that the outside of them may be clean also.

"Woe to you, scribes and Pharisees, hypocrites! For you are like whitewashed tombs which indeed appear beautiful outwardly, but inside are full of dead men's bones and all uncleanness. Even so you also outwardly appear righteous to men, but inside you are full of hypocrisy and lawlessness.

"Woe to you, scribes and Pharisees, hypocrites! Because you build the tombs of the prophets and adorn the monuments of the righteous, and say, 'If we had lived in the days of our fathers, we would not have been partakers with them in the blood of the prophets.'

"You are witnesses against yourselves that you are sons of those who murdered the prophets. Take the full measure, then, of your fathers' guilt. Serpents, brood of vipers! How can you escape the condemnation of hell?"

Matthew stood quivering, awaiting Jesus' sure arrest, but he was startled when the Master suddenly began weeping.

"O Jerusalem, Jerusalem!" Jesus cried out. "You're the one who kills the prophets and stones those who are sent to her! How often I wanted to gather your children together, as a hen gathers her chicks under her wings, but you were not willing! You shall see Me no more till you say, *'Blessed is He who comes in the name of the Lord!'*"

MATTHEW WAS RELIEVED when Jesus stopped preaching and the crowd began to dissipate. He and the others rushed to His side, and as they departed, Jesus gestured to the buildings of the temple. "Do you not see all these things? Assuredly, I say to you, not one stone shall be left here upon another that shall not be thrown down."

As they left the city, Matthew kept looking back, expecting an arresting party. He tried to hurry the others along. Jesus appeared headed for the Mount of Olives, but the destination didn't matter to Matthew, as long as Jesus was away from the eyes of the scribes and Pharisees He had so boldly called out.

When Jesus finally sat in the shade and privacy of the Mount of Olives, the disciples settled in with Him away from the people. "Tell us," Thomas said, "when will these things be? What will be the sign of Your coming and of the end of the age?"

Jesus said, "Take heed that no one deceives you. For many will come in My name, saying, 'I am the

Christ,' and will deceive many. And you will hear of wars and rumors of wars. See that you are not troubled; for all these things must come to pass, but the end is not yet. For nation will rise against nation, and kingdom against kingdom. And there will be famines, pestilences, and earthquakes in various places. All these are the beginning of sorrows.

"Then they will deliver you up to tribulation and kill you, and you will be hated by all nations for My name's sake. And then many will be offended, will betray one another, and will hate one another. Then many false prophets will rise up and deceive many. And because lawlessness will abound, the love of many will grow cold. But he who endures to the end shall be saved. And this gospel of the kingdom will be preached in all the world as a witness to all the nations, and then the end will come."

Jesus fell silent, and as Matthew sat there with his brother, he whispered, "Does not the Master seem weary?"

James nodded. "I fear His demise is nigh. All this talk of the end."

"Sometimes," Matthew said, "I wish I were more like Peter or the brothers Zebedee. No wonder the Lord has called them the 'Sons of Thunder.' In righteous anger I want to strike out against Jesus' enemies and thwart whatever plan they have for Him. But I more fear hindering the will of God."

James smiled sadly. "Rest assured, brother, we are powerless to do that."

And Jesus continued: "As the lightning comes from the east and flashes to the west, so also will the coming of the Son of Man be. Immediately after the tribulation of those days, the sun will be darkened and the moon will not give its light; the stars will fall from heaven, and the powers of the heavens will be shaken. Then the sign of the Son of Man will appear in heaven and all the tribes of the earth will mourn as they see the Son of Man coming on the clouds of heaven with power and great glory. He will send His angels with a great sound of a trumpet, and they will gather together His elect from the four winds, from one end of heaven to the other. Heaven and earth will pass away, but My words will by no means pass away."

Peter, sounding exasperated, said, "But when, Lord, when? How long?"

"Of that day and hour no one knows, not even the angels of heaven, but My Father only. But as the days of Noah were, so also will the coming of the Son of Man be. In the days before the flood they were eating and drinking, marrying and giving in marriage, until the day Noah entered the ark and the flood came and took them all away. So also will the coming of the Son of Man be.

"Two men will be in the field: one will be taken and the other left. Two women will be grinding at the mill: one will be taken and the other left. Watch, therefore, for you do not know what hour your Lord is coming. Therefore you also be ready, for the Son of Man is coming at an hour you do not expect.

"When the Son of Man comes in His glory and all the holy angels with Him, He will sit on the throne of His glory. All the nations will be gathered before Him, and He will separate them one from another, as a shepherd divides his sheep from the goats. He will set the sheep on His right hand and the goats on the left. Then the King will say to those on His right hand, 'Come, you blessed of My Father, inherit the kingdom prepared for you from the foundation of the world: for I was hungry and you gave Me food; I was thirsty and you gave Me drink; I was a stranger and you took Me in; I was naked and you clothed Me; I was sick and you visited Me; I was in prison and you came to Me.'

"Then the righteous will answer Him, saying, 'Lord, when did we see You hungry and feed You, or thirsty and give You drink? When did we see You a stranger and take You in, or naked and clothe You? Or when did we see You sick, or in prison, and come to You?'

"And the King will answer, 'Assuredly, I say to you, inasmuch as you did it to one of the least of these My brethren, you did it to Me.'

"Then He will say to those on the left hand,

'Depart from Me, you cursed, into the everlasting fire prepared for the devil and his angels: for I was hungry and you gave Me no food; I was thirsty and you gave Me no drink; I was a stranger and you did not take Me in, naked and you did not clothe Me, sick and in prison and you did not visit Me.'

"Then they will answer Him, saying, 'Lord, when did we see You hungry or thirsty or a stranger or naked or sick or in prison, and did not minister to You?'

"And He will say, 'Assuredly, I say to you, inasmuch as you did not do it to one of the least of these, you did not do it to Me.'

"And these will go away into everlasting punishment, but the righteous into eternal life."

WHEN JESUS FINISHED His discourse about the future, Matthew wished he had time to reread everything he had written. But now the Master turned His disciples' attention to the near future, and Matthew wanted to make sure he captured all of it.

"You know," Jesus said, "that after two days is the Passover, and the Son of Man will be delivered up to be crucified."

"Lord," Peter said, "forgive me, but we don't want to hear this."

"The will of My Father must be done. Even now the chief priests, the scribes, and the elders of the people are assembled at the palace of the high priest, Caiaphas, and are plotting to take Me by trickery and kill Me. They will put it off until after the feast, lest there be an uproar among the people."

TWENTY-FIVE

On the first day of the Feast of the Unleavened Bread, the disciples asked Jesus where He wanted them to prepare for Him to eat the Passover meal. He sent them into Jerusalem to a house where they were to say that "the Teacher says, 'My time is at hand; I will keep the Passover at your house with My disciples.'"

They were provided a room atop the house of a widow named Mary and her teen son, Mark. When evening had come, Jesus sat down with the twelve. As they were eating, He said, "Assuredly, I say to you, one of you will betray Me."

Matthew could barely breathe. Surely he would not betray his Master. He said, "Lord, is it I?"

And the others, also looking sorrowful, began to say to Him, "Lord, is it I?"

Jesus said, "He who dipped his hand with Me in the dish will betray Me. The Son of Man indeed goes just as it is written of Him, but woe to that man by whom the Son of Man is betrayed! It would have been good for that man if he had not been born."

Matthew and the others stared at Judas Iscariot who had dipped his bread into the bowl at the same time as Jesus. Judas said, "Rabbi, is it I?"

Jesus said, "You have said it."

Judas ran out, and Matthew knew the others were as shocked as he. For several minutes no one spoke.

Then, as they were eating, Jesus took bread, blessed and broke it, and gave it to the disciples and said, "Take, eat; this is My body." Then He took the cup and gave thanks and gave it to them, saying, "Drink from it, all of you. For this is My blood of the new covenant, which is shed for many for the remission of sins."

He led them in the singing of a hymn, but to Matthew it sounded like a funeral dirge. His friends had pale, vacant looks. When Jesus rose and made His way down the stairs and out of the city toward the Mount of Olives, they followed, somber and quiet.

Jesus said, "All of you will be made to stumble because of Me this night, for it is written: *'I will strike the Shepherd, and the sheep of the flock will be scattered.'"*

Matthew did not want to believe it of himself. Could he not stand with His Lord after all this time?

"But after I have been raised," Jesus said, "I will go before you to Galilee."

Peter stopped in the path and shook his head, saying, "Even if all are made to stumble because of You, I will never be made to stumble."

"Oh, Peter," Jesus said. "Assuredly, I say to you that this night, before the rooster crows, you will deny Me three times."

"No! Even if I have to die with You, I will not deny You!"

"Nor will I!" Matthew said.

And so said all the others.

Jesus led them to the Garden of Gethsemane, where He told Matthew and seven of the others to wait for Him while He took with Him Peter and James and John and went to pray. After a short while Matthew and the others heard Him chastising the three for falling asleep while He was praying. Twice more this happened, and it struck Matthew that the Lord sounded most disappointed and weary.

"My soul is exceedingly sorrowful, even to death. Stay here and watch with Me." He fell on His face, and prayed, "O My Father, if it is possible, let this cup pass from Me; nevertheless, not as I will, but as You will."

Finally Jesus came to His disciples and said, "Behold, the hour is at hand, and the Son of Man is being betrayed into the hands of sinners. See, My betrayer is at hand."

There stood Judas with a great multitude of men carrying swords and clubs. He moved from among them and approached Jesus. "Greetings, Rabbi!" he said, and kissed Him.

Jesus said sadly, "Friend, why have you come?"

But before Judas could respond, the others rushed Jesus and seized him. Peter drew a sword and lunged at a servant of the high priest, slicing off his ear.

"Put your sword in its place," Jesus said, immediately healing the man. "For all who take the sword will perish by the sword. Do you not think I could pray right now to My Father and He would provide Me with more than twelve legions of angels? But how, then, could the Scriptures be fulfilled?"

As the mob began to pull at Jesus, He said, "Have you come out as against a robber with swords and clubs to take Me? I sat daily with you, teaching in the temple, and you did not seize Me."

In that instant Matthew felt paralyzed with fear. In his mind he was transported to childhood when the king's men had thundered up to his house and slaughtered his baby brother. He hated this, didn't want it, wanted to be brave like Peter and take on any and all who threatened his Master.

But the crowd was raucous and threatening, and as they shouted and cursed and surged around Jesus, Matthew saw some of his friends flee. It couldn't be! Suddenly the mob turned on Matthew.

"Are you one of His?" a soldier demanded.

Matthew couldn't speak. He shuddered at the thought that if he had been able, he would have denied it, denied Him. Horrified at himself, Matthew saw other soldiers coming his way. Even Peter was in full flight, and Matthew turned and ran.

He sprinted until he could barely breathe, stealing away into the darkness of the garden, as far as he could from the danger. And from the Lord. He fell to his knees, sobbing. Matthew could not even pray.

Where was James? Peter? John? Any of them? Did no one have the courage to stand with the Man they knew to be the Son of God? Matthew could not imagine ever forgiving himself. Judas had betrayed Jesus. Peter was to deny Him. Matthew was no better.

Where could he go? Back to the upper room? What would he say? What could he do?

In the distance by the light of torches the crowd led Jesus back into the city. Matthew had never felt so devastated and alone, even during all his years as a bitter tax collector. With no destination, he followed the procession from afar.

Matthew was startled at a shaky voice from behind a tree. "They're taking Him to the high priest."

"Peter!"

"I'm so ashamed!"

"But you stood up to them! You—"

"Not for long. And I was chastised even for that. Jesus told us this night was coming and that He must do the will of His Father. But no, I knew better. I was going to make all things right."

"I too ran, my friend. We all did."

"It's not too late, Matthew. He must not be left alone. Come."

Matthew followed Peter at a brisk pace until they nearly caught the crowd. The boisterous men forced Jesus inside the gate of Caiaphas's home and Matthew found himself separated from Peter, six or seven rows of onlookers from where the fisherman stood at the fence near a charcoal fire. When the gate opened Matthew could see that Peter was swept in with some of the servants, and he could see past him to where the scribes and elders had gathered.

The gate closed again, but the crowd pressed against it, Matthew in their midst. He had lost sight of Peter but knew he had to be nearby. The council was hearing testimony against Jesus, and Matthew wanted to cry out at the injustice of it when a false witness took Jesus' words out of context and said, "This fellow said, 'I am able to destroy the temple of God and to build it in three days.'"

From outside Matthew saw Caiaphas rise and thunder, "Do You answer nothing? What is it this man testifies against You?"

But Jesus did not answer.

The high priest shouted, "I put You under oath by the living God: Tell us if You are the Christ, the Son of God!"

Matthew heard Jesus' soft reply: "It is as you said. Nevertheless, I say to you, hereafter you will see the Son of Man sitting at the right hand of the Power, and coming on the clouds of heaven."

With that Caiaphas tore his clothes and railed, "He has spoken blasphemy! What further need do we have of witnesses? Look, now you have heard His blasphemy! What do you think?"

The council responded, "He is deserving of death."

As Matthew maneuvered for position, tears streaming down his cheeks, members of the council spat in Jesus' face and beat Him with rods, and others struck Him with their hands, saying, "Prophesy to us, Christ! Who is the one who struck You?"

Matthew caught sight of Peter just beyond him in the courtyard. A servant girl came to him and said, "You also were with Jesus of Galilee."

Peter said loudly, "I do not know what you are saying!" And he stood to leave.

But as he reached the gateway, not far from where Matthew stood, another girl saw him and said, "This fellow also was with Jesus of Nazareth."

Peter swore and said, "I do not know the Man!"

As he hurried through the gate and past Matthew, looking like a crazy person, a man said, "Surely you are one of them, for your speech betrays you. You are a Galilean too!"

Again Peter cursed and swore, saying, "I do not know the Man!"

And immediately a rooster crowed.

Peter was on the run now, sobbing loudly, and Matthew lit out after him and overtook him, grabbing his shoulder. "God forgive me, Peter, I would have done the same!"

But Peter shook him off, fell to the ground, and wept bitterly.

What manner of men are we? Matthew wondered.

EVENTUALLY PETER ROSE and he and Matthew trudged back to the garden, where they started a small fire and sat silent and dejected. Soon Matthew's brother and Thomas found them, sitting and shaking their heads.

"I abandoned my Lord," James said pitifully. "I am not worthy to live."

"We all did," Peter said. "We are most miserable."

About an hour later John crept out of the darkness. "I saw your fire," he said, his voice quavering. "The others are afar off over the ridge. We are all lamenting our cowardice."

"Go and bring them," Peter said, "and we will plot together what we might do now."

"It is no excuse and nothing can make me feel better," Matthew's brother said, "but thus it was prophesied that the Son of Man would be left alone by those closest to Him."

"You're right," Peter said. "It does not help. We have sinned egregiously against our Lord. We must resolve to stand with Him now until the end. Some of you who are not known to the multitude must get close enough to determine where they are taking Him."

"I will go," Matthew said, and a few others also volunteered.

"You are known, Matthew," Peter said. "I saw the soldiers confront you at His capture."

"I no longer care," Matthew said. "My life is worth nothing to me now."

"Very well," Peter said. "You and your brother and Thomas go in the morning then, and bring us word."

TWENTY-SIX

Matthew and the others spent a fitful night back at the home of Mary and her son. It seemed no one slept much, worried as they were about Jesus and humiliated at their own cowardice. Matthew woke before dawn, bathed in a frigid nearby stream, and set out early for the middle of the city with his brother and Thomas. There they learned that the chief priests and elders of the people had plotted against Jesus to put Him to death. Word was that they had bound Him and led Him away to deliver Him to Pontius Pilate, the governor.

As they headed toward the governor's estate,

Thomas said he thought he had heard someone say something about Judas, so he left the brothers and ran to see what he could learn. He soon returned to them.

"Rumor has it that Judas brought back some thirty pieces of silver the chief priests and elders had paid him for identifying Jesus, saying, 'I have sinned by betraying innocent blood.'

"They said, 'What is that to us?' Then he threw down the pieces of silver in the temple and went out and hanged himself."

"How awful," James said, stopping to gather himself. "I confess there were times in the night last night that I was tempted to do harm to myself."

"Me, too," Matthew said. "I never would have connived to betray my Lord, but I feel little better after having deserted Him. We must show our repentance with boldness now."

Thomas said, "People are saying the elders would not put the tainted money in their treasury, so they are going to buy a field with it where they can bury strangers."

"That was prophesied, Matthew," James said. "Remember? Jeremiah wrote, '*And they took the thirty pieces of silver, the value of Him who was priced, and gave them for the potter's field . . .*'"

WHEN THE TRIO ARRIVED at Pilate's palace and watched from the back of the crowd, Jesus was already standing before the governor.

Pilate said, "Are You the King of the Jews?"

Jesus said, "It is as you say."

The chief priests and elders came forward, leveling all sorts of charges, including blasphemy, sedition, conspiracy to overthrow the government, and violating the Sabbath.

When Jesus did not respond, Pilate said, "Do you not hear how many things they testify against You?"

Jesus answered not one word, and Matthew thought Pilate looked amazed. The governor shook his head and addressed the crowd. "You know it has been my tradition during the feast to release to you one prisoner, whomever you wish! This Jesus gives us an option along with Barabbas, who, as you know, has been with us a long time. Whom do you want me to release to you? Barabbas, or this Jesus who is called Christ?"

For a moment Matthew allowed himself a flash of hope. Was it possible? Might the crowd ask for Jesus? If they did, he could tell by the resolute looks on the faces of his brother and Thomas that they would never again allow anyone to harm the Lord. They would rush the crowd, the soldiers, the centurions, the governor's staff, anyone. They would deliver Jesus from this mob or die trying.

But the chief priests and elders fanned out among the multitude, cajoling them to ask for Barabbas to be released.

"No!" Matthew cried, and the other two joined in. "Release Jesus! Jesus!"

But they were shouted down until the governor raised a hand to silence the crowd. "Which of the two do you want me to release to you today?"

Matthew and Thomas and James's plaintive cries were drowned out by the crowd as it roared as one, "Barabbas! Barabbas! Give us Barabbas!"

They continued until Pilate again silenced them with a wave. He was smiling now. "What then shall I do with this man, Jesus, who is called Christ?"

To Matthew's horror, the crowd began shouting and chanting, "Let Him be crucified!"

Pilate's smile faded. He raised both arms. "Why, what evil has He done?"

The people cried out all the more, "Let Him be crucified! Crucify Him!"

Now Pilate looked stricken and it seemed to Matthew that the governor was alarmed as he surveyed the crowd. They were jostling and surging forward, and the man had to fear a rising tumult. He signaled for an aide to bring him a bowl of water, and as soon as it arrived he made a show of washing his hands. As he dried them he said, "I am innocent of the blood of this just Person. What you choose to do with Him now is on you."

"Yes! Yes!" the people shouted. "His blood be on us and on our children!"

Pilate released Barabbas, who ran into the crowd leaping and laughing. And as the three disciples watched, Jesus was scourged and sent off with a contingent of soldiers. Matthew, James, and Thomas followed from a distance as they took Jesus into the Praetorium and gathered the whole garrison around Him.

Matthew wanted to cover his eyes, but he could not turn away as they stripped Jesus and put a scarlet robe on Him. He recoiled in horror when they twisted a crown of thorns and pressed it down upon His head, causing blood to stream down His face.

Someone put a reed in His right hand, and they all bowed before Him and jeered, "Hail, King of the Jews!"

Had they not seen Him heal? Had they not heard Him preach and teach and prophesy and express profound truth never uttered before? How could they do this? Disagree with Him, oppose Him, even charge Him with speaking out publicly against the religious leaders . . . but this? Why did they have to scorn Him and mock Him? And how could He be sentenced to die?

Then they spat on Him, and one took the reed and struck Him on the head. Finally they tore off the robe and put His own clothes back on Him and led Him away. The crossbeam of the contraption on which He was to hang they settled heavily on His shoulders, and though He staggered several steps under it, it proved too much and He stumbled. The soldiers recruited a man from within the crowd to come forward and carry His cross.

It was all Matthew could do to put one foot in front of the other and he and his brother and friend followed the taunting crowd down the dusty roads and outside the city. The sun was rising in a cloudless sky as Jesus staggered along, pushed and prodded by the crowd and by the soldiers.

Matthew pressed a coin into a lad's hand and bade him race to the house of Mary and her son and tell the disciples there that Jesus was headed to Golgotha, the "Place of the Skull." How he had wished he had something different to report, that he would have had time to go back and dine with Jesus' friends again as they awaited His fate. This was all happening too fast, and Matthew felt helpless.

Two other men were to be crucified that day, and Matthew recoiled as they were laid out on their crosses and their legs and feet nailed to the wood with great spikes. They shrieked in pain and cursed as their crosses were lifted over holes in the ground, then roughly dropped in. This caused their flesh to tear against the spikes and they wailed all the more, blood cascading down their bodies. They had to press with their feet and force their weight up and off their lungs to breathe, and the effort appeared pure torture.

IT WAS ANOTHER HOUR before Jesus was laid out on His cross, and by then His mother stood afar off with many women who had followed Jesus from Galilee and had ministered to Him. Among them were Mary Magdalene, Mary the mother of James and Joses, and the mother of Zebedee's sons.

The rest of the disciples had also arrived, and Matthew found it curious that they did not stand together. Even he parted from Thomas and James, as if each man was to experience this alone. John hurried to the side of Jesus' mother. She and her party all hid their faces when Jesus was nailed to the cross and cried out in agony.

When His cross was dropped into the ground some in the crowd cheered. Others moaned in sympathy. Matthew saw Jesus talking with the men hanging on either side of Him, and then He asked for something to drink. A sponge was lifted up to Him, but even the smell of it made Him turn His head away and He did not drink.

At the foot of the cross soldiers cast lots, the winner claiming Jesus' clothes. Later James would tell Matthew that this too was a fulfilled prophecy: *"They divided My garments among them, and for My clothing they cast lots."*

Then the soldiers sat to watch the three men die.

As the horrible day progressed and the sun mercilessly beat on all assembled, eventually the soldiers made a rough-hewn sign and hoisted it and nailed it above Jesus' head. It read: THIS IS JESUS THE KING OF THE JEWS.

Many in the crowd pointed and wagged their heads and called out, "You who destroy the temple and build it in three days, save Yourself! If You are the Son of God, come down from the cross!"

Likewise the chief priests, mocking with the scribes and elders, shouted, "He saved others; Himself He cannot save. If He is the King of Israel, let Him now come down from the cross, and we will believe Him. He trusted in God; let God deliver Him now if He will have Him; for He said, 'I am the Son of God.'"

Suddenly the sun was blotted out and though it was noon, the place turned dark as night for three hours. The wind blew cold, and Matthew pulled his cloak tighter around him, trembling and praying for His Lord, wishing this nightmare would end.

Finally, at about the ninth hour of the day, three in the afternoon, Jesus cried out with a loud voice, "Eli, Eli, lama sabachthani?" which Matthew knew was Aramaic for *My God, My God, why have You forsaken Me?"*

Some who watched said they thought He was calling for Elijah, and one of them ran and took a sponge and put it on a reed, holding it up to Him and again offering Him to drink. But others said, "Let Him alone; let us see if Elijah will come to save Him."

Matthew suddenly found himself on his knees,

finally realizing what Jesus had meant when He told him that one day He would experience Matthew's pain. Matthew had suffered the loss of his beloved baby brother, and that had nearly ruined his entire life. Now God was losing His only Son, and ironically Jesus felt rejected by Him.

"God, forgive me!" Matthew sobbed.

And Jesus cried out again with a loud voice, and He bowed His head and died.

At that instant the earth began to quake and the silence was shattered by the thunderous sound of rocks splitting. People scattered screaming or fell to the ground, hiding their heads. A centurion shouted, "Surely this Man was the Son of God!"

Matthew stayed right where he was, watching, waiting, wondering if God would immediately avenge the death of His Son.

As the sky cleared and the sun reappeared, the centurions mounted their skittish horses and stood watch at the crosses, making sure no one tried to steal the bodies. Presently a young man came running from Jerusalem to announce to the scribes and Pharisees: "At the moment of the earthquake, the veil in the temple was rent in two from top to bottom! And along the way I passed cemeteries where graves had burst open and dead men were raised, walking toward the gates of the city!"

Matthew did not know what to make of this, but

despite his curiosity, he would not leave the Place of the Skull. He stayed until evening, when a rich man, who identified himself as Joseph of Arimathea, came and showed the centurions a scroll from Pilate.

"I was a follower of Jesus," he said, "and I asked the governor if I could bury the body. See, here, all is in order, and that is Pilate's seal."

"Very well, sir," the centurion said. "But where do you plan to take it?"

"To what was meant to be my own tomb nearby," he said. "It was recently hewn out of the rock."

"Is it secure?" the centurion said. "Everyone knows that this man claimed He would rise again after three days. We can't have His friends spiriting away the body and claiming He arose."

"There is an extremely large stone that can be rolled to cover the entrance."

Mary and her friends helped Joseph lower the body, and he wrapped it in a clean linen cloth and carefully laid it on a cart. Matthew followed alone as the small assemblage made its way to a garden tomb. Once Jesus had been laid in it, Joseph asked Matthew's help in rolling the large stone against the door.

When Joseph departed, Matthew turned to see Mary Magdalene and the other Mary sitting opposite the tomb. He did not know what to say. He merely nodded, then slowly made his way back to the upper room where the rest of the disciples had gathered.

There was much lamenting and weeping, but they were also joined by previously dead friends who had been resurrected from their graves at Jesus' death. And they all marveled.

TWENTY-SEVEN

The next day Matthew was sitting and talking with two men who had risen from their graves the day before, fascinated by their tales of having been in paradise. Peter had sent three other disciples into the city to see if any more danger was in store for the followers of Jesus. These reported back that the chief priests and Pharisees had gathered with Pilate, reminding him that Jesus was a deceiver who had predicted that He would rise again after three days. They told the governor that zealous followers of Jesus had dug up graves and claimed people had been resurrected.

Soon Pilate commanded that the tomb be made secure until the third day, lest His disciples come by night and steal Him away and tell people He had risen from the dead. Pilate actually explained himself by saying that he didn't want a new deception to be worse than the first. He told the Roman guards to make the grave as secure as they knew how. Matthew and some of the others stole away and crept near the garden tomb, hidden in the trees. In truth Roman centurions were there supervising the sealing of the stone. They left a full garrison to guard the area.

MATTHEW HAD NO IDEA what the future held for him. He was grieving deeply over His Lord, as all the disciples were. Some spoke of going into other regions and teaching and preaching about the kingdom, praying that they still had the power to perform miracles, with which Jesus had imbued them.

Thomas said, "But what are we to say when people ask where this Man is now?"

"That He is in heaven."

"God is in heaven too, and they have ignored Him. Gradually the fame of Jesus will fade and the stories—yes, even of His healing the sick— will be forgotten. We will be the only ones left who truly believe He was the Son of God."

Matthew wanted to tell everyone of Jesus, what he had learned, how he had been forgiven, what he believed about the future. But with Jesus gone it was as if any power to preach, and certainly to heal, had left him. Had he lost his faith? He didn't believe so. But he had lost his Master and his Lord. After finding true life after so many years, he felt he was back where he started.

Oh, he was a different man, he knew that. He could never go back to tax collecting. Besides that Rome would never have him again, he had no stomach for that kind of work. Perhaps he would let the fishermen teach him their trade. They seemed to be the only ones who had something to which they could return. James and John's father still ran their small fishing concern, and relatives had also continued Peter and Andrew's enterprise.

There was talk from the hostess of the house where they were staying that her son meant to accompany Mary Magdalene and the other Mary to the tomb following the Sabbath, the morning of the first day of the week.

"For what purpose?" Matthew said. "Have they not seen it? It is a lovely spot, but they will not be allowed in to tend to the Lord's body. Not only has the stone been rolled in front of the entrance—I helped do it myself—but the Romans have sealed it. There will be little the women can do but sit."

"Perhaps that is all they wish to do," Mark's mother said. "Sit and remember."

"I cannot imagine that will be easy with the Roman guards milling about. If I were one of the women, I would be hard-pressed not to think evil thoughts toward these men."

"Oh, Matthew," she said with a kind smile, "that's not the way of the Master."

"I know. But the pain is too fresh."

"And sharp," she said, sighing. "This is so hard."

MATTHEW HAD had trouble resting since the crucifixion and had spent many of the hours of the night tossing and turning and often rising and pacing—only to find his brother and many of his friends doing the same. But that evening he found himself weary beyond measure. The trauma of the preceding days had caught up with him, and though it was his turn to trade his spot on a pliable wooden bench and recline on the hard stone floor of the upper room with a half dozen or so of the others, he was soon fast asleep.

Matthew did not awaken until dawn, when he heard young Mark scurrying about, complaining that he had overslept and that the Marys had left for the tomb without him. He watched the lad quickly dress and light out for the garden tomb.

Despite that he felt he could use a couple of more hours of sleep, Matthew found himself overcome with compassion for his sleeping friends. They were as bereaved as he, and it struck him that he had rarely thought of the feelings of anyone but himself before he met Jesus. He padded down to see if the mistress of the house was about and whether he could help her prepare the morning meal. He found her in the guest parlor, sitting and gazing out the window.

"A beautiful morning," he said, then had to apologize when he realized he had startled her.

"Oh, it's all right, Matthew. I need to get moving anyway. Andrew had some salted fish delivered last night and I must be about roasting it for breakfast."

"May I help?"

"I have bread baking, if you could watch that and bring it out when it's ready." She paused. "I envy you, you know."

"You envy me?"

She nodded. "That you can see the day as beautiful. It is, of course. I know that. But it does not soothe me, does not bring me pleasure."

"Me either, really. I was just making conversation."

"But I also envy that you got to know the Master. He loved you all so."

"He loved you and Mark too."

"I know," she said, rising. "But I rarely got any time with him. He was most kind to me and to the women who followed Him from Galilee. But we all would say we did not know Him as you men did. The bond between you all was something very special."

Matthew did not know what to say. It had always impressed him the way Jesus seemed to treat everyone the same. He was no respecter of persons. He was as kind and patient with children as He was with their parents. He was as gracious and grateful to the women around Him as to the men. And whether a man had been a fisherman or a tax collector, He treated him the same as He would have a man known in the city as one with real stature.

Matthew chuckled in spite of himself. In truth,

Jesus was hardly impressed with people in power and said so at almost every opportunity. And as quickly as Matthew had chuckled he fought a sob rising in his throat. It was Jesus' very directness, His honesty, His probing truth that had gotten Him killed.

Matthew shook his head as he slid the golden brown loaves from the hearth oven. Jesus would tell Him that it wasn't the Romans or Jews who had crucified Him but that He had willingly given Himself up to do the will of His Father. There was so much about the Lord Matthew wished he knew.

He followed Mary up the stairs with the loaves and the roasted fish, leaving her just outside the door as he entered to rouse the others. They appeared grateful for the sustenance and spoke kindly to Mary as she entered and helped serve.

THE DISCIPLES WERE nearly finished eating when they heard what sounded like thunder in the distance and the whole place was shaken. One table slid several feet across the floor and a bench pitched over, causing several men to fall.

"An earthquake?" one said.

"A tremor following the one from the other day."

They sat and waited to see if more were to follow, and when none did, they gingerly went back to eating.

Several minutes later Matthew heard excited

voices and footsteps on the stairs. Several rose to peer out and others looked frightened, as if they believed the authorities were coming after them. Mary opened the door to her son and the other two Marys, who swept past her, faces beaming and eyes afire.

"There was an earthquake!" they said.

"We know," Peter said.

"An angel of the Lord descended from heaven and rolled back the stone from the tomb and sat on it!" Mary of Magdala said. "His countenance was like lightning, and his clothing as white as snow."

"You're mad!" Thomas said.

"We're not. It is as we have said!"

"What of the Roman guards?"

"They shook for fear and fainted like dead men," the other Mary said.

Peter squinted at them and cocked his head. "But you were braver than they?"

Mary Magdalene said, "Not until the angel told us, 'Do not be afraid, for I know that you seek Jesus who was crucified. He is not here; for He is risen, as He said. Come, see the place where the Lord lay.'"

"Craziness!"

"Lunacy!"

"And did you go?"

"Of course we did! His grave clothes were there, but He was not, for He has risen!"

"I don't believe it."

"You're dreaming!"

"No! The angel told us to go quickly and tell you that He is risen from the dead, and indeed He is going before you into Galilee; there you will see Him."

"This cannot be! Swear by heaven that you are telling us the truth!"

"There's more! As we ran from there to come and tell you, behold, Jesus met us on the way, saying, 'Rejoice!' "

"You are most deluded! You two had better sit and regain your senses!"

"No! Believe us! It's true, gentlemen! We fell at His feet and worshiped Him!"

"Did He say anything else?"

"Yes! He told us to not be afraid, and He said, as the angel had, that we were to go and tell His brethren to go to a certain mount in Galilee that you would know, 'and there they will see Me.' Do you know it and will you go?"

Matthew wanted so badly to believe. These women wouldn't lie, would they? Of course not. But they could have been deceived. They wanted Jesus alive as much as anyone.

"Whatever shall we do?" Matthew said.

"Whatever shall we do?" Peter mocked him with a huge smile. "I don't know about you, but I am going to Galilee! And yes, I know the mount of which He speaks."

"You believe them?" Thomas said.

"I don't know what to think," Peter said. "But whether I believe them or not, I will not take the chance of missing Jesus, risen from the grave. Who is going with me?"

"I daresay we all are," Matthew said, grabbing his cloak and making for the door.

"We have a long journey ahead," Peter said. "Andrew, arrange for beasts and a cart. We must go straightaway!"

AN HOUR LATER as they hurried along, the disciples saw a contingent of Roman soldiers telling a crowd, "His disciples came at night and stole Him away while we slept."

Matthew told Peter he would catch up to the group and to continue on. He waited until the crowd scattered, then he pulled one of the soldiers off to the side.

"What really happened, friend? I know some of His disciples, and they were nowhere near the tomb last night."

The man looked around, then pulled out his coin pouch and rattled it. "The earth shook and an angel from heaven appeared and rolled the stone away, and we were sore afraid. When we told the chief priests and elders what happened, they conspired together and paid us all handsomely to tell this story. They said that if it reached the governor's ears that we had failed in our duty—punishable by death, I might add—they would appease him and make us secure."

Matthew ran to catch up with the others.

"It's true!" he said. "It's true! I just heard it from another eyewitness!"

"Let us make haste," Peter said. "Imagine soon seeing the Lord again!"

"I'll believe it when I see it," Thomas muttered.

Matthew couldn't deny that despite all he had seen and heard, he was sympathetic to Thomas. He wanted it to be true so badly—and the Lord had predicted this very thing.

But could it be? He had seen many signs and wonders and miracles over the past few years. Why couldn't this also be true? As he hurried along, Matthew allowed himself more faith with each step. All he wanted was to see his Friend and his Lord again. Yet what would he say if and when he saw Him? He was so ashamed at his own lack of faith and courage that he feared he would just hang his head.

Had he only trusted the Lord and believed that He would rise as He said, Matthew would have been afraid of nothing in the Garden of Gethsemane that night.

TWENTY-EIGHT

Matthew was intrigued by the attitudes of his friends as they finally reached Galilee and began to climb the familiar mount where Jesus had preached and taught and healed so many. Some of the disciples quickened their pace, smiling, talking excitedly. Believing. But others looked dubious, even frightened.

Peter led the way, of course. Matthew found himself hoping it was true and that the risen Jesus would really be there, almost as much for Peter's sake as for his own. How sorely disappointed Peter would be if it was not true after all.

Matthew turned to his brother. "Do you believe it, James?"

His brother shook his head. "I want to so badly. The Scriptures prophesied this and He Himself predicted it also. But my faith is so weak."

"You of all people! A student of the law!"

"I know. I just don't know what I'll do if He is not here. What will become of us, Matthew? Where will we go? What will we do? You cannot collect taxes again. I will certainly not be welcomed back into the temple in Jerusalem."

Matthew laughed. "Did Father teach you nothing of his trade? You could open a shop!"

"You're talking nonsense now, brother," James said, holding out his hands, palms up, as he hurried along. "Do these look like the hands of a craftsman? Not a callus in sight. I will be relegated to being a scribe."

"You can copy all that I have written and we can get others to do the same. That way we will spread the truth and the history of Jesus. People will find it hard to believe unless they witnessed it as we did, but His words must go out."

James appeared distracted and turned. "Where is Thomas? He was here a moment ago."

Matthew stopped and looked back. "He's here. Surely. I spoke with him not an hour ago. But we can't wait. I would not want to be the last to arrive if the Lord awaits us."

"There he is!" James said. "Thomas! Make haste!"

Thomas trudged along alone. He waved acknowledgment but did not speed up.

"I'll get him," Matthew said. "You catch up to the others. Just don't let them leave us."

"I dare say they will not be listening to me as we get closer," James said.

By the time Matthew reached Thomas, the man had stopped and was sitting on a rock.

"Now is no time to rest, friend. Do you need a walking stick? A hand?"

"I need to not go," Thomas muttered.

"What? Why?"

"Because if Jesus is there He will know of my lack of faith. The others are so trusting, so eager."

"And you're skeptical?"

"I'm not! It's just—I don't know! I wish I could believe without seeing as so many of you others do. The Lord knows us, knows our minds and hearts. He has proven this over and over. I was there when He died, Matthew. You know I was. I saw them nail Him to that cross, and I saw them pierce Him with a sword. I will not believe until I see the nail marks in His hands and feet and the wound in His side."

"Come, Thomas! None of us will know for sure until we see Him! You don't want to miss this."

"It's not true. You *all* believe it. You all have faith. If He is not there and I am right, I will be as disappointed as the rest. But if He is there, He will know my heart."

"He knows your heart whether you are there or not. He knows you even if *He* is not there but is in heaven with His Father! Now come, please."

"I'm sorry, Matthew. I cannot. You go."

Matthew looked into the distance. The others were getting too far ahead. "I am not a young man, Thomas. I must hasten if I am to catch them."

"Go! Really. Go. I will be right here when you all return, and if you swear it's true, then I will believe."

"No, you won't! You said yourself that you had to see His scars! How will you see if you do not come?"

"I'm not coming."

"And I must go."

"Go."

Matthew hated to leave his friend. He knew what Thomas was going through, because he himself was conflicted, as he knew they all—perhaps with the exception of Peter—must be. He wanted to see Jesus, and nothing could keep him from it. But he was also desperate not to be disappointed. If Jesus was not there, it would be like seeing Him die again. And Matthew did not believe he could endure that.

MATTHEW'S HEART POUNDED as he trotted along the road, and he was grateful to see that James must have asked Peter to wait for him. The eight men had stopped just before the last rise that led to where Jesus had taught and healed so many times.

When Matthew arrived, Peter said, "Catch your breath, old man. Just a little more climbing. Do we all believe?"

"I do," John said. "But does it matter? He will be there or not be there regardless what any of us thinks."

"I know He will be there," Peter said. "And what of Thomas?"

Matthew shook his head. "Allow the man to take his own counsel," he said.

"Ready?" Peter said, and they all nodded.

The fisherman led the way, and as soon as he reached the summit, he called out, "My Lord and my God!" and began running. Matthew and the others rushed to keep up.

And there was Jesus, sitting on a rock, arms outstretched. "My friends," He said.

Peter fell at his feet, weeping. "Lord, forgive me! I did as you said I would do, and I am wretched with shame!"

Jesus reached for Peter as the others fell at His feet. He embraced the man while everyone else exulted, "You're alive!"

"It's You!"

"You are risen as You said!"

Matthew found no words. He just wept as he reached for Jesus and saw the nail-scarred hands that he knew would convince even Thomas.

Jesus whispered, "Matthew, do not worry about him. When you are gathered for a meal, I will come to you, and then he will see and believe."

"Lord," Peter said, "will you now set up your kingdom and overthrow Rome and the religious leaders of Jerusalem?"

"No," Jesus said. "I am here only a short time longer before I go to My Father. I have told you about the end. Watch and wait. My kingdom is not of this world."

He instructed the disciples to go and tell others that He was alive, "and I will visit you again."

But none wanted to leave His side. And so He taught them and encouraged them before sending them on their way.

MATTHEW AND THE OTHERS continued to rejoice as they descended, and when they reached Thomas it was obvious that he was embarrassed about not having gone with them. All excitedly told him of what they had seen and heard, and while he could not deny so many witnesses, their excitement seemed to make him only more resolute.

"Unless I see in His hands the print of the nails, and put my finger into the print of the nails, and put my hand into His side, I will not believe."

EIGHT DAYS LATER the disciples were again inside eating, and Thomas with them. Suddenly Jesus appeared in the midst of them and said, "Peace to you!"

They fell to their knees, many of them frightened, even though they had seen Him little more than a week before. That He had appeared though the door was shut had startled them.

Jesus said, "Thomas, reach your finger here, and look at My hands; and reach your hand here, and put it into My side. Do not be unbelieving, but believing."

Thomas, kneeling, said, "My Lord and my God!"

Jesus reached for Him and helped him stand. "Thomas, because you have seen Me, you have believed. Blessed are those who have not seen and yet have believed."

Jesus turned to face the others. "Why are you troubled? And why do doubts arise in your hearts? Behold My hands and My feet, that it is I Myself. Handle Me and see, for a spirit does not have flesh and bones as you see I have."

Still startled and overcome with joy at seeing Him again, Matthew and the others just stared and smiled. And Jesus said, "Have you any food here?"

So they gave Him a piece of a broiled fish and some honeycomb, and He ate. "These are the words which I spoke to you while I was still with you, that all things must be fulfilled which were written in the Law of Moses and the Prophets and the Psalms concerning Me. Thus it is written, and thus it was necessary for the Christ to suffer and to rise from the dead the third day, and that repentance and remission of sins should be preached in His name to all nations, beginning at Jerusalem.

"And you are witnesses of these things. Behold, I send the Promise of My Father upon you; but I want you to tarry in the city of Jerusalem until you are endued with power from on high. Now, come and follow Me."

As they rose to follow Him out, Matthew was

reminded of the day about three years before when Jesus had beckoned him alone and said, "Follow Me."

While he had immediately risen and followed, leaving his old life behind, and while he had sensed that nothing in his life would ever again be the same, he had to admit that he had had no idea what his discipleship would entail. Matthew had witnessed the greatest miracles ever performed, had heard teaching so profound and so contradictory to the common wisdom of the age that he knew he had been in the very presence of the Son of God.

Despite all that, he had lost his faith and courage when Jesus was seized, but the Master had understood and forgiven him. And now to see the risen Christ yet again and to be taught by Him, well, Matthew felt a confidence and faith and resolve that could never be shaken.

As Jesus had died for him and for the sins of the world, Matthew believed he would die for Jesus. He would copy all his notes and all the sayings and teachings of Jesus and see that they were disseminated as far and as wide as possible.

Jesus led the disciples out as far as Bethany, and suddenly He stopped and lifted His hands and blessed them, saying, "All authority has been given to Me in heaven and on earth. Go therefore and make disciples of all the nations, baptizing them in the name of the Father and of the Son and of the Holy Spirit, teaching them to observe all things that I have commanded you; and lo, I am with you always, even to the end of the age."

As soon as He finished speaking, He parted from them and was carried up into heaven before their very eyes.

Peter said, "Let us worship Him and return to Jerusalem with great joy. Let us be continually in the temple praising and blessing God."

They made haste back into the city, telling everyone about the risen Christ.

EPILOGUE

After Jesus' ascension and the founding of His Church on the day of Pentecost, Matthew used his copious notes to compile the sayings of Jesus—which many believe became the basis for his gospel.

THOUSANDS OF NEW BELIEVERS, SOME WHO HAD HEARD HIM AND MANY WHO HAD NOT, CLAMORED FOR HIS PROFOUND SAYINGS, COPIED FROM MATTHEW'S HARD WORK OVER NEARLY THREE YEARS.

THE GOSPEL
OF MATTHEW

MATTHEW

The Genealogy of Jesus Christ

1 The book of the genealogy of Jesus Christ, the Son of David, the Son of Abraham:

2 Abraham begot Isaac, Isaac begot Jacob, and Jacob begot Judah and his brothers. 3 Judah begot Perez and Zerah by Tamar, Perez begot Hezron, and Hezron begot Ram. 4 Ram begot Amminadab, Amminadab begot Nahshon, and Nahshon begot Salmon. 5 Salmon begot Boaz by Rahab, Boaz begot Obed by Ruth, Obed begot Jesse, 6 and Jesse begot David the king.

David the king begot Solomon by her *who had been the wife*[a] of Uriah. 7 Solomon begot Rehoboam, Rehoboam begot Abijah, and Abijah begot Asa.[a] 8 Asa begot Jehoshaphat, Jehoshaphat begot Joram, and Joram begot Uzziah. 9 Uzziah begot Jotham, Jotham begot Ahaz, and Ahaz begot Hezekiah. 10 Hezekiah begot Manasseh, Manasseh begot Amon,[a] and Amon begot Josiah. 11 Josiah begot Jeconiah and his brothers about the time they were carried away to Babylon.

12 And after they were brought to Babylon, Jeconiah begot Shealtiel, and Shealtiel begot Zerubbabel. 13 Zerubbabel begot Abiud, Abiud

---

1:6 [a]Words in italic type have been added for clarity. They are not found in the original Greek. **1:7** [a]NU–Text reads *Asaph.* **1:10** [a]NU–Text reads *Amos.*

begot Eliakim, and Eliakim begot Azor. [14]Azor begot Zadok, Zadok begot Achim, and Achim begot Eliud. [15]Eliud begot Eleazar, Eleazar begot Matthan, and Matthan begot Jacob. [16]And Jacob begot Joseph the husband of Mary, of whom was born Jesus who is called Christ.

[17]So all the generations from Abraham to David *are* fourteen generations, from David until the captivity in Babylon *are* fourteen generations, and from the captivity in Babylon until the Christ *are* fourteen generations.

Christ Born of Mary

[18]Now the birth of Jesus Christ was as follows: After His mother Mary was betrothed to Joseph, before they came together, she was found with child of the Holy Spirit. [19]Then Joseph her husband, being a just *man,* and not wanting to make her a public example, was minded to put her away secretly. [20]But while he thought about these things, behold, an angel of the Lord appeared to him in a dream, saying, "Joseph, son of David, do not be afraid to take to you Mary your wife, for that which is conceived in her is of the Holy Spirit. [21]And she will bring forth a Son, and you shall call His name JESUS, for He will save His people from their sins."

[22]So all this was done that it might be fulfilled which was spoken by the Lord through the prophet, saying: [23]*"Behold, the virgin shall be with child,*

and bear a Son, and they shall call His name Immanuel,"[a] which is translated, "God with us."

[24]Then Joseph, being aroused from sleep, did as the angel of the Lord commanded him and took to him his wife, [25]and did not know her till she had brought forth her firstborn Son.[a] And he called His name JESUS.

Wise Men from the East

2 Now after Jesus was born in Bethlehem of Judea in the days of Herod the king, behold, wise men from the East came to Jerusalem, [2]saying, "Where is He who has been born King of the Jews? For we have seen His star in the East and have come to worship Him."

[3]When Herod the king heard *this,* he was troubled, and all Jerusalem with him. [4]And when he had gathered all the chief priests and scribes of the people together, he inquired of them where the Christ was to be born.

[5]So they said to him, "In Bethlehem of Judea, for thus it is written by the prophet:

[6]　*'But you, Bethlehem, in the land of Judah,*
　Are not the least among the rulers of Judah;
　For out of you shall come a Ruler
　Who will shepherd My people Israel.'"[a]

1:23 [a]Isaiah 7:14. Words in oblique type in the New Testament are quoted from the Old Testament. **1:25** [a]NU–Text reads *a Son.* **2:6** [a]Micah 5:2

313

⁷Then Herod, when he had secretly called the wise men, determined from them what time the star appeared. ⁸And he sent them to Bethlehem and said, "Go and search carefully for the young Child, and when you have found *Him,* bring back word to me, that I may come and worship Him also."

⁹When they heard the king, they departed; and behold, the star which they had seen in the East went before them, till it came and stood over where the young Child was. ¹⁰When they saw the star, they rejoiced with exceedingly great joy. ¹¹And when they had come into the house, they saw the young Child with Mary His mother, and fell down and worshiped Him. And when they had opened their treasures, they presented gifts to Him: gold, frankincense, and myrrh.

¹²Then, being divinely warned in a dream that they should not return to Herod, they departed for their own country another way.

The Flight into Egypt

¹³Now when they had departed, behold, an angel of the Lord appeared to Joseph in a dream, saying, "Arise, take the young Child and His mother, flee to Egypt, and stay there until I bring you word; for Herod will seek the young Child to destroy Him."

¹⁴When he arose, he took the young Child and His mother by night and departed for Egypt, ¹⁵and

was there until the death of Herod, that it might be fulfilled which was spoken by the Lord through the prophet, saying, *"Out of Egypt I called My Son."*[a]

Massacre of the Innocents

[16]Then Herod, when he saw that he was deceived by the wise men, was exceedingly angry; and he sent forth and put to death all the male children who were in Bethlehem and in all its districts, from two years old and under, according to the time which he had determined from the wise men. [17]Then was fulfilled what was spoken by Jeremiah the prophet, saying:

[18] *"A voice was heard in Ramah,*
Lamentation, weeping, and great mourning,
Rachel weeping for her children,
Refusing to be comforted,
Because they are no more."[a]

The Home in Nazareth

[19]Now when Herod was dead, behold, an angel of the Lord appeared in a dream to Joseph in Egypt, [20]saying, "Arise, take the young Child and His mother, and go to the land of Israel, for those who sought the young Child's life are dead." [21]Then he arose, took the young Child and His mother, and came into the land of Israel.

2:15 [a]Hosea 11:1 **2:18** [a]Jeremiah 31:15

22But when he heard that Archelaus was reigning over Judea instead of his father Herod, he was afraid to go there. And being warned by God in a dream, he turned aside into the region of Galilee. 23And he came and dwelt in a city called Nazareth, that it might be fulfilled which was spoken by the prophets, "He shall be called a Nazarene."

John the Baptist Prepares the Way

3 In those days John the Baptist came preaching in the wilderness of Judea, 2and saying, "Repent, for the kingdom of heaven is at hand!" 3For this is he who was spoken of by the prophet Isaiah, saying:

"The voice of one crying in the wilderness:
'Prepare the way of the LORD;
*Make His paths straight.' "*a

4Now John himself was clothed in camel's hair, with a leather belt around his waist; and his food was locusts and wild honey. 5Then Jerusalem, all Judea, and all the region around the Jordan went out to him 6and were baptized by him in the Jordan, confessing their sins.

7But when he saw many of the Pharisees and Sadducees coming to his baptism, he said to them, "Brood of vipers! Who warned you to flee from

---

3:3 aIsaiah 40:3

the wrath to come? [8]Therefore bear fruits worthy of repentance, [9]and do not think to say to yourselves, 'We have Abraham as *our* father.' For I say to you that God is able to raise up children to Abraham from these stones. [10]And even now the ax is laid to the root of the trees. Therefore every tree which does not bear good fruit is cut down and thrown into the fire. [11]I indeed baptize you with water unto repentance, but He who is coming after me is mightier than I, whose sandals I am not worthy to carry. He will baptize you with the Holy Spirit and fire.[a] [12]His winnowing fan *is* in His hand, and He will thoroughly clean out His threshing floor, and gather His wheat into the barn; but He will burn up the chaff with unquenchable fire."

John Baptizes Jesus

[13]Then Jesus came from Galilee to John at the Jordan to be baptized by him. [14]And John *tried to* prevent Him, saying, "I need to be baptized by You, and are You coming to me?"

[15]But Jesus answered and said to him, "Permit *it to be so* now, for thus it is fitting for us to fulfill all righteousness." Then he allowed Him.

[16]When He had been baptized, Jesus came up immediately from the water; and behold, the heavens were opened to Him, and He[a] saw the Spirit of God descending like a dove and alighting

3:11 [a]M–Text omits *and fire.* 3:16 [a]Or *he.*

317

upon Him. [17]And suddenly a voice *came* from heaven, saying, "This is My beloved Son, in whom I am well pleased."

Satan Tempts Jesus

4 Then Jesus was led up by the Spirit into the wilderness to be tempted by the devil. [2]And when He had fasted forty days and forty nights, afterward He was hungry. [3]Now when the tempter came to Him, he said, "If You are the Son of God, command that these stones become bread."

[4]But He answered and said, "It is written, *'Man shall not live by bread alone, but by every word that proceeds from the mouth of God.'*"[a]

[5]Then the devil took Him up into the holy city, set Him on the pinnacle of the temple, [6]and said to Him, "If You are the Son of God, throw Yourself down. For it is written:

'He shall give His angels charge over you,'

and,

*'In their hands they shall bear you up,
Lest you dash your foot against a stone.'*"[a]

[7]Jesus said to him, "It is written again, *'You shall not tempt the LORD your God.'*"[a]

4:4 [a]Deuteronomy 8:3 4:6 [a]Psalm 91:11, 12
4:7 [a]Deuteronomy 6:16

⁸Again, the devil took Him up on an exceedingly high mountain, and showed Him all the kingdoms of the world and their glory. ⁹And he said to Him, "All these things I will give You if You will fall down and worship me."

¹⁰Then Jesus said to him, "Away with you,ᵃ Satan! For it is written, *'You shall worship the LORD your God, and Him only you shall serve.'"ᵇ*

¹¹Then the devil left Him, and behold, angels came and ministered to Him.

Jesus Begins His Galilean Ministry

¹²Now when Jesus heard that John had been put in prison, He departed to Galilee. ¹³And leaving Nazareth, He came and dwelt in Capernaum, which is by the sea, in the regions of Zebulun and Naphtali, ¹⁴that it might be fulfilled which was spoken by Isaiah the prophet, saying:

15 *"The land of Zebulun and the land of Naphtali,*
> *By the way of the sea, beyond the Jordan, Galilee of the Gentiles:*
16 *The people who sat in darkness have seen a great light,*
> *And upon those who sat in the region and shadow of death*
> *Light has dawned."ᵃ*

4:10 ᵃM–Text reads *Get behind Me.*   ᵇDeuteronomy 6:13
4:16 ᵃIsaiah 9:1, 2

¹⁷From that time Jesus began to preach and to say, "Repent, for the kingdom of heaven is at hand."

Four Fishermen Called as Disciples

¹⁸And Jesus, walking by the Sea of Galilee, saw two brothers, Simon called Peter, and Andrew his brother, casting a net into the sea; for they were fishermen. ¹⁹Then He said to them, "Follow Me, and I will make you fishers of men." ²⁰They immediately left *their* nets and followed Him.

²¹Going on from there, He saw two other brothers, James *the son* of Zebedee, and John his brother, in the boat with Zebedee their father, mending their nets. He called them, ²²and immediately they left the boat and their father, and followed Him.

Jesus Heals a Great Multitude

²³And Jesus went about all Galilee, teaching in their synagogues, preaching the gospel of the kingdom, and healing all kinds of sickness and all kinds of disease among the people. ²⁴Then His fame went throughout all Syria; and they brought to Him all sick people who were afflicted with various diseases and torments, and those who were demon-possessed, epileptics, and paralytics; and He healed them. ²⁵Great multitudes followed Him—from Galilee, and *from* Decapolis, Jerusalem, Judea, and beyond the Jordan.

The Beatitudes

5 And seeing the multitudes, He went up on a mountain, and when He was seated His disciples came to Him. ²Then He opened His mouth and taught them, saying:

3 "Blessed *are* the poor in spirit,
   For theirs is the kingdom of heaven.
4 Blessed *are* those who mourn,
   For they shall be comforted.
5 Blessed *are* the meek,
   For they shall inherit the earth.
6 Blessed *are* those who hunger and thirst
   for righteousness,
   For they shall be filled.
7 Blessed *are* the merciful,
   For they shall obtain mercy.
8 Blessed *are* the pure in heart,
   For they shall see God.
9 Blessed *are* the peacemakers,
   For they shall be called sons of God.
10 Blessed *are* those who are persecuted
   for righteousness' sake,
   For theirs is the kingdom of heaven.

¹¹"Blessed are you when they revile and persecute you, and say all kinds of evil against you falsely for My sake. ¹²Rejoice and be exceedingly glad, for great *is* your reward in heaven,

for so they persecuted the prophets who were before you.

Believers Are Salt and Light

13"You are the salt of the earth; but if the salt loses its flavor, how shall it be seasoned? It is then good for nothing but to be thrown out and trampled underfoot by men.

14"You are the light of the world. A city that is set on a hill cannot be hidden. 15Nor do they light a lamp and put it under a basket, but on a lampstand, and it gives light to all *who are* in the house. 16Let your light so shine before men, that they may see your good works and glorify your Father in heaven.

Christ Fulfills the Law

17"Do not think that I came to destroy the Law or the Prophets. I did not come to destroy but to fulfill. 18For assuredly, I say to you, till heaven and earth pass away, one jot or one tittle will by no means pass from the law till all is fulfilled. 19Whoever therefore breaks one of the least of these commandments, and teaches men so, shall be called least in the kingdom of heaven; but whoever does and teaches *them,* he shall be called great in the kingdom of heaven. 20For I say to you, that unless your righteousness exceeds *the righteousness* of the scribes and Pharisees, you will by no means enter the kingdom of heaven.

Murder Begins in the Heart

21"You have heard that it was said to those of old, '*You shall not murder,*[a] and whoever murders will be in danger of the judgment.' 22But I say to you that whoever is angry with his brother without a cause[a] shall be in danger of the judgment. And whoever says to his brother, 'Raca!' shall be in danger of the council. But whoever says, 'You fool!' shall be in danger of hell fire. 23Therefore if you bring your gift to the altar, and there remember that your brother has something against you, 24leave your gift there before the altar, and go your way. First be reconciled to your brother, and then come and offer your gift. 25Agree with your adversary quickly, while you are on the way with him, lest your adversary deliver you to the judge, the judge hand you over to the officer, and you be thrown into prison. 26Assuredly, I say to you, you will by no means get out of there till you have paid the last penny.

Adultery in the Heart

27"You have heard that it was said to those of old,[a] '*You shall not commit adultery.*'[b] 28But I say to you that whoever looks at a woman to lust for

5:21 [a]Exodus 20:13; Deuteronomy 5:17 **5:22** [a]NU–Text omits *without a cause.* **5:27** [a]NU–Text and M–Text omit *to those of old.* [b]Exodus 20:14; Deuteronomy 5:18

her has already committed adultery with her in his heart. [29]If your right eye causes you to sin, pluck it out and cast *it* from you; for it is more profitable for you that one of your members perish, than for your whole body to be cast into hell. [30]And if your right hand causes you to sin, cut it off and cast *it* from you; for it is more profitable for you that one of your members perish, than for your whole body to be cast into hell.

Marriage Is Sacred and Binding

[31]"Furthermore it has been said, 'Whoever divorces his wife, let him give her a certificate of divorce.' [32]But I say to you that whoever divorces his wife for any reason except sexual immorality[a] causes her to commit adultery; and whoever marries a woman who is divorced commits adultery.

Jesus Forbids Oaths

[33]"Again you have heard that it was said to those of old, 'You shall not swear falsely, but shall perform your oaths to the Lord.' [34]But I say to you, do not swear at all: neither by heaven, for it is God's throne; [35]nor by the earth, for it is His footstool; nor by Jerusalem, for it is the city of the great King. [36]Nor shall you swear by your head, because you cannot make one hair white or black. [37]But let your 'Yes' be 'Yes,' and your 'No,'

5:32 [a]Or *fornication*.

'No.' For whatever is more than these is from the evil one.

Go the Second Mile

38"You have heard that it was said, '*An eye for an eye and a tooth for a tooth.*'ᵃ 39But I tell you not to resist an evil person. But whoever slaps you on your right cheek, turn the other to him also. 40If anyone wants to sue you and take away your tunic, let him have *your* cloak also. 41And whoever compels you to go one mile, go with him two. 42Give to him who asks you, and from him who wants to borrow from you do not turn away.

Love Your Enemies

43"You have heard that it was said, '*You shall love your neighbor*ᵃ and hate your enemy.' 44But I say to you, love your enemies, bless those who curse you, do good to those who hate you, and pray for those who spitefully use you and persecute you,ᵃ 45that you may be sons of your Father in heaven; for He makes His sun rise on the evil and on the good, and sends rain on the just and on the unjust. 46For if you love those who love you, what reward have you? Do not even the tax collectors do

---

5:38 ᵃExodus 21:24; Leviticus 24:20; Deuteronomy 19:21 **5:43** ᵃCompare Leviticus 19:18. **5:44** ᵃNU–Text omits three clauses from this verse, leaving, *"But I say to you, love your enemies and pray for those who persecute you."*

the same? ⁴⁷And if you greet your brethren^a only, what do you do more *than others?* Do not even the tax collectors^b do so? ⁴⁸Therefore you shall be perfect, just as your Father in heaven is perfect.

Do Good to Please God

6 "Take heed that you do not do your charitable deeds before men, to be seen by them. Otherwise you have no reward from your Father in heaven. ²Therefore, when you do a charitable deed, do not sound a trumpet before you as the hypocrites do in the synagogues and in the streets, that they may have glory from men. Assuredly, I say to you, they have their reward. ³But when you do a charitable deed, do not let your left hand know what your right hand is doing, ⁴that your charitable deed may be in secret; and your Father who sees in secret will Himself reward you openly.^a

The Model Prayer

⁵"And when you pray, you shall not be like the hypocrites. For they love to pray standing in the synagogues and on the corners of the streets, that they may be seen by men. Assuredly, I say to you, they have their reward. ⁶But you, when you pray, go into your room, and when you have shut your door, pray to your Father who *is* in the secret *place;* and your Father who sees in secret will

5:47 ^aM–Text reads *friends.* ^bNU–Text reads *Gentiles.*
6:4 ^aNU–Text omits *openly.*

reward you openly.[a] [7]And when you pray, do not use vain repetitions as the heathen *do*. For they think that they will be heard for their many words.

[8]"Therefore do not be like them. For your Father knows the things you have need of before you ask Him. [9]In this manner, therefore, pray:

Our Father in heaven,
Hallowed be Your name.
[10] Your kingdom come.
Your will be done
On earth as *it is* in heaven.
[11] Give us this day our daily bread.
[12] And forgive us our debts,
As we forgive our debtors.
[13] And do not lead us into temptation,
But deliver us from the evil one.
For Yours is the kingdom and the power and
the glory forever. Amen.[a]

[14]"For if you forgive men their trespasses, your heavenly Father will also forgive you. [15]But if you do not forgive men their trespasses, neither will your Father forgive your trespasses.

Fasting to Be Seen Only by God
[16]"Moreover, when you fast, do not be like the hypocrites, with a sad countenance. For they dis-

6:6 [a]NU–Text omits *openly*. **6:13** [a]NU–Text omits *For Yours* through *Amen*.

figure their faces that they may appear to men to be fasting. Assuredly, I say to you, they have their reward. [17]But you, when you fast, anoint your head and wash your face, [18]so that you do not appear to men to be fasting, but to your Father who *is* in the secret *place;* and your Father who sees in secret will reward you openly.[a]

Lay Up Treasures in Heaven
[19]"Do not lay up for yourselves treasures on earth, where moth and rust destroy and where thieves break in and steal; [20]but lay up for yourselves treasures in heaven, where neither moth nor rust destroys and where thieves do not break in and steal. [21]For where your treasure is, there your heart will be also.

The Lamp of the Body
[22]"The lamp of the body is the eye. If therefore your eye is good, your whole body will be full of light. [23]But if your eye is bad, your whole body will be full of darkness. If therefore the light that is in you is darkness, how great *is* that darkness!

You Cannot Serve God and Riches
[24]"No one can serve two masters; for either he will hate the one and love the other, or else he will be loyal to the one and despise the other. You cannot serve God and mammon.

6:18 [a]NU–Text and M–Text omit *openly.*

Do Not Worry

25"Therefore I say to you, do not worry about your life, what you will eat or what you will drink; nor about your body, what you will put on. Is not life more than food and the body more than clothing? 26Look at the birds of the air, for they neither sow nor reap nor gather into barns; yet your heavenly Father feeds them. Are you not of more value than they? 27Which of you by worrying can add one cubit to his stature?

28"So why do you worry about clothing? Consider the lilies of the field, how they grow: they neither toil nor spin; 29and yet I say to you that even Solomon in all his glory was not arrayed like one of these. 30Now if God so clothes the grass of the field, which today is, and tomorrow is thrown into the oven, *will He* not much more *clothe* you, O you of little faith?

31"Therefore do not worry, saying, 'What shall we eat?' or 'What shall we drink?' or 'What shall we wear?' 32For after all these things the Gentiles seek. For your heavenly Father knows that you need all these things. 33But seek first the kingdom of God and His righteousness, and all these things shall be added to you. 34Therefore do not worry about tomorrow, for tomorrow will worry about its own things. Sufficient for the day *is* its own trouble.

Do Not Judge

7 "Judge not, that you be not judged. ²For with what judgment you judge, you will be judged; and with the measure you use, it will be measured back to you. ³And why do you look at the speck in your brother's eye, but do not consider the plank in your own eye? ⁴Or how can you say to your brother, 'Let me remove the speck from your eye'; and look, a plank *is* in your own eye? ⁵Hypocrite! First remove the plank from your own eye, and then you will see clearly to remove the speck from your brother's eye.

⁶"Do not give what is holy to the dogs; nor cast your pearls before swine, lest they trample them under their feet, and turn and tear you in pieces.

Keep Asking, Seeking, Knocking

⁷"Ask, and it will be given to you; seek, and you will find; knock, and it will be opened to you. ⁸For everyone who asks receives, and he who seeks finds, and to him who knocks it will be opened. ⁹Or what man is there among you who, if his son asks for bread, will give him a stone? ¹⁰Or if he asks for a fish, will he give him a serpent? ¹¹If you then, being evil, know how to give good gifts to your children, how much more will your Father who is in heaven give good things to those who ask Him! ¹²Therefore, what-

ever you want men to do to you, do also to them, for this is the Law and the Prophets.

The Narrow Way

13"Enter by the narrow gate; for wide *is* the gate and broad *is* the way that leads to destruction, and there are many who go in by it. 14Because[a] narrow *is* the gate and difficult *is* the way which leads to life, and there are few who find it.

You Will Know Them by Their Fruits

15"Beware of false prophets, who come to you in sheep's clothing, but inwardly they are ravenous wolves. 16You will know them by their fruits. Do men gather grapes from thornbushes or figs from thistles? 17Even so, every good tree bears good fruit, but a bad tree bears bad fruit. 18A good tree cannot bear bad fruit, nor *can* a bad tree bear good fruit. 19Every tree that does not bear good fruit is cut down and thrown into the fire. 20Therefore by their fruits you will know them.

I Never Knew You

21"Not everyone who says to Me, 'Lord, Lord,' shall enter the kingdom of heaven, but he who does the will of My Father in heaven. 22Many will say to Me in that day, 'Lord, Lord, have we not prophesied in Your name, cast out demons in Your name,

7:14 [a]NU–Text and M–Text read *How . . . !*

and done many wonders in Your name?' ²³And then I will declare to them, 'I never knew you; depart from Me, you who practice lawlessness!'

Build on the Rock

²⁴"Therefore whoever hears these sayings of Mine, and does them, I will liken him to a wise man who built his house on the rock: ²⁵and the rain descended, the floods came, and the winds blew and beat on that house; and it did not fall, for it was founded on the rock.

²⁶"But everyone who hears these sayings of Mine, and does not do them, will be like a foolish man who built his house on the sand: ²⁷and the rain descended, the floods came, and the winds blew and beat on that house; and it fell. And great was its fall."

²⁸And so it was, when Jesus had ended these sayings, that the people were astonished at His teaching, ²⁹for He taught them as one having authority, and not as the scribes.

Jesus Cleanses a Leper

8 When He had come down from the mountain, great multitudes followed Him. ²And behold, a leper came and worshiped Him, saying, "Lord, if You are willing, You can make me clean."

³Then Jesus put out *His* hand and touched him, saying, "I am willing; be cleansed." Immediately his leprosy was cleansed.

^{4}And Jesus said to him, "See that you tell no one; but go your way, show yourself to the priest, and offer the gift that Moses commanded, as a testimony to them."

Jesus Heals a Centurion's Servant

^{5}Now when Jesus had entered Capernaum, a centurion came to Him, pleading with Him, ^{6}saying, "Lord, my servant is lying at home paralyzed, dreadfully tormented."

^{7}And Jesus said to him, "I will come and heal him."

^{8}The centurion answered and said, "Lord, I am not worthy that You should come under my roof. But only speak a word, and my servant will be healed. ^{9}For I also am a man under authority, having soldiers under me. And I say to this *one,* 'Go,' and he goes; and to another, 'Come,' and he comes; and to my servant, 'Do this,' and he does *it.*"

^{10}When Jesus heard *it,* He marveled, and said to those who followed, "Assuredly, I say to you, I have not found such great faith, not even in Israel! ^{11}And I say to you that many will come from east and west, and sit down with Abraham, Isaac, and Jacob in the kingdom of heaven. ^{12}But the sons of the kingdom will be cast out into outer darkness. There will be weeping and gnashing of teeth." ^{13}Then Jesus said to the centurion, "Go your way; and as you have believed, *so* let it be done for you." And his servant was healed that same hour.

Peter's Mother-in-Law Healed

[14]Now when Jesus had come into Peter's house, He saw his wife's mother lying sick with a fever. [15]So He touched her hand, and the fever left her. And she arose and served them.[a]

Many Healed in the Evening

[16]When evening had come, they brought to Him many who were demon-possessed. And He cast out the spirits with a word, and healed all who were sick, [17]that it might be fulfilled which was spoken by Isaiah the prophet, saying:

*"He Himself took our infirmities
And bore our sicknesses."*[a]

The Cost of Discipleship

[18]And when Jesus saw great multitudes about Him, He gave a command to depart to the other side. [19]Then a certain scribe came and said to Him, "Teacher, I will follow You wherever You go."

[20]And Jesus said to him, "Foxes have holes and birds of the air *have* nests, but the Son of Man has nowhere to lay *His* head."

[21]Then another of His disciples said to Him, "Lord, let me first go and bury my father."

[22]But Jesus said to him, "Follow Me, and let the dead bury their own dead."

8:15 [a]NU–Text and M–Text read *Him.* **8:17** [a]Isaiah 53:4

Wind and Wave Obey Jesus

²³Now when He got into a boat, His disciples followed Him. ²⁴And suddenly a great tempest arose on the sea, so that the boat was covered with the waves. But He was asleep. ²⁵Then His disciples came to *Him* and awoke Him, saying, "Lord, save us! We are perishing!"

²⁶But He said to them, "Why are you fearful, O you of little faith?" Then He arose and rebuked the winds and the sea, and there was a great calm. ²⁷So the men marveled, saying, "Who can this be, that even the winds and the sea obey Him?"

Two Demon-Possessed Men Healed

²⁸When He had come to the other side, to the country of the Gergesenes,^a there met Him two demon-possessed *men,* coming out of the tombs, exceedingly fierce, so that no one could pass that way. ²⁹And suddenly they cried out, saying, "What have we to do with You, Jesus, You Son of God? Have You come here to torment us before the time?"

³⁰Now a good way off from them there was a herd of many swine feeding. ³¹So the demons begged Him, saying, "If You cast us out, permit us to go away^a into the herd of swine."

³²And He said to them, "Go." So when they had come out, they went into the herd of swine. And

---

8:28 ^aNU–Text reads *Gadarenes.* **8:31** ^aNU–Text reads *send us.*

suddenly the whole herd of swine ran violently down the steep place into the sea, and perished in the water.

33Then those who kept *them* fled; and they went away into the city and told everything, including what *had happened* to the demon-possessed *men.* 34And behold, the whole city came out to meet Jesus. And when they saw Him, they begged *Him* to depart from their region.

Jesus Forgives and Heals a Paralytic

9 So He got into a boat, crossed over, and came to His own city. 2Then behold, they brought to Him a paralytic lying on a bed. When Jesus saw their faith, He said to the paralytic, "Son, be of good cheer; your sins are forgiven you."

3And at once some of the scribes said within themselves, "This Man blasphemes!"

4But Jesus, knowing their thoughts, said, "Why do you think evil in your hearts? 5For which is easier, to say, '*Your* sins are forgiven you,' or to say, 'Arise and walk'? 6But that you may know that the Son of Man has power on earth to forgive sins"—then He said to the paralytic, "Arise, take up your bed, and go to your house." 7And he arose and departed to his house.

8Now when the multitudes saw *it,* they marveleda and glorified God, who had given such power to men.

9:8 aNU–Text reads *were afraid.*

Matthew the Tax Collector

⁹As Jesus passed on from there, He saw a man named Matthew sitting at the tax office. And He said to him, "Follow Me." So he arose and followed Him.

¹⁰Now it happened, as Jesus sat at the table in the house, *that* behold, many tax collectors and sinners came and sat down with Him and His disciples. ¹¹And when the Pharisees saw *it,* they said to His disciples, "Why does your Teacher eat with tax collectors and sinners?"

¹²When Jesus heard *that,* He said to them, "Those who are well have no need of a physician, but those who are sick. ¹³But go and learn what *this* means: *'I desire mercy and not sacrifice.'*ᵃ For I did not come to call the righteous, but sinners, to repentance."ᵇ

Jesus Is Questioned About Fasting

¹⁴Then the disciples of John came to Him, saying, "Why do we and the Pharisees fast often,ᵃ but Your disciples do not fast?"

¹⁵And Jesus said to them, "Can the friends of the bridegroom mourn as long as the bridegroom is with them? But the days will come when the bridegroom will be taken away from them, and then they will fast. ¹⁶No one puts a piece of

---

9:13 ᵃHosea 6:6 ᵇNU–Text omits *to repentance.*
9:14 ᵃNU–Text brackets *often* as disputed.

unshrunk cloth on an old garment; for the patch pulls away from the garment, and the tear is made worse. [17]Nor do they put new wine into old wineskins, or else the wineskins break, the wine is spilled, and the wineskins are ruined. But they put new wine into new wineskins, and both are preserved."

A Girl Restored to Life and a Woman Healed

[18]While He spoke these things to them, behold, a ruler came and worshiped Him, saying, "My daughter has just died, but come and lay Your hand on her and she will live." [19]So Jesus arose and followed him, and so *did* His disciples.

[20]And suddenly, a woman who had a flow of blood for twelve years came from behind and touched the hem of His garment. [21]For she said to herself, "If only I may touch His garment, I shall be made well." [22]But Jesus turned around, and when He saw her He said, "Be of good cheer, daughter; your faith has made you well." And the woman was made well from that hour.

[23]When Jesus came into the ruler's house, and saw the flute players and the noisy crowd wailing, [24]He said to them, "Make room, for the girl is not dead, but sleeping." And they ridiculed Him. [25]But when the crowd was put outside, He went in and took her by the hand, and the girl arose. [26]And the report of this went out into all that land.

Two Blind Men Healed

²⁷When Jesus departed from there, two blind men followed Him, crying out and saying, "Son of David, have mercy on us!"

²⁸And when He had come into the house, the blind men came to Him. And Jesus said to them, "Do you believe that I am able to do this?"

They said to Him, "Yes, Lord."

²⁹Then He touched their eyes, saying, "According to your faith let it be to you." ³⁰And their eyes were opened. And Jesus sternly warned them, saying, "See *that* no one knows *it.*" ³¹But when they had departed, they spread the news about Him in all that country.

A Mute Man Speaks

³²As they went out, behold, they brought to Him a man, mute and demon-possessed. ³³And when the demon was cast out, the mute spoke. And the multitudes marveled, saying, "It was never seen like this in Israel!"

³⁴But the Pharisees said, "He casts out demons by the ruler of the demons."

The Compassion of Jesus

³⁵Then Jesus went about all the cities and villages, teaching in their synagogues, preaching the gospel of the kingdom, and healing every sickness

and every disease among the people.[a] 36But when He saw the multitudes, He was moved with compassion for them, because they were weary[a] and scattered, like sheep having no shepherd. 37Then He said to His disciples, "The harvest truly *is* plentiful, but the laborers *are* few. 38Therefore pray the Lord of the harvest to send out laborers into His harvest."

The Twelve Apostles

10 And when He had called His twelve disciples to *Him,* He gave them power *over* unclean spirits, to cast them out, and to heal all kinds of sickness and all kinds of disease. 2Now the names of the twelve apostles are these: first, Simon, who is called Peter, and Andrew his brother; James the *son* of Zebedee, and John his brother; 3Philip and Bartholomew; Thomas and Matthew the tax collector; James the *son* of Alphaeus, and Lebbaeus, whose surname was[a] Thaddaeus; 4Simon the Cananite,[a] and Judas Iscariot, who also betrayed Him.

Sending Out the Twelve

5These twelve Jesus sent out and commanded them, saying: "Do not go into the way of the

---

9:35 [a]NU–Text omits *among the people.* 9:36 [a]NU–Text and M–Text read *harassed.* 10:3 [a]NU–Text omits *Lebbaeus, whose surname was.* 10:4 [a]NU–Text reads *Cananaean.*

Gentiles, and do not enter a city of the Samaritans. [6]But go rather to the lost sheep of the house of Israel. [7]And as you go, preach, saying, 'The kingdom of heaven is at hand.' [8]Heal the sick, cleanse the lepers, raise the dead,[a] cast out demons. Freely you have received, freely give. [9]Provide neither gold nor silver nor copper in your money belts, [10]nor bag for *your* journey, nor two tunics, nor sandals, nor staffs; for a worker is worthy of his food.

[11]"Now whatever city or town you enter, inquire who in it is worthy, and stay there till you go out. [12]And when you go into a household, greet it. [13]If the household is worthy, let your peace come upon it. But if it is not worthy, let your peace return to you. [14]And whoever will not receive you nor hear your words, when you depart from that house or city, shake off the dust from your feet. [15]Assuredly, I say to you, it will be more tolerable for the land of Sodom and Gomorrah in the day of judgment than for that city!

Persecutions Are Coming

[16]"Behold, I send you out as sheep in the midst of wolves. Therefore be wise as serpents and harmless as doves. [17]But beware of men, for they will deliver you up to councils and scourge you in their synagogues. [18]You will be brought before

---

10:8 [a]NU–Text reads *raise the dead, cleanse the lepers;* M–Text omits *raise the dead.*

governors and kings for My sake, as a testimony to them and to the Gentiles. [19]But when they deliver you up, do not worry about how or what you should speak. For it will be given to you in that hour what you should speak; [20]for it is not you who speak, but the Spirit of your Father who speaks in you.

[21]"Now brother will deliver up brother to death, and a father *his* child; and children will rise up against parents and cause them to be put to death. [22]And you will be hated by all for My name's sake. But he who endures to the end will be saved. [23]When they persecute you in this city, flee to another. For assuredly, I say to you, you will not have gone through the cities of Israel before the Son of Man comes.

[24]"A disciple is not above *his* teacher, nor a servant above his master. [25]It is enough for a disciple that he be like his teacher, and a servant like his master. If they have called the master of the house Beelzebub,[a] how much more *will they call* those of his household! [26]Therefore do not fear them. For there is nothing covered that will not be revealed, and hidden that will not be known.

Jesus Teaches the Fear of God

[27]"Whatever I tell you in the dark, speak in the light; and what you hear in the ear, preach on the housetops. [28]And do not fear those who kill the

10:25 [a]NU–Text and M–Text read *Beelzebul.*

body but cannot kill the soul. But rather fear Him who is able to destroy both soul and body in hell. [29]Are not two sparrows sold for a copper coin? And not one of them falls to the ground apart from your Father's will. [30]But the very hairs of your head are all numbered. [31]Do not fear therefore; you are of more value than many sparrows.

Confess Christ Before Men

[32]"Therefore whoever confesses Me before men, him I will also confess before My Father who is in heaven. [33]But whoever denies Me before men, him I will also deny before My Father who is in heaven.

Christ Brings Division

[34]"Do not think that I came to bring peace on earth. I did not come to bring peace but a sword. [35]For I have come to *'set a man against his father, a daughter against her mother, and a daughter-in-law against her mother-in-law';* [36]and *'a man's enemies will be those of his own household.'*[a] [37]He who loves father or mother more than Me is not worthy of Me. And he who loves son or daughter more than Me is not worthy of Me. [38]And he who does not take his cross and follow after Me is not worthy of Me. [39]He who finds his life will lose it, and he who loses his life for My sake will find it.

10:36 [a]Micah 7:6

A Cup of Cold Water

40"He who receives you receives Me, and he who receives Me receives Him who sent Me. 41He who receives a prophet in the name of a prophet shall receive a prophet's reward. And he who receives a righteous man in the name of a righteous man shall receive a righteous man's reward. 42And whoever gives one of these little ones only a cup of cold *water* in the name of a disciple, assuredly, I say to you, he shall by no means lose his reward."

John the Baptist Sends Messengers to Jesus

11 Now it came to pass, when Jesus finished commanding His twelve disciples, that He departed from there to teach and to preach in their cities.

2And when John had heard in prison about the works of Christ, he sent two of[a] his disciples 3and said to Him, "Are You the Coming One, or do we look for another?"

4Jesus answered and said to them, "Go and tell John the things which you hear and see: 5*The* blind see and *the* lame walk; *the* lepers are cleansed and *the* deaf hear; *the* dead are raised up and *the* poor have the gospel preached to them. 6And blessed is he who is not offended because of Me."

7As they departed, Jesus began to say to the mul-

11:2 [a]NU–Text reads *by* for *two of.*

titudes concerning John: "What did you go out into the wilderness to see? A reed shaken by the wind? [8]But what did you go out to see? A man clothed in soft garments? Indeed, those who wear soft *clothing* are in kings' houses. [9]But what did you go out to see? A prophet? Yes, I say to you, and more than a prophet. [10]For this is *he* of whom it is written:

> *'Behold, I send My messenger before Your face,*
> *Who will prepare Your way before You.'*[a]

[11]"Assuredly, I say to you, among those born of women there has not risen one greater than John the Baptist; but he who is least in the kingdom of heaven is greater than he. [12]And from the days of John the Baptist until now the kingdom of heaven suffers violence, and the violent take it by force. [13]For all the prophets and the law prophesied until John. [14]And if you are willing to receive *it,* he is Elijah who is to come. [15]He who has ears to hear, let him hear!

[16]"But to what shall I liken this generation? It is like children sitting in the marketplaces and calling to their companions, [17]and saying:

> 'We played the flute for you,
>   And you did not dance;
> We mourned to you,
>   And you did not lament.'

11:10 [a]Malachi 3:1

¹⁸For John came neither eating nor drinking, and they say, 'He has a demon.' ¹⁹The Son of Man came eating and drinking, and they say, 'Look, a glutton and a winebibber, a friend of tax collectors and sinners!' But wisdom is justified by her children.'"^a

Woe to the Impenitent Cities

²⁰Then He began to rebuke the cities in which most of His mighty works had been done, because they did not repent: ²¹"Woe to you, Chorazin! Woe to you, Bethsaida! For if the mighty works which were done in you had been done in Tyre and Sidon, they would have repented long ago in sackcloth and ashes. ²²But I say to you, it will be more tolerable for Tyre and Sidon in the day of judgment than for you. ²³And you, Capernaum, who are exalted to heaven, will be^a brought down to Hades; for if the mighty works which were done in you had been done in Sodom, it would have remained until this day. ²⁴But I say to you that it shall be more tolerable for the land of Sodom in the day of judgment than for you."

Jesus Gives True Rest

²⁵At that time Jesus answered and said, "I thank You, Father, Lord of heaven and earth, that You have hidden these things from *the* wise and pru-

---

11:19 ^aNU–Text reads *works.* **11:23** ^aNU–Text reads *will you be exalted to heaven? No, you will be.*

dent and have revealed them to babes. ^{26}Even so, Father, for so it seemed good in Your sight. ^{27}All things have been delivered to Me by My Father, and no one knows the Son except the Father. Nor does anyone know the Father except the Son, and *the one* to whom the Son wills to reveal *Him.* ^{28}Come to Me, all *you* who labor and are heavy laden, and I will give you rest. ^{29}Take My yoke upon you and learn from Me, for I am gentle and lowly in heart, and you will find rest for your souls. ^{30}For My yoke *is* easy and My burden is light."

Jesus Is Lord of the Sabbath

12 At that time Jesus went through the grain-fields on the Sabbath. And His disciples were hungry, and began to pluck heads of grain and to eat. ^{2}And when the Pharisees saw *it,* they said to Him, "Look, Your disciples are doing what is not lawful to do on the Sabbath!"

^{3}But He said to them, "Have you not read what David did when he was hungry, he and those who were with him: ^{4}how he entered the house of God and ate the showbread which was not lawful for him to eat, nor for those who were with him, but only for the priests? ^{5}Or have you not read in the law that on the Sabbath the priests in the temple profane the Sabbath, and are blameless? ^{6}Yet I say to you that in this place there is *One* greater than the temple. ^{7}But if you had known what *this* means, *'I desire mercy and not sacrifice,'*[a] you would not have condemned the guiltless. [8]For the Son of Man is Lord even[a] of the Sabbath."

Healing on the Sabbath

[9]Now when He had departed from there, He went into their synagogue. [10]And behold, there was a man who had a withered hand. And they asked Him, saying, "Is it lawful to heal on the Sabbath?"—that they might accuse Him.

[11]Then He said to them, "What man is there among you who has one sheep, and if it falls into a pit on the Sabbath, will not lay hold of it and lift *it* out? [12]Of how much more value then is a man than a sheep? Therefore it is lawful to do good on the Sabbath." [13]Then He said to the man, "Stretch out your hand." And he stretched *it* out, and it was restored as whole as the other. [14]Then the Pharisees went out and plotted against Him, how they might destroy Him.

Behold, My Servant

[15]But when Jesus knew *it,* He withdrew from there. And great multitudes[a] followed Him, and He healed them all. [16]Yet He warned them not to make Him known, [17]that it might be fulfilled which was spoken by Isaiah the prophet, saying:

12:7 [a]Hosea 6:6 **12:8** [a]NU–Text and M–Text omit *even*. **12:15** [a]NU–Text brackets *multitudes* as disputed.

¹⁸ *"Behold! My Servant whom I have chosen,*
My Beloved in whom My soul is well
  pleased!
I will put My Spirit upon Him,
And He will declare justice to the Gentiles.
¹⁹ *He will not quarrel nor cry out,*
Nor will anyone hear His voice in the
  streets.
²⁰ *A bruised reed He will not break,*
And smoking flax He will not quench,
Till He sends forth justice to victory;
²¹ *And in His name Gentiles will trust."*[a]

A House Divided Cannot Stand

²²Then one was brought to Him who was demon-possessed, blind and mute; and He healed him, so that the blind and[a] mute man both spoke and saw. ²³And all the multitudes were amazed and said, "Could this be the Son of David?"

²⁴Now when the Pharisees heard *it* they said, "This *fellow* does not cast out demons except by Beelzebub,[a] the ruler of the demons."

²⁵But Jesus knew their thoughts, and said to them: "Every kingdom divided against itself is brought to desolation, and every city or house divided against itself will not stand. ²⁶If Satan casts out Satan, he is divided against himself. How then will his kingdom stand? ²⁷And if I cast

12:21 [a]Isaiah 42:1–4 **12:22** [a]NU–Text omits *blind and.*
12:24 [a]NU–Text and M–Text read *Beelzebul.*

out demons by Beelzebub, by whom do your sons cast *them* out? Therefore they shall be your judges. 28But if I cast out demons by the Spirit of God, surely the kingdom of God has come upon you. 29Or how can one enter a strong man's house and plunder his goods, unless he first binds the strong man? And then he will plunder his house. 30He who is not with Me is against Me, and he who does not gather with Me scatters abroad.

The Unpardonable Sin

31"Therefore I say to you, every sin and blasphemy will be forgiven men, but the blasphemy *against* the Spirit will not be forgiven men. 32Anyone who speaks a word against the Son of Man, it will be forgiven him; but whoever speaks against the Holy Spirit, it will not be forgiven him, either in this age or in the *age* to come.

A Tree Known by Its Fruit

33"Either make the tree good and its fruit good, or else make the tree bad and its fruit bad; for a tree is known by *its* fruit. 34Brood of vipers! How can you, being evil, speak good things? For out of the abundance of the heart the mouth speaks. 35A good man out of the good treasure of his heart[a] brings forth good things, and an evil man out of the evil treasure brings forth evil things. 36But I say to you that for every idle word men may

12:35 [a]NU–Text and M–Text omit *of his heart.*

speak, they will give account of it in the day of judgment. ³⁷For by your words you will be justified, and by your words you will be condemned."

The Scribes and Pharisees Ask for a Sign
³⁸Then some of the scribes and Pharisees answered, saying, "Teacher, we want to see a sign from You."

³⁹But He answered and said to them, "An evil and adulterous generation seeks after a sign, and no sign will be given to it except the sign of the prophet Jonah. ⁴⁰For as Jonah was three days and three nights in the belly of the great fish, so will the Son of Man be three days and three nights in the heart of the earth. ⁴¹The men of Nineveh will rise up in the judgment with this generation and condemn it, because they repented at the preaching of Jonah; and indeed a greater than Jonah *is* here. ⁴²The queen of the South will rise up in the judgment with this generation and condemn it, for she came from the ends of the earth to hear the wisdom of Solomon; and indeed a greater than Solomon *is* here.

An Unclean Spirit Returns
⁴³"When an unclean spirit goes out of a man, he goes through dry places, seeking rest, and finds none. ⁴⁴Then he says, 'I will return to my house from which I came.' And when he comes, he finds *it* empty, swept, and put in order. ⁴⁵Then he goes

and takes with him seven other spirits more wicked than himself, and they enter and dwell there; and the last *state* of that man is worse than the first. So shall it also be with this wicked generation."

Jesus' Mother and Brothers Send for Him

⁴⁶While He was still talking to the multitudes, behold, His mother and brothers stood outside, seeking to speak with Him. ⁴⁷Then one said to Him, "Look, Your mother and Your brothers are standing outside, seeking to speak with You."

⁴⁸But He answered and said to the one who told Him, "Who is My mother and who are My brothers?" ⁴⁹And He stretched out His hand toward His disciples and said, "Here are My mother and My brothers! ⁵⁰For whoever does the will of My Father in heaven is My brother and sister and mother."

The Parable of the Sower

13 On the same day Jesus went out of the house and sat by the sea. ²And great multitudes were gathered together to Him, so that He got into a boat and sat; and the whole multitude stood on the shore.

³Then He spoke many things to them in parables, saying: "Behold, a sower went out to sow. ⁴And as he sowed, some *seed* fell by the wayside; and the birds came and devoured them. ⁵Some fell

on stony places, where they did not have much earth; and they immediately sprang up because they had no depth of earth. ⁶But when the sun was up they were scorched, and because they had no root they withered away. ⁷And some fell among thorns, and the thorns sprang up and choked them. ⁸But others fell on good ground and yielded a crop: some a hundredfold, some sixty, some thirty. ⁹He who has ears to hear, let him hear!"

The Purpose of Parables

¹⁰And the disciples came and said to Him, "Why do You speak to them in parables?"

¹¹He answered and said to them, "Because it has been given to you to know the mysteries of the kingdom of heaven, but to them it has not been given. ¹²For whoever has, to him more will be given, and he will have abundance; but whoever does not have, even what he has will be taken away from him. ¹³Therefore I speak to them in parables, because seeing they do not see, and hearing they do not hear, nor do they understand. ¹⁴And in them the prophecy of Isaiah is fulfilled, which says:

'Hearing you will hear and shall not under-
  stand,
And seeing you will see and not perceive;
15 *For the hearts of this people have grown dull.*
  Their ears are hard of hearing,

And their eyes they have closed,
Lest they should see with their eyes and hear
with their ears,
Lest they should understand with their
hearts and turn,
So that I should[a] *heal them.* ,[b]

¹⁶But blessed *are* your eyes for they see, and your ears for they hear; ¹⁷for assuredly, I say to you that many prophets and righteous *men* desired to see what you see, and did not see *it,* and to hear what you hear, and did not hear *it.*

The Parable of the Sower Explained

¹⁸"Therefore hear the parable of the sower: ¹⁹When anyone hears the word of the kingdom, and does not understand *it,* then the wicked *one* comes and snatches away what was sown in his heart. This is he who received seed by the wayside. ²⁰But he who received the seed on stony places, this is he who hears the word and immediately receives it with joy; ²¹yet he has no root in himself, but endures only for a while. For when tribulation or persecution arises because of the word, immediately he stumbles. ²²Now he who received seed among the thorns is he who hears the word, and the cares of this world and the deceitfulness of riches choke the word, and he becomes unfruitful. ²³But he who received seed

---

13:15 [a]NU–Text and M–Text read *would.* [b]Isaiah 6:9, 10

on the good ground is he who hears the word and understands *it,* who indeed bears fruit and produces: some a hundredfold, some sixty, some thirty."

The Parable of the Wheat and the Tares

24Another parable He put forth to them, saying: "The kingdom of heaven is like a man who sowed good seed in his field; 25but while men slept, his enemy came and sowed tares among the wheat and went his way. 26But when the grain had sprouted and produced a crop, then the tares also appeared. 27So the servants of the owner came and said to him, 'Sir, did you not sow good seed in your field? How then does it have tares?' 28He said to them, 'An enemy has done this.' The servants said to him, 'Do you want us then to go and gather them up?' 29But he said, 'No, lest while you gather up the tares you also uproot the wheat with them. 30Let both grow together until the harvest, and at the time of harvest I will say to the reapers, "First gather together the tares and bind them in bundles to burn them, but gather the wheat into my barn."' "

The Parable of the Mustard Seed

31Another parable He put forth to them, saying: "The kingdom of heaven is like a mustard seed, which a man took and sowed in his field, 32which indeed is the least of all the seeds; but when it is grown it is greater than the herbs and becomes a tree, so that the birds of the air come and nest in its branches."

The Parable of the Leaven
33Another parable He spoke to them: "The kingdom of heaven is like leaven, which a woman took and hid in three measures[a] of meal till it was all leavened."

Prophecy and the Parables
34All these things Jesus spoke to the multitude in parables; and without a parable He did not speak to them, 35that it might be fulfilled which was spoken by the prophet, saying:

"I will open My mouth in parables;
I will utter things kept secret from the foun-
  dation of the world."[a]

The Parable of the Tares Explained
36Then Jesus sent the multitude away and went into the house. And His disciples came to Him, saying, "Explain to us the parable of the tares of the field."

37He answered and said to them: "He who sows the good seed is the Son of Man. 38The field is the world, the good seeds are the sons of the kingdom,

---

13:33 [a]Greek *sata*, approximately two pecks in all.
13:35 [a]Psalm 78:2

but the tares are the sons of the wicked *one*. ³⁹The enemy who sowed them is the devil, the harvest is the end of the age, and the reapers are the angels. ⁴⁰Therefore as the tares are gathered and burned in the fire, so it will be at the end of this age. ⁴¹The Son of Man will send out His angels, and they will gather out of His kingdom all things that offend, and those who practice lawlessness, ⁴²and will cast them into the furnace of fire. There will be wailing and gnashing of teeth. ⁴³Then the righteous will shine forth as the sun in the kingdom of their Father. He who has ears to hear, let him hear!

The Parable of the Hidden Treasure
⁴⁴"Again, the kingdom of heaven is like treasure hidden in a field, which a man found and hid; and for joy over it he goes and sells all that he has and buys that field.

The Parable of the Pearl of Great Price
⁴⁵"Again, the kingdom of heaven is like a merchant seeking beautiful pearls, ⁴⁶who, when he had found one pearl of great price, went and sold all that he had and bought it.

The Parable of the Dragnet
⁴⁷"Again, the kingdom of heaven is like a dragnet that was cast into the sea and gathered some of every kind, ⁴⁸which, when it was full,

they drew to shore; and they sat down and gathered the good into vessels, but threw the bad away. ⁴⁹So it will be at the end of the age. The angels will come forth, separate the wicked from among the just, ⁵⁰and cast them into the furnace of fire. There will be wailing and gnashing of teeth."

⁵¹Jesus said to them,^a "Have you understood all these things?"

They said to Him, "Yes, Lord."^b

⁵²Then He said to them, "Therefore every scribe instructed concerning^a the kingdom of heaven is like a householder who brings out of his treasure *things* new and old."

Jesus Rejected at Nazareth

⁵³Now it came to pass, when Jesus had finished these parables, that He departed from there. ⁵⁴When He had come to His own country, He taught them in their synagogue, so that they were astonished and said, "Where did this *Man* get this wisdom and *these* mighty works? ⁵⁵Is this not the carpenter's son? Is not His mother called Mary? And His brothers James, Joses,^a Simon, and Judas? ⁵⁶And His sisters, are they not all with us? Where then did this *Man* get all these things?" ⁵⁷So they were offended at Him.

But Jesus said to them, "A prophet is not without honor except in his own country and in

---

13:51 ^aNU–Text omits *Jesus said to them.* ^bNU–Text omits *Lord.* 13:52 ^aOr *for.* 13:55 ^aNU–Text reads *Joseph.*

his own house." ⁵⁸Now He did not do many mighty works there because of their unbelief.

John the Baptist Beheaded

14 At that time Herod the tetrarch heard the report about Jesus ²and said to his servants, "This is John the Baptist; he is risen from the dead, and therefore these powers are at work in him." ³For Herod had laid hold of John and bound him, and put *him* in prison for the sake of Herodias, his brother Philip's wife. ⁴Because John had said to him, "It is not lawful for you to have her." ⁵And although he wanted to put him to death, he feared the multitude, because they counted him as a prophet.

⁶But when Herod's birthday was celebrated, the daughter of Herodias danced before them and pleased Herod. ⁷Therefore he promised with an oath to give her whatever she might ask.

⁸So she, having been prompted by her mother, said, "Give me John the Baptist's head here on a platter."

⁹And the king was sorry; nevertheless, because of the oaths and because of those who sat with him, he commanded *it* to be given to *her.* ¹⁰So he sent and had John beheaded in prison. ¹¹And his head was brought on a platter and given to the girl, and she brought *it* to her mother. ¹²Then his disciples came and took away the body and buried it, and went and told Jesus.

Feeding the Five Thousand

¹³When Jesus heard *it,* He departed from there by boat to a deserted place by Himself. But when the multitudes heard it, they followed Him on foot from the cities. ¹⁴And when Jesus went out He saw a great multitude; and He was moved with compassion for them, and healed their sick. ¹⁵When it was evening, His disciples came to Him, saying, "This is a deserted place, and the hour is already late. Send the multitudes away, that they may go into the villages and buy themselves food."

¹⁶But Jesus said to them, "They do not need to go away. You give them something to eat."

¹⁷And they said to Him, "We have here only five loaves and two fish."

¹⁸He said, "Bring them here to Me." ¹⁹Then He commanded the multitudes to sit down on the grass. And He took the five loaves and the two fish, and looking up to heaven, He blessed and broke and gave the loaves to the disciples; and the disciples gave to the multitudes. ²⁰So they all ate and were filled, and they took up twelve baskets full of the fragments that remained. ²¹Now those who had eaten were about five thousand men, besides women and children.

Jesus Walks on the Sea

²²Immediately Jesus made His disciples get into the boat and go before Him to the other side, while

He sent the multitudes away. ²³And when He had sent the multitudes away, He went up on the mountain by Himself to pray. Now when evening came, He was alone there. ²⁴But the boat was now in the middle of the sea,^a tossed by the waves, for the wind was contrary.

²⁵Now in the fourth watch of the night Jesus went to them, walking on the sea. ²⁶And when the disciples saw Him walking on the sea, they were troubled, saying, "It is a ghost!" And they cried out for fear.

²⁷But immediately Jesus spoke to them, saying, "Be of good cheer! It is I; do not be afraid."

²⁸And Peter answered Him and said, "Lord, if it is You, command me to come to You on the water."

²⁹So He said, "Come." And when Peter had come down out of the boat, he walked on the water to go to Jesus. ³⁰But when he saw that the wind *was* boisterous,^a he was afraid; and beginning to sink he cried out, saying, "Lord, save me!"

³¹And immediately Jesus stretched out *His* hand and caught him, and said to him, "O you of little faith, why did you doubt?" ³²And when they got into the boat, the wind ceased.

³³Then those who were in the boat came and^a worshiped Him, saying, "Truly You are the Son of God."

14:24 ^aNU–Text reads *many furlongs away from the land.*
14:30 ^aNU–Text brackets *that* and *boisterous* as disputed.
14:33 ^aNU–Text omits *came and.*

Many Touch Him and Are Made Well

³⁴When they had crossed over, they came to the land of^a Gennesaret. ³⁵And when the men of that place recognized Him, they sent out into all that surrounding region, brought to Him all who were sick, ³⁶and begged Him that they might only touch the hem of His garment. And as many as touched *it* were made perfectly well.

Defilement Comes from Within

15 Then the scribes and Pharisees who were from Jerusalem came to Jesus, saying, ²"Why do Your disciples transgress the tradition of the elders? For they do not wash their hands when they eat bread."

³He answered and said to them, "Why do you also transgress the commandment of God because of your tradition? ⁴For God commanded, saying, *'Honor your father and your mother'*;^a and, *'He who curses father or mother, let him be put to death.'*^b ⁵But you say, 'Whoever says to his father or mother, "Whatever profit you might have received from me *is* a gift *to God*"— ⁶then he need not honor his father or mother.'^a Thus you have made the commandment^b of God of no effect by your tra-

---

14:34 ^aNU–Text reads *came to land at.* **15:4** ^aExodus 20:12; Deuteronomy 5:16 ^bExodus 21:17 **15:6** ^aNU–Text omits *or mother.* ^bNU–Text reads *word.*

dition. ⁷Hypocrites! Well did Isaiah prophesy about you, saying:

8 'These people draw near to Me with their mouth,
   And[a] honor Me with their lips,
   But their heart is far from Me.
9 And in vain they worship Me,
   Teaching as doctrines the commandments of men.'"[a]

¹⁰When He had called the multitude to *Himself*, He said to them, "Hear and understand: ¹¹Not what goes into the mouth defiles a man; but what comes out of the mouth, this defiles a man."

¹²Then His disciples came and said to Him, "Do You know that the Pharisees were offended when they heard this saying?"

¹³But He answered and said, "Every plant which My heavenly Father has not planted will be uprooted. ¹⁴Let them alone. They are blind leaders of the blind. And if the blind leads the blind, both will fall into a ditch."

¹⁵Then Peter answered and said to Him, "Explain this parable to us."

¹⁶So Jesus said, "Are you also still without understanding? ¹⁷Do you not yet understand that

15:8 [a]NU–Text omits *draw near to Me with their mouth, And.* **15:9** [a]Isaiah 29:13

whatever enters the mouth goes into the stomach and is eliminated? [18]But those things which proceed out of the mouth come from the heart, and they defile a man. [19]For out of the heart proceed evil thoughts, murders, adulteries, fornications, thefts, false witness, blasphemies. [20]These are *the things* which defile a man, but to eat with unwashed hands does not defile a man."

A Gentile Shows Her Faith

[21]Then Jesus went out from there and departed to the region of Tyre and Sidon. [22]And behold, a woman of Canaan came from that region and cried out to Him, saying, "Have mercy on me, O Lord, Son of David! My daughter is severely demon-possessed."

[23]But He answered her not a word.

And His disciples came and urged Him, saying, "Send her away, for she cries out after us."

[24]But He answered and said, "I was not sent except to the lost sheep of the house of Israel."

[25]Then she came and worshiped Him, saying, "Lord, help me!"

[26]But He answered and said, "It is not good to take the children's bread and throw *it* to the little dogs."

[27]And she said, "Yes, Lord, yet even the little dogs eat the crumbs which fall from their masters' table."

[28]Then Jesus answered and said to her, "O

woman, great *is* your faith! Let it be to you as you desire." And her daughter was healed from that very hour.

Jesus Heals Great Multitudes

29Jesus departed from there, skirted the Sea of Galilee, and went up on the mountain and sat down there. 30Then great multitudes came to Him, having with them *the* lame, blind, mute, maimed, and many others; and they laid them down at Jesus' feet, and He healed them. 31So the multitude marveled when they saw *the* mute speaking, *the* maimed made whole, *the* lame walking, and *the* blind seeing; and they glorified the God of Israel.

Feeding the Four Thousand

32Now Jesus called His disciples to *Himself* and said, "I have compassion on the multitude, because they have now continued with Me three days and have nothing to eat. And I do not want to send them away hungry, lest they faint on the way."

33Then His disciples said to Him, "Where could we get enough bread in the wilderness to fill such a great multitude?"

34Jesus said to them, "How many loaves do you have?"

And they said, "Seven, and a few little fish."

35So He commanded the multitude to sit down

on the ground. [36]And He took the seven loaves and the fish and gave thanks, broke *them* and gave *them* to His disciples; and the disciples *gave* to the multitude. [37]So they all ate and were filled, and they took up seven large baskets full of the fragments that were left. [38]Now those who ate were four thousand men, besides women and children. [39]And He sent away the multitude, got into the boat, and came to the region of Magdala.[a]

The Pharisees and Sadducees Seek a Sign

16 Then the Pharisees and Sadducees came, and testing Him asked that He would show them a sign from heaven. [2]He answered and said to them, "When it is evening you say, '*It will be* fair weather, for the sky is red'; [3]and in the morning, '*It will be* foul weather today, for the sky is red and threatening.' Hypocrites![a] You know how to discern the face of the sky, but you cannot *discern* the signs of the times. [4]A wicked and adulterous generation seeks after a sign, and no sign shall be given to it except the sign of the prophet[a] Jonah." And He left them and departed.

The Leaven of the Pharisees and Sadducees

[5]Now when His disciples had come to the other side, they had forgotten to take bread. [6]Then Jesus

---

15:39 [a]NU–Text reads *Magadan*. **16:3** [a]NU–Text omits *Hypocrites*. **16:4** [a]NU–Text omits *the prophet*.

said to them, "Take heed and beware of the leaven of the Pharisees and the Sadducees."

7And they reasoned among themselves, saying, "*It is* because we have taken no bread."

8But Jesus, being aware of *it,* said to them, "O you of little faith, why do you reason among yourselves because you have brought no bread?a 9Do you not yet understand, or remember the five loaves of the five thousand and how many baskets you took up? 10Nor the seven loaves of the four thousand and how many large baskets you took up? 11How is it you do not understand that I did not speak to you concerning bread?—*but* to beware of the leaven of the Pharisees and Sadducees." 12Then they understood that He did not tell *them* to beware of the leaven of bread, but of the doctrine of the Pharisees and Sadducees.

Peter Confesses Jesus as the Christ
13When Jesus came into the region of Caesarea Philippi, He asked His disciples, saying, "Who do men say that I, the Son of Man, am?"

14So they said, "Some *say* John the Baptist, some Elijah, and others Jeremiah or one of the prophets."

15He said to them, "But who do you say that I am?"

16Simon Peter answered and said, "You are the Christ, the Son of the living God."

16:8 aNU–Text reads *you have no bread.*

[17]Jesus answered and said to him, "Blessed are you, Simon Bar-Jonah, for flesh and blood has not revealed *this* to you, but My Father who is in heaven. [18]And I also say to you that you are Peter, and on this rock I will build My church, and the gates of Hades shall not prevail against it. [19]And I will give you the keys of the kingdom of heaven, and whatever you bind on earth will be bound in heaven, and whatever you loose on earth will be loosed[a] in heaven."

[20]Then He commanded His disciples that they should tell no one that He was Jesus the Christ.

Jesus Predicts His Death and Resurrection

[21]From that time Jesus began to show to His disciples that He must go to Jerusalem, and suffer many things from the elders and chief priests and scribes, and be killed, and be raised the third day.

[22]Then Peter took Him aside and began to rebuke Him, saying, "Far be it from You, Lord; this shall not happen to You!"

[23]But He turned and said to Peter, "Get behind Me, Satan! You are an offense to Me, for you are not mindful of the things of God, but the things of men."

Take Up the Cross and Follow Him

[24]Then Jesus said to His disciples, "If anyone desires to come after Me, let him deny himself,

---

16:19 [a]Or *will have been bound . . . will have been loosed.*

and take up his cross, and follow Me. 25For whoever desires to save his life will lose it, but whoever loses his life for My sake will find it. 26For what profit is it to a man if he gains the whole world, and loses his own soul? Or what will a man give in exchange for his soul? 27For the Son of Man will come in the glory of His Father with His angels, and then He will reward each according to his works.28Assuredly, I say to you, there are some standing here who shall not taste death till they see the Son of Man coming in His kingdom."

Jesus Transfigured on the Mount

17Now after six days Jesus took Peter, James, and John his brother, led them up on a high mountain by themselves; 2and He was transfigured before them. His face shone like the sun, and His clothes became as white as the light. 3And behold, Moses and Elijah appeared to them, talking with Him. 4Then Peter answered and said to Jesus, "Lord, it is good for us to be here; if You wish, let usa make here three tabernacles: one for You, one for Moses, and one for Elijah."

5While he was still speaking, behold, a bright cloud overshadowed them; and suddenly a voice came out of the cloud, saying, "This is My beloved Son, in whom I am well pleased. Hear Him!" 6And when the disciples heard it, they fell on their faces and were greatly afraid. 7But Jesus

17:4 aNU–Text reads I will.

came and touched them and said, "Arise, and do not be afraid." [8]When they had lifted up their eyes, they saw no one but Jesus only.

[9]Now as they came down from the mountain, Jesus commanded them, saying, "Tell the vision to no one until the Son of Man is risen from the dead."

[10]And His disciples asked Him, saying, "Why then do the scribes say that Elijah must come first?"

[11]Jesus answered and said to them, "Indeed, Elijah is coming first[a] and will restore all things. [12]But I say to you that Elijah has come already, and they did not know him but did to him whatever they wished. Likewise the Son of Man is also about to suffer at their hands." [13]Then the disciples understood that He spoke to them of John the Baptist.

A Boy Is Healed

[14]And when they had come to the multitude, a man came to Him, kneeling down to Him and saying, [15]"Lord, have mercy on my son, for he is an epileptic[a] and suffers severely; for he often falls into the fire and often into the water. [16]So I brought him to Your disciples, but they could not cure him."

[17]Then Jesus answered and said, "O faithless and perverse generation, how long shall I be with

17:11 [a]NU–Text omits *first.* **17:15** [a]Literally *moonstruck.*

you? How long shall I bear with you? Bring him here to Me." [18]And Jesus rebuked the demon, and it came out of him; and the child was cured from that very hour.

[19]Then the disciples came to Jesus privately and said, "Why could we not cast it out?"

[20]So Jesus said to them, "Because of your unbelief;[a] for assuredly, I say to you, if you have faith as a mustard seed, you will say to this mountain, 'Move from here to there,' and it will move; and nothing will be impossible for you. [21]However, this kind does not go out except by prayer and fasting."[a]

Jesus Again Predicts His Death and Resurrection

[22]Now while they were staying[a] in Galilee, Jesus said to them, "The Son of Man is about to be betrayed into the hands of men, [23]and they will kill Him, and the third day He will be raised up." And they were exceedingly sorrowful.

Peter and His Master Pay Their Taxes

[24]When they had come to Capernaum,[a] those who received the *temple* tax came to Peter and said, "Does your Teacher not pay the *temple* tax?"

[25]He said, "Yes."

17:20 [a]NU–Text reads *little faith*. **17:21** [a]NU–Text omits this verse. **17:22** [a]NU–Text reads *gathering together*. **17:24** [a]NU–Text reads *Capharnaum* (here and elsewhere).

And when he had come into the house, Jesus antic-ipated him, saying, "What do you think, Simon? From whom do the kings of the earth take customs or taxes, from their sons or from strangers?"

26Peter said to Him, "From strangers."

Jesus said to him, "Then the sons are free. 27Nevertheless, lest we offend them, go to the sea, cast in a hook, and take the fish that comes up first. And when you have opened its mouth, you will find a piece of money;a take that and give it to them for Me and you."

Who Is the Greatest?

18 At that time the disciples came to Jesus, saying, "Who then is greatest in the kingdom of heaven?"

2Then Jesus called a little child to Him, set him in the midst of them, 3and said, "Assuredly, I say to you, unless you are converted and become as little children, you will by no means enter the kingdom of heaven. 4Therefore whoever humbles himself as this little child is the greatest in the kingdom of heaven. 5Whoever receives one little child like this in My name receives Me.

Jesus Warns of Offenses

6"Whoever causes one of these little ones who believe in Me to sin, it would be better for him if

17:27 aGreek *stater*, the exact amount to pay the temple tax (didrachma) for two

a millstone were hung around his neck, and he were drowned in the depth of the sea. [7]Woe to the world because of offenses! For offenses must come, but woe to that man by whom the offense comes!

[8]"If your hand or foot causes you to sin, cut it off and cast *it* from you. It is better for you to enter into life lame or maimed, rather than having two hands or two feet, to be cast into the everlasting fire. [9]And if your eye causes you to sin, pluck it out and cast *it* from you. It is better for you to enter into life with one eye, rather than having two eyes, to be cast into hell fire.

The Parable of the Lost Sheep

[10]"Take heed that you do not despise one of these little ones, for I say to you that in heaven their angels always see the face of My Father who is in heaven. [11]For the Son of Man has come to save that which was lost.[a]

[12]"What do you think? If a man has a hundred sheep, and one of them goes astray, does he not leave the ninety-nine and go to the mountains to seek the one that is straying? [13]And if he should find it, assuredly, I say to you, he rejoices more over that *sheep* than over the ninety-nine that did not go astray. [14]Even so it is not the will of your Father who is in heaven that one of these little ones should perish.

18:11 [a]NU–Text omits this verse.

Dealing with a Sinning Brother

15"Moreover if your brother sins against you, go and tell him his fault between you and him alone. If he hears you, you have gained your brother. 16But if he will not hear, take with you one or two more, that *'by the mouth of two or three witnesses every word may be established.'*a 17And if he refuses to hear them, tell *it* to the church. But if he refuses even to hear the church, let him be to you like a heathen and a tax collector.

18"Assuredly, I say to you, whatever you bind on earth will be bound in heaven, and whatever you loose on earth will be loosed in heaven.

19"Again I saya to you that if two of you agree on earth concerning anything that they ask, it will be done for them by My Father in heaven. 20For where two or three are gathered together in My name, I am there in the midst of them."

The Parable of the Unforgiving Servant

21Then Peter came to Him and said, "Lord, how often shall my brother sin against me, and I forgive him? Up to seven times?"

22Jesus said to him, "I do not say to you, up to seven times, but up to seventy times seven. 23Therefore the kingdom of heaven is like a certain king who wanted to settle accounts with his

---

18:16 aDeuteronomy 19:15 **18:19** aNU–Text and M–Text read *Again, assuredly, I say.*

servants. ²⁴And when he had begun to settle accounts, one was brought to him who owed him ten thousand talents. ²⁵But as he was not able to pay, his master commanded that he be sold, with his wife and children and all that he had, and that payment be made. ²⁶The servant therefore fell down before him, saying, 'Master, have patience with me, and I will pay you all.' ²⁷Then the master of that servant was moved with compassion, released him, and forgave him the debt.

²⁸"But that servant went out and found one of his fellow servants who owed him a hundred denarii; and he laid hands on him and took *him* by the throat, saying, 'Pay me what you owe!' ²⁹So his fellow servant fell down at his feet[a] and begged him, saying, 'Have patience with me, and I will pay you all.'[b] ³⁰And he would not, but went and threw him into prison till he should pay the debt. ³¹So when his fellow servants saw what had been done, they were very grieved, and came and told their master all that had been done. ³²Then his master, after he had called him, said to him, 'You wicked servant! I forgave you all that debt because you begged me. ³³Should you not also have had compassion on your fellow servant, just as I had pity on you?' ³⁴And his master was angry, and delivered him to the torturers until he should pay all that was due to him.

18:29 [a]NU–Text omits *at his feet.* [b]NU–Text and M–Text omit *all.*

³⁵"So My heavenly Father also will do to you if each of you, from his heart, does not forgive his brother his trespasses.''^a

Marriage and Divorce

19 Now it came to pass, when Jesus had finished these sayings, *that* He departed from Galilee and came to the region of Judea beyond the Jordan. ²And great multitudes followed Him, and He healed them there.

³The Pharisees also came to Him, testing Him, and saying to Him, "Is it lawful for a man to divorce his wife for *just* any reason?"

⁴And He answered and said to them, "Have you not read that He who made^a *them* at the beginning *'made them male and female,'*^b ⁵and said, *'For this reason a man shall leave his father and mother and be joined to his wife, and the two shall become one flesh.'*^a ⁶So then, they are no longer two but one flesh. Therefore what God has joined together, let not man separate."

⁷They said to Him, "Why then did Moses command to give a certificate of divorce, and to put her away?"

⁸He said to them, "Moses, because of the hardness of your hearts, permitted you to divorce your wives, but from the beginning it was not so. ⁹And I say to you, whoever divorces his wife, except for

---

18:35 ^aNU–Text omits *his trespasses.* **19:4** ^aNU–Text reads *created.* ^bGenesis 1:27; 5:2 **19:5** ^aGenesis 2:24

sexual immorality,[a] and marries another, commits adultery; and whoever marries her who is divorced commits adultery."

10His disciples said to Him, "If such is the case of the man with *his* wife, it is better not to marry."

Jesus Teaches on Celibacy

11But He said to them, "All cannot accept this saying, but only *those* to whom it has been given: 12For there are eunuchs who were born thus from *their* mother's womb, and there are eunuchs who were made eunuchs by men, and there are eunuchs who have made themselves eunuchs for the kingdom of heaven's sake. He who is able to accept *it,* let him accept *it."*

Jesus Blesses Little Children

13Then little children were brought to Him that He might put *His* hands on them and pray, but the disciples rebuked them. 14But Jesus said, "Let the little children come to Me, and do not forbid them; for of such is the kingdom of heaven." 15And He laid *His* hands on them and departed from there.

Jesus Counsels the Rich Young Ruler

16Now behold, one came and said to Him, "Good[a] Teacher, what good thing shall I do that I may have eternal life?"

17So He said to him, "Why do you call Me

19:9 [a]Or *fornication.* **19:16** [a]NU–Text omits *Good.*

good?ᵃ No one *is* good but One, *that is,* God.ᵇ But if you want to enter into life, keep the commandments."

¹⁸He said to Him, "Which ones?"

Jesus said, " *'You shall not murder,' 'You shall not commit adultery,' 'You shall not steal,' 'You shall not bear false witness,'* ¹⁹*'Honor your father and your mother,'*ᵃ and, *'You shall love your neighbor as yourself.'"*ᵇ

²⁰The young man said to Him, "All these things I have kept from my youth.ᵃ What do I still lack?"

²¹Jesus said to him, "If you want to be perfect, go, sell what you have and give to the poor, and you will have treasure in heaven; and come, follow Me."

²²But when the young man heard that saying, he went away sorrowful, for he had great possessions.

With God All Things Are Possible

²³Then Jesus said to His disciples, "Assuredly, I say to you that it is hard for a rich man to enter the kingdom of heaven. ²⁴And again I say to you, it is easier for a camel to go through the eye of a needle than for a rich man to enter the kingdom of God."

19:17 ᵃNU–Text reads *Why do you ask Me about what is good?* ᵇNU–Text reads *There is One who is good.* **19:19** ᵃExodus 20:12–16; Deuteronomy 5:16–20 ᵇLeviticus 19:18 **19:20** ᵃNU–Text omits *from my youth.*

^{25}When His disciples heard *it,* they were greatly astonished, saying, "Who then can be saved?"

^{26}But Jesus looked at *them* and said to them, "With men this is impossible, but with God all things are possible."

^{27}Then Peter answered and said to Him, "See, we have left all and followed You. Therefore what shall we have?"

^{28}So Jesus said to them, "Assuredly I say to you, that in the regeneration, when the Son of Man sits on the throne of His glory, you who have followed Me will also sit on twelve thrones, judging the twelve tribes of Israel. ^{29}And everyone who has left houses or brothers or sisters or father or mother or wife[a] or children or lands, for My name's sake, shall receive a hundredfold, and inherit eternal life. ^{30}But many *who are* first will be last, and the last first.

The Parable of the Workers in the Vineyard

20 "For the kingdom of heaven is like a landowner who went out early in the morning to hire laborers for his vineyard. ^{2}Now when he had agreed with the laborers for a denarius a day, he sent them into his vineyard. ^{3}And he went out about the third hour and saw others standing idle in the marketplace, ^{4}and said to them, 'You also go into the vineyard, and whatever is right I will give you.' So they went. ^{5}Again

19:29 [a]NU–Text omits *or wife.*

he went out about the sixth and the ninth hour, and did likewise. ⁶And about the eleventh hour he went out and found others standing idle,^a and said to them, 'Why have you been standing here idle all day?' ⁷They said to him, 'Because no one hired us.' He said to them, 'You also go into the vineyard, and whatever is right you will receive.'^a

⁸"So when evening had come, the owner of the vineyard said to his steward, 'Call the laborers and give them *their* wages, beginning with the last to the first.' ⁹And when those came who *were hired* about the eleventh hour, they each received a denarius. ¹⁰But when the first came, they supposed that they would receive more; and they likewise received each a denarius. ¹¹And when they had received *it,* they complained against the landowner, ¹²saying, 'These last *men* have worked *only* one hour, and you made them equal to us who have borne the burden and the heat of the day.' ¹³But he answered one of them and said, 'Friend, I am doing you no wrong. Did you not agree with me for a denarius? ¹⁴Take *what is* yours and go your way. I wish to give to this last man *the same* as to you. ¹⁵Is it not lawful for me to do what I wish with my own things? Or is your eye evil because I am good?' ¹⁶So the last will be first, and the first last. For many are called, but few chosen."^a

---

20:6 ^aNU–Text omits *idle.* **20:7** ^aNU–Text omits the last clause of this verse. **20:16** ^aNU–Text omits the last sentence of this verse.

Jesus a Third Time Predicts His Death and Resurrection

[17]Now Jesus, going up to Jerusalem, took the twelve disciples aside on the road and said to them, [18]"Behold, we are going up to Jerusalem, and the Son of Man will be betrayed to the chief priests and to the scribes; and they will condemn Him to death, [19]and deliver Him to the Gentiles to mock and to scourge and to crucify. And the third day He will rise again."

Greatness Is Serving

[20]Then the mother of Zebedee's sons came to Him with her sons, kneeling down and asking something from Him.

[21]And He said to her, "What do you wish?"

She said to Him, "Grant that these two sons of mine may sit, one on Your right hand and the other on the left, in Your kingdom."

[22]But Jesus answered and said, "You do not know what you ask. Are you able to drink the cup that I am about to drink, and be baptized with the baptism that I am baptized with?"[a]

They said to Him, "We are able."

[23]So He said to them, "You will indeed drink My cup, and be baptized with the baptism that I am baptized with;[a] but to sit on My right hand and on

---

20:22 [a]NU–Text omits *and be baptized with the baptism that I am baptized with.* **20:23** [a]NU–Text omits *and be baptized with the baptism that I am baptized with.*

My left is not Mine to give, but *it is for those* for whom it is prepared by My Father."

24And when the ten heard *it,* they were greatly displeased with the two brothers. 25But Jesus called them to *Himself* and said, "You know that the rulers of the Gentiles lord it over them, and those who are great exercise authority over them. 26Yet it shall not be so among you; but whoever desires to become great among you, let him be your servant. 27And whoever desires to be first among you, let him be your slave— 28just as the Son of Man did not come to be served, but to serve, and to give His life a ransom for many."

Two Blind Men Receive Their Sight

29Now as they went out of Jericho, a great multitude followed Him. 30And behold, two blind men sitting by the road, when they heard that Jesus was passing by, cried out, saying, "Have mercy on us, O Lord, Son of David!"

31Then the multitude warned them that they should be quiet; but they cried out all the more, saying, "Have mercy on us, O Lord, Son of David!"

32So Jesus stood still and called them, and said, "What do you want Me to do for you?"

33They said to Him, "Lord, that our eyes may be opened." 34So Jesus had compassion and touched their eyes. And immediately their eyes received sight, and they followed Him.

The Triumphal Entry

21 Now when they drew near Jerusalem, and came to Bethphage,[a] at the Mount of Olives, then Jesus sent two disciples, [2]saying to them, "Go into the village opposite you, and immediately you will find a donkey tied, and a colt with her. Loose *them* and bring *them* to Me. [3]And if anyone says anything to you, you shall say, 'The Lord has need of them,' and immediately he will send them."

[4]All[a] this was done that it might be fulfilled which was spoken by the prophet, saying:

5   *"Tell the daughter of Zion,*
    'Behold, your King is coming to you,
    Lowly, and sitting on a donkey,
    A colt, the foal of a donkey.' "[a]

[6]So the disciples went and did as Jesus commanded them. [7]They brought the donkey and the colt, laid their clothes on them, and set *Him*[a] on them. [8]And a very great multitude spread their clothes on the road; others cut down branches from the trees and spread *them* on the road. [9]Then the multitudes who went before and those who followed cried out, saying:

21:1 [a]M–Text reads *Bethsphage.* **21:4** [a]NU–Text omits *All.* **21:5** [a]Zechariah 9:9 **21:7** [a]NU–Text reads *and He sat.*

"Hosanna to the Son of David!
*'Blessed is He who comes in the name of the
  LORD!'*[a]
Hosanna in the highest!"

¹⁰And when He had come into Jerusalem, all the city was moved, saying, "Who is this?"

¹¹So the multitudes said, "This is Jesus, the prophet from Nazareth of Galilee."

Jesus Cleanses the Temple

¹²Then Jesus went into the temple of God[a] and drove out all those who bought and sold in the temple, and overturned the tables of the money changers and the seats of those who sold doves. ¹³And He said to them, "It is written, *'My house shall be called a house of prayer,'*[a] but you have made it a *'den of thieves.'"*[b]

¹⁴Then *the* blind and *the* lame came to Him in the temple, and He healed them. ¹⁵But when the chief priests and scribes saw the wonderful things that He did, and the children crying out in the temple and saying, "Hosanna to the Son of David!" they were indignant ¹⁶and said to Him, "Do You hear what these are saying?"

And Jesus said to them, "Yes. Have you never read,

21:9 [a]Psalm 118:26 **21:12** [a]NU–Text omits *of God.*
21:13 [a]Isaiah 56:7 [b]Jeremiah 7:11

'Out of the mouth of babes and nursing
infants
You have perfected praise'?"[a]

17Then He left them and went out of the city to
Bethany, and He lodged there.

The Fig Tree Withered
18Now in the morning, as He returned to the city,
He was hungry. 19And seeing a fig tree by the road,
He came to it and found nothing on it but leaves,
and said to it, "Let no fruit grow on you ever
again." Immediately the fig tree withered away.

The Lesson of the Withered Fig Tree
20And when the disciples saw *it,* they marveled,
saying, "How did the fig tree wither away so
soon?"
21So Jesus answered and said to them,
"Assuredly, I say to you, if you have faith and do
not doubt, you will not only do what was done to
the fig tree, but also if you say to this mountain,
'Be removed and be cast into the sea,' it will be
done. 22And whatever things you ask in prayer,
believing, you will receive."

Jesus' Authority Questioned
23Now when He came into the temple, the chief
priests and the elders of the people confronted

21:16 [a]Psalm 8:2

Him as He was teaching, and said, "By what authority are You doing these things? And who gave You this authority?"

24But Jesus answered and said to them, "I also will ask you one thing, which if you tell Me, I likewise will tell you by what authority I do these things: 25The baptism of John—where was it from? From heaven or from men?"

And they reasoned among themselves, saying, "If we say, 'From heaven,' He will say to us, 'Why then did you not believe him?' 26But if we say, 'From men,' we fear the multitude, for all count John as a prophet." 27So they answered Jesus and said, "We do not know."

And He said to them, "Neither will I tell you by what authority I do these things.

The Parable of the Two Sons

28"But what do you think? A man had two sons, and he came to the first and said, 'Son, go, work today in my vineyard.' 29He answered and said, 'I will not,' but afterward he regretted it and went. 30Then he came to the second and said likewise. And he answered and said, 'I *go,* sir,' but he did not go. 31Which of the two did the will of *his* father?"

They said to Him, "The first."

Jesus said to them, "Assuredly, I say to you that tax collectors and harlots enter the kingdom of God before you. 32For John came to you in the way of righteousness, and you did not believe him; but tax collectors and harlots believed him; and when you saw *it,* you did not afterward relent and believe him.

The Parable of the Wicked Vinedressers

33"Hear another parable: There was a certain landowner who planted a vineyard and set a hedge around it, dug a winepress in it and built a tower. And he leased it to vinedressers and went into a far country. 34Now when vintage-time drew near, he sent his servants to the vinedressers, that they might receive its fruit. 35And the vinedressers took his servants, beat one, killed one, and stoned another. 36Again he sent other servants, more than the first, and they did likewise to them. 37Then last of all he sent his son to them, saying, 'They will respect my son.' 38But when the vinedressers saw the son, they said among themselves, 'This is the heir. Come, let us kill him and seize his inheritance.' 39So they took him and cast *him* out of the vineyard and killed *him.*

40"Therefore, when the owner of the vineyard comes, what will he do to those vinedressers?"

41They said to Him, "He will destroy those wicked men miserably, and lease *his* vineyard to other vinedressers who will render to him the fruits in their seasons."

42Jesus said to them, "Have you never read in the Scriptures:

'The stone which the builders rejected
Has become the chief cornerstone.
This was the LORD's doing,
And it is marvelous in our eyes'?[a]

43"Therefore I say to you, the kingdom of God will be taken from you and given to a nation bearing the fruits of it. 44And whoever falls on this stone will be broken; but on whomever it falls, it will grind him to powder."

45Now when the chief priests and Pharisees heard His parables, they perceived that He was speaking of them. 46But when they sought to lay hands on Him, they feared the multitudes, because they took Him for a prophet.

The Parable of the Wedding Feast

22 And Jesus answered and spoke to them again by parables and said: 2"The kingdom of heaven is like a certain king who arranged a marriage for his son, 3and sent out his servants to call those who were invited to the wedding; and they were not willing to come. 4Again, he sent out other servants, saying, 'Tell those who are invited, "See, I have prepared my dinner; my oxen and fatted cattle *are* killed, and all things *are* ready. Come to the wedding."' 5But they made light of it and went their ways, one to his own farm, another to his business. 6And the rest

21:42 [a]Psalm 118:22–23

seized his servants, treated *them* spitefully, and killed *them.* ⁷But when the king heard *about it,* he was furious. And he sent out his armies, destroyed those murderers, and burned up their city. ⁸Then he said to his servants, 'The wedding is ready, but those who were invited were not worthy. ⁹Therefore go into the highways, and as many as you find, invite to the wedding.' ¹⁰So those servants went out into the highways and gathered together all whom they found, both bad and good. And the wedding *hall* was filled with guests.

¹¹"But when the king came in to see the guests, he saw a man there who did not have on a wedding garment. ¹²So he said to him, 'Friend, how did you come in here without a wedding garment?' And he was speechless. ¹³Then the king said to the servants, 'Bind him hand and foot, take him away, and[a] cast *him* into outer darkness; there will be weeping and gnashing of teeth.'

¹⁴"For many are called, but few *are* chosen."

The Pharisees: Is It Lawful
to Pay Taxes to Caesar?

¹⁵Then the Pharisees went and plotted how they might entangle Him in *His* talk. ¹⁶And they sent to Him their disciples with the Herodians, saying, "Teacher, we know that You

---

22:13 [a]NU–Text omits *take him away, and.*

are true, and teach the way of God in truth; nor do You care about anyone, for You do not regard the person of men. [17]Tell us, therefore, what do You think? Is it lawful to pay taxes to Caesar, or not?"

[18]But Jesus perceived their wickedness, and said, "Why do you test Me, *you* hypocrites? [19]Show Me the tax money."

So they brought Him a denarius.

[20]And He said to them, "Whose image and inscription *is* this?"

[21]They said to Him, "Caesar's."

And He said to them, "Render therefore to Caesar the things that are Caesar's, and to God the things that are God's." [22]When they had heard *these words,* they marveled, and left Him and went their way.

The Sadducees: What About the Resurrection?

[23]The same day the Sadducees, who say there is no resurrection, came to Him and asked Him, [24]saying: "Teacher, Moses said that if a man dies, having no children, his brother shall marry his wife and raise up offspring for his brother. [25]Now there were with us seven brothers. The first died after he had married, and having no offspring, left his wife to his brother. [26]Likewise the second also, and the third, even to the seventh. [27]Last of all the woman died also. [28]Therefore, in the resur-

rection, whose wife of the seven will she be? For they all had her."

²⁹Jesus answered and said to them, "You are mistaken, not knowing the Scriptures nor the power of God. ³⁰For in the resurrection they neither marry nor are given in marriage, but are like angels of God^a in heaven. ³¹But concerning the resurrection of the dead, have you not read what was spoken to you by God, saying, ³²*'I am the God of Abraham, the God of Isaac, and the God of Jacob'*^a God is not the God of the dead, but of the living." ³³And when the multitudes heard *this,* they were astonished at His teaching.

The Scribes: Which Is the First Commandment of All?

³⁴But when the Pharisees heard that He had silenced the Sadducees, they gathered together. ³⁵Then one of them, a lawyer, asked *Him a question,* testing Him, and saying, ³⁶"Teacher, which *is* the great commandment in the law?"

³⁷Jesus said to him, " *'You shall love the LORD your God with all your heart, with all your soul, and with all your mind.'*^a ³⁸This is *the* first and great commandment. ³⁹And *the* second *is* like it: *'You shall love your neighbor as yourself.'*^a ⁴⁰On these two commandments hang all the Law and the Prophets."

22:30 ^aNU–Text omits *of God.* **22:32** ^aExodus 3:6, 15 **22:37** ^aDeuteronomy 6:5 **22:39** ^aLeviticus 19:18

Jesus: How Can David Call
His Descendant Lord?

[41]While the Pharisees were gathered together, Jesus asked them, [42]saying, "What do you think about the Christ? Whose Son is He?"

They said to Him, "*The Son* of David."

[43]He said to them, "How then does David in the Spirit call Him '*Lord,*' saying:

[44] '*The LORD said to my Lord,*
"*Sit at My right hand,*
Till I make Your enemies Your footstool" 'a

[45]If David then calls Him '*Lord,*' how is He his Son?" [46]And no one was able to answer Him a word, nor from that day on did anyone dare question Him anymore.

Woe to the Scribes and Pharisees

23 Then Jesus spoke to the multitudes and to His disciples, [2]saying: "The scribes and the Pharisees sit in Moses' seat. [3]Therefore whatever they tell you to observe,a *that* observe and do, but do not do according to their works; for they say, and do not do. [4]For they bind heavy burdens, hard to bear, and lay *them* on men's shoulders; but they *themselves* will not move them with one of their fingers. [5]But all their works they do to be seen by

22:44 aPsalm 110:1 23:3 aNU–Text omits *to observe*.

men. They make their phylacteries broad and enlarge the borders of their garments. ⁶They love the best places at feasts, the best seats in the synagogues, ⁷greetings in the marketplaces, and to be called by men, 'Rabbi, Rabbi.' ⁸But you, do not be called 'Rabbi'; for One is your Teacher, the Christ,ᵃ and you are all brethren. ⁹Do not call anyone on earth your father; for One is your Father, He who is in heaven. ¹⁰And do not be called teachers; for One is your Teacher, the Christ. ¹¹But he who is greatest among you shall be your servant. ¹²And whoever exalts himself will be humbled, and he who humbles himself will be exalted.

¹³"But woe to you, scribes and Pharisees, hypocrites! For you shut up the kingdom of heaven against men; for you neither go in *yourselves,* nor do you allow those who are entering to go in. ¹⁴Woe to you, scribes and Pharisees, hypocrites! For you devour widows' houses, and for a pretense make long prayers. Therefore you will receive greater condemnation.ᵃ

¹⁵"Woe to you, scribes and Pharisees, hypocrites! For you travel land and sea to win one proselyte, and when he is won, you make him twice as much a son of hell as yourselves.

¹⁶"Woe to you, blind guides, who say, 'Whoever swears by the temple, it is nothing; but

---

23:8 ᵃNU–Text omits *the Christ.* **23:14** ᵃNU–Text omits this verse.

whoever swears by the gold of the temple, he is obliged *to perform it.*' [17]Fools and blind! For which is greater, the gold or the temple that sanctifies[a] the gold? [18]And, 'Whoever swears by the altar, it is nothing; but whoever swears by the gift that is on it, he is obliged *to perform it.*' [19]Fools and blind! For which is greater, the gift or the altar that sanctifies the gift? [20]Therefore he who swears by the altar, swears by it and by all things on it. [21]He who swears by the temple, swears by it and by Him who dwells[a] in it. [22]And he who swears by heaven, swears by the throne of God and by Him who sits on it.

[23]"Woe to you, scribes and Pharisees, hypocrites! For you pay tithe of mint and anise and cummin, and have neglected the weightier *matters* of the law: justice and mercy and faith. These you ought to have done, without leaving the others undone. [24]Blind guides, who strain out a gnat and swallow a camel!

[25]"Woe to you, scribes and Pharisees, hypocrites! For you cleanse the outside of the cup and dish, but inside they are full of extortion and self-indulgence.[a] [26]Blind Pharisee, first cleanse the inside of the cup and dish, that the outside of them may be clean also.

[27]"Woe to you, scribes and Pharisees, hypocrites! For you are like whitewashed tombs

23:17 [a]NU–Text reads *sanctified.* **23:21** [a]M–Text reads *dwelt.* **23:25** [a]M–Text reads *unrighteousness.*

which indeed appear beautiful outwardly, but inside are full of dead *men's* bones and all uncleanness. [28]Even so you also outwardly appear righteous to men, but inside you are full of hypocrisy and lawlessness.

[29]"Woe to you, scribes and Pharisees, hypocrites! Because you build the tombs of the prophets and adorn the monuments of the righteous, [30]and say, 'If we had lived in the days of our fathers, we would not have been partakers with them in the blood of the prophets.'

[31]"Therefore you are witnesses against yourselves that you are sons of those who murdered the prophets. [32]Fill up, then, the measure of your fathers' *guilt.* [33]Serpents, brood of vipers! How can you escape the condemnation of hell? [34]Therefore, indeed, I send you prophets, wise men, and scribes: *some* of them you will kill and crucify, and *some* of them you will scourge in your synagogues and persecute from city to city, [35]that on you may come all the righteous blood shed on the earth, from the blood of righteous Abel to the blood of Zechariah, son of Berechiah, whom you murdered between the temple and the altar. [36]Assuredly, I say to you, all these things will come upon this generation.

Jesus Laments over Jerusalem
[37]"O Jerusalem, Jerusalem, the one who kills the prophets and stones those who are sent to her!

How often I wanted to gather your children together, as a hen gathers her chicks under *her* wings, but you were not willing! [38]See! Your house is left to you desolate; [39]for I say to you, you shall see Me no more till you say, *'Blessed is He who comes in the name of the LORD!'"*[a]

Jesus Predicts the Destruction of the Temple

24 Then Jesus went out and departed from the temple, and His disciples came up to show Him the buildings of the temple. [2]And Jesus said to them, "Do you not see all these things? Assuredly, I say to you, not *one* stone shall be left here upon another, that shall not be thrown down."

The Signs of the Times
and the End of the Age

[3]Now as He sat on the Mount of Olives, the disciples came to Him privately, saying, "Tell us, when will these things be? And what *will be* the sign of Your coming, and of the end of the age?"

[4]And Jesus answered and said to them: "Take heed that no one deceives you. [5]For many will come in My name, saying, 'I am the Christ,' and will deceive many. [6]And you will hear of wars and rumors of wars. See that you are not troubled; for all[a] *these things* must come to pass, but the end is not yet. [7]For nation will rise against nation, and kingdom against kingdom. And there will be

---

23:39 [a]Psalm 118:26 **24:6** [a]NU–Text omits *all*.

famines, pestilences,ᵃ and earthquakes in various places. ⁸All these *are* the beginning of sorrows.

⁹"Then they will deliver you up to tribulation and kill you, and you will be hated by all nations for My name's sake. ¹⁰And then many will be offended, will betray one another, and will hate one another. ¹¹Then many false prophets will rise up and deceive many. ¹²And because lawlessness will abound, the love of many will grow cold. ¹³But he who endures to the end shall be saved. ¹⁴And this gospel of the kingdom will be preached in all the world as a witness to all the nations, and then the end will come.

The Great Tribulation

¹⁵"Therefore when you see the *'abomination of desolation,'*ᵃ spoken of by Daniel the prophet, standing in the holy place" (whoever reads, let him understand), ¹⁶"then let those who are in Judea flee to the mountains. ¹⁷Let him who is on the housetop not go down to take anything out of his house. ¹⁸And let him who is in the field not go back to get his clothes. ¹⁹But woe to those who are pregnant and to those who are nursing babies in those days! ²⁰And pray that your flight may not be in winter or on the Sabbath. ²¹For then there will be great tribulation, such as has not been since the beginning of the world until this time,

24:7 ᵃNU–Text omits *pestilences*. **24:15** ᵃDaniel 11:31; 12:11

no, nor ever shall be. ²²And unless those days were shortened, no flesh would be saved; but for the elect's sake those days will be shortened.

²³"Then if anyone says to you, 'Look, here *is* the Christ!' or 'There!' do not believe *it*. ²⁴For false christs and false prophets will rise and show great signs and wonders to deceive, if possible, even the elect. ²⁵See, I have told you beforehand.

²⁶"Therefore if they say to you, 'Look, He is in the desert!' do not go out; *or* 'Look, *He is* in the inner rooms!' do not believe *it*. ²⁷For as the lightning comes from the east and flashes to the west, so also will the coming of the Son of Man be. ²⁸For wherever the carcass is, there the eagles will be gathered together.

The Coming of the Son of Man

²⁹"Immediately after the tribulation of those days the sun will be darkened, and the moon will not give its light; the stars will fall from heaven, and the powers of the heavens will be shaken. ³⁰Then the sign of the Son of Man will appear in heaven, and then all the tribes of the earth will mourn, and they will see the Son of Man coming on the clouds of heaven with power and great glory. ³¹And He will send His angels with a great sound of a trumpet, and they will gather together His elect from the four winds, from one end of heaven to the other.

The Parable of the Fig Tree

32"Now learn this parable from the fig tree: When its branch has already become tender and puts forth leaves, you know that summer *is* near. 33So you also, when you see all these things, know that it[a] is near—at the doors! 34Assuredly, I say to you, this generation will by no means pass away till all these things take place. 35Heaven and earth will pass away, but My words will by no means pass away.

No One Knows the Day or Hour

36"But of that day and hour no one knows, not even the angels of heaven,[a] but My Father only. 37But as the days of Noah *were,* so also will the coming of the Son of Man be. 38For as in the days before the flood, they were eating and drinking, marrying and giving in marriage, until the day that Noah entered the ark, 39and did not know until the flood came and took them all away, so also will the coming of the Son of Man be. 40Then two *men* will be in the field: one will be taken and the other left. 41Two *women will be* grinding at the mill: one will be taken and the other left. 42Watch therefore, for you do not know what hour[a] your Lord is coming. 43But know this, that if the master of the house had known what hour the thief

---

24:33 [a]Or *He.*   24:36 [a]NU–Text adds *nor the Son.*
24:42 [a]NU–Text reads *day.*

would come, he would have watched and not allowed his house to be broken into. ⁴⁴Therefore you also be ready, for the Son of Man is coming at an hour you do not expect.

The Faithful Servant and the Evil Servant
⁴⁵"Who then is a faithful and wise servant, whom his master made ruler over his household, to give them food in due season? ⁴⁶Blessed *is* that servant whom his master, when he comes, will find so doing. ⁴⁷Assuredly, I say to you that he will make him ruler over all his goods. ⁴⁸But if that evil servant says in his heart, 'My master is delaying his coming,' ^a ⁴⁹and begins to beat *his* fellow servants, and to eat and drink with the drunkards, ⁵⁰the master of that servant will come on a day when he is not looking for *him* and at an hour that he is not aware of, ⁵¹and will cut him in two and appoint *him* his portion with the hypocrites. There shall be weeping and gnashing of teeth.

The Parable of the Wise and Foolish Virgins
25 "Then the kingdom of heaven shall be likened to ten virgins who took their lamps and went out to meet the bridegroom. ²Now five of them were wise, and five *were* foolish. ³Those who *were* foolish took their lamps and took no oil with them, ⁴but the wise took oil in their vessels

24:48 ^aNU–Text omits *his coming.*

with their lamps. ^{5}But while the bridegroom was delayed, they all slumbered and slept.

^{6}"And at midnight a cry was *heard:* 'Behold, the bridegroom is coming;^{a} go out to meet him!' ^{7}Then all those virgins arose and trimmed their lamps. ^{8}And the foolish said to the wise, 'Give us *some* of your oil, for our lamps are going out.' ^{9}But the wise answered, saying, '*No,* lest there should not be enough for us and you; but go rather to those who sell, and buy for yourselves.' ^{10}And while they went to buy, the bridegroom came, and those who were ready went in with him to the wedding; and the door was shut.

^{11}"Afterward the other virgins came also, saying, 'Lord, Lord, open to us!' ^{12}But he answered and said, 'Assuredly, I say to you, I do not know you.'

^{13}"Watch therefore, for you know neither the day nor the hour^a in which the Son of Man is coming.

The Parable of the Talents

^{14}"For *the kingdom of heaven is* like a man traveling to a far country, *who* called his own servants and delivered his goods to them. ^{15}And to one he gave five talents, to another two, and to another one, to each according to his own ability; and immediately he went on a journey. ^{16}Then he who had received the five talents went and traded with them, and made another five talents. ^{17}And like-

---

25:6 ^{a}NU–Text omits *is coming.* **25:13** ^{a}NU–Text omits the rest of this verse.

wise he who *had received* two gained two more also. 18But he who had received one went and dug in the ground, and hid his lord's money. 19After a long time the lord of those servants came and settled accounts with them.

20"So he who had received five talents came and brought five other talents, saying, 'Lord, you delivered to me five talents; look, I have gained five more talents besides them.' 21His lord said to him, 'Well *done,* good and faithful servant; you were faithful over a few things, I will make you ruler over many things. Enter into the joy of your lord.' 22He also who had received two talents came and said, 'Lord, you delivered to me two talents; look, I have gained two more talents besides them.' 23His lord said to him, 'Well *done,* good and faithful servant; you have been faithful over a few things, I will make you ruler over many things. Enter into the joy of your lord.'

24"Then he who had received the one talent came and said, 'Lord, I knew you to be a hard man, reaping where you have not sown, and gathering where you have not scattered seed. 25And I was afraid, and went and hid your talent in the ground. Look, *there* you have *what is* yours.'

26"But his lord answered and said to him, 'You wicked and lazy servant, you knew that I reap where I have not sown, and gather where I have not scattered seed. 27So you ought to have deposited my money with the bankers, and at my coming I would have received back my own with interest. ^{28}So take the talent from him, and give *it* to him who has ten talents.

^{29}'For to everyone who has, more will be given, and he will have abundance; but from him who does not have, even what he has will be taken away. ^{30}And cast the unprofitable servant into the outer darkness. There will be weeping and gnashing of teeth.'

The Son of Man Will Judge the Nations

^{31}"When the Son of Man comes in His glory, and all the holy^a angels with Him, then He will sit on the throne of His glory. ^{32}All the nations will be gathered before Him, and He will separate them one from another, as a shepherd divides *his* sheep from the goats. ^{33}And He will set the sheep on His right hand, but the goats on the left. ^{34}Then the King will say to those on His right hand, 'Come, you blessed of My Father, inherit the kingdom prepared for you from the foundation of the world: ^{35}for I was hungry and you gave Me food; I was thirsty and you gave Me drink; I was a stranger and you took Me in; ^{36}I *was* naked and you clothed Me; I was sick and you visited Me; I was in prison and you came to Me.'

^{37}"Then the righteous will answer Him, saying, 'Lord, when did we see You hungry and feed *You,* or thirsty and give *You* drink? ^{38}When did we see

25:31 ^{a}NU–Text omits *holy.*

You a stranger and take *You* in, or naked and clothe *You?* ³⁹Or when did we see You sick, or in prison, and come to You?' ⁴⁰And the King will answer and say to them, 'Assuredly, I say to you, inasmuch as you did *it* to one of the least of these My brethren, you did *it* to Me.'

⁴¹"Then He will also say to those on the left hand, 'Depart from Me, you cursed, into the everlasting fire prepared for the devil and his angels: ⁴²for I was hungry and you gave Me no food; I was thirsty and you gave Me no drink; ⁴³I was a stranger and you did not take Me in, naked and you did not clothe Me, sick and in prison and you did not visit Me.'

⁴⁴"Then they also will answer Him,^a saying, 'Lord, when did we see You hungry or thirsty or a stranger or naked or sick or in prison, and did not minister to You?' ⁴⁵Then He will answer them, saying, 'Assuredly, I say to you, inasmuch as you did not do *it* to one of the least of these, you did not do *it* to Me.' ⁴⁶And these will go away into everlasting punishment, but the righteous into eternal life."

The Plot to Kill Jesus

26 Now it came to pass, when Jesus had finished all these sayings, *that* He said to His disciples, ²"You know that after two days is the Passover, and the Son of Man will be delivered up to be crucified."

25:44 ^aNU–Text and M–Text omit *Him.*

³Then the chief priests, the scribes,ᵃ and the elders of the people assembled at the palace of the high priest, who was called Caiaphas, ⁴and plotted to take Jesus by trickery and kill *Him.* ⁵But they said, "Not during the feast, lest there be an uproar among the people."

The Anointing at Bethany

⁶And when Jesus was in Bethany at the house of Simon the leper, ⁷a woman came to Him having an alabaster flask of very costly fragrant oil, and she poured *it* on His head as He sat *at the table.* ⁸But when His disciples saw *it,* they were indignant, saying, "Why this waste? ⁹For this fragrant oil might have been sold for much and given to *the* poor."

¹⁰But when Jesus was aware of *it,* He said to them, "Why do you trouble the woman? For she has done a good work for Me. ¹¹For you have the poor with you always, but Me you do not have always. ¹²For in pouring this fragrant oil on My body, she did *it* for My burial. ¹³Assuredly, I say to you, wherever this gospel is preached in the whole world, what this woman has done will also be told as a memorial to her."

Judas Agrees to Betray Jesus

¹⁴Then one of the twelve, called Judas Iscariot, went to the chief priests ¹⁵and said, "What are you

26:3 ᵃNU–Text omits *the scribes.*

willing to give me if I deliver Him to you?" And they counted out to him thirty pieces of silver. [16]So from that time he sought opportunity to betray Him.

Jesus Celebrates Passover with His Disciples
[17]Now on the first *day of the Feast* of the Unleavened Bread the disciples came to Jesus, saying to Him, "Where do You want us to prepare for You to eat the Passover?"

[18]And He said, "Go into the city to a certain man, and say to him, 'The Teacher says, "My time is at hand; I will keep the Passover at your house with My disciples."' "

[19]So the disciples did as Jesus had directed them; and they prepared the Passover.

[20]When evening had come, He sat down with the twelve. [21]Now as they were eating, He said, "Assuredly, I say to you, one of you will betray Me."

[22]And they were exceedingly sorrowful, and each of them began to say to Him, "Lord, is it I?"

[23]He answered and said, "He who dipped *his* hand with Me in the dish will betray Me. [24]The Son of Man indeed goes just as it is written of Him, but woe to that man by whom the Son of Man is betrayed! It would have been good for that man if he had not been born."

[25]Then Judas, who was betraying Him, answered and said, "Rabbi, is it I?"

He said to him, "You have said it."

Jesus Institutes the Lord's Supper

26And as they were eating, Jesus took bread, blessed[a] and broke *it,* and gave *it* to the disciples and said, "Take, eat; this is My body."

27Then He took the cup, and gave thanks, and gave *it* to them, saying, "Drink from it, all of you. 28For this is My blood of the new[a] covenant, which is shed for many for the remission of sins. 29But I say to you, I will not drink of this fruit of the vine from now on until that day when I drink it new with you in My Father's kingdom."

30And when they had sung a hymn, they went out to the Mount of Olives.

Jesus Predicts Peter's Denial

31Then Jesus said to them, "All of you will be made to stumble because of Me this night, for it is written:

'I will strike the Shepherd,
And the sheep of the flock will be scattered.'[a]

32But after I have been raised, I will go before you to Galilee."

33Peter answered and said to Him, "Even if all are made to stumble because of You, I will never be made to stumble."

26:26 [a]M–Text reads *gave thanks for.* **26:28** [a]NU–Text omits *new.* **26:31** [a]Zechariah 13:7

³⁴Jesus said to him, "Assuredly, I say to you that this night, before the rooster crows, you will deny Me three times."

³⁵Peter said to Him, "Even if I have to die with You, I will not deny You!"

And so said all the disciples.

The Prayer in the Garden

³⁶Then Jesus came with them to a place called Gethsemane, and said to the disciples, "Sit here while I go and pray over there." ³⁷And He took with Him Peter and the two sons of Zebedee, and He began to be sorrowful and deeply distressed. ³⁸Then He said to them, "My soul is exceedingly sorrowful, even to death. Stay here and watch with Me."

³⁹He went a little farther and fell on His face, and prayed, saying, "O My Father, if it is possible, let this cup pass from Me; nevertheless, not as I will, but as You *will.*"

⁴⁰Then He came to the disciples and found them sleeping, and said to Peter, "What! Could you not watch with Me one hour? ⁴¹Watch and pray, lest you enter into temptation. The spirit indeed *is* willing, but the flesh *is* weak."

⁴²Again, a second time, He went away and prayed, saying, "O My Father, if this cup cannot pass away from Me unless^a I drink it, Your will be done." ⁴³And He came and found them asleep again, for their eyes were heavy.

26:42 ^aNU–Text reads *if this may not pass away unless.*

⁴⁴So He left them, went away again, and prayed the third time, saying the same words. ⁴⁵Then He came to His disciples and said to them, "Are *you* still sleeping and resting? Behold, the hour is at hand, and the Son of Man is being betrayed into the hands of sinners. ⁴⁶Rise, let us be going. See, My betrayer is at hand."

Betrayal and Arrest in Gethsemane

⁴⁷And while He was still speaking, behold, Judas, one of the twelve, with a great multitude with swords and clubs, came from the chief priests and elders of the people.

⁴⁸Now His betrayer had given them a sign, saying, "Whomever I kiss, He is the One; seize Him." ⁴⁹Immediately he went up to Jesus and said, "Greetings, Rabbi!" and kissed Him.

⁵⁰But Jesus said to him, "Friend, why have you come?"

Then they came and laid hands on Jesus and took Him. ⁵¹And suddenly, one of those *who were* with Jesus stretched out *his* hand and drew his sword, struck the servant of the high priest, and cut off his ear.

⁵²But Jesus said to him, "Put your sword in its place, for all who take the sword will perish^a by the sword. ⁵³Or do you think that I cannot now pray to My Father, and He will provide Me with more than twelve legions of angels? ⁵⁴How then

26:52 ^aM–Text reads *die.*

could the Scriptures be fulfilled, that it must happen thus?"

⁵⁵In that hour Jesus said to the multitudes, "Have you come out, as against a robber, with swords and clubs to take Me? I sat daily with you, teaching in the temple, and you did not seize Me. ⁵⁶But all this was done that the Scriptures of the prophets might be fulfilled."

Then all the disciples forsook Him and fled.

Jesus Faces the Sanhedrin

⁵⁷And those who had laid hold of Jesus led *Him* away to Caiaphas the high priest, where the scribes and the elders were assembled. ⁵⁸But Peter followed Him at a distance to the high priest's courtyard. And he went in and sat with the servants to see the end.

⁵⁹Now the chief priests, the elders,ᵃ and all the council sought false testimony against Jesus to put Him to death, ⁶⁰but found none. Even though many false witnesses came forward, they found none.ᵃ But at last two false witnessesᵇ came forward ⁶¹and said, "This *fellow* said, 'I am able to destroy the temple of God and to build it in three days.'"

⁶²And the high priest arose and said to Him,

26:59 ᵃNU–Text omits *the elders*. 26:60 ᵃNU–Text puts a comma after *but found none*, does not capitalize *Even*, and omits *they found none*. ᵇNU–Text omits *false witnesses*.

"Do You answer nothing? What *is it* these men testify against You?" [63]But Jesus kept silent. And the high priest answered and said to Him, "I put You under oath by the living God: Tell us if You are the Christ, the Son of God!"

[64]Jesus said to him, "*It is as* you said. Nevertheless, I say to you, hereafter you will see the Son of Man sitting at the right hand of the Power, and coming on the clouds of heaven."

[65]Then the high priest tore his clothes, saying, "He has spoken blasphemy! What further need do we have of witnesses? Look, now you have heard His blasphemy! [66]What do you think?"

They answered and said, "He is deserving of death."

[67]Then they spat in His face and beat Him; and others struck *Him* with the palms of their hands, [68]saying, "Prophesy to us, Christ! Who is the one who struck You?"

Peter Denies Jesus, and Weeps Bitterly

[69]Now Peter sat outside in the courtyard. And a servant girl came to him, saying, "You also were with Jesus of Galilee."

[70]But he denied it before *them* all, saying, "I do not know what you are saying."

[71]And when he had gone out to the gateway, another *girl* saw him and said to those *who were* there, "This *fellow* also was with Jesus of Nazareth."

72But again he denied with an oath, "I do not know the Man!"

73And a little later those who stood by came up and said to Peter, "Surely you also are *one* of them, for your speech betrays you."

74Then he began to curse and swear, *saying,* "I do not know the Man!"

Immediately a rooster crowed. 75And Peter remembered the word of Jesus who had said to him, "Before the rooster crows, you will deny Me three times." So he went out and wept bitterly.

Jesus Handed Over to Pontius Pilate

27 When morning came, all the chief priests and elders of the people plotted against Jesus to put Him to death. 2And when they had bound Him, they led Him away and delivered Him to Pontiusa Pilate the governor.

Judas Hangs Himself

3Then Judas, His betrayer, seeing that He had been condemned, was remorseful and brought back the thirty pieces of silver to the chief priests and elders, 4saying, "I have sinned by betraying innocent blood."

And they said, "What *is that* to us? You see *to it!*"

5Then he threw down the pieces of silver in the temple and departed, and went and hanged himself.

27:2 aNU–Text omits *Pontius.*

⁶But the chief priests took the silver pieces and said, "It is not lawful to put them into the treasury, because they are the price of blood." ⁷And they consulted together and bought with them the potter's field, to bury strangers in. ⁸Therefore that field has been called the Field of Blood to this day.

⁹Then was fulfilled what was spoken by Jeremiah the prophet, saying, *"And they took the thirty pieces of silver, the value of Him who was priced, whom they of the children of Israel priced,* ¹⁰*and gave them for the potter's field, as the LORD directed me."*[a]

Jesus Faces Pilate

¹¹Now Jesus stood before the governor. And the governor asked Him, saying, "Are You the King of the Jews?"

Jesus said to him, *"It is as* you say." ¹²And while He was being accused by the chief priests and elders, He answered nothing.

¹³Then Pilate said to Him, "Do You not hear how many things they testify against You?" ¹⁴But He answered him not one word, so that the governor marveled greatly.

Taking the Place of Barabbas

¹⁵Now at the feast the governor was accustomed to releasing to the multitude one prisoner whom they wished. ¹⁶And at that time they had a noto-

27:10 [a]Jeremiah 32:6–9

rious prisoner called Barabbas.[a] [17]Therefore, when they had gathered together, Pilate said to them, "Whom do you want me to release to you? Barabbas, or Jesus who is called Christ?" [18]For he knew that they had handed Him over because of envy.

[19]While he was sitting on the judgment seat, his wife sent to him, saying, "Have nothing to do with that just Man, for I have suffered many things today in a dream because of Him."

[20]But the chief priests and elders persuaded the multitudes that they should ask for Barabbas and destroy Jesus. [21]The governor answered and said to them, "Which of the two do you want me to release to you?"

They said, "Barabbas!"

[22]Pilate said to them, "What then shall I do with Jesus who is called Christ?"

They all said to him, "Let Him be crucified!"

[23]Then the governor said, "Why, what evil has He done?"

But they cried out all the more, saying, "Let Him be crucified!"

[24]When Pilate saw that he could not prevail at all, but rather *that* a tumult was rising, he took water and washed *his* hands before the multitude, saying, "I am innocent of the blood of this just Person.[a] You see *to it.*"

27:16 [a]NU–Text reads *Jesus Barabbas.* 27:24 [a]NU–Text omits *just.*

²⁵And all the people answered and said, "His blood *be* on us and on our children."

²⁶Then he released Barabbas to them; and when he had scourged Jesus, he delivered *Him* to be crucified.

The Soldiers Mock Jesus

²⁷Then the soldiers of the governor took Jesus into the Praetorium and gathered the whole garrison around Him. ²⁸And they stripped Him and put a scarlet robe on Him. ²⁹When they had twisted a crown of thorns, they put *it* on His head, and a reed in His right hand. And they bowed the knee before Him and mocked Him, saying, "Hail, King of the Jews!" ³⁰Then they spat on Him, and took the reed and struck Him on the head. ³¹And when they had mocked Him, they took the robe off Him, put His *own* clothes on Him, and led Him away to be crucified.

The King on a Cross

³²Now as they came out, they found a man of Cyrene, Simon by name. Him they compelled to bear His cross. ³³And when they had come to a place called Golgotha, that is to say, Place of a Skull, ³⁴they gave Him sour[a] wine mingled with gall to drink. But when He had tasted *it,* He would not drink.

27:34 [a]NU–Text omits *sour.*

³⁵Then they crucified Him, and divided His garments, casting lots,ᵃ that it might be fulfilled which was spoken by the prophet:

"They divided My garments among them,
*And for My clothing they cast lots."*ᵇ

³⁶Sitting down, they kept watch over Him there. ³⁷And they put up over His head the accusation written against Him:

THIS IS JESUS THE KING OF THE JEWS.

³⁸Then two robbers were crucified with Him, one on the right and another on the left.

³⁹And those who passed by blasphemed Him, wagging their heads ⁴⁰and saying, "You who destroy the temple and build *it* in three days, save Yourself! If You are the Son of God, come down from the cross."

⁴¹Likewise the chief priests also, mocking with the scribes and elders,ᵃ said, ⁴²"He saved others; Himself He cannot save. If He is the King of Israel,ᵃ let Him now come down from the cross, and we will believe Him.ᵇ ⁴³He trusted in God; let

---

27:35 ᵃNU–Text and M–Text omit the rest of this verse. ᵇPsalm 22:18 **27:41** ᵃM–Text reads *with the scribes, the Pharisees, and the elders.* **27:42** ᵃNU–Text reads *He is the King of Israel!* ᵇNU–Text and M–Text read *we will believe in Him.*

Him deliver Him now if He will have Him; for He said, 'I am the Son of God.'"

⁴⁴Even the robbers who were crucified with Him reviled Him with the same thing.

Jesus Dies on the Cross

⁴⁵Now from the sixth hour until the ninth hour there was darkness over all the land. ⁴⁶And about the ninth hour Jesus cried out with a loud voice, saying, "Eli, Eli, lama sabachthani?" that is, *"My God, My God, why have You forsaken Me?"*ᵃ

⁴⁷Some of those who stood there, when they heard *that,* said, "This Man is calling for Elijah!" ⁴⁸Immediately one of them ran and took a sponge, filled *it* with sour wine and put *it* on a reed, and offered it to Him to drink.

⁴⁹The rest said, "Let Him alone; let us see if Elijah will come to save Him."

⁵⁰And Jesus cried out again with a loud voice, and yielded up His spirit.

⁵¹Then, behold, the veil of the temple was torn in two from top to bottom; and the earth quaked, and the rocks were split, ⁵²and the graves were opened; and many bodies of the saints who had fallen asleep were raised; ⁵³and coming out of the graves after His resurrection, they went into the holy city and appeared to many.

⁵⁴So when the centurion and those with him, who were guarding Jesus, saw the earthquake and

27:46 ᵃPsalm 22:1

the things that had happened, they feared greatly, saying, "Truly this was the Son of God!"

55And many women who followed Jesus from Galilee, ministering to Him, were there looking on from afar, 56among whom were Mary Magdalene, Mary the mother of James and Joses,[a] and the mother of Zebedee's sons.

Jesus Buried in Joseph's Tomb

57Now when evening had come, there came a rich man from Arimathea, named Joseph, who himself had also become a disciple of Jesus. 58This man went to Pilate and asked for the body of Jesus. Then Pilate commanded the body to be given to him. 59When Joseph had taken the body, he wrapped it in a clean linen cloth, 60and laid it in his new tomb which he had hewn out of the rock; and he rolled a large stone against the door of the tomb, and departed. 61And Mary Magdalene was there, and the other Mary, sitting opposite the tomb.

Pilate Sets a Guard

62On the next day, which followed the Day of Preparation, the chief priests and Pharisees gathered together to Pilate, 63saying, "Sir, we remember, while He was still alive, how that deceiver said, 'After three days I will rise.' 64Therefore command that the tomb be made

27:56 [a]NU–Text reads *Joseph.*

secure until the third day, lest His disciples come by night[a] and steal Him *away,* and say to the people, 'He has risen from the dead.' So the last deception will be worse than the first."

⁶⁵Pilate said to them, "You have a guard; go your way, make *it* as secure as you know how." ⁶⁶So they went and made the tomb secure, sealing the stone and setting the guard.

He Is Risen

28 Now after the Sabbath, as the first *day* of the week began to dawn, Mary Magdalene and the other Mary came to see the tomb. ²And behold, there was a great earthquake; for an angel of the Lord descended from heaven, and came and rolled back the stone from the door,[a] and sat on it. ³His countenance was like lightning, and his clothing as white as snow. ⁴And the guards shook for fear of him, and became like dead *men.*

⁵But the angel answered and said to the women, "Do not be afraid, for I know that you seek Jesus who was crucified. ⁶He is not here; for He is risen, as He said. Come, see the place where the Lord lay. ⁷And go quickly and tell His disciples that He is risen from the dead, and indeed He is going before you into Galilee; there you will see Him. Behold, I have told you."

27:64 [a]NU–Text omits *by night.* **28:2** [a]NU–Text omits *from the door.*

[8]So they went out quickly from the tomb with fear and great joy, and ran to bring His disciples word.

The Women Worship the Risen Lord

[9]And as they went to tell His disciples,[a] behold, Jesus met them, saying, "Rejoice!" So they came and held Him by the feet and worshiped Him. [10]Then Jesus said to them, "Do not be afraid. Go *and* tell My brethren to go to Galilee, and there they will see Me."

The Soldiers Are Bribed

[11]Now while they were going, behold, some of the guard came into the city and reported to the chief priests all the things that had happened. [12]When they had assembled with the elders and consulted together, they gave a large sum of money to the soldiers, [13]saying, "Tell them, 'His disciples came at night and stole Him *away* while we slept.' [14]And if this comes to the governor's ears, we will appease him and make you secure." [15]So they took the money and did as they were instructed; and this saying is commonly reported among the Jews until this day.

The Great Commission

[16]Then the eleven disciples went away into Galilee, to the mountain which Jesus had

28:9 [a]NU–Text omits the first clause of this verse.

appointed for them. [17]When they saw Him, they worshiped Him; but some doubted.

[18]And Jesus came and spoke to them, saying, "All authority has been given to Me in heaven and on earth. [19]Go therefore[a] and make disciples of all the nations, baptizing them in the name of the Father and of the Son and of the Holy Spirit, [20]teaching them to observe all things that I have commanded you; and lo, I am with you always, *even* to the end of the age." Amen.[a]

28:19 [a]M–Text omits *therefore*. **28:20** [a]NU–Text omits *Amen*.

Center Point Publishing
600 Brooks Road ● PO Box 1
Thorndike ME 04986-0001 USA

(207) 568-3717

US & Canada:
1 800 929-9108
www.centerpointlargeprint.com